# Outstanding praise for James Driggers and *Lovesick*!

"Jim Driggers's *Lovesick* is a collection of novellas that are just as heartbreaking as they are wise, just as beautiful as they are devastating. While spanning nearly the entire 20th century and tackling some of our nation's greatest social and cultural issues, *Lovesick* anchors its heart to the fictional town of Morris, South Carolina, and its collection of seemingly eccentric citizens whose traumas, loves, and comedic turns simultaneously charm and repulse us, and that's what good—dare I say great—fiction is supposed to do. *Lovesick* does this in spades. Like Allan Gurganus and Doris Betts, Jim Driggers gives us small-town life in a way that reveals big, heartfelt ideas and universal themes."
—Wiley Cash, *New York Times* bestselling author of
*A Land More Kind Than Home*

"In *Lovesick*, Jim Driggers takes us behind polite surfaces across a century as old plantation land turns into subdivisions, unraveling the concealed tragedy next door, the romantic yearning behind a tabloid scandal, and the scheming and sacrifice hidden between the lines of a legendary Southern cookbook. Witty, compassionate, yet unrelenting, Driggers knows what ties a fatal love knot: the object of forbidden love may be indifferent, unworthy, or just plain poisonous, but what matters to the lovestruck is to give all and so find a way to be, however briefly, truly alive."
—Lynne Barrett, author of *Magpies*

"We may think we know some of the personages that populate James Driggers's tour de force, *Lovesick*. Here is the overweight insurance salesman, the sisters jealous of each other, the shiny-hair evangelist, and the faded Southern belle. But then we watch them think and do things we could never have imagined. There's a hint of Erskine Caldwell here—with a strong dash of Grand Guignol. We may never understand, but we are *convinced*. Yes, he gets away with it."
—Fred Chappell, author of *Look Back All the Green Valley*

"Like a swiftly moving train rolling through the deep South, *Lovesick* takes you on an incredible journey filled with history, lies and deceit. I couldn't put it down."
—Lisa Jackson, #1 *New York Times* bestselling author

Please turn the page for more advance praise for
James Driggers and *Lovesick*

**More advance praise for James Driggers and *Lovesick***

"*Lovesick* is aptly titled. These four interrelated novellas, each a bit more twisted than its predecessor, hinge on lovesickness of one kind or another. The characters live in a South where violence blooms like ditch lilies along an unpaved road. Not for the faint of heart, these stories will not quickly fade from the reader's memory."
—Wayne Caldwell, author of *Requiem by Fire*

"While James Driggers's ensemble of unforgettable characters are unified by the blood-soaked daggers of lust, greed, and ungovernable passion, *Lovesick* is ultimately a gorgeous exploration of humanity—our sorrow and hope, loneliness and joy, and above all, love, how it lifts us, and how irrecoverably lost and shattered we are without it."
—Patrick Michael Finn

# LOVESICK

## JAMES DRIGGERS

KENSINGTON BOOKS
www.kensingtonbooks.com

KENSINGTON BOOKS are published by

Kensington Publishing Corp.
119 West 40th Street
New York, NY 10018

All Kensington titles, imprints, and distributed lines are available at
special quantity discounts for bulk purchases for sales promotion, pre-
miums, fund-raising, and educational or institutional use.

Special book excerpts or customized printings can also be created to fit
specific needs. For details, write or phone the office of the Kensington
Special Sales Manager: Kensington Publishing Corp., 119 West 40th
Street, New York, NY 10018. Attn. Special Sales Department. Phone:
1-800-221-2647.

Kensington and the K logo Reg. U.S. Pat. & TM Off.

eISBN-13: 978-1-61773-476-2
eISBN-10: 1-61773-476-4
First Kensington Electronic Edition: April 2015

ISBN-13: 978-1-61773-475-5
ISBN-10: 1-61773-475-6
First Kensington Trade Paperback Printing: April 2015

10  9  8  7  6  5  4  3  2  1

Printed in the United States of America

We two boys together clinging,
One the other never leaving,
Up and down the roads going—North and South excursions
  making,
Power enjoying—elbows stretching—fingers clutching,
Arm'd and fearless—eating, drinking, sleeping, loving.

—Walt Whitman

# Acknowledgments

Writing a story may be a personal endeavor, but it is not a solitary one. There have been many talented hands, generous hearts who have helped along the way. Without them, this book would not be. Deepest thanks then to:

John Scognamiglio, my editor at Kensington Publishing, for his guidance and enthusiasm.

Mitchell Waters, my agent at Curtis Brown, Ltd., for his belief in me, in my writing, and for helping find the book its best and right home.

The team at Kensington involved in the production of the book: Paula Reedy and copy editor Sheila Higgins; Vida Engstrand and Karen Auerbach, who guided the publicity and marketing for the book.

The New South Wales Writers Centre and my friends there— Julie Chevalier, Sue Booker, Heather, Linda Christensen—who workshopped the very first story in the collection and helped me remember so much of what I love about writing is the company of other writers.

Tom Mendicino, who took me under his wing when I needed a mentor and offered not only great advice, but helped open doors that I had no access to.

My dear friend and colleague, Eileen Crowe, who helped shape these stories with her keen insights and observations.

Pat O'Cain and Rhoda Groce for comprehensive edits on the preliminary manuscript.

Early readers Cynn Chadwick ("just write the damn thing"), Dawn McCann, Jeff Glick, Gary Zinik, who gave me confidence to keep writing.

Katrina Ronneburger, who produced the image of "The Lady in the White Hat"; Miss Merle for serving as the model for the image (and for what a true Southern lady of grace and distinction should be).

Phil, my husband and best friend, who is my first and most trusted reader.

And my writing students, who continually teach me to encounter story, character, and the blank page in new, unexpected, and exciting ways.

*The lovesick, the betrayed, and the jealous all smell alike.*

—Sidonie-Gabrielle Colette

# Contents

Butcher, the Baker  /  1

The Brambles  /  107

Sandra and the Snake Handlers  /  175

M.R. Vale  /  235

# Butcher, the Baker

# 1

# smothered chicken . . .

The winter sky hugged the earth like a tight-fitting lid on a pot. Butcher felt trapped inside this bleak landscape, oppressed; standing alone on the back steps of the Residence, everywhere he looked there was only cold. In every direction, flat clouds pressed hard against the dull horizon, the trees bare and lifeless silhouettes against sheet-metal gray. Though it was early morning, there was no discernable sun, and as a result, the dim light leveled everything to a sadness.

It seemed to Butcher that he had spent the best part of his life inside this gray, that his life could be pieced together like scraps from a newspaper article:

- First, there was the boy struggling to plow the pitiable sandy soil he and his mam had 'cropped back in Morris, South Carolina.

- Then, when she had passed, there was the youth chasing freedom into the army at the first call to enlist, only to find himself buried deep inside the steel belly of a ship that bore him to France and the Great War.

- Then, there was the war itself, where death and misery floated like smoke over everything.

- And finally, when he returned home to find that the war had made no difference for him, that he was still just a nigger to all those he had fought to protect, there was the soldier whose anger had killed a man in an alley behind a clip joint only to find himself buried once more—this time locked in a prison for nearly ten years.

He had been barely eighteen when he had gone to war—it had been seventeen years since. A second lifetime. Both equally hard, though now he knew what to expect, and so it didn't wear on him as much. He knew everybody suffered—it was impossible to escape it. Sometimes you caught a lucky break. Sometimes you didn't, so you dealt with what you had. He'd been raised poor and was used to living hand to mouth. Nothing new in that. Besides, he was better off than many.

He'd been in Fayetteville now for over two years, first having wandered through the South after the war, drifting from one job to the next till he got hired to cook for the railroad. During the riots of '19, he'd thought himself fortunate to stay out of trouble. He'd been working for the Southern Railroad traveling between Charleston and Memphis; though the worst of the troubles had been in the North, there had been martial law for a time in Charleston. Black veterans, mainly navy men, had been killed by gangs of whites, some of them veterans as well. A great many others had ended up in jail. For him, it was all in the timing. He understood the anger, the frustration, the resentment on both sides—the whites scared of the black migration taking over the jobs in the factories, the blacks tired of just taking the scraps of what was deemed to be their share. Butcher was glad to see his brothers standing up and fighting back. But when the rioting began over the summer, he was in the dining car kitchen riding from Charleston to Memphis, from Memphis to Charleston. Each leg took one day; he did three trips a week, so the only news he had came from the porters and brakemen. If he had a day off, he spent it drunk and then sleeping off the booze till it was time to get back on the train. Some men worked the train for the travel—the chance to see new things. Having traveled across the ocean and back again, Butcher figured he had seen as much as he ever wanted to see. Some men worked the train because it made them feel important, especially those who got to put on a starched jacket and hoist the baggage of the white passengers. Butcher had worn a uniform and knew there was no privilege to be found in that. He worked the train because it meant he had some money, and he knew that money was all that counted for anything.

In '22, he had been in the wrong place—a honky-tonk on the outskirts of Wilmington. He was drinking, drunk again, and challenged by a man to a fight. Butcher didn't remember much—there was gambling, dice, and accusations of cheating. And there was a woman as well. All of this had been read back to him in the judge's papers at the trial. The woman, a tall, statuesque gal with skin as smooth and black as her silk dress, had testified that Butcher accused her man, whose name was Johnson Everetts, of cheating at craps. She said both men had pulled knives and there was a fight. Butcher couldn't argue with that. He always carried a weapon—had learned to have protection on him when walking the backstreets of Brest, back to the barracks after visiting the brothel. She said she had screamed when she saw Johnson stabbed, and when she said that Butcher had stabbed Johnson in the chest, there was a flash of memory—Butcher could feel the pressure as the knife punctured flesh, then pressed against bone, but only slightly so that it too gave way until the knife lodged in Johnson Everetts's heart. They'd sent him to Caledonia for ten years. Butcher knew it would have been longer if Johnson Everetts had had a family or had been a man of reputation. He was lucky in that regard. Lucky that the judge saw the case as just another two niggers cutting each other. Lucky that Johnson was not a white man.

When he arrived at Caledonia, he feared he might be put to work in one of the road camps, which was where they put most black men, transported every few days to a new stretch of road in a cage with five or six other men. There they would dig and scrape the hillsides to make way for the highway, only to be herded back into their cage for the night, covered over with large flaps of canvas to keep out the cold. He knew if he were forced to live like that for long, he would go crazy or die or be killed just trying to escape. So, when they were cataloging him into the system, he told the boss on duty he had been employed in both the army and on the rail as a cook. Told him he knew what it took to work in a kitchen, knew how to take orders, and knew how to give them as well. Told the boss he could cook anything. That he would make sure the boss's favorite dishes would be on the menu if given the opportunity. The boss said he had always been partial to corn fritters and smothered chicken and gravy.

It was as simple as that. Give the man what he wanted. Butcher worked in the kitchen for the whole ten years he was on the inside, and by the time he was released, he had made a name for himself—his cobbler, his country hash, his biscuits. There were fields and gardens around the prison, and Butcher cooked the harvest, preserving fruit and vegetables for the winters. Even the sorriest prisoner would tell you that the one thing Caledonia had going for it was the food.

He'd been back to his home, Morris, South Carolina, where he was born and lived as a boy, only once after he was released, back to visit his mam's grave, back to see if there was any work for him in surroundings that were at least familiar. What he found was those who lived on a rented farm trying to 'crop couldn't make a living that amounted to more than a chicken scratching in the dirt. Those who worked for wages didn't fare much better. After the cemetery, he sought out the four-room cabin where he had lived with his mam. He followed the dirt road, running near the railroad tracks past the Deegan farm. He was surprised to see the house deserted, a funeral wreath strung on the front gate. He tried to recall the Deegans, could picture the old man and his wife sitting up on the porch, a straw hat pulled down over Mr. Deegan's eyes while he slept in his rocking chair. They had a son only a year or two older than Butcher. Occasionally, he would shout out a "hello" as Butcher passed by. Butcher had walked this road as a boy, remembered the smoky cough from trains as they passed in the distance, freight trains and passenger trains. He had never thought about leaving then, had never imagined working on the train, but then he never imagined his mam dying so young either. As the Deegan farm disappeared behind him, he watched the house he had shared with his mam grow out of the horizon as he crested a small hill. It had never been painted, but nevertheless, it was respectable enough—like a dozen others just like it spread out over the plots of the families who rented them.

A gravel path outlined by stones set one against another led from the front steps about twenty feet and stopped. A small attempt at a yard. He noticed that there had been a small shed added to the rear. There were children in the yard, white children, playing a game with a stick and a ball. When they saw him walking toward the house, the girl ran inside. She reappeared almost immediately, followed out by her father, a tall, lanky young man in overalls. His wife, the girl's mother, stayed on the porch at the door. They were all suspicious of him, but Butcher could also see relief. He posed no threat.

"Is there something I can help you with?" the man asked. The girl, who was older than the boy, stood close behind her father. He swatted her back toward the house. "Get up on the porch there with your mamma. Get. This ain't none of your bidness."

Butcher introduced himself. "I just come round to visit my mam's grave," he said. "Thought I would bring her some flowers. Thought I would walk out this way. We used to rent round here." Butcher stopped short of telling the man that this house had been his. Didn't want to say the man was raising his children in a place once belonged to blacks. Didn't want to shame him. But Butcher could see that the man knew this. Times were hard for everyone.

"Looks like some trouble had fallen on the Deegans," he said.

"Fewer troubles than most," said the man. "Old man and woman have been dead a while. The son hanged hisself almost two years ago. Couldn't see how to make the farm work for him. They took his missus away—went still as a stone after he died. Just sat there on the porch day after day. Wouldn't speak. Finally, her kinfolk came and took her away. Left the farm to just rot. I heard tell that it had been sold."

"Well, I hope whoever bought it can make a go of it."

"I doubt anyone's ever made too much of anything off this land," the man said.

"You got that right," said Butcher. "The rich man gets it all. Always has."

The man pointed to the shed. "See them boards. I bought them myself. Nailed 'em up there just a little bit loose. If we move, I'll just pull 'em down and take 'em with me. What's mine belongs to me."

Butcher tipped his hat to the man and toward the porch, and left. He knew there was nothing left there for him. That it was just a place he had once lived. So, he went to Fayetteville because there was an army base there. There were CCC camps there. There was work there. People would need to eat. He would cook for them.

The whole country was out of work—white and black, one as poor as the next—but Butcher was determined to find a job. He had a letter of introduction from the head boss at Caledonia, and he focused on those places where they were serving large numbers of people. He visited the CCC camp, and the director was impressed with his letter, but the camp reminded Butcher too much of the army. He had only found the Volunteers of America relief house by accident, looking for a place to stay for the night. They took him on in the kitchen, and because there was so much turnover not only with the men, but the staff as well, it only took him about six months to become the head cook. The position was answerable only to the director and because he was head cook, the VOA also provided him lodging—a small room, but it was his alone. Butcher was a large man, a little over six feet tall, and the room was only slightly larger than the cell he had occupied in prison, so it was cramped, and since it was on the top floor of the Residence, as everyone who lived there called it, one wall sloped down low to knee height and he had to bend down if he walked on that side of the room. But there was a window. And there were no bars. And he was free to come and go when he pleased. And it was separated from the dorms for the men who stayed in the Residence while looking for work in Fayetteville, or till they realized there was no work to be had and moved on in search of work in

Wilmington or Charleston or some other town. Sometimes they were there for a week or more, sometimes only overnight. The VOA also paid him a salary—six bucks a week. Which Butcher knew was good for these parts—especially for colored. One of the men staying at the Residence had gotten work at one of the mills inspecting hosiery, and he was tickled to have a salary of eight and a half a week.

Plus, Butcher ate for free. The Director of the Residence, a high-strung, thin, bespeckled ex-professor who was employed by the VOA, and whom Butcher suspected was also a three-letter man because of his habit of standing with his hands cocked on his hips when he was trying to speak emphatically and with purpose, had made a point of telling him that meals were included. But Butcher had been around a kitchen long enough to know the cook always eats for free.

Still, he didn't mind if he thought the director was playing up to him. Butcher knew the VOA saw him as a valued commodity. Didn't want to lose him. They served three meals a day, seven days a week. Butcher could stretch the budget so that even though the soup was sometimes little more than broth or the gravy was little more than flavored drippings, he always managed to make it seem like more. He was a damn fine cook and when he put his hand to pastry, there was no one who could hold a candle to him. He could take the thinnest broth and fatten it up with enough soft pastry so that no one thought twice there was only a skerrick of meat. He would nestle a towering golden biscuit in a puddle of gravy so that by the time a hungry man had finished sopping his plate, the greasy film coating his lips held only the satisfying memory of breakfast. Sunday mornings, he always made sweet buns or fried fresh doughnuts with a warm cinnamon and powdered sugar glaze, and on those nights when there was only soup for dinner, any man could have as many helpings as he wanted.

He had been offered a job at one of the penny restaurants on Robeson Street and though the pay had been better, working there meant he would have had to find a room. Here, though he had his private space, he was never isolated. The Residence was alive with comings and goings, of people, of challenges. True, the

VOA was charity with a foundation in scripture, but it was still run like a business, and he merely lived over the store. It helped him to hang on to the dream that someday he would do just that. Live over the store, like the bakers and bistro owners he had seen in Brest. And since the VOA perceived itself as doing a "good work," living there also helped keep him on the straight and narrow. No drinking allowed. That was the rule. He had seen it enforced enough to know not to test it. Besides, as they say, he had a problem with the drink. He was smart enough to know it. It had fueled his courage when he joined the army. And it had caused the death of Johnson Everetts in a bar one night after the war. He was happy to stay where he was until he had his own store. His own shop. At night, after he had showered and gone to his room for the night, he would lie on top of his bed, his hands interlaced behind his head, his head resting on his pillow, and he would dream.

The VOA Residence was more than just a soup kitchen. They served three squares a day. He had gotten trained that way in the army. It was his routine for the ten years he had been on the inside as well. There was never enough money, but the director was dogged in his search for donations, and had created a board of "Miss Anns" culled from several local women's clubs and charitable organizations who had agreed to adopt the VOA as their own personal charitable mission, happy to assist those who had even less than they did. At least they were still able to hold to a pretense of prosperity even if their dresses were out of fashion and their hats were several years old, merely redressed with a new ribbon or a silk flower. Still, they were happy to help pass the plate or ask for contributions from their husbands and friends when there were too many men to feed and not enough money to feed them with.

They were exceedingly flattering. On his pies, his cake, his cobblers, his stews, his gravies. Some would even ask him for a pie to take home with them if company was coming. Lemon meringue, buttermilk custard, chocolate chess. They always made sure to bring their own pie pan. They told him they didn't want to put him out in case he needed it for the Residence. He knew, however, they just intended to pass his pie off as their own. That didn't bother him. They acted as if they were paying him a compliment, to take what he had made and claim it—that it somehow legitimized it, gave it worth. Butcher also recognized there was some truth in that idea. His value in this world was determined by someone other than himself. He had learned that in the war, on the rail, in prison. Get what you can get. Nothing's free. Over the two years, with his salary and his pies, he had managed to save almost $500. When he had enough, he planned to take the money and buy himself a storefront, and turn it into a bistro or a café like those he had seen in Brest. And he would sell baked goods to anyone who wanted them. Pies, cakes, bread. The ladies on the board from the VOA would shop at his store or they would send their maids to bring something home. He would even bake a pie in their tin if they wanted. As long as they paid. Set a value on it. Valued him.

Butcher looked out across the horizon. It was later, but only slightly brighter. In his hand he held a scrap of paper. He folded it up and tucked it back into his shirt pocket, which is where he kept it. "Fucking cold," he muttered as he threw the dregs of his coffee out across the back steps. Butcher knew he needed money. More money than he had. He wanted money. A great sum of money. And Butcher had a plan for how he was going to get it. All he needed now was a partner.

# 2

# Sally Lunn bread . . .

The director had dedicated a small parlor off the main common area of the Residence for the board of women to use for their meetings, which they did every other Thursday. The women had taken great pride in their meeting room, as he knew women were wont to do with such things, decorating it with bric-a-brac from their own homes to lessen the austerity of the straight-backed chairs and small mahogany pedestal table and breakfront that served as the only furniture in the room. Now there was a floor lamp with a fringed shade, a lace cloth for the table, odd mismatched pieces of china from their cupboards. One of the women had also donated a watercolor done by her niece titled *Hestia at the Hearth*.

The director would meet with them to go over the finances, discuss donations, plan meals for special events like Thanksgiving and Christmas. It had become the custom that Butcher would bake something for them: sticky bread or a tea cake if they met in the morning, perhaps a shortbread or a burnt custard if they met in the afternoon. They had all gathered, their chairs arranged in a loose semicircle, when he brought in a freshly baked Sally Lunn, some sweet butter, and a pot of homemade peach jam. Mrs. Katherine Fisher, the unofficial leader of the board, poured tea and directed

Butcher to leave the bread on the table. All the members of the board were there. In addition to Miss Katherine, there was Marie Wilkins, Margaret Adcock, Thelma Russell, Elizabeth Bookshire, Ruth Jennings, and Virginia Yeager. And next to her, the director. Butcher knew them all, had listened to the director complain about them collectively and individually, had heard about their husbands and their children, had studied them in the months he had worked at the VOA, knew the pecking order.

Miss Katherine was married to the President of the Piedmont Security and Trust, and as the wife of a banker, she commanded the respect of the other women. She was a broad, heavyset woman with a determined jawline and an unswerving eye. Butcher knew her to be no-nonsense. She was not prone to fashion as were most of the "Miss Anns"—she would often wear the same frock, a simple pleated chocolate shirtwaist with a squared bodice adorned only by a pearl brooch. She was practical in her shoes as well, Butcher had observed. Where the other ladies would have heels with straps or shiny patent leathers, Miss Katherine always wore a simple pair of rounded flat heels. She looked ready for business. Her only luxury was the heavy fur she brought with her at the first hint of cold and wore well into the spring. Butcher also watched how the other women reacted to, honored the wealth the coat represented.

"Thank you, George," she said, eying the tray with the bread. "Is that a Sally Lunn? What a treat. My mother-in-law makes one, but she does hers in an angel cake pan. I am sure yours will rival it if anyone's can. Has it cooled? I don't want to slice it too fresh. When bread is too hot, you can't slice it. It will only press it down. And did you bring a serrated knife?"

"I took it out of the oven 'bout half an hour ago," Butcher replied. "It should be fine to slice, but still warm enough to spread the butter. I brought you a knife—if you want, I can slice it for you."

"No, that won't be necessary," she said. "I think Mrs. Wilkins can do the honors." Butcher placed the tray on the table as Miss Marie, round as a cookie jar with two brightly colored dots of rouge circled on her cheeks, jumped to Miss Katherine's command.

Butcher knew he could not leave until he was dismissed by the director, needed to be available should there be a question about the state of affairs in the kitchen. He showed Miss Marie where to cut.

"I think you should be able to get eight slices," he said, "if nobody minds the heel."

"If you make it in an angel cake pan, George, then no one has to get the heel end," noted Miss Katherine.

"The heel will do for me," said the director.

"And for me as well," said Miss Virginia. Butcher recognized the concession. Miss Virginia was the newest member of the group, having been awarded admission only four months earlier. She was the widow of a war hero, her husband killed at the second battle for the Marne, the director had told him. What troubled Butcher was the awareness that while the rest of the women seemed cut of a whole cloth, he could not figure Miss Virginia. She didn't act like the others. She didn't look like the others. She was pale as a moonbeam, and even in the coldest weather, she fancied lighter tones—ice blue, eggshell, sage or sherbet green—unlike the drab browns and olives of the other women. Butcher felt she wished to stand apart from them somehow, wondered if it was simply that she did not want to be deemed matronly. However, there was something else to her, something hidden. Her dresses were tailored to showcase her slim waist, and whereas they all had their hair pulled back into a loose bun or topknot, her blond hair was cut short and curled in a deep-set finger wave. She plucked her eyebrows and smoothed them with a pencil into thin arches above her watery blue eyes. Butcher had the impression that if the sun caught her at the right angle she might be translucent. He could also see the relationship between her and these other women was one of mutual distrust. It was obvious—these women did not like her, and she did not care for them. She moved among them, but was not one of them. She deferred to them in polite society, but would not be a guest in any of their homes unless it would be to fill a table as the escort for a single officer from the army base.

"This cuts like a dream," said Miss Marie. "I don't know how you do it, George. It is light as a cloud, but it has texture as well."

Then to the ladies, "Unless there is objection, I will put jam and butter on each plate." There was a murmur of consent as she passed the plates. Miss Virginia and the director received theirs last. The women balanced the plates expertly on their laps, holding cups of hot tea in their hands.

"If I could bake like this, I know what I would be doing," said Miss Thelma.

"Yes, and what is that?" asked Miss Katherine as she poured the final cup of tea for herself and lowered herself into her chair.

"Why, I would be entering my recipes in the Mystic White Flour contest. I would be applying to become *The Lady in the White Hat*."

"There is only one problem with that," said Miss Ruth. "I've tasted your biscuits."

There was some good-natured laughter, to which Miss Thelma replied, "Yes, it is good I can still afford to have a cook. I think the judge would starve if Leena ever left us."

Butcher stood to the side of the director, waiting for an opportunity to address any questions. Sometimes, they would ask for his report first thing and he would be free of them; other days, he would be forced to stand, head bowed, hands folded in front while they ate and gossiped and sipped their tea. Today, they took little notice of him, the conversation having turned to the baking contest.

Miss Elizabeth, who also served on the WCTU, had no time for the contest since they specifically allowed the use of alcohol.

"But, Elizabeth, it isn't like they are promoting drinking," said Miss Ruth. "It is only a flavoring. I am as temperance as the next, but I have never had a fruit cake or a Lane cake that wasn't made better with a drop of shinny."

Miss Elizabeth wasn't moved. She merely humphed, "It is a line, Ruth. And either you cross it or you don't. Get people used to the taste in a sweet cake, then they will be wanting more. Besides, my sister-in-law has met Colonel Clayton Claiborne II"—she paused to clarify for those not familiar with the name—"the President of the Mystic White Flour Company. She says he has strong associations with the Klan. Not to mention that whoever does this would be like a common salesgirl. Imagine having your likeness on a sack of flour."

Butcher was familiar with the contest, since a flyer came in every sack of Mystic White. It was the same flyer he had tucked into his pocket:

### *Are You The Lady in the White Hat?*

Mystic White Flour is searching for the ideal Southern Woman to represent the best of Southern Womanhood— delicacy, purity, softness, and strength.

Qualities that also describe Mystic White Flour, milled from only the finest, soft white flour.

*A Southern Tradition . . .*

*. . . Born from Our Southern Heritage*

The winner will receive a cash prize of $2500 and a one-year contract with Mystic White Flour as "The Lady in the White Hat."

First runner-up will receive a *Brand-New! All Gas! Porcelain & Heavy Cast-Iron Metal!* Magic Chef Oven!

All finalists will receive a one-year supply of Mystic White baking products.

On the back of the flyer was the list of rules:

1. Each entrant should submit a short biography and a photograph, and her favorite "signature" recipe made with Mystic White Flour or Mystic White Self-Rising Flour. Recipes should be in keeping with the tastes of women in the South and should not employ exotic or foreign ingredients. *Note:* Alcohol is permitted only as a flavoring in limited amounts.

2. Finalists should be available to appear in Atlanta during the third week of June 1935.

3. Finalists will be judged on the following:
   - Interview, personality, and poise
   - Menu planning
   - Baking demonstration

4. Each finalist will be expected to pay her own travel expenses to Atlanta. Hotel room and board during the competition will be complimentary.

5. Contest open to any woman of true Southern descent.

6. All contestants should be of highest moral quality.

7. Recipes must be original (or adapted to a family tradition) and will be judged on criteria outlined below:
   - Taste
   - Appearance
   - Creativity
   - Consumer appeal

8. Decision of the judges is final in all matters relating to this contest.

What Butcher could do with that money! It would be more than enough to fund his bistro, his café. He would even be able to compete in a city where people knew about food, somewhere like Savannah or even New Orleans. How unfair to dress up one of these hollow "Miss Anns" who only pretended to know how to cook, when he . . . when he . . . was actually deserving. The system was rigged against him. Had always been, he knew. But if he was clever . . .

"George?"

The director's voice shook him from his contemplation.

"Yessir."

"Mrs. Fisher was asking about the hams she had donated for Christmas."

"I'm down to the last two."

"Already," said Miss Katherine. "Why, I declare. You must be serving these men ham biscuits every day. I thought surely that they might at least last till Easter." She dabbed crumbs and a spot of jam from her lips.

Butcher wanted to walk over to her, to grab her by her throat and shake her hard till her tight gray bun fell loose down her back and her teeth rattled in her head. He had scraped and scrimped with the four hams she had donated to the Residence, had served each man a mere sliver on Christmas Day, and then chopped just a small amount into his New Year's Hoppin' John. He wanted to scream at her about the hundreds of ways he worked to serve the men something that even resembled real food—how just last week he had been forced to press black-eyed peas into patties so they would at least look like meat.

"I can assure you, Mrs. Fisher, the men do not eat ham every morning," said the director. "I eat with them every day, and though George does a good job of working with what we have, the meals are far from fancy."

Butcher thought back to the brothel when he was in Brest, how Maude had taken him down one morning for breakfast with the whores. He remembered the smell of the freshly baked bread and the fried sausages and the coffee. The prism of bottled vinegars and oils lining the shelves, glinting in the morning light. Maude fed him cheese and bread. There was enough for all—barely, but enough. Outside there was war and death and hunger. But inside,

each was happy, glad, eager to share. It made him want to cry—
that these bitches had so much, that he had so little. That he
wanted only his part. That one of them, or one of a hundred or
thousand just like them, would win a contest that he could win if
only he was allowed to enter.

"I suppose," said Miss Katherine. "But times are hard for us all—
and hams don't grow on trees, now do they?" The ladies laughed at
this.

"No, ma'am," he said. "I'll work to make them last. Till Easter.
And I appreciate the kindness you all do for us here. All the men
do." He tried to hide the contempt in his face, was afraid to look
around the room. "Now, I need to get back to the kitchen."

"Of course," said Miss Katherine.

"Thank you, George," said the director.

George lifted his head and in turning, caught the eye of Miss
Virginia. "If you don't mind, I would like to speak to you when we
are finished here," she said.

"Yes, ma'am. I'll be in the kitchen or the boss can come and get
me if you want." Butcher figured she had some baking for him—
the first time she ever requested something. But there was more to
it. He imagined, or maybe it was just wishing he told himself, that
she knew what he was thinking. There seemed to be an instant
when their eyes met and she understood.

He was right. She did understand. Virginia watched as the cook
shuffled out toward the kitchen. How these women bored her. She
had to take a small nip of brandy just to endure those mornings the
board met to discuss their good deeds accomplished as a result of
their good breeding and their well-made marriages. Some of them
came from local church groups, some from the YWCA, or the
WTCU. One common denominator was that they all belonged to
the United Daughters of the Confederacy. Without that birthright,
you need not apply.

Women like this perplexed Virginia. She did not understand
how they could be satisfied with the profits of a bake sale. It baf-
fled her how they gloated over a mediocre performance at a piano
recital by one of their daughters or brooded over the slight if suffi-

cient notice wasn't paid to it in the society column of the paper. It wasn't that she was a stranger to society, wasn't that she hadn't been born to a pedigreed background that even Katherine Fisher admired. No. If asked, she would tell you in great detail about her voice lessons as a girl, how she sang once for the Governor's Ball. She would describe the fabric of the dress she wore to her debutante cotillion, and how she had a silk magnolia pinned at the waist. If pressed, she would tell you that she had been born into one of the better families in South Carolina. Her grandfather, Herbert Blankenship, had been a successful merchant with a large rice plantation near Charleston. He had served with distinction with Generals Gilmore and Beauregard during the War of Secession before being killed securing a victory in the defense of the Charleston Harbor in 1863. She still had in her possession the letter, written in General Gilmore's own hand to her grandmother, describing the nobility and valor of her grandfather's death.

Her father had been granted a full scholarship to the University of South Carolina, and was a prominent attorney until his untimely death. Bad investments and shiftless scallywags had driven her mother to her grave as well. It was a sad story, familiar enough to most of the women she had chosen to associate with. Virginia had crafted it well, perfected the telling of it, so that she grew misty-eyed when she recounted the loss of family, of property, of position. The women would hold her hand, dab at their eyes, and nod in sympathy.

The story was also a lie, a grand fabrication. She had been born Jenny Duff. She had married Henry "Harry" Yeager in 1918. She had taken the name of Blankenship when she read it on a memorial plaque when she had visited Charleston. She also knew Charleston was too difficult a town for her to break into—people knew about your past, could smell your breeding. These dumb clucks in Fayetteville hadn't a clue about who she was, where she really came from. They only knew what she wanted them to know, what they wanted to hear, wanted to believe. So when she had arrived in Fayetteville, let it slip at the hairdressers one afternoon that she was the granddaughter of a Confederate martyr, a member in good standing of the United Daughters of the Confederacy, they were obliged to invite her to tea, to join their clubs, to serve as the escort to one of the endless stream of officers stationed at Fort Bragg.

It was easy enough to blend the lie into the fabric of truth, like a brightly colored thread. And she was experienced enough as an actress to pull off the part. She had run away from the South as a girl—from the poverty, from the drunken wretch of a father who wanted only to beat her until he found her good enough to mount. She briefly joined a circus passing through town, then later worked in a minstrel show. She could sing a little, was quick to learn a routine, and was willing to do whatever she needed. One man, after all, was pretty much just like the next. While working with a traveling vaudeville show, she and her friend Dorothea developed a comedy sketch "School Daze," which was reported in a paper as being "a cracker!" and she had dreams of perhaps one day even working in New York.

She had been married briefly in the hullaballoo of the war, but that had been a marriage of necessity for her. Harry Yeager had been crazy in love for her, following her around like a sad puppy at the entrance to the hotel where the vaudeville company was quartered when playing his town. Poor Harry had believed all the claptrap they sang back in those days: "Keep the Home Fires Burning," "Pack up Your Troubles," and "It's a Long Way to Tipperary," even though she knew he didn't have the slightest notion of where Tipperary could be found on a map. Harry Yeager had come around at a time when she needed him, and so she married him, and sent him off to war. She promised she would "keep the home fires burning," and he was dippy enough to believe her. And he did her the greatest of all services. He got himself shot in the head on the riverbank of the Marne. He had provided her with a small income accorded to the widow of a war hero and a small degree of respectability that granted her admission to military bases. But there were thousands of women in her situation, and she was not content to just make do on what she had. Not willing to be a face in the crowd of war widows.

So when they were playing Charleston, and Dorothea told her that she was breaking up the act to get married to the colored ventriloquist, it came almost as a flash from the sky to her. She would reinvent herself. Take the parts that were respectable enough and add to them, like a potter making a bowl. A vessel. Yes, she would create a new self, and she would be the vessel for her. And so Jenny Yeager née Jenny Duff became Virginia Blankenship Yeager of the Charleston Blankenships.

When the meeting had ended and the women had said their good-byes, Virginia had the director lead her to the kitchen to see the cook. He was chopping vegetables for a stew or a soup, she couldn't tell which.

He stopped chopping as they entered, wiped his large hands on a cloth tucked into the right side of his pants.

"George," said the director. "Mrs. Yeager has a small matter to discuss with you."

"A favor really," said Virginia. "I am entertaining tomorrow evening. And I was hoping I could get you to make a pie for me. I will pay you for your time and materials of course."

"Is there something special you want?" asked Butcher.

"As a matter of fact, there is." Virginia paused to look at the director. "I don't need to bore you with my baking requests. And I am sure you must have a thousand things that command your attention. But I do thank you for your assistance." She extended an ivory-gloved hand to the director, who, understanding he was dismissed, excused himself. "Now, where was I?" she continued.

"You have a request," said Butcher.

"Yes," she said. "I have a small bag of pecans that I was hoping you might be able to turn into a pie for me. My friend Major Gleeson is a great fan of the Karo pie, and he will be joining me tomorrow night for supper. I wanted to have something special, and I know that sometimes you make things for the ladies."

"Did you bring a plate to bake it in?"

"No. Did I need to?"

"Most times they bring their own dish."

"No," she said, understanding the implication of what he said. "I am happy to give you credit for the pie, George. Major Gleeson is not courting me for my baking expertise. I'm afraid I am really a terrible cook." She smiled at him, and Butcher was impressed by this small confession. "About the best I can do in a pinch are salmon croquettes with mustard sauce. Fortunately, tomorrow is Friday, so I will be able to get by with fish for supper."

Butcher thought of the rows of canned salmon in the pantry. It was abundant, cheap, and he served it for dinner every Friday night. "Did you bring the pecans?" Saying the word, Butcher noted the difference in the way they each pronounced it: She had said *puh-kahn* with the emphasis on the second half of the word; he had always called them *pea-cans*.

"No, I wanted to make sure you could do it for me first," she said. "I can have my girl bring them around this evening if you need."

"That'll do," he said. "I'll pick the nut meat after supper tonight and roll out the crust in the morning. She can pick it up sometime after lunch. If she comes around three o'clock, it should still be warm for supper."

"Thank you so much," she said. "That is very generous of you. And how much will I owe you?"

"Six bits," he said. "That should do."

"And I'm sure it would be a bargain at twice that."

That afternoon, he had just cut out the biscuits for dinner and had brushed them with buttermilk. There was a soft knocking at the door and he looked to see a young woman standing there—Miss Virginia's maid, he assumed. He opened the door and held it to keep it from being blown back by the breeze. The woman had no hat or scarf, even though it was still cold, and she wore a cheap cloth asparagus-colored coat. When she looked up at him, he realized she was no more than a girl really—sixteen, maybe seventeen at best, so young to be in service. But working for a white woman of even moderate means would have to be better than what she had left behind. What surprised Butcher more than her age, however, was her beauty. She was a mulatto, possibly octoroon, and her skin held only the slightest tint, like coffee with cream. Her features were delicate, refined, and she had soft greenish brown eyes, which made him think of an unripe pear. She held a small, greasy paper sack in front of her like an offering.

"I'm from Mrs. Yeager's," she said. "I brought the pecans for the pie. Are you the baker?" Butcher could see that she wore no gloves, her legs were bare, and she shivered with the cold.

"Come in here where it's warm," Butcher said. He took the sack from her and looked inside. "I reckon there's enough here," he said. "But it'll be more Karo than nut meat, that's for sure." Butcher nodded to the stove. "I have fresh coffee if you want."

"No," said the girl. "I have errands to run. She will be wanting to know where I am. She's anxious as a cat today. She's spent all afternoon laying out her clothes for tomorrow evening. I'll have to be home in time to help her with her bath." Butcher thought she looked too young to be so haggard.

"This must be an important dinner," said Butcher.

"She thinks the major is going to propose to her. Take her away from here. He's got a commission to take him to Missouri." Panic flared in her green-brown eyes—it was obvious she had spoken too quickly.

Butcher smiled to let her know he was not a threat. He offered her a cruller that he had saved for himself from breakfast. She took it and began nibbling on the corner of the fried dough. "What's your name, anyhow?" he asked.

"Mona," she said.

"Mona what?"

"Just Mona."

Butcher figured she thought he was trying to make a pass at her, probably had men of all races pitching her. "Well, Miss Mona, the way I see it, we're all trying to get someplace else from here."

"I hate it here," she said. "Hate it. Wish we never had come here. Nothing here but rednecks and shit-kickers."

"And where was you before you was here?"

"Around."

"Well, that covers a lot of ground."

"I've lived in the North," she said. "That's where I was born. I plan to go back there when I'm able. Or maybe West. Missouri is at least a step."

"So, you reckon she will take you with her if she gets married?"

"She better."

"Then I best make sure this is a pie that'll do the trick. Sprinkle a little magic into it so the major goes crazy in love. So crazy he will fall down and roll on the floor and beg Miss Virginia to marry him and go with him to Missouri."

The girl flashed a slight smile at him. Butcher wanted her to know that she need not fear him. "There may be a scarf here I can loan you to help fight this wind. Folks is always leaving stuff behind."

"Thank you, no," she said. "I can bear it."

Butcher could tell even this simple kindness was not lost on her. "You tell Miss Virginia I'll have her pie ready for you to pick up by three o'clock tomorrow afternoon."

"Yes, sir, Mr. . . . ."

"George Butcher," he said, bowing down toward her. "But friends all just call me Butcher."

"Three o'clock," she said. "I will see you then, Mr. George Butcher." As she opened the door to leave, she gave him another smile—this one fuller, which made him suddenly scared and excited and sad all at once. And as the door closed behind her, he could hear her call out, "And thank you for the doughnut, Mr. Butcher. Butcher, the baker."

# 3

# Karo pie . . .

It was after six the next evening when Butcher arrived at Miss Virginia's house. He had the pie ready by three, made a fresh pot of coffee, and even dished up a bit of the rice pudding he had made for the evening meal in anticipation of the girl's arrival. He had remembered the shy smile of the girl when he offered her the cruller and wanted to make her smile again. Nothing more. But she never came. Not at 3:30, not at 4:00, not at 4:30. Dinner for the men was from 5 to 6, so he busied himself with the final preparations, though his mind was only half on his job. He had been stood up. They had ordered a pie from him and then just sloughed him off. It made him mad. Though he was able to glean most of the ingredients from the pantry of the Residence, he had to use his own supply of Karo and vanilla. He had put so much into this pie—it *mattered* to him that she like it—this was more than just the money. He wanted to impress her with it. Show her what he was capable of. What he was worth.

When he could see the line for dinner beginning to dwindle, he handed over the finishing duties to the crew. It would be easy enough for them to finish up without him. He spoke to the director about the pie, telling him he wasn't sure if he had been supposed to deliver it. That maybe he had gotten things confused.

"George, now, that is very careless of you. These women ask very little from us and give us a great deal in return."

Butcher apologized for his mistake and said if he could have the address, he would run it over to them. "It will be in time for dessert," he said. "And I have kept it warm on the rack."

"Yes, take it to her," he said, handing him the address on a paper torn from a yellow pad. "And you should not charge her for it. Tell her that is your way of making amends."

The route was familiar enough. To get to Haymount, he walked past the Old Market, which though not built for slavery, certainly witnessed the buying and selling of slaves on its steps. Now, farmers pulled wagons there to sell vegetables. Butcher walked there several times a week to see if there were any bargains; often, he was able to get a better price because of the quantity he could afford. It had taken him a while to find the house, though. She didn't live on one of the broader, more prominent streets like Hay or Green like most of the other "Miss Anns," but was back a couple of blocks on Arsenal. As he studied the numbers, looking for the correct one, he held the pie wrapped in a kitchen towel and could feel its warmth in the chill evening.

He thought it strange that though it was already getting dim, there were no lights on in the front parlor. He walked to the back door, expecting there to be lights. But there were not. He was sure he had the correct address, so he knocked on the door. He could hear a rumbling as a chair scraped against the linoleum. An orangish-colored lamp came on, and through the glass of the door Butcher could see Miss Virginia walking unsteadily toward him. She had on a garishly colored satin robe, like something out of a Charlie Chan. When she opened the door, Butcher couldn't believe it, but she was definitely blind drunk.

"Miss Virginia, it's me, George from the VOA. I brought you your pie."

It took a moment for the words to register with her, but then she realized who he was. "Shit. The pie," she said, smoothing her hair back from her face. "Well, might as well bring it in." She pushed the screen door open for him and then stepped back into the kitchen. He followed her inside. She turned on an overhead light and the sudden glare of the bulb overhead drew everything in sharp angles and shadows. He looked around on the counters to see that dinner had been started, but abandoned.

Miss Virginia walked back in with her pocketbook open, digging for her change purse.

"How much did you say?"

"Six bits."

She handed him a dollar, then waved with the back of her hand. "You can keep the extra for your trouble." Then, pointing to the pie, she said, "Put that anywhere. Throw it in the goddamn yard for all I care. The queen declares there will be no need for pie tonight. No need for dessert, no need for dinner. It's all ruined." Then she fell into one of the chairs at the kitchen table and began to cry. He could tell she was not a woman used to crying, and her breath came in quick gasps as she tried to hold back the tears but couldn't. She put her hands up to her cheeks as if she could press the flow back into her eyes, and when that didn't work, gave up, laid her head on the table, and sobbed. It was as if she had forgotten he was standing there not four feet away looking at her—or that she didn't care.

He let her cry. He went to the stove and made coffee. He knew she would need some. He also wondered where the girl was, why she wasn't here. By the time the coffee had percolated, Virginia had stopped crying. She raised her head, running her hands through her hair, and then wiped her nose and eyes with the sleeve from her gown.

"Where's Mona?" she asked.

"There wasn't anybody here but you since I got here." He set the coffee cup down in front of her.

"The little bitch better keep her head low if she knows what's good for her. A millstone." Then louder, to no one: "A millstone."

She noticed Butcher again. "I must look a fright. Why is it no one ever thinks to put a mirror in the kitchen? If you would like to have some coffee, please help yourself. There's some milk in the icebox if you take it light," she said. "If you don't mind"—she pointed to an open bottle of hooch on the counter—"I think I could use a bit of 'sweetener' in mine." He handed her the bottle and poured a cup of coffee for himself. She sighed, then more to herself than him, said, "She made a real mess of it."

Butcher wasn't quite sure what to do. It wasn't unusual for white women to talk in front of him as if he were a dimwitted child or a pet, acting as if he were incapable of comprehending the matters about which they spoke. He didn't collect information as some of the help would do; it made him uncomfortable to hear such intimacies. Still, he imagined this might be useful to him—she was vulnerable, approachable.

"With your friend, the major."

"The major—I'm afraid I won't be seeing any more of him. Jesus, what a crumb he turned out to be. Yes, he's given me the kiss-off, I'm afraid. I can tell you one thing, George, whoever said 'honesty is the best policy' was full of hooey."

Butcher laughed. "The way I've seen it, is the one who owns it is the one who says what it is. The rest of us just play by their rules."

"Yes," she said. "We are not the ones to make the rules—I am sure you know that better than most."

"I'm sorry about the major," Butcher said. "The girl, Mona, told me you two were going to be married. Said she hoped you was all gonna leave here."

Fire flashed in Miss Virginia's eyes. "She told you that, did she? Well, she had no right. And the little bitch certainly managed to gum up the works so that wouldn't happen."

Butcher remembered what the girl had said about not being left behind. "Has she run off as well?"

Miss Virginia laughed. "God, I couldn't get rid of her if I wanted to. She's hiding around here somewhere."

He didn't say anything, gave her an opportunity to continue. The shot of whiskey had relaxed her so the words poured out as if she needed to tell them.

"It's complicated, that's all. You see, Mona is the daughter of a dear friend of mine, a woman now deceased. Her father didn't want anything to do with her. He couldn't raise a child. Dorothea asked me to take her. I couldn't refuse."

"I thought she was your maid."

"She is my maid," said Virginia. "It is an arrangement. I care for her. I provide for her. She cooks for me, for us. Runs errands. You do understand I cannot travel around with the mixed-race child of my dead friend without some reason. That much would seem to be obvious."

Butcher thought about it. It made sense. It wasn't right, he knew. But it did make sense. A light-skinned girl like Mona would have a hard time of it on her own, unable to claim her mother's race, not really part of her father's. Maybe this woman had done the best by the girl that she could.

The whiskey and coffee had begun to put a bit of color into Virginia's cheeks. She pulled her robe close up around her throat. "Mona insisted that I tell the major the truth about her so that if he and I did get engaged, there would be no question about her coming with us to his new post. I agreed. Now look what that got me. Everything ruined." She sighed again and smiled. He could tell she had regained herself. "I am sorry to have been so . . . expansive . . . in my emotions. I trust . . ."

"This is none of my business," he said.

"Thank you. Thank you for bringing the pie. I am sure it is delicious. I am sorry it will go to waste."

"I can cut you a slice. It might do you good to eat something," he said.

"Perhaps," she said. "I haven't eaten anything, and it doesn't look like I'll be getting dinner."

He turned away from her as he sliced a piece, larger than he should have, and lifted it gently from the pan to a plate.

"Then I should let you get back to the Residence. I have no idea what time it is. I am going to take a hot bath to soothe my nerves."

But Butcher wasn't done. He knew this was the time. When he saw her again with the ladies, she would never acknowledge what had passed between them, knew she might possibly be steeled against him even. It was now or never.

"Miss Virginia, there is something I would like to talk to you about."

"Yes, George. What is that?"

Butcher set the pie down in front of her. He knew the pie was perfect, could feel it as he rolled the dough that morning, could smell it in the roasted edges of the pecans as he took it out of the oven, could sense it in the slight *give* of the thickened syrup and sugar and eggs as he sliced the piece for her. "I was wondering if you ever thought that you might want to be 'The Lady in the White Hat'?"

# 4

# angel biscuits . . .

The note read simply:

*Secured employment.*
*GB*

Virginia understood the cryptic message, recognized George's hand—she had copied enough from the small notebook of recipes he kept to know it instantly. It had been over three months since that night in the kitchen when he had proposed the idea. He had been gone for just over three weeks, and in less than one week she was due to travel to Atlanta. She had to smile. The plan had worked—she was one of eight finalists in the Mystic White Flour Company's contest. One of eight ladies to become *The* Lady.

When Butcher had first explained it to her, she could see the logic in it, understood the possibility. "It's a recipe," he said, holding the notebook out to her. "And I got hundreds here. I can teach you to make 'em—you don't have to cook 'em all. Make one or two. Maybe three or four tops. I can teach you that."

"But why me?"

"You have a style," he said. When she didn't respond, he offered, "I don't mean offense by that."

"No," she said. "I understand that much—they aren't looking for Auntie Lou or a mammy. They want to sell a certain image."

"Style," he repeated.

"This would be cheating. Is that what you are proposing to me, George?"

"It ain't cheating if the game is rigged, and this sure as hell is a closed game," he said. "I could cook circles around any one of the Miss Anns who will enter the contest. But I'm not the . . . *image*, as you put it."

Virginia studied him. He was a large man, not too tall, but solidly built. He had beautiful hands, kept his nails trimmed and buffed. She thought that curious about a man. He had a soft smile, but his eyes betrayed him with their sadness. She understood what he meant—even here, these women shut her out, sensed her as an outsider and treated her just. It appealed to her to have an opportunity to leapfrog over the bitches. The Blankenships would be rushing to know her, to remember her, to claim her. It would provide her status, stature, social heft. It would definitely give her an advantage.

"The Lady in the White Hat," she said.

"Not cheating, really," he said. "You would be the one to make the recipe. I would give you some of mine and teach you to make them. Don't worry. I would choose things that was easy."

"I must strike you as somewhat inept," she said. She tried to toss it off as a quip.

"No, ma'am," he said. "That's not it. It's about keeping it simple. Think on this. I was at the picture show a couple of Saturdays ago, and the newsreel had a part about the 'modern housewife.' Said what she wants more than anything else is convenience." He paused for a moment to let the full effect of that settle over her, then added, "Easy is convenient." He smiled, now fuller.

"Yes," she said. "I suppose you have a point. What are you expecting to get from this, George? I don't imagine you are doing this for charity or for the comfort of the American housewife."

He was unapologetic. "I want the money," he said. "Plain as that."

"You would be placing a great deal of trust in me."

"I'm a lot of things," he said. "A white woman ain't one of 'em. I need a partner."

"And I would do all of this in return for what? Certainly you do not expect the whole sum?

"I would be happy with a split. I was thinking maybe sixty-forty. They're my recipes after all."

"Fifty-fifty," she said. "Like you said, I have the style." And with that, their bargain began to take shape.

The initial phase of the contest required that she submit a short letter about herself and why she would be a suitable candidate to represent the company. Virginia knew which bits to play in her letter—made sure to mention that she was the widow of a war hero. She was proud of her DOC membership. She mentioned the work she did with the group in Fayetteville at the Residence. Butcher agreed, mentioning the VOA was a plus. The group was all about charity, but the religious part was vague and broadminded enough not to offend anyone.

They were to also include a signature recipe. For that, there had been no discussion. George had taught her to make his biscuits—his angel biscuits.

"You got two types of biscuits," he said. "Powder or yeast. My biscuit has both, so you can mix it up and keep it cold in the icebox. Don't have to mix fresh dough in the morning. Convenient. The yeast gives it texture, the powder keeps it soft. Also, biscuits come in two styles: dropped or rolled.

"When I was a girl, we would have beaten biscuits," she said.

"Hard tack," he said. "We ate 'em in the army as well. Times is hard enough without the misery of a beaten biscuit."

"I can't argue with you there," she said.

"Now," he continued, "I don't much care for the dropped, unless it's on a cobbler. The rolled are just more elegant. You can cut them whatever size you want."

"A rolled biscuit," she repeated. "I should have an assortment of biscuit cutters."

"Yes," he said. "Those are easy enough to come by. In a pinch, you can use the lip of a cup, but a sharper edge is better. Cuts the dough instead of pressing it out."

She copied the recipe from his notebook. His script was straightforward, without flourish—practical. She had no difficulty in reading it. Nevertheless, he kept looking over her shoulder to make sure she had the measurements correct. "Now, my mam, she could mix and measure in her hands—had the feel for it. That's how she taught me. I can do it, too, but that takes time to learn. So I figured all these out for you. Did the measurements till you learn. Made sure they were right. You have some room to vary a bit if you're making a gravy or a stew. But not with baking. Plus, you can taste a stew. With a biscuit, you can mix it up so it looks just like it did every time before, but if you got one or two things off, you might as well bake a pie made of road apples. Taste will be about the same."

Before they ever began to bake, he had her learn the measurements by heart. She would pour a tablespoon of salt into her palm. "Feel it. See how it looks when you cup your hand or if you have your hand held flat." Then they would pour the salt back into a bowl and she would scoop what she imagined was the same amount. When she would get it wrong, he would chastise her: "You have to know this, Miss Virginia. Like when I was in the army. They had us put together our rifles and take 'em apart again a hundred times. So you could do it in your sleep. Then they took 'em all away from us when we left basic. It's one thing to teach a colored man to put together a gun, it's another to let him have one in his hands."

She practiced the measurements daily for the entire week after her first lesson, and he seemed pleased enough with her when he returned. The making of the biscuits proved more difficult. The lard had to be chilled, cubed, chilled again. It took a while for her to get the sizes correct. And then there was the cutting in. He sifted flour, sugar, salt, and baking powder into a bowl and crumbled the chilled white lard on top. "Some will want to use self-rising flour," he said. "I don't believe in it myself. Like to add my own salt and my own baking powder." When he spoke about the ingredients, he seemed somehow to be more alive, like each element's purpose was special to him.

Then, picking two dinner knives from the drawer, he began crisscrossing them rapidly, the gentle zing of the blades barely touching as he incorporated the lard into the flour. When he handed her the knives, he indicated she should repeat the motion.

She tried, but failed miserably at it. After a half-dozen botched attempts, Mona pulled a small pastry blender from the drawer.

"It's what I use," she said. "It's what they will use. Stop being such a show-off."

George relented. Virginia couldn't help but notice how he deferred to Mona in such details, acted as if he wanted to please her, win her approval. It bothered Virginia that he was twice the girl's age, but there was nothing she could do about that. Mona had been the go-between in arranging the cooking lessons. She would carry a note to the Residence with a request for a cake or a pie—usually one George had prearranged with her. George would bring the item at an appointed time and then give Virginia a lesson. Mona would sit watching, slunk into a chair, drinking coffee or nibbling at the cake or pie George had brought. An ill breeze hovered in the air between Virginia and the girl. Virginia knew that Butcher could feel it, and worked hard to include her in the conversation. Whenever he asked whether she liked it, she would shrug. "I like store bought," she would say sometimes, and Virginia had the distinct impression it was meant just to goad him. He always took the bait.

"Phew! There isn't a store-bought pastry that can hold a candle to this, little miss. Just can't do it."

"A cake from the store is sweeter."

"That's because all it is, is sugar. Sugar and spit. You can't buy this in a store—unless it was a store where I sold this. Maybe you just need another slice to tell how good it is." And he would smile at the girl, who would readily accept the pastry from him. Virginia could tell she enjoyed the attention. When Mona would relax toward him a bit, Virginia could see what attracted him. Her beauty. How hard that was for her. Mona, of course, had no concept of it, and Virginia knew that it was only in the losing of a thing that it became invaluable. She struggled now to make her appearance what it should be, but she knew she was no longer young. No longer the ingénue. Time for parts that required more skill.

Virginia had to agree with Butcher about his pies and cakes. His baking was extraordinary. Cakes seemed to melt away in her mouth. If there was frosting, it wasn't just sticky goo holding the layers together, but possessed its own delicate, complementary character. George said that a cake was like a necklace. The layers were the jewels, but the frosting was the chain. "You wouldn't tie a diamond around your neck with a piece of twine," he said. Every detail mattered to him, was instrumental. He demanded that she adopt the same attitude. Bowl after bowl of flour and lard went into the trash. The nuggets of lard were too large, too mushy, too *something*. Virginia thought she would never get it right, but finally after many failed attempts, she mastered the technique, so the lard blended into the flour like tiny pea-sized pearls.

But even that accomplishment was short-lived, for with each foothold gained came a new challenge. Next came the wet ingredients. He showed her how to determine the correct water temperature so she could tell it was okay to crumble the fresh yeast cake into it—too hot or too cold would kill the yeast. "It's a living thing. You have to remember that. And if you notice any little specks of mold on it, toss it out—it's going off." He showed her how to add vinegar to milk to sour it. "Buttermilk is always best, but you can't always get it. This works almost as well. And it's a good trick to have up your sleeve." The yeast and sour milk were combined, and he stirred them into the flour just so the mixture held together. "Too much mixing and the biscuits will be tough."

After that came the kneading. He turned the whole bowl onto the countertop, which had been dusted with flour. He took a long metal spoon from the drawer and pressed it to the back of her hand. "Feel how cool this is," he said. "This is how you want your hand to feel. Some people have a natural coolness to them. My mam had it. I don't, so I try to cool my hands a bit before touching the dough. Want to keep it cool, keep that lard from melting from the heat of your hand." Instinctively, she thrust her hand out toward him. She thought of how the women from the DOC would react to her holding her hand for this colored man to inspect.

"It'll do," he said, touching his fingertips to her palm. "A little on the cool side, and you have a soft surface. No calluses." He showed her how to knead the dough, quickly, but firmly, using only five or six quick thrusts with the base of her hand, turning the dough after each push. The dough ball was then gathered and put in a large bowl, covered in cellophane, and put into the icebox. "Let it rest for a spell," he said. "You'd be good to roll 'em out for dinner. But you can do a double batch in the afternoon, bake the second half in the morning."

She peeked several times at the dough resting gently in the bowls in the icebox after he left. Trying to see if there was a difference between the one she had assembled and his. He was right, she realized. All that work, and it was impossible to tell how the end result would be. There was something else, though—she was excited to know if she could do this. Wanted to succeed at it.

When he returned several days later, he brought a long wooden rolling pin and an assortment of cutters for her—smooth tin rings with handles. They did not look new. When she asked him, he said, "Real cooks have things they use for a long time. Find something they like and they keep it. These have some age on them. Can't have you showing up with something with the price tag still on it. Wouldn't look right."

Holding the tapered wood in her hands, running her hand over its smooth surface, she was impressed by his constant attention to detail. "It's from France," he said. "I got it in the war. It will let you feel the dough better. . . ."

"So you don't press it down," she said.

"Yes," he said, smiling. "You understand."

Again, using it correctly was no small feat. After kneading the dough again briefly, he showed her how to roll the dough in consistent, steady strokes, turning the dough each time "so that it didn't get worked too much in one direction." Then they cut the dough into circles.

"Stamp 'em out without twisting," he said, slicing into the

dough and pulling back with the tin cutter in an almost mechanical action. "As close together as possible. Any dough that's left, then you can fit back together, roll again, and finish stamping." He placed the cut pieces onto a greased sheet pan. "Put them close together in the pan so they rise up and not out," he said. Then, brushing the tops with melted butter, he added, "Give 'em a kiss with the butter, cover them, and let them rise again. The butter will keep them soft and help them brown better. Use the big ring for cutting out biscuits for dinner or if you're going to serve them in gravy. The little one is good if you want to stuff them with something."

"Like Katherine Fisher's ham."

He just grunted. It pleased her to know that Katherine Fisher's comments had annoyed him.

While they waited for the biscuits to rise, she had Mona make coffee for them all. George, meanwhile, continued with the lesson, stressing to her how the oven had to be hot so the biscuits would cook quickly. When he pulled the biscuits from the oven, they looked perfect to her—a honeyed brown on top. But even that wasn't enough for George. He took one of the blistering biscuits from the pan and held it up so she could inspect the bottom as well. "Top is golden, the bottom is tan," he said. "That's when you know it's done." He then took a knife and sliced it open so the steam floated up into the room. He poured a drizzle of molasses over each half, then offered her and Mona the plate. "Unless you want me to run down to the store and see if they have one better than this for you," he said with a slight nod to Mona. While she and Mona ate their biscuits in silence at the table, he stood at the counter, watching them, his own plate balanced in his left hand, using his right to hold the remainder of the biscuit to sop up any molasses that had dripped onto the plate. She could tell he wanted her reaction.

"Angel biscuits," she said. "It's a good name for them."

# 5

# popovers with homemade preserves . . .

Butcher had been working at the Plantation House Hotel going on just a month. When he first sought employment, he was willing to take anything they had available—custodial, bellhop, it didn't matter. He had not asked the Director of the Residence for a reference and would probably not have gotten one either considering he quit without notice—just packed his bags during the night, served breakfast, and had lunch started when he told the director he was leaving.

"I made up the menu for the rest of the week. The boys should be able to follow it—nothing new on there. And William can take charge till you find someone better—he might even be the one to promote if he doesn't let them push him around."

The director just sat behind his desk, silent, like he was waiting for Butcher to deliver the punch line to a joke. When none came, he said, "Well, this is a fine how-to-do. What is it, George? Has someone offered you a better position? I thought you might have a bit more loyalty in you than that."

Butcher enjoyed how the boss always wanted to make it seem like you working for him was really him doing you a favor. "No, sir, it's just that it's time for me to be moving on."

"You're not in trouble now, are you? I won't have the police showing up here looking for you?"

"No, sir. Just time to be going. Butcher handed him a slip. "I calculated my wages through yesterday."

"And if I was to do an inventory."

Butcher stiffened. "You would find everything there that is supposed to be there. I packed myself some sandwiches for the road, but that is no more than I would do for any man moving on. Go and check the pantry if you want."

Butcher could see the director knew he wasn't going to take accusations of shortages or thievery, so he didn't push it, let the matter drop. But he still wasn't done. "I will have to pay you from petty cash, which means more paperwork for me," he said. "You will have to sign a voucher—don't want you saying I didn't pay you."

"I'll sign whatever you need," said Butcher. "Write it out."

As the director made out the form, Butcher noticed how his hands shook. "And don't imagine that you can parade back in here after a week or two of drinking and whoring wanting your job back."

"Won't be coming back," Butcher said. He clenched his fists tight to hold in his anger at the little squeak of a man. He didn't need trouble. Just wanted to disappear. He had already purchased his ticket on the afternoon's Southern Crescent, and when the director had handed over the cash, Butcher collected his belongings and walked to the station to wait for the train. He had thought the girl might come to wish him good-bye, but she didn't.

Though Butcher was reluctant to admit it, the fondness he had felt for her had begun to run to something deeper. He had little experience with women, had really only bedded Maude for a brief time when he was deployed. But he could feel the same tug of desire with the girl. Maude wasn't much like Mona, her features less delicate, coarser. But she was still just a girl when he had known her, an experienced whore at seventeen. Her age hadn't mattered to him then—little more than a boy himself after all. Still, whenever her image would creep from the recesses of his memory, he always remembered her as little more than a kid, her nightgown pulled down over her shoulder to reveal her small, firm breasts, her black hair falling in thick curls down her back. When she would crawl onto him in the bed or in a chair, she could drape herself over him so that she felt little more than a coverlet, and when he took her hand into his, her fingers barely reached beyond the flat surface of his palm. She told him her mother was Romanian, a gypsy, but he didn't know if this were the truth or a fiction she had fabricated for herself and her customers. He had chosen her from the group of women in the house—not because she was the prettiest, not because she was the youngest. It wasn't that he just wanted to fuck her, though fuck her he did. Those afternoons, nights, early mornings before dawn could travel back to him without warning over the years in the quiet of his room, the emptiness of his prison cell. When he would give himself over to the memory, feel his meat firm up in his hand, he would touch himself, remembering the softness of her skin like peach flesh, or the smell between her legs—sweet like melon. When he had known Maude, he imagined he had been her only lover, that though she still took the money each time he came, with him somehow it was more than that. He wanted to possess her, and wanted her to love him in that way as well. He was ripe for plucking.

There had been a period of time in Brest, after the war was officially over, that men remained in the town, waiting to be shipped home. Butcher and the other black servicemen were among the last to return home. Though he was still expected to show up to cook for his shifts, regulations relaxed, everyone seemed to breathe a bit easier, and the bosses turned a blind eye to many infractions that would have otherwise carried punishment. Perhaps it was the reward for having won. Or perhaps it was a small compensation for having survived. Butcher had not seen battle, but he had surely seen the war. They were all little more than frightened boys when they arrived in France, himself included. Every day was much like the one before—new arrivals waiting to be shipped out to the front lines. Wounded soldiers waiting to return home. All needed to eat. All came into the mess tents. The new arrivals were easy to spot in their clean uniforms, barely broken-in boots. Some blustered and postured bravely, assuming the stance of what they imagined a soldier should be. Some sat silently, writing letters home, trying to establish a link between where they were heading and what they had left behind. Those who were fortunate enough to come back to the port from the front in one piece did not posture, did not pose. They had learned that being a soldier meant only not getting your head blown off or being quick enough to grab your gas mask and praying it would work. Red Cross workers sat on the benches taking dictation from the ones who could not write, the ones who had been blinded or maimed. Others had to be fed because their hands shook too badly to hold the food. Yes, Butcher had seen the war.

But when the armistice was signed and Kaiser Wilhelm was nothing more than fodder for impressions by some of the rowdier boys, the mood in Brest changed. Men no longer polished rifles or fiddled with gear, instead choosing to sit in the sun for hours drinking wine brought in from the countryside. In the evenings, they visited cafés and bars and brothels. Many of the houses set up elaborate buffets, or what seemed elaborate to the men living on army rations. In the dining room of the house where Maude worked, they kept a table laid out for the men. A deep mahogany pedestal table sat in the center of the room. Some nights, Laurent the cook covered it with a worn linen tablecloth with blue striping so faded that it almost seemed to disappear. In the corner of the room, there was a hutch where the regulars could keep a bottle of cognac or absinthe. Laurent, or more typically Helaine, who actually owned the house, would mark the bottles and tuck them away for safekeeping. Bottles of beer and wine were always on hand, and Helaine made sure each man purchased something to drink either before going upstairs or when returning. She did not have to work hard—the servicemen were ready to drink before fucking, ready to eat and drink more afterward. Laid out on the table were platters of sliced ham and sausages; thick, crusty bread, and cheese—some so soft and ripe that they melted like candle wax, others so hard that they curled like wood shavings when you scraped the block with a knife. American dollars made purchasing supplies easy, and the cost of some bread and cheese was a pittance compared to what the men paid for the women.

Butcher was enthralled, captivated by the display. When Butcher had been coming to the house long enough to be considered a regular customer, or perhaps after Maude had let it be known that he was special to her, Laurent made a point to tell him what certain things were.

The pale, quivering white sausage was a boudin blanc—made with milk and cognac. The deep burgundy black was boudin noir— an infinitely more delicate version of the spicy blood sausage like he had eaten as a boy. Pâté could be made from almost anything— duck or chicken livers, pork or veal, seasoned with pepper and herbs, wrapped in a glistening skin of aspic. Butcher had never seen such things, had never imagined such things existed. But now that he knew, he could not learn enough. Laurent welcomed him as a pupil, and though the language was difficult, Laurent would show Butcher something, tell him the name and Butcher would write it down in his book, often accompanied by a rough sketch. Sometimes, after he had fucked Maude, Butcher would dress and climb back down the narrow staircase from the second floor and peek into the kitchen where Laurent would be making bread for the next morning. Sometimes she complained that he came for the cooking and not for her. Butcher tried to assure her it wasn't so. He wanted her. Desired her. Wanted to be with her. But he wanted the world of Laurent as well. He had begun to imagine a life like Laurent and Helaine's—so that Maude would not have to be a whore. Perhaps it would be an inn. Maybe a café. And he could cook for whomever would stop by for the night or for a meal.

It was easy for him to dream of those times in Brest as he sat in his uniform in the service area back of the kitchen at the Plantation House or wandered into the hotel kitchen. Though his title was Porter's Assistant, he served more as a jack-of-all-trades, helping the bellhops if they needed an extra hand with luggage. He would also run trays of food to guests from the kitchen or fetch a newspaper if requested. It was a perfect job for him. He could be everywhere, anywhere—unnoticed, unobtrusive as a chair in the lobby of the hotel. Most often, he worked the 4 PM to midnight shift, but when one of the boys wanted a morning or night off, he was always happy to take a morning or night shift as well. In a small room next to the service elevator, they provided a cot and a chair, so he was free to relax unless the night porter needed him. Because of the hours, that wasn't often. Some of the boys said that when Colonel Claiborne's friends would take over the hotel,

"Then they gonna run you all night long. And never tip. White cracker sons of bitches think they still own us."

Butcher had learned a great deal about how the hotel operated from these men who waited around for orders. Butcher had learned chatter in these circumstances was always pretty much the same, whether you were in the army or sitting in the service hallway outside the kitchen of the Plantation House Hotel. Men liked to talk about women, liked to brag about sex, but they also liked to complain about their jobs. He also learned a great deal about Colonel Clayton Claiborne II, the hotel owner.

"Ain't no colored man ever gonna do anything in this hotel except tote and fetch," said Matthew, a man only slightly older than Butcher, but who had worked at the hotel for well over a decade. When pressed why he stayed for so long, he told Butcher the same story he had heard so often—where else was he to go? What better was there out there? Here there was a paycheck, even if there was no opportunity.

"What about the kitchen?" Butcher asked. He had purposefully avoided asking for work in the kitchen, didn't want to draw attention to himself. "There's plenty of boys working in there. Maybe you could move up."

"Line cook is about the top of the hill, and at least here I can sit a spell if I want. The rest is left to cutting and slicing and washing and peeling," said Matthew. "I guess Colonel Claiborne figures the black will get cooked out of it before it gets served to a guest." Matthew laughed, but when Butcher didn't respond, Matthew continued. "He's Klan through and through, brother. The joke is after his friends check out after one of their gatherings, they have to replace all the sheets in the hotel."

"Go on, now. You know they don't meet here," Butcher said.

"No, he's much too crafty for that," said Matthew. "But everybody knows. He doesn't make any secret he hates us all. Wouldn't have any black man here in a position to give an order."

Butcher knew it was true. Could see it in the faces of the maids or the bellhops and of the kitchen crew when he had to wait for a tray to be made to take to a guest. The cooks were all men, like men he had worked with in the army. Men who made food as if they worked on an assembly line stamping out a pattern with a die. The creativity all lay with the sole white man in the kitchen, Roland, the head cook in the hotel. A small, fiery-tempered man with remote ties to New Orleans, Roland claimed he had apprenticed at Antoine's, and prided himself on the menu. Though he cooked very little himself, he would inspect the plates as they came up to be loaded on a tray. If something didn't meet with his approval, it was discarded—often he would simply smash the plate into the wall.

"Goddammit. We ain't serving shit on a shingle here. Give me another one without the sauce running all over the goddamn plate. This ain't gravy, you black bastards. Don't slop it on like you were feeding a bunch of niggers. We got the top of the line of Atlanta society out front. Try to act with some sense and some idea of what it means to be civilized."

And almost immediately, another plate, with sauce ladled on to his satisfaction, would appear. Butcher knew this man, or better this type of man, well: He was a low-rent white man with a small bit of skill and knew how to make that work for him. Butcher had met this type of man before—a sergeant, a conductor, a guard. Such a man also made sure he exercised a very firm hand over everyone around him to show he wasn't afraid to use whatever power had been awarded to him. Here in Atlanta, Butcher had seen men fired or humiliated for the smallest of errors. After all, as Matthew had said, to whom were these boys going to complain? If they didn't like being called shiftless, or lazy, or good-for-nothing, then "there's the door. Thank you very much." And there would be a line of men ready to take their place, eager to get paid for the privilege of the insult.

But Roland was right. The pride of Atlanta society did come calling at Plantation House. The dining room was usually full not only with guests, but also with local people who could afford to eat out or wanted to celebrate a special occasion. There was no heart in this food, but Butcher had to admit that at least they did manage to serve it hot—he knew that when you were serving to order that could be a challenge. They dressed it up so that it looked nice, served it under little silver lids that the waiters would remove in unison when a table was served. It was all for show, but it worked. Butcher couldn't help but think how different it would be when he was the man in charge again, only this time with a kitchen of his own.

In the evenings after the kitchen was closed, and the dishwashers had finished cleaning for the night, and the night porter was napping behind the front desk, Butcher was free to explore the kitchen on his own. He loved especially to wander into the pastry room, a section of the kitchen set off from the rest of the kitchen by two swinging doors. During the afternoons, the doors to the pastry room would be propped open for easy access, and no matter how noisy or dirty or crowded the kitchen itself was—waiters calling out orders, the cooks yelling to each other on the line to fire a course, Roland barking loud above the rest—the pastry room was always ordered, quiet, serene. It was the only place in the kitchen where women were allowed to work, and Butcher noted even Ronald treated these women, even though every one of them was black, with a certain deference. The women cranked out pies, cakes, cobblers, banana pudding, biscuits, rolls, tea cakes without seeming to ever raise even a slight dust of flour. Butcher could feel these women in the pastry room deep in the night, long after they had gone for the day, could feel the heart and love that they put into these dishes to be sliced and sold to strangers. He understood what that meant to them, and he drew strength from it. He was tempted to make something for them, morning bread fresh from the oven when they arrived. A mysterious gesture of love and appreciation. But he knew he could not risk it.

The hotel, and the kitchen in particular, had been busy getting ready for the arrival of "Colonel Claiborne's Ladies," which is what everyone called the women who were coming to compete in the Mystic White contest. Butcher feigned ignorance, appeared disinterested in the contest, though the topic was certainly the buzz. Very little of it was flattering to Claiborne or the women.

"Wonder if they know they gonna have to fuck him to win that contest. They should be calling it The Lady in the White Knickers."

"Maybe he'll just have 'em make doughnuts on his old-man pecker pole."

"The only white hat they gonna be wearing is a Klan hood."

Butcher ignored the chatter, concerned himself with the layout of the baking room, where each of the women would prepare her recipe for judging. Once the initial recipe had been accepted, the contest rules became more complex. There were several categories that had to be covered: biscuits/rolls, batter, pie crust, cake, cookie. Also, each recipe was to be a part of a larger menu, and while Butcher had painstakingly mapped out the details for each meal, it had not been easy. Virginia was terrified of all the multiple components, and he had fought with her over what to include for each menu—she was not confident she could make any/most/all of the items he suggested. However, he was just as adamant that she could learn. "Besides," he said, referring to the guidelines, "it says 'each contestant will choose recipes that best showcase her abilities as a cook and as a hostess.' They aren't gonna ask you to make anything that ain't on this list. This isn't about making you look bad. And I am here to make you look good." He coaxed, he prodded, and soon they had crafted the three required menus for submission.

### *Menu One—Weekend Breakfast*

Half a Grapefruit with Maraschino Cherry
Shirred Eggs
Sausage
Fried Potatoes
Popovers with Homemade Preserves
Coffee

Virginia had wanted to do waffles or pancakes since that would satisfy the batter requirements, but Butcher insisted on the popovers. "Every one of those women is gonna make a waffle. Or eggs and grits with biscuits and gravy. You have to do something different. Separate yourself from the crowd. Don't want to just plop a mess of grits on the plate—I don't care how good they are. You might as well be slopping a hog. A popover is as simple as a pancake batter, but it is like eating a cloud. Plus, I will give you some homemade preserves to serve along with it. Just tell them you brought 'em from your own pantry. That will impress them. Besides, won't be anyone to question you about that. And it will show you have skills beyond just baking."

"But we spent so much time with the biscuits," she complained. "Am I just to abandon those now?"

"We can do the biscuits for the Sunday dinner," he said.

### Menu Two—Sunday Dinner

Cream of Tomato Soup
Fried Chicken
Mashed Potatoes and Gravy
Garden Peas
Biscuits
Coconut Cake

"This one's got flour in the chicken breading, a cake, and the biscuits, so you have three things to show," he said, holding three fingers in the air. "Plus, chicken for Sunday dinner will make them think you are a lady of real refinement."

"I am a lady of real refinement," she snapped back.

"A lady of means," he said. "A chicken is not as easy to come by as a piece of pork or stew beef. You watch. Those other women will have a mock turtle soup and call it sophisticated."

"I could never make all of this in a million years," she complained. "It's too much."

"You won't have to make it all," he replied. "I guarantee they are only going to be interested in what you tell them you can bake. You have to sell them on the idea of it. And when you roll out those angel biscuits, they probably will just write you the check right there and then on the spot."

The final menu—*Ladies' Luncheon*—had proved the most cantankerous of all. Butcher had wanted to do a cold menu, which he explained to Virginia would show her to be a hostess who knew how to plan ahead. The problem was that as the centerpiece to the menu, he had proposed a baked pâté in aspic, which would fulfill the pie crust requirement, but also something he said was so refined that it would elevate her to an entirely different level. Virginia protested no sane woman would ever attempt such a thing.

"That's just because they couldn't think of it. Won't imagine a savory pie. They will all be doing lemon meringue or peach or chocolate chess. I guarantee it," said Butcher. "And this is as simple as the pie crust really. Ain't nothing more than minced pork baked in a shell. A meatloaf when you get down to it. It's just when you slice it that it shows off." Butcher had seen Laurent slice one to lay out on a platter for the dining room at the brothel. Spiced ground pork encased in a shimmering golden pool of aspic surrounded by a delicate, flaky pastry. He had called it a country pâté (*pâté de campagne*). Butcher didn't think there was anything country about it. It was the most pleasing dish he had ever seen—worthy of a king or queen.

He had finally convinced her, but only after Mona had taken his side. They had fallen into a rhythm again, he sensed.

"Remember when we had the chicken liver spread on toast?" she asked. "You said how much you liked that—how elegant it was. Pâté of chicken livers," she said, as if scrolling the words through her memory. "It was on the menu at the hotel."

"Where was that?" asked Butcher.

"Before we were in Fayetteville," she said. "We were staying in a hotel in—"

"What difference does it make?" said Virginia. "Yes, I remember the chicken liver spread. Perhaps you are right. It would make a good impression. But you can't call it anything that sounds foreign. That will sound like I'm putting on airs. And *country* just sounds . . . well, so *common*."

And so the final menu fell into place.

### Menu Three—Ladies' Luncheon

Tomato Juice Cocktail with Celery
Waldorf Salad
Farmhouse Pâté in Pastry
Chilled Asparagus
Shortbreads with Berries and Cream

Butcher liked that Mona had taken his side against her boss, tried not to imagine that it meant more than it did. Tried to squash down the feeling that he had become sweet on her. He had missed her since he had left Fayetteville, and he was looking forward to her arrival in Atlanta. She had awakened something in him, and though he was surely twice her age, she had made him feel like a young man again.

He agreed to work any shifts that were available in the days before and during the contest. He had no idea when exactly Mona and Miss Virginia would arrive, and it came almost as a surprise when Mona opened the door to the room when Butcher had been sent to deliver afternoon tea. She motioned to the table in front of the window.

"Put it down over there," she said. "And don't worry about pouring. I will do that for Miss Virginia." Then, closing the door behind him, she added, "Don't you look a sight all dressed up in a uniform."

"It's hotter than Hades, I can tell you that," said Butcher. "And it scratches like hell." Miss Virginia stood in the corner in a simple celery-colored dress. She was as still as a mannequin in a window, but he could tell she was nervous from the way she held her hands, clasping and unclasping them in front of her.

"Good afternoon, George," she said.

"Good afternoon, Miss Virginia. I hope you had an easy travel."

"Pleasant enough. So how are things here?"

"Some of the ladies started arriving yesterday. They ain't been going out much, though. I guess most everybody is keeping to themselves."

"Waiting for the opening reception to make an entrance," she said.

"I saved these for you," he said, pulling a neatly folded stack of newspaper articles from his pocket. "They have been writing about all of you and the contest in the paper. It gives the names of everyone who is coming. And the schedule of how the contest will run."

"I have the schedule," she said. "They sent that to me last week. The names as well. But it was kind of you to go to the trouble. Who knows? Perhaps there is something here that might be of use."

"Maybe so," said Butcher, turning to Mona. "And how are you enjoying Atlanta, little miss?"

However, before Mona could reply, Virginia interjected. "I don't mean to interrupt this reunion, but it might not be appropriate for us to be receiving the colored help in our hotel room," she said.

"I understand," said Butcher. "Besides, I have work to do myself. Everyone here is on high alert, like when the general would come to address the soldiers. Y'all are a big deal." He opened the door and in an exaggerated voice repeated the words that he had been told to say to all guests, "Welcome to Atlanta. If there is anything we can do to assist you in your stay, please let one of the staff know."

After George closed the door, Virginia motioned to Mona. "Pour me a cup of that tea, will you, sweetie? And put just a drop in it to help settle my nerves?" Virginia sat in the overstuffed upholstered chair by the window and began to read the clippings Butcher had brought her. She started with the most recent, which was from the *Journal* from the previous Sunday:

## OUT AND ABOUT WITH JOCELYN

### More than a Cooking Contest:
### The Best Will Rise to the Top

*By Jocelyn Hind Crowley, Society Editor*

Dear Readers,

In an event that is sure to have housewives and society mavens alike across the region buzzing like bees in a hive, this weekend brings to Atlanta one of the season's most highly anticipated events: the Mystic White Flour Company's search for *The Lady in the White Hat*. Clayton Claiborne II, President of Mystic White, says he is hosting the competition to find the model of Southern womanhood, who will represent the company for the next year: "Someone

who holds the ideals of family, honor, and home as sacred." The competition, he continues, is not just
about cooking. "It is about preserving the principles
that represent us as Southerners." *Colonel* Claiborne,
as he is known to his friends, has spared no expense
in mounting the contest, opening the doors to his
grand Plantation House Hotel for the ladies and spe-
cially invited guests, including yours truly.

As we have noted in previous columns, festivities
begin on Thursday afternoon at a tea and fashion
show where each contestant will model a white hat of
her own design. I am looking forward to seeing how
each woman will customize this "crowning" acces-
sory as a reflection of her personality. Members of our
own chapter of the DOC will serve as honorary am-
bassadors for the event, and I will be on hand to interview the ladies about their menus (*Weekend Breakfast,
Sunday Dinner*, and *Ladies' Luncheon*) and their ideas
on what makes a successful and gracious hostess.

And did I tell you, faithful readers, the colonel has
also asked me to be one of the esteemed panel of
judges? That is an honor, indeed, considering that
the other two members of the judging competition
will be the Plantation House's renowned Chef
Roland and the colonel himself. The way to a man's
heart may be through his appetite, but I imagine
they may welcome a bit of feminine insight to help
them in their considerations.

The ladies are traveling from all regions of
Dixie—from as far north as Richmond and from deep
in the heart of Texas—to be here. Their interests and
profiles show what an exemplary field of competitors
has been chosen:

**Muriel Sallis** lives in Richmond, Virginia, and devotes her free time to maintaining gravesites of the
fallen Confederate heroes.

**Jubal Hart,** from Abilene, Texas, says that her grandchildren are her pride and joy, and her favorite people to cook for.

**Virginia Yeager** hails from Fayetteville, North Carolina, where the war widow devotes her days to charity.

**Cornelia "Neelie" Bryson,** a native of Mobile, Alabama, tells us that she enjoys cooking for church socials where her squash casserole is always a favorite.

**Inez Honeycutt** has traveled from Chattanooga, Tennessee, where she works as a third-grade teacher. Inez also teaches Sunday school and sings in the choir at church.

**Wadena Chastain** represents our own fair state and hails from Savannah. Not a surprise that she says peach pie is her favorite.

**Patricia "Patsy" Smith** resides in Walterboro, South Carolina, where she tends her garden and raises prize-winning flowers. She is also an avid cake decorator.

**Martha Humphrey** comes from Meridian, Mississippi, and is a gold-star mother. Her chocolate pound cake recipe was the one her son always requested.

Good luck to all these extraordinary women, and remember . . .

Jocelyn will be your eyes and ears for this momentous and historic event, just as she is for all things of social importance in Atlanta.

Virginia dropped the clipping on the table and swept the whole bunch of them to the floor with her hand. She picked up her tea.

"Aren't you going to read the rest of them?" asked Mona.

"Why bother," said Virginia. "They're all the same. These

bitches or the ones back in Fayetteville. They all think that just because their daddy or granddaddy fought and died for the Confederacy that they deserve some special attention. They make me sick to my stomach. Why don't you draw a hot bath for me? I want to rest before the reception this afternoon."

Virginia closed her eyes and could hear the water running in the bath. What a bunch of dolts, she thought to herself. A bunch of stuck-up society bags with dreams of grandeur. She would wipe the floor with them. It would be almost as easy as making a batch of Butcher's popovers. He had been right about those. They were so simple, she could now probably make them blindfolded. And they were perfect every time—the shell would pull apart gently only to melt in your mouth when it had cooled a bit. Yes, easy as Butcher's popovers. No, not Butcher's, she corrected herself. My popovers. Miss Virginia's popovers.

# 6

# Lane cake . . .

The reception was scheduled to begin at three, but Virginia knew some would want to be late to create interest. Virginia thought it not wise to show up late for a job interview, for she understood that was what this hustle and show was about: It was an audition. She had been on enough of those to know what worked. There were always categories of girls—some too eager, some absolutely unqualified, and those with an attitude as enticing as vinegar. But there were a couple of girls every time who knew they could have the job if they wanted it. She could see it in the way they carried themselves, the way they sat, the way they quietly drew attention to themselves. They usually did get the job.

George had that attitude. He knew he could cook any of these women straight out the back door of any kitchen. And she agreed that he probably was correct. But this was about more than who could make the best biscuit. She recognized that from the initial request for a photo. These women would run a gamut of sizes, shapes, dispositions, but there was one thing of which she was certain—they would all be white women of a certain age and background.

For the tea, they had each been asked to wear a hat of their "own creation or personalization" as a "statement of her originality and unique character." Virginia had found a picture in *Photoplay* of

Constance Bennett wearing a wide-brimmed straw hat with a satin ribbon that she liked, so she took the picture to the milliner at Belk Brothers Department Store, and together they fashioned a similar version for her. Virginia's hat was also made of white straw, but there was no crown. The milliner wove creamy apricot ribbon around to form a latticework top. "Like a pie," she said, tying a ribbon around to hide her stitch work. And for a pin to hold the ribbon there was one topped with silver filigreed wings like a butterfly . . . or an angel. *Angel biscuits.* Virginia thought it simple and sophisticated. That was going to be how she presented herself. Like the girl who knew she could have this part if she wanted it.

The reception was to be held in the Ladies' Lounge of the hotel just off the main dining room and opposite the Gentlemen's Lounge. The room was light, breezy, an extravaganza of wicker and chintz upholstery in contrast to what she supposed were the deep leathers and wood of the Gentlemen's Lounge. The room buzzed with women, the elite of Atlanta society, all dressed in summer silks, their fashionable best. Here to see her. It made her happy to think that. For the occasion, Virginia had chosen a cream-colored charmeuse with a pleated apricot bodice to match the ribbon in her hat. She studied the room briefly, then walked to the women sitting at the registration table.

"Good afternoon," she said, extending her gloved hand to the woman in charge. "I am Virginia Yeager."

The woman behind the table introduced herself as Florence Gaffney and her friend, who seemed slightly hard of hearing, as Mrs. Bethel Talbot Walker. Florence Gaffney leaned toward Virginia as if sharing a confidence, "The Talbot Walkers are one of Atlanta's finest. Her grandfather was killed in the Battle of Atlanta just around the corner somewhere." Virginia made sure to seem suitably impressed and gave a warm hello to the old woman. Florence Gaffney continued, "Some of the ladies have already arrived and are gathered by the punch bowl or looking at the seating arrangement." She pointed to the row of chairs at the front of the room, facing the audience. "I'm afraid they have you all lined up in a row like a firing squad."

"More of a semicircle," said Virginia. "Perhaps some of us will manage to get out alive."

"I think it has something to do with the newspaper woman, so that she can ask you all questions. And I am sure you will do just fine. Now, if you don't mind, I must pin this dreadful name tag on you. Why they gave this job to me, I'll never know. Don't let me do any damage. There now. That doesn't look too bad."

"Thank you," said Virginia. "I think I might have a sip of punch. It is awfully warm today."

"Do," said Mrs. Talbot Walker of the Atlanta Talbot Walkers. "It's temperance. And the best of luck to you."

In a quick head count, Virginia could spot five other ladies. She tried to size them up. Which ones were just incompetent, which would be too eager to please, which ones would be difficult or needy? She was not the last. As she made her way to the punch bowl, a woman arrived at the registration table with Mrs. Gaffney and Mrs. Talbot Walker. Virginia took a glass of sparkling punch and a napkin, and studied the arrangement of the chairs. Their names were printed on cards taped to the back—it *was* rather like a firing squad, she agreed. She thought about wandering to the semicircle, but her attention was diverted by a commotion at the door. The last woman had entered the room. And what a woman. For a moment, Virginia felt as if she might burst into laughter at the sheer spectacle of her. Her dress was totally inappropriate in these surroundings. She wore a boldly printed floral silk lounge dress with a Bertha ruffle with a fitted bodice and short sleeves. Even worse, she had pinned a silk hydrangea inside the bosom of her dress, so that it looked as if it were blooming there. But most conspicuous was the hat. She had taken what appeared to be two white cloche-style hats and stitched them together, one on top of the other so they resembled a cake where the layers had gone slightly cockeyed. Around the hat she had sewn or pinned bunches of cherries. She paraded into the room with her arms out in front of her and slightly to the side, palms down in an imitation of a Ziegfeld girl. Virginia could see the soft flesh wagging underneath her arms.

"Hi, y'all," she called out to everyone. "The circus has arrived."

She paused for a moment. "I'm Wadena, but you all can call me Elaine Cake." Then she paused again, pointing to her hat. "Get it? A Lane cake?" She laughed again, broadly, and some of the ladies applauded.

"How clever she is," said a woman near where Virginia stood. "And what an outgoing personality."

Virginia thought, yes, the circus had indeed arrived. And brought with it her competition.

One of the women from the local DOC asked the women to take their places in the circle of chairs. It was time to begin the official program. Virginia was seated between Jubal Hart and Inez Honeycutt. Jubal had fashioned a bonnet for herself, and when she saw that Virginia was looking at it, she said she was always inspired by her granny who wore a bonnet, so she wanted to honor her. Virginia could tell by the cut of her clothes that Jubal was out of her league here—a woman who probably volunteered to make chicken salad for every church function and, therefore, had a favorable reputation among a very small group of women who were happy enough to have decent chicken salad made for them on a regular basis. On the other hand, Inez was hard country, nothing more. Virginia had seen this type of woman often enough. Her shoes were old and did not match her dress, which was probably borrowed. Her hat was white straw like Virginia's, but it was flat as a pancake and sat atop her head as if she were balancing a tray where perched a veritable cornucopia of wax fruit. Wadena Chastain sat opposite Virginia in the circle of chairs, almost a mirror image in her Lane cake hat. She didn't settle in right away, fidgeting like a small girl at a recital, smoothing her skirt over her legs and adjusting her hat. They were small gestures, but Virginia could tell she was nervous, a bit on edge, ready to begin. When she looked across at Virginia, she cocked her head slightly like an animal in the zoo that enjoys being watched. She flashed a smile and shrugged her shoulders as if to ask what was happening next.

Then, as if on cue, the local DOC representative, who also turned out to be the president of the local chapter, Mrs. Margaret Wheeler, thanked the committee responsible for hosting the tea, then recognized all the officers present from their club. These small pleasantries formed the foundation of the women's clubs, Virginia knew. Each woman needed just a moment in the sun so she could show off her hat, her hairdo, her latest frock. It would give the women of the Atlanta DOC fodder for months. Mrs. Wheeler then introduced Jocelyn Hind Crowley from the paper, who would interview them and also serve as a judge. She also introduced Roland, the chef of the Plantation House. After each name was presented, there was polite applause.

Then Mrs. Wheeler took a deep breath and gathered herself up for her official welcoming speech. Fortunately, it was mercifully short about the virtue of women in general and the virtues of Southern women in particular. Then, she added, "But none of this would be possible without the vision, the support, and the generosity of our sponsor, the President of Mystic White Flour, Colonel Clayton Claiborne II."

The surprise of Clayton Claiborne was that he was not what she had expected. Virginia thought the name sounded almost like a bit of stagecraft, a politician in a melodrama. Seersucker and a full head of white hair. Gregarious, a bit pompous, exaggerated. The Clayton Claiborne who walked through the door, however, more closely resembled an accountant or an undertaker.

He was nearly bald, but combed wisps of hair up and around to the top of his head where they lay like discarded thread. He wore a dark suit, too hot for summer, and though it was expensive, it did not fit him well. There was open space between his neck and shirt collar, and he wore spectacles. As for age, Virginia had not a clue— he could have been forty or four hundred. She thought he looked very much like a fairy-tale troll sprung to life.

Claiborne thanked Mrs. Wheeler and took out a sheet of paper with his prepared remarks. His voice was high-pitched, nasal, with a deep Southern drawl that identified him as Georgia born and bred.

"Ladies of Atlanta and ladies who are guests of Atlanta," he said, acknowledging first the audience and then the circle of contestants. "This is a very special occasion. A special occasion, indeed. I want to welcome you all to the Plantation House Hotel where we will, before the weekend is over, choose one of these women to be the official representative of the Mystic White Flour Company.

"As you know, Mystic White is a family business, started by my grandfather. We have always prided ourselves on milling the softest white flour that money can buy. We are the flour of the Southern lady."

There was a slight murmur of applause from the group. Claiborne looked up from his statement. "I hope I wasn't sounding too much like an advertisement," he said. "But this is my heritage. There is a joke that says, 'If you were to slice Clay Claiborne's finger, he would bleed white.' There may be some truth in that. And Mystic White is a part of your heritage as well. Every time you use it to bake a cake or a biscuit. To show your family how much you care."

Virginia looked out over the audience. The women seemed genuinely moved by this notion. That what they were doing each day mattered.

"Now there are two women who cooked for me when I was a boy," Claiborne continued. My mamma was one of them, and the other was my black mammy. I loved them both, put flowers on both their graves, God rest their souls, but who do you suppose I want to have be the representative of my company—the picture of the Southern woman we send out to the world?

"I know you ladies know what I am talking about. Some will put a colored man or a black mammy on a box and call it Southern. 'Jimmy Crack Corn' and all that nonsense. Well, it ain't my South. My South is you ladies. And your sisters and your aunts and your cousins and your daughters. And your daughters' daughters.

"You all hold the heart of the South in your hands. I applaud your work and your sacrifice. Mystic White Flour celebrates all of you by choosing one of you to represent each of you."

The ladies of Atlanta applauded loudly as Claiborne concluded his remarks. The muffled thump of gloved hands. Virginia could not help but smile. If Claiborne sought a champion, then that is what she would be. There was probably less than a span of fifteen years in age among them all, but she was the prettiest of these contestants—that was obvious. She was the most stylish. The most sophisticated. She could sense the wariness of the women around her. If Wadena was a parade float, then she was a sculpture. She knew this feeling, had experienced it before when she mingled in their midst. She had not had friends really since Dorothea. She didn't have time for it—life on her own took all she had. Besides, women did not take to her, trust her, like her. She supposed they feared she might become entangled with one of their husbands, and that could never be allowed. And so they would invite her to dinner, to cocktails if they were liberal. But only to fill out a table. Never as a friend for supper. The wives had it wrong, though— Virginia was not interested in *their* husbands. She wanted more than what these women had. She wanted a husband of her own who would take her someplace where she could become her own creation. Women did it all the time in plays and movies. All it took was imagination and bit of flair.

This time was different somehow, Virginia realized. Now she could cook. This made her like one of them—or at least would make them think she was like them. When she became The Lady, she would perform it like a part, like a role played by Constance Bennett or Irene Dunne. And just as the women wanted to be them, they would want to be like her. When she became The Lady, these women would perhaps be uneasy around her, but it would not be out of fear she was going to steal their husbands. In fact, she imagined they would offer the husbands up if The Lady asked it. These women now in the audience were trying to imagine what it must be like to be her—and Virginia understood what those girls in the auditions knew. This was hers for the taking.

Claiborne made his way around the circle beginning on the far side away from Virginia. He said something to each woman, wished them well. She tried to judge if he lingered with Wadena Chastain, but wasn't certain. And since he had his back directly to her, Wadena's face was hidden from her.

When he reached her, Virginia had to lean her head back slightly to hold him full faced in front of her.

"That is a very dramatic hat, Mrs. Yeager," he said.

"You don't think it gilds the lily?"

"Impossible."

"What a kind thing to say. Please call me Virginia—as my friends do."

"Very well, Miss Virginia." She noted that he did not return the offer to call him by his Christian name. Instead, he added, "I seem to recall that your maiden name was Blankenship. That is a fine family, indeed. I went to Emory with Lionel Blankenship."

"A distant cousin no doubt," Virginia interjected. "As they say, stick a pushpin into a low-country map of the Carolinas and you're likely to hit a Blankenship."

"Yes, well, a fine family. I am certainly looking forward to getting to know you more over the weekend. The best of luck to you." She thought that ever so slightly his hand held hers just a bit more tightly than was proper. Then he was off to Jubal Hart and her bonnet. Virginia wondered how many times she would be forced to hear that recitation.

When he had greeted all the contestants, Claiborne introduced Roland to tell them about how the program would unfold.

"In a few minutes, Miss Crowley is going to ask you some questions and then have her photographer take some pictures of all of you for the paper," he said. "Tomorrow, I'm afraid, will not be as glamorous. We will meet tomorrow morning at eight-thirty AM in the kitchen for the first round of the competition. Each of you will make an item from your breakfast menu. If you only submitted one item, you must make that. If you submitted two selections, you may choose which one. You will have two hours to prepare your dish and then Mr. Claiborne, Miss Crowley, and myself will taste, compare, and judge. At that time, four of you will be eliminated."

There was an audible gasp from somewhere in the room.

"Goodness," said Inez Honeycutt. "Eliminated. How humiliating to just be told to go home."

Roland held his hand up to silence the chatter. "Yes, the competition is very real. After lunch, the remaining four contestants will meet at two o'clock to prepare an item from her Sunday Dinner menu. The same rules as for breakfast apply, except you will have three hours to make your dinner entry. That should give those of you who wish to make a cake or a pie plenty of time. We will eliminate two more contestants after this round.

"The championship round will take place on Saturday morning, where the final two contestants will make an item from her Ladies' Luncheon menu. Again, contestants will be given three hours to prepare the dish. We will announce the winner at a reception held here on Saturday afternoon at four o'clock. You may use any special pie plates, molds, or cooking equipment that you may have brought with you. We will supply all other ingredients including, of course, Mystic White Flour, both plain and self-rising."

There was a feeble attempt at laughter, but Virginia could tell his announcement had caught many of the women off guard, could read the surprise and indignation on several faces, though the women tried to conceal their emotions. She thought Muriel Sallis might just stand up and march right out of the room. These women were not used to being so much on display, and they did not like it. This struck at their vanity—to be called out in public as the worst at something they took pride in. It was like being told your child was ugly. It just wasn't done.

Roland concluded, "If you have any questions for me, please see me after the photo session. We will have a tour of the kitchen, and I will do whatever I can to assist you." He returned to his seat as one of the photographers pulled a chair up to the edge of the circle for the reporter. In the lull, Wadena Chastain confided to the group in an exaggerated stage whisper. "My brother Bobby won a pig once at the fair. Had to wrassle a boy for it, though. At least we don't have to wrassle."

"At least not yet," answered one of the women. But Virginia couldn't tell which one. She was running recipes in her head, planning her strategy. She had no intention of leaving now that she had arrived.

# 7

# pound cake . . .

The call for a tray to be delivered to Miss Virginia's room came just after seven o'clock. One of the other boys was in line to take it, but Butcher asked if he could step up.

"Not a problem," said Walter. "These ladies don't tip much no ways."

Butcher managed to sneak a bit of pound cake on the tray for Mona. He knew how much she liked sweets. It was a small gesture, but he hoped she would notice.

When the girl opened the door to the room, Butcher saw Virginia seated in the chair by the window in her stocking feet, sipping a highball, her eyes closed. He put the tray on the table and waited. For a moment, he wasn't sure she was even going to greet him.

Mona spoke on his behalf. "Mr. Butcher is here to see you, ma'am."

Virginia raised her head and opened her eyes. He could see she was slightly tipsy. Not as drunk as the night in her kitchen, but she had had a nip. He wondered if it was a signal things had gone badly.

"George, thank you for bringing our supper tray."

"Weren't no problem. Glad to do it."

He stood for a moment, unsure what to do. He looked to Mona for help.

"He wants to know about the reception. Tell him."

Virginia smiled. "Yes, the reception. I was just drinking a toast to myself. I was a huge success if I do say so."

"That's good news indeed. You'll be baking in the morning I suppose."

"We're all baking in the morning," she said. "All the ladies are on display in the morning baking for breakfast. Or does a waffle count as baking? You were right, you know. Three of them are doing waffles. Poor Jubal Hart is making pancakes. She'll probably wear that god-awful bonnet of hers as well. Two are making biscuits. The very fact I am doing something different should give me some advantage."

"Just like I told you," he said, smiling. "You bring the popover pans with you? They got muffin tins down in the kitchen, but they won't hold the heat. And make sure they have the ingredients out for you—they need to be at room temperature."

"I have the popover pans. And I have spoken to Roland about the ingredients. Please, George, do not ask me about food. I have listened to women do nothing else but talk food all afternoon. I feel like I have been battered and fried and baptized in gravy. Wadena Chastain is making cake doughnuts. Isn't that clever? Why didn't you think of cake doughnuts, George?"

"A doughnut is more variable. You have to time them just right or they get tough."

"Don't you love it, Mona? You see, like I said—he has an answer for every question. George is a walking food encyclopedia. Answer me this, George. What is the most important item in your kitchen—and you can't say stove."

"I don't know. My recipe book, I suppose."

"You don't know. Your recipe book. Well, then, let me tell you that you would have not done very well in the interview portion of our competition, Mr. Butcher. The ladies of Atlanta want to know what you treasure, need to know what it says about you. Miss Jocelyn Hind Crowley wants them to know. It's her job to tell them. Inez Honeycutt said it was her Bible. Martha Humphrey said it was the medal from her dead son, which she keeps framed by his picture."

"What did you say?" George asked.

"I told them it was my mirror. You should have seen the looks I got from those sows." Then she began to act out the scene for him.

" 'A mirror, Mrs. Yeager?' asked Miss Jocelyn Hind Crowley. 'What function does that serve?' "

" 'I may spend the afternoon in the kitchen, Miss Crowley,' I said. 'But when it is time to serve the meal, the only powder I want on my nose is face powder, not baking powder. A cook should be every bit as attractive as her food.' I thought of that right on the spot. Wasn't that witty of me? I thought about that night in the kitchen when I wanted a mirror. It just came to me."

"Yes, ma'am," he said. "That was sure a smart answer. Not one I would have thought of."

"You may have the ideas about the food, George, but I am bringing something to the equation as well."

"Yes, ma'am, you do. That's for sure." He hesitated, not wanting to leave, but knowing he had only a short time. "I brought Miss Mona a bit of cake. It wasn't on the order, but I put it on."

"That was very sweet of you, George. But you don't want to do things that might call attention to yourself. What if you had gotten caught?"

"I was real careful, Miss Virginia. And I was wondering if Miss Mona might want to take a walk after you all have your supper. I will be off by nine, and I could walk her around to show her a little of the town. I'm sure she must be tired of being cooped up in here all day and night."

Before Mona could speak, Virginia answered. "As I said, it is probably not a good idea for you to do anything that might call attention to yourself or to associate you with . . . us. Mona is fine to stay here with me."

Butcher tried to read Mona's expression. Was she angry? Embarrassed? Either way, he could tell that Virginia was not concerned with the girl.

"Besides, I will need her help to get ready for bed. She always helps to see me to bed, don't you, Mona? Now, George, it may be best for you to get back to the kitchen."

"I was wondering if there was anything I could do . . . you know. To help."

"Do you want to grease the pan for me, George? Do you want to stand over my shoulder and make sure I have the measurements right? Sorry, but you are just going to have to keep out of sight for now. If there is anything I need from you, I will let you know. Do you understand that?"

"Yes, ma'am."

"Stop being such a nervous Nellie. You make me nervous, too. I practiced the recipes every day after you left. Didn't I, Mona?"

"Yes, she did. Biscuits and more biscuits."

"Things could not be going better. I know I have impressed the judges. I would say that Colonel Claiborne is even a bit smitten with me. Can you imagine? He is perfectly dreadful. He has no hair to speak of, but he still has dandruff. How is that possible? George, you have to trust me now. You have to step away from it."

George nodded to them both and left. Outside the door, he felt the past rush over him like the breeze from a ceiling fan. It was the same shut out feeling he had back in Brest when he had visited Maude on a night when he was not scheduled to visit. He had started drinking in the afternoon and began to miss her. He stumbled his way along the familiar streets. However, when he arrived he discovered she was already occupied entertaining a local dairy farmer. Everyone in the house was in the dining room and parlor, drinking and toasting. Maude had become engaged to the dairy farmer that very afternoon. Butcher knew she had other men, but this was different—the fact that she loved someone else, wanted to marry him was not a consideration. He tried to fight the dairy farmer, whose name he did not know, until several of the men along with Laurent pinned his arms and threw him out the door onto the street.

Laurent tried to explain that it was for the best, that Butcher would be leaving soon anyway. Butcher knew this was true, but it did not console him. Laurent told Butcher the farmer was the one who supplied all the dairy for the house, all milk and cream, the butter, the eggs. "He has bartered them with us for a long time," he said. "He has had his eye on Maude for a while. Besides, I am the one you should feel sorry for," he laughed, trying to lighten the mood. "Now I will have to pay cash for everything." Butcher didn't think the joke was funny. "I am in love with her." "I wish you could be happy for her. This is a good match. If you really do love her, you will understand this. You will step away."

Butcher could feel that he was ready to cry, so he clambered up from the street and declared that he would never return. Butcher told Laurent that he and Helaine and Maude and her dairyman could all go to hell. Fuck 'em all.

Laurent told Butcher that perhaps it would be best if he did not return to the brothel. And if he tried, he would throw him out. Butcher knew he did not need to threaten. He would never return, never see Maude again, but he never forgot the feeling of being cast away. It was the same thing he felt now outside the door to Virginia's room. But hadn't he known it would come to this—that he had to trust her? What else was there?

When he returned to the kitchen, he got a reprimand from Roland for taking too long with the order. "I bet you snuck off to take a smoke break, didn't you? We got orders here that need to go out. So learn to move your sorry black ass faster, or you will find you won't have a job here." Butcher pushed his anger, his hurt deeper. He delivered half a dozen more trays before the end of his shift without complaint.

When he had changed out of the hotel uniform into his own clothes, as he came out from the dressing room, he saw Mona standing by the back stairs, near the service elevator. She wore a pale yellow sweater that glowed golden in the light from the milk-glass shade on the stairs. She was waiting on him. She had come for their walk.

"Did she change her mind?" he asked.

"Who knows what her mind is? She's gone to sleep. I just picked up the key and walked out the door."

"Snuck out the door, I betcha."

"I wanted to thank you for the cake."

"Would you like to go take a walk with me?" he asked. He wanted to walk with her, maybe put his arm around her, tried to imagine if she would let him kiss her.

"I can't go far. Maybe we can walk to the corner and back," she suggested.

Outside, the air was thick with warmth.

"Humid night," he said.

"I hate it down here," she said.

"It's no worse than Fayetteville. I bet it's hot there now, too."

"I hate it there, too."

"Where is it, then, you want to be that's not one of them places?" he asked.

"Away from her," she said.

"You can just leave her. You're old enough. I bet a great many women would be happy to have someone like you in their employ. Does she treat you bad?"

"Good enough for a servant girl—fetch this, make me this, clean up my mess. She don't hit me as much as she used to. But she don't like me much. That I know."

"Sad to say, it's going to be that way anywhere you work for a white woman. It just is."

They walked the rest of the way to the corner in silence, looked at the empty intersection, and turned to walk back. "But it shouldn't be," she said. Butcher looked down into her eyes and he knew what she was going to tell him was something he already knew, something he had known all along. "I think she's my mother."

They didn't go back to the hotel. Instead, they walked in silence until they came to a coffee shop he knew that served late in the evening, catching trade from the hotels and restaurants when workers finished a shift. They found a booth near the back. They ordered only coffee.

As she raised her eyes toward him, he was reminded of the afternoon he first met her. He could not help himself, but reached across the table and took her hands in his. He thought of his own mam, how she would stroke his shoulder as he stood on a box at the table in the kitchen, watching her cook, sometimes helping her with small tasks—stirring a bowl of batter, whipping eggs. He thought, too, of Maude, how she told him her family had left her with Helaine and Laurent, traded her for food, supplies. Mona did not pull away, but left her hands in his, quivering like a rabbit or small bird trapped and too frightened to fight.

"I have never been courted, Mr. Butcher," she said. "I don't really know what to do."

"But you know I care for you."

"Yes," she said. "I know."

"I would watch out for you," he said. "I would never force you."

She pulled her hands away and placed them in her lap.

"Then we will give it time. To be honest, I haven't courted much myself. Let's just give it some time. About the other. You said you think Miss Virginia is your mam. What makes you believe that?" he asked.

"She hates me, calls me her albatross, her millstone. But even so, she would never turn me out—and there were some hard times before we got to Fayetteville. Some hard times. But she always kept me close, even when there was no need for her to have a child with her. At least not until the major."

"She told the major the truth about you?"

"No," she said. "The afternoon he was supposed to come to supper I asked her what was going to happen to me if he proposed. She said I was free to come along with them as long as it was convenient for everyone involved.

"When I asked her what that meant, she said I could come or I could go—she had done her duty by me, that she had made sacrifices aplenty for me, and she had been on her own younger than me. That's when I told her that I knew. What I think."

"What did she say?"

"She told me that I was crazy. Told me that she had helped her friend by taking me in. But when I ask her about Dorothea, she doesn't ever have anything to say. Where she came from. Who her people were. Why is that? If I was this woman's child, don't you think she would want me to know that?"

"Maybe there isn't anything to tell."

"I know it, Mr. Butcher. I know it. Anyway, we had a terrible row. I told her I would tell the major if she didn't."

"And did you?"

Mona smiled, but only slightly. "Didn't have to. As we were fighting, the major came by. I'm not sure why. But he heard it all. And he left. Plain and simple. I hid from her. She started drinking and was so angry that I knew she would hit me if she could find me. I heard her calling and calling. But then you stepped in. Brought her the pie. She said it was like the sky opened up and she saw a rainbow that night when you came to the house. A rainbow with a pot of gold."

Butcher could tell from her face that there was more.

"She's a liar, Mr. Butcher. She don't care for no one but herself."

"But why are you telling me this?" Butcher asked.

"When she drinks, she talks. Doesn't remember what she tells me, what she says. She laughs about how you think she is just going to hand over half that prize money. That once she gets it, she is free and clear all the way to California."

Butcher wondered why the walls of the café didn't fall away from him, why the buildings around them didn't suddenly crumble from their foundations. He had taught this woman, trusted her.

"Don't say that, Miss Mona. I worked with her. Partnered with her. She knows she couldn't have done any of this without me."

"But now she can. And if she wins, I swear you won't see nothing of her but hind parts and elbows."

Butcher wanted to throw the ceramic mug against the wall, watch it smash. "She owes me," he said.

"She owes us both," said Mona.

# 8

# aspic . . .

When Virginia woke, Mona had already set out a breakfast tray for her—just coffee and a roll. Her two day dresses hung on the back of the closet door: One was a simple yellow shirtwaist; the other was a lilac summer dress, pleated in the front and with capelet sleeves. On the dresser lay a faceted blue glass brooch and earrings she planned to wear with the summer dress, a multicolored flowered rhinestone pin to wear against the buttercream shirtwaist. Which to wear? She quickly decided on the yellow. It was straightforward enough for a day of cooking, but still would set her apart from the mob. She had also purchased an embroidered pleated bib apron to show her practical mindedness. Though everything depended on her performance today, she was not nervous. She was ready. Mona sat in the chair by the window, drinking coffee, staring mindlessly out the window.

"What time is it? How long do I have before I need to be downstairs?"

Mona stopped staring, checked her watch. "It's just past seven. What time do you want to leave?"

"I would like to be in the kitchen by eight-fifteen at the latest. I would like a chance to get everything ready so I can use all the time allotted. The popover batter must rest for as long as possible before I bake them. I assume they will want us to start as close to eight-thirty as we can."

"I have your clothes ready for you. I would think you would want the yellow today."

It irritated Virginia that the girl knew her so well. "Yes, the yellow for today. I will save the lilac for tomorrow. It fits me nicer across the bosom and will show up better in photographs."

When Mona didn't say anything, Virginia continued, "I am sure they will want to photograph the winner." She pointed to the coffee on the tray. "Bring me my coffee here. I will have it here in bed."

Mona set the tray next to the bed and poured the coffee in silence.

"You don't think I can win this, do you? You probably don't want me to win it."

Mona walked back to the window and flung herself into the chair.

"Out with it," said Virginia. "I know you have something on your mind. An opinion on the matter. Get it out. I don't need any distractions today."

"I think you could win. Mr. Butcher taught you well. I know if you win, then you gonna toss me on the road like a sack of trash."

"I would never just turn you out, Mona. I would help you get established somewhere. But you are nearly grown. And I have my own life."

Neither spoke for a moment. Virginia sipped her coffee. "This is awfully bitter."

"That's because there isn't any hooch in it."

Virginia put the saucer on the night table delicately. "I should come over there and slap the blue Jesus out of you. You have no right to speak to me like that. No right. But I have other fish to fry today. I told you I would set you up. I do not need permission from you to have my own life. I looked out for you—I didn't have to do that."

"Didn't you?"

"No. No, I didn't. And you don't have one ounce of gratitude for the sacrifices I have made for you."

Virginia struggled not to cry. She refused to lose her composure.

To lose this battle. But the girl was just like her in that regard—resolute in her stubborn steadfastness. Finally, Mona spoke. "You will have two and half thousand dollars," she said. "How much you planning to give me?"

"I hadn't thought of an amount. Perhaps five hundred dollars. That would seem a generous sum."

Mona looked at her as if pondering the amount.

"Maybe I would have it all," said Mona.

"You must be crazy," Virginia said, throwing off the bedcovers, jumping to the floor. "All of it? Why would I go through all this? Learn all this? And then hand the winnings over to you."

"How fast did the major leave when he thought I was your daughter? How long they gonna let you wear the white hat when they hear about me?"

"You would do that? You would take it all from me."

"No. No, I wouldn't," said Mona. "I would leave you five hundred dollars. As you said, it would be a generous sum."

Virginia was still shaking slightly as she stepped into the kitchen, a jar of apricot preserves cradled in her apron, which was folded on top of the popover pan. She balanced the pan in front of her awkwardly—this would have been one thing that Mona could have done for her, help her carry this gear down to the kitchen. Several of the women including Wadena had colored maids, so it would not have been inappropriate. The poorer women were assisted by daughters, nieces, sisters, friends. Virginia felt as if the air whispered about her as she made her way to her designated station. In addition to the cooking supplies, she also carried a small clutch purse, containing only some powder and lipstick and her flask. She found one of the women from the local DOC, a hostess, to help her tie her apron in back. Who knows, thought Virginia. It might even work to her advantage—she knew the story would be repeated: "I tell you, she had no one at all to help her."

It was just past 8:30 when Roland came in, shooed the maids and relatives from the kitchen, and gave them their starting instructions: "We had a walk-through yesterday, but if you forget something, please ask me, or ask one of the pastry cooks from the hotel here to help you find what you need. Do not just go off rummaging. Not all of you are using an oven, so you shouldn't have to share. So let's begin. I judge that it is nearly a quarter till nine, and since there is not a clock in here, I will also serve as the timekeeper. You are all probably a bit nervous, and not used to cooking in such a big space, so we can round up to nine o'clock. That means your presentations won't be until eleven. I will give you a countdown at each hour, then half hour, fifteen, ten, five minutes."

"Would any of you like to pray before we begin?" asked Inez. "I thought it might be a good idea for us to come together as sisters and have a brief prayer. I would be happy to lead." The women joined hands in a circle in the center of the room—Virginia flanked by Neelie Bryson and Martha Humphrey. From the way she prayed, Virginia judged Inez to be Holiness. She asked Jesus to give fire in the ovens, not only for their biscuits, but also for their souls. She asked Jesus to help them stir their batters with a joyous heart. Virginia prayed that Inez be eliminated after the first round.

When she went back to her station, she remembered what Butcher had told her, how he made her practice each recipe in the same way he told her he had practiced with his gun as a new recruit in the army. The steps were nearly automatic now—a pleasant distraction from the encounter with Mona. She heated the milk slowly on the stove, stirring it gently, then removed it from the burner to cool just before it came to a boil. She dropped soft butter into the hot milk so it would melt. In a large mixing bowl, certainly larger than any she had used at home, she sifted together flour, salt, baking powder, a touch of sugar. She made sure to first scoop the flour into a cup until it overflowed and then leveled it off with a knife. Butcher had reminded her again and again of the importance of this step—too much flour and the popovers would be tough. Too little, they would collapse. Next, she beat together eggs, and when the milk had cooled, she stirred them in. She then combined the milk and the eggs with the flour into a relatively smooth batter. "The lumps will even out," Butcher had told her. "Don't want to overbeat it. Nothing wrong with a few lumps." Finally, she added a small splash of vanilla, something Butcher claimed was his own trick. "It gives 'em just a touch of mystery.

Like the perfume you wear. Don't quite know what it is, but it is pleasant." It surprised Virginia that he would speak to her so personally, but knew he felt the food allowed them such intimacies. Now Virginia had to let the batter rest. "Forty-five minutes minimum," said Butcher. "An hour if you can stand it. But remember, the pans have to heat first, then they have to bake for forty minutes." Virginia counted backward from eleven o'clock. The extra fifteen minutes would allow her to leave the batter to rest for the full hour. It would also provide her with ten full minutes on either side of the baking to fill the pans and then to put them on the plate.

Most of the women busied themselves with a test batch of their biscuits or pancakes or waffles. Some were obviously frustrated with the scale of the kitchen, off balance. She watched Wadena drop a circle of dough into the sizzling oil in the cast-iron fryer on her stove. "This flame is too hot," she said to no one in particular. "It'll burn the outside and leave the inside raw."

Virginia motioned to the hostess who had helped her before. "My batter needs to rest before I can bake," she said. "I thought I might take a minute to walk out in the lobby."

"Do you need someone to assist you?" the woman asked.

"No," said Virginia. "I can find my way. I just want to get some air."

"I'll stay close at hand," said the hostess. "Don't want to leave it unattended for too long. I will just keep an eye on it for you till you get back." Virginia was a bit surprised by the implication that someone might tamper with her batter. Would she do the same if given an opportunity? Turn the heat up so high under Wadena's doughnuts that they would crisp like cinders? It frustrated her she wasn't free to return to her own room, but she did want to find a private spot for just a moment or two. Long enough to take a sip if her nerves demanded.

As she made her way from the kitchen into the dining room and lobby of the hotel, she was reminded of the theater, the world backstage where everything was orchestrated chaos and noise, while out front, there were no signs that anything beyond these walls even existed. People sat chatting, sipping coffee in the lobby, reading the *Constitution*. She thought briefly about slipping into the Ladies' Lounge but knew it would be crowded with the friends and families of her competition. She hesitated in front of the door when she saw Clayton Claiborne emerge from the Gentleman's Lounge. He motioned to her to join him.

"Miss Virginia. This is a surprise. I would expect you to be in the kitchen making something . . . delicious."

"I hope it will be," she said. "I am making popovers. And I brought some homemade preserves to serve with them. But the batter has to rest a bit. Gives the dough time to relax. I thought I might as well do the same."

"Delightful," he said. "If you have a moment, I would consider it a great privilege to have you sit with me for a visit. I will order a beverage. We have coffee, tea—I can order something cool for you if you prefer."

"What would you be having?" Virginia asked.

"Well," said Claiborne, "I must confess a fondness for the Ramos Fizz. But I don't want to tempt you with spirits if you are not so inclined."

"A Fizz would be perfection," she said, removing her gloves.

Claiborne motioned to one of the colored workers nearby—Virginia was relieved it wasn't George—and told him to bring the drinks. "And be snappy about it," he said. "My friend has only a short time with me." After the man had left, Claiborne turned to her. He was still as homely as she remembered, but seemed oblivious to the fact; she also thought him to be a bit of a fop, like a gentleman's valet in a Ginger Rogers comedy. She knew it didn't matter what he looked like or how queer he was—all that mattered was who he was. "As a young man, a dear friend of the family took me to New Orleans for an extended visit over Carnival and Mardi Gras. I can still see the boys at The Stag Saloon mixing up batches of Ramos Fizz all day and night, shaking and shaking those shiny metallic urns till I thought their arms would fall off or they would turn into butter like Little Black Sambo. It may just be the fondness of memory for certain places or times, but I do sometimes enjoy one in the morning when I do not have business concerns."

The server returned almost immediately with the drinks. After he set them down, Claiborne asked, "Miss Virginia, how long do you have for this break?"

"I really should be back at work no later than quarter till ten."

Claiborne took his watch from his vest and addressed the waiter: "Boy, what is your name?"

"Matthew, sir."

"Matthew, I assume you can tell time."

"Yes, sir."

"Well, then, Matthew, I am going to have you stand over there where I can see you, and I am going to give you this watch to hold. And when it is twenty-two minutes till ten, not a minute before or after, then I want you to bring the watch back to me. Not a minute before or after—otherwise, there will be the devil to pay."

"Yes, sir."

After Matthew had walked to the other side of the room, positioning himself beside a potted palm, Claiborne retrieved his drink. "They have to be good for something," he said. "I guess a clock is about as good a thing as any."

"By why twenty-two minutes till the hour?"

"I like to give them an odd time to tell," he said, smiling. "You would be surprised how often they get it confused."

"And then . . ."

"Makes the day a bit more interesting. But Matthew's a good boy. Smart as they come. He won't make a mistake."

"You know him. . . ."

"I know all the staff at my hotel," he said. "White and colored. But they don't need to know that, do they?"

He raised his glass to her: "You understand, Miss Virginia, that should you win this contest, you and I will be working very closely together."

"Yes, I suppose we would," she said. She could not discern the direction of his remarks, wanted to get out in front of them, avoid an awkward encounter. After all, he was one third of the voting— hell, he might even hold all the cards for all she knew. She sipped her drink. The gin floated through her on a cloud of white froth. "This is delicious," she remarked.

"May I tell you something?" Claiborne asked.

"Certainly, Colonel Claiborne. As you said, you may be my boss here very shortly."

"Yes. Yes, indeed I may. You know, you strike me as different from these women. Somehow I have a hard time imagining you putting up preserves in the summer, getting up early to make batter for breakfast. You would seem more to me the type of lady who would have those things served to her."

"Times are hard for us all," she said. "It is important to be resourceful. And I have only a widow's pension to live on. It is a godsend, but it doesn't go far, I can assure you."

"Still," he said, "you strike me as a woman with a level of sophistication that is absent from some of our other contestants."

Virginia thought of Wadena and her cake hat. She thought of Jubal's bonnet. "It wouldn't be very becoming of me, Colonel Claiborne, to comment on my competitors. Why, just not more than an hour ago, Inez Honeycutt led us all in a lovely prayer of sisterhood. I think you are wicked to tempt me to speak disparagingly of them."

"Yes," he said, "I suppose I am. But Mystic White belongs to me. And I am a man used to getting what I want."

Virginia understood he was laying out terms here for her. "And what is it you want from this, Colonel Claiborne? What will The Lady in the White Hat bring to you?"

"She will be the representative of my company."

"Yes," said Virginia, "and that is something I would be honored to do. But the contest. The publicity."

"Yes," he replied with a smile. "The publicity. It's an image, Miss Virginia. We will become the flour of the refined Southern lady. Pure Southern, if you will. And by doing that for Mystic White, it will also enhance my image."

"How so, sir?"

"As I said, the contest winner and I will work very closely together."

"I believe the contract terms are for a year."

She thought he looked at her with a slight bit of astonishment, that she would have even an awareness of such a thing. "Yes, for one year. To start. Who is to say what would happen after that?"

"I suppose all things are negotiable," she said.

"I have many dreams, Miss Virginia," Claiborne said, leaning over toward her as if sharing an intimacy. "Business is just one of them. You may be interested to know that some folks—people with influence and connections—have encouraged me to turn my attentions to politics. God knows, with all that is happening in the world, so much is slipping away from us. But it would be difficult to entertain those notions as a bachelor. There is too much importance placed on the image of family for that. I would hope that whoever is chosen to represent Mystic White Flour will also be available to assist me. Would be available . . ."

Virginia stiffened in the chair. "I hope, sir, that you understand this business arrangement would be simply that."

"Indeed," he said. "But as you said yourself—all things are negotiable."

Virginia was suddenly aware that Matthew was standing next to them.

"Sorry to interrupt you, sir, but it is twenty-two to ten," he said, holding the watch out to Claiborne for verification.

"So it is," Claiborne said. "Thank you, Matthew. If you will escort Miss Virginia back to the kitchen." Claiborne did not rise from his chair, but extended his hand to her. She took his hand, and again noticed that he held it for an improper amount of time. She knew this was no accident. It was a test. She did not flinch or pull away, waited for him to release her.

"Thank you for the beverage, Colonel Claiborne," she said.

"The first of many, I hope," he replied.

She saw Claiborne again that morning in the dining room as he and Roland and Jocelyn Hind Crowley sampled the items that had been placed for them to taste and made comments. Looking at Claiborne, it was hard to imagine him as a senator or possibly even governor. But he did have money. He did have power. And what would that do for her?

After the judges conferred, Roland delivered the verdict: "The following ladies will stay to compete," he said. "Wadena Chastain, Muriel Sallis, Virginia Yeager, and Jubal Hart. To our other contestants, thank you very much."

Inez Honeycutt burst into tears on the spot. Neelie Bryson simply walked to the table and picked up her plate of rejected waffles and tossed the whole kit and caboodle into the trash on her way out the door. "I should have never entered such a carnival sideshow," she said. "My family warned me."

"But your waffles were delicious, Mrs. Bryson," Jocelyn Hind Crowley called out after her. "It's just that Mrs. Sallis put sour cream and chopped nuts into hers. A very original approach."

Roland gave Jocelyn Hind Crowley a look so dark that she stopped talking and took her place back in line. "As I said," he continued, "we thank all of you for your efforts. And Mystic White flour will be sending you a year's supply of flour."

The gift seemed of little consolation to the discarded women who looked as if they had just been told the last lifeboat had been filled. Too bad that all hope for them had now been abandoned. Slowly they made their way to consoling daughters, nieces, sisters, friends. To the four remaining women, Roland said, "The next round will begin at two o'clock and will last three hours. If you will confirm with me before you leave for lunch what you will be baking, I will make sure everything you need is waiting for you. And congratulations."

Claiborne didn't speak to any of the winners, but the women all hugged one another.

"I am so thrilled," said Jubal Hart. "When I saw all the fancy things that you all were making—and I just had pancakes."

"But you were the only one with pancakes," said Wadena Chastain. "That was the difference. Waffles were the low suit today. I could have told you this morning that only one waffle would be chosen. Chopped nuts—who knew, Muriel?" She then looked to Virginia. "And those popovers were a grand idea," she said. "Plus, using your own preserves—inspired. I must find out from you how you make them." When Virginia didn't offer any recipe tips, Wadena continued. "We have to watch out for this one, ladies," she said to Inez and Muriel. "She didn't just come to play. She came to win."

Virginia didn't linger longer than necessary to chat with the women, eager to return upstairs. When she arrived, she discovered the room had been cleaned, but Mona wasn't anywhere to be found. Fortunately, her bag was in the wardrobe. Everything ordered, in its place. She was not gone for good, but this was not like her. Virginia tried not to panic, but she had difficulty even in getting out of her dress alone. Mona took care of these things for her—helped her dress, drew her bath, poured her coffee. The windows were closed and all the air seemed to have been sucked out of the room. She found it hard to breathe. But she forced herself to settle, opened the window, changed into her dressing gown.

And she ordered a tray. She could only hope that it was Butcher who delivered it.

When he put the tray down on the table, she felt a sudden tenderness toward him, like a music student who has mastered a difficult piece and wants the teacher to take pride in the accomplishment. She would have embraced him, but knew she could not.

"I am on to the next round," she said.

"I heard," he replied. "I also heard you had time with the man himself."

"Yes," she said. "Totally by coincidence. He is such a curiosity. So absolutely sure of himself. But such a . . ." She sighed, catching herself. "But I shouldn't say. It sounds like there is a veritable network of information going on behind the scenes."

"That's why I came, isn't it? To see. To hear."

"So they do comment on us," she said.

"It's of high interest," he replied.

"Did you see the popovers, George? They baked up just as golden as could be. Roland even commented on the vanilla. Called it a note. Said it helped to make them sing. I saw that Crowley woman write it down. It will probably be in the newspaper."

"I didn't see 'em," he said. "But I heard the cooks say they all liked the preserves that came with 'em."

"Yes," she said. "The preserves were a nice touch."

It struck her suddenly as odd that he hadn't looked for, asked for Mona.

"I think Mona has deserted me," she said.

He didn't reply.

"George," she said. "I had a terrible fight with Mona this morning. Now she is gone. Something could happen to her. She is not nearly as tough as she makes out."

"She'll be okay," he said. "You can trust that."

"If you know where she is, then you need to send her back to me."

Butcher didn't say anything.

"There is a great deal of pressure on me," she continued. "I need to have her here to assist me." She sat, smoothing the dressing gown down over her legs. "Don't you understand, you dolts, that if I don't win, then no one gets anything. Do you know she has demanded the majority of the winnings? What would she do with that great a sum? Am I to assume that she is going to split this with you? What makes you think she is any more trustworthy than I am?"

Butcher lowered his head, avoiding her eyes. "I think everyone is just watching out for themselves."

"Fine," she said. "And where will that get you—us? Send her back to me. When it is over, then we will decide what to do. But you both cannot desert me now." She put her head in her hands and began to cry.

He felt suddenly ashamed now of the slip of paper in his jacket, a letter he had written to Clayton Claiborne that read:

*Mr. Clayton Claiborne,*
*My name is George Butcher and I work*
*for you in this hotel. I am also associated*
*with Mrs. Virginia Yeager. She is*
*indebted to me for the recipes she has used*
*to compete in the contest.*

*George Butcher*

He had intended to show it to her, to frighten her that if she thought she could run out on him, that he knew ways to get at her as well. Mona had wanted him to put in about her being Miss Virginia's daughter, but Butcher would not. "This is just business," he told her. "The other is personal between the two of you."

If the crying was an act for him, Butcher could not tell. She seemed genuinely distraught.

"I will talk to her," he said. "You are right. We need to all hang together here until this is over."

Virginia stopped crying. "Thank you," she said.

"I don't get off until nine o'clock or so tonight. You will be on your own this afternoon."

Virginia seemed full of new energy. "Certainly. Not a problem. Just as long as she is here tonight. I don't want to be here by myself. And to help me in the morning. Then, when this is over, as you said, we will work out a solution that is equitable for each of us."

"If I may say, Miss Virginia, I don't think it is the money she is concerned with."

"You know, don't you, that it doesn't matter what I tell her. She will believe what she wants. But tell her to come back tonight and then she and I will talk."

"Yes, ma'am," he said. "And I know you will do a good job with the biscuits. Nothing to be worried about there."

Butcher collected food trays for the first part of the afternoon, so he was only in the kitchen sporadically as the women competed in the second round. When it was time for the judging, the chef motioned to him to come and carry a plate for one of the women, a thin birdlike woman whose face seemed all contrary angles. Butcher's prediction proved accurate about the biscuits. Even from a distance, he could tell they were perfect, and when the judges announced the finalists, Miss Virginia was one of the two. She didn't look at him, just gave a nod of appreciation to the judges. The other finalist, a short, plump woman with enormous breasts, clapped her hands together and gave a shout when her name was called. The chef thanked the women and told them they would meet again in the morning for the final round. However, before the room cleared, Butcher saw Virginia approach the chef and Colonel Claiborne and the woman from the newspaper.

After a few minutes, the chef held up his hand and motioned for everyone to be silent.

"Folks," he said. "Mrs. Yeager has just presented me with an unusual circumstance. For her final dish, she will be making aspic, which will need to be refrigerated overnight before it can be sliced."

One of the women near to where Butcher stood said, "Aspic. In this heat?"

Her friend replied, "She probably just stares at it to cool it down. Such an icy disposition."

They both laughed quietly at their private joke as Roland continued.

"We have conferred, and we are going to allow Mrs. Yeager to prepare her dish this evening. She says she will be happy to have a short break and then begin."

There was a small burst of applause for her efforts.

"Miss Chastain, I trust this is acceptable to you."

"Lord, yes," said the woman. "I don't care who cooks when."

There was more applause for her generosity.

"Very well, then," said Chef Roland. "I have five-thirty PM. Mrs. Yeager, if you will return to the kitchen by seven, then you should be able to begin. It will be a late night, I'm afraid—and you will have to have your dish finished by ten PM to abide by the three-hour time limit. I have other obligations, but I will discuss with Colonel Claiborne and Miss Crowley as to what we need to do so you will not have to be all by yourself in the kitchen."

When the crowd had dispersed, Butcher and several other men crumbed the tables and checked to see if any cloths needed to be changed. When the men began to eat the leftover food, Butcher asked if they shouldn't return at least some of it to the kitchen so the cooks might taste it. "If we eat all this now, there won't be another slice of pie that ever comes in our direction," he said. In truth, he wanted to know what the pastry cooks thought of his biscuits. He took his time, scraping trays and stacking plates so he could watch as the women from the pastry room gathered to dissect the biscuits remaining. He could not hear their comments but could discern a general hum of approval. It satisfied him.

It was only a short while before Chef Roland appeared in the main kitchen again. Butcher was not surprised to see the woman from the newspaper following closely, but what was remarkable was that Colonel Claiborne also walked in behind the chef. Butcher had never seen him in the service areas of the hotels. Roland excused himself and went to the table where Miss Virginia's supplies had been laid out for her. He checked things off on a list he carried with him, calling out to make sure what wasn't on the table was in the refrigerator. Butcher noticed that he seemed to be particularly well-behaved. There was no cursing tonight in front of Claiborne. No smashed plates. After all, thought Butcher, the plates really belonged to Claiborne and he might not take too kindly to seeing them tossed against a wall.

The swinging door from the dining room opened slightly, and Miss Virginia entered the kitchen. She was still in her yellow dress, Butcher noted, though she looked worn down from the heat and effort of the day. She seemed to have trouble opening the door, like a child pushing a heavy weight, and Butcher could tell from the flush in her cheeks that she had been drinking.

If she saw him, she didn't let on, but went straight to Claiborne and the chef, her hand extended. "I appreciate so much this courtesy," she said. "I hope I am not putting anyone out."

"Not at all," said Chef Roland. "The kitchen will close at nine, so there will be people here working till then. However, the last hour may be a bit lonely."

This did not sit well with the newspaper woman. "I don't think it is appropriate, sir, that Mrs. Yeager be left here by herself. Besides, there are rules to follow, and someone has to keep time."

"I understand that, Miss Crowley, but do you think it necessary to babysit Mrs. Yeager? I think we can trust her."

Miss Crowley's face flamed red. "I wasn't implying anything like that," she said. "But . . ."

"I agree with Miss Crowley," said Claiborne. "It would not be proper to abandon Mrs. Yeager here. We are asking one of these women to become the spokeswoman for my company. She is not applying for a job as a scullery maid." He looked toward Virginia. "Tell me, Miss Virginia, do you have a companion here with you, someone who might sit here with you this evening?"

Virginia looked back at Claiborne but also let her eyes meet Butcher's, like she had done that morning in the Residence. Butcher knew that she had been aware of him all along. "I am afraid I gave my maid the afternoon off to visit an aunt who lives here," she said. "She hasn't returned."

"And the hostesses from the DOC have all gone home," said Miss Crowley. "They were here all day and will be back early in the morning as well." Then, as if afraid she would be commandeered, she added, "I must go to the newspaper to turn in my copy from today. I am late now as it is."

Claiborne considered the situation. "What do we need—someone to tell her when the time is up? That would seem simple enough." Claiborne looked first to Virginia and then over to Butcher.

"Boy," he said. "Come over here."

Butcher walked to Claiborne, the chef, and the newspaper woman.

"What is your name, son?" Claiborne asked.

"George," Butcher said.

"Can you tell time, George?" Claiborne asked.

"Yes, sir," said Butcher.

"Well, I hope so, because if you're lying to me, there will be the devil to pay, I can tell you that, George," said Claiborne, removing a large pocket watch from his vest. He handed the watch to Butcher.

"Now, what time is it, George?"

Butcher looked at the watch face. "It is five minutes till seven."

"Good," said Claiborne, winking at Virginia. "I love me a nigger that can tell the time. Now, George, here is what I'm going to do. I am going to give you this watch, and I want you to go and sit on that stool over there. One of the other boys will run your trays tonight. I want you to sit on that stool and look at this watch, and when it is quarter till ten, then I want you to come and get me in the Gentlemen's Lounge. Do you think you can do that, George?"

"Yes, sir," said Butcher.

"Colonel Claiborne," interjected Jocelyn Crowley. "Do you think this is proper?"

"Proper?" asked Claiborne.

"I mean, to leave her here—alone with . . ."

"George," said Claiborne, waving a hand toward Butcher, "George isn't going to bother anyone, are you, George?"

Butcher knew better than to speak. He lowered his eyes to the floor and shook his head.

But Claiborne was happy to have the attention of those around him and continued. "Because if he dared even so much as sniff in her direction, he knows what that would mean. Besides, we don't employ field hands here, Miss Crowley. George will behave himself."

Clayton stepped in close to George and spoke in a loud whisper. "Now, if she needs to know the time, she will ask you. But I don't want you to speak to her, to interfere with her in any way. If she tells me you have spoken to her or been impolite to her, then you will be a sorry fellow I can assure you. And don't believe I won't ask her either. Miss Virginia, will it suit you to have this boy serve as your timepiece?"

Virginia hesitated for a moment, but replied softly, "Yes."

Butcher took his place on the stool with the watch in his hand as Virginia began preparing the pâté. Claiborne, the chef, and the newspaper woman talked for a few minutes before losing interest in her and George. The swoosh of the swinging door carried with it Claiborne's final comment as they departed: "They have to be good for something. I guess a clock is as good a thing as any."

Butcher sat staring at the floor for several minutes, making sure they would not return. In the main kitchen, he could hear the chatter of cooks as they plated foods, happy to be free from Chef Roland's supervision, certain they would be able to shut the kitchen down a bit early. Butcher remembered those nights from the army, from the kitchen in the Residence, even from the kitchen at Caledonia, after the rush of service had ended and there hung around the kitchen a general easiness.

"My thoughts are all muddled," Miss Virginia interrupted.

"You've had a long day," said Butcher. "I could get you some coffee if you want. It might help."

"Yes," said Virginia. "Actually, a bit of coffee might do the trick. But you were told not to move."

"I'll just go to the door," he said, which he did. He motioned to one of the men in the kitchen, and in a very short time, a coffee service was delivered. He wasn't surprised when she poured a shot from a flask into the cup.

"Miss Virginia," he said. "There are a lot of steps to this recipe. I'm not sure . . ."

"You know the contest they really need to have," she said. "Let all these women sit around sipping sherry for an hour, then make them prepare a whole meal. That would be closer to the heart of it, don't you think?"

"If I may say, Miss Virginia, you shouldn't be wasting time on the filling just yet. Remember, the dough has got to chill, and the aspic will need time to clear. And baking time is an hour."

She let out a tremendous sigh, then turned to face him squarely.

"I can't do it," she said.

"You have to," he replied.

"I am tired, George. My head is spinning. I just want to sit down. Maybe I should do to you what Mona has done to me—just withdraw. Make you carry the entire burden for a while. Who has helped me, George? I ask you that. Who has helped me?"

"It's just a little bit more, Miss Virginia. Then it will all be done."

But he could tell he made no progress with her. "Seriously, George, why don't you make this? You know you would love to. When they cut into it in the morning and they all *ooh* and *aah* over it, then you will know it will be you they are *oohing* and *aahing* over, not me."

"Miss Virginia, if we were to get caught . . ."

"Who is going to come in here and check on us? The men are

out in the Gentlemen's Lounge for the rest of the evening, and you heard that little simp from the paper. She has a deadline. George, this is an opportunity for you."

She was right. It would be a pleasure to create this final dish, to know that it was his work that was being judged. But it was risky.

"I will sit here by the door," she said. "And keep watch. Or do you just want to be Clayton Claiborne's timepiece?"

Butcher undid the buttons on his uniform, laying the jacket on the end of the table, leaving him just in his undershirt. "I can't cook in that thing," he said. "It confines me too much."

"Try wearing a girdle sometime," said Virginia, as she climbed onto the stool by the door. "Now hurry. We don't have any time to spare."

Butcher took a moment to survey the layout of the ingredients for the pastry crust, then began to gather them together. He was transported back to her kitchen in Fayetteville, demonstrating to her the first time how the dish was made. He traveled further, back to Brest, back to the kitchen with Laurent, when he watched and learned the secret of the dish. Outside the swinging doors, the kitchen grew silent as they crew finished their work and slipped out into the night.

How good it felt to have his hands dusty with flour, to feel the soft dough as it gave to the push of his palm. It seemed like only a matter of moments before he had lined the mold with the pastry, filled it with the meat mixture, and put the whole thing into the oven to bake. He poured the aspic through a sieve and marveled at the amber liquid as it cooled. He cleaned up the station, stacking empty bowls and pans in the sink. He knew better than to wash them, however. Knew that task would have been left for someone else.

When the pâté emerged from the oven, he took his own blade from his pocket, unsheathed it, and cut a small hole no larger than a dime in the top so steam could escape. When it had cooled slightly, he would ladle the aspic into a funnel inserted into the hole and then use the blade to reinsert the lid. Unless you knew where he cut, it would be nearly impossible to tell that the crust had been broken. They were nearly there.

He could tell from the way she tried hard not to lean that she was a bit wobbly on the stool.

"Miss Virginia," he said. "You will need . . ." He hesitated. "You will need a few minutes to gather yourself before I go and collect Colonel Claiborne. You want to look your best when they come to see you."

"Tell me, George," she said. "Why did you choose me for this?"

"I told you when I first spoke to you about it," he replied.

"Yes, that I had a style. But there had to be more to it."

"Maybe I could sense that you were hungry, that you wanted things beyond what was in front of you," he said. "I would watch you in the meetings back at the Residence. You wanted people to look at you. I watched how they regarded you. You were not like them. These women do this because this is who they are."

"And I was putting on a show."

"Yes."

"Yes," she said. "That is the truth. I am a fraud."

"No," he told her. "Not now. Not anymore. Like you said, today it was you who did all this, who carried all the weight."

"When we first began, I thought that I could never learn all the steps. I would watch you and see how you did things that seemed so effortless, but when I tried them . . . Well, I don't have to re-mind you how many things went into the trash. But I learned to love it," she said, and he could see the truth in her pale blue eyes. "And now I do. I love it. It is a gift you have given to me," she said. She raised herself off the stool and stumbled. He caught her, held her. She didn't resist.

There was the soft suck of air as the swinging door to the pastry room opened, and then there was the sudden sickening realization that they were not alone. As Butcher released Virginia, they turned to see Wadena Chastain standing full frame in the door. Virginia stepped away from him, but they both knew it was too late. They had been discovered.

Butcher forgot that he was standing in his undershirt with his arms around a white woman. He forgot about his folded uniform jacket. He forgot about Clayton Claiborne's watch in his pocket. He forgot about everything. He simply walked past Wadena. Walked out of the room. Walked out of the kitchen. Out of the hotel into the night.

For a moment, neither woman spoke. Finally, Wadena said, "I came down to see if you might like to join me for a nightcap when you are done. I had my maid mix a pitcher of Brandy Daisies, and I have some sandwiches. I don't imagine you have eaten."

Virginia turned her attention to the pâté and to the container of golden aspic. "You are so kind to think of me," she said. "I simply have to ladle this in through the funnel and put it into the icebox to set up for tomorrow." She tried to spoon the mixture into the funnel, but her hands shook so violently that a great deal of it spilled onto the counter.

"I can see that I am making you nervous," said Wadena. "I will expect you when you finish. I am on the third floor—Room 307."

"Yes," said Virginia, trying to sound nonchalant. "I will be there directly. As soon as I am finished."

When Virginia was alone, she went to the sink where Butcher had placed the dirty pots and baking sheets. She turned the cold water on full and held a clean towel under the running water, which she used to wipe the sweat from her neck and face. How cool and refreshing the cloth felt. She covered the pâté with a bit of tin foil and collected the items George had left behind, his coat, a knife. She was in a mess she knew, but she also knew that she was not one to let mere circumstance determine the course of her life. Something would come to her. A solution. A way out. It always did. There had been Henry Yeager when she needed him to help her out of a pickle. And then George. Just when things looked their most bleak. She needed some time. She would talk to Wadena. Size up the situation.

She turned out the light in the pastry room and made her way through the darkened kitchen to the service elevator.

Wadena opened the door to the room as soon as she knocked.

The room was larger than Virginia's—a suite. There was a settee and matching wingback chairs. Wadena motioned to them. Virginia sat, Butcher's jacket folded over her hands like a muff, as Wadena poured a drink for each of them. As she positioned herself in one of the wingbacks, Wadena lit a cigarette.

Virginia sipped the cool drink, the alcohol soothing her nerves.

"Makes things easier, doesn't it?" Wadena said.

"Yes," said Virginia. "It has been a very long day."

"Well," said Wadena. "I have a whole pitcher of 'em. Drink as much as you want. Ain't no one here but me and you. We have all night to get this mess sorted out."

"Where is your girl?"

"My maid? She stays down at the colored hotel. Doesn't yours?"

"No," said Virginia. "She stays with me."

"Oh," replied Wadena. "Maybe that's where you developed the habit. I mean sleeping with the help, my dear. It doesn't get much more common than that."

"It's not like that," said Virginia. "It is not what you think."

"I don't give a crap what it *is*," said Wadena. "All I care about is what it looks like—what it means. The two are rarely consistent."

Virginia thought of the deception she and George had engineered. "Yes," she said. "I think I know what you mean."

"No, my dear, I don't think you do. For example, why does everyone refer to Clayton Claiborne as colonel? Was he in the war?"

"I don't know."

"It was a nickname that came from his time at boarding school when he was appointed to some piddly-ass position of authority because of his family's wealth. The way I heard it told is he was such a bossy-pants that everyone just started calling him Colonel Claiborne as a joke. But he liked it. Nurtured it. Encouraged people to call him that. And now, ask anyone about Colonel Clayton Claiborne, they could tell you which battles he fought in. Hell, he will probably be buried with full military honors when the time comes. The fantasy he has wielded for himself has become the truth."

"What is it you want?"

"Well, that is pretty simple, don't you think?" Wadena blew a puff of smoke up into the room where it was caught by the breeze from the ceiling fan. "I want to win this contest. Become *The Lady*. Won't that be a hoot? I know you want that, too. But this isn't simply about one of us having our picture on a sack of flour," she said.

"Yes," Virginia stammered. "I had an idea of that."

"What is the one thing we all have in common—apart from the fact that we are all white and not destitute." When Virginia didn't answer, she continued. "We are all single. Widows, church spinsters, each of us a variation on the theme. Clayton Claiborne is courting a wife. Spinning a new yarn. Plans to present her in all the trappings that his money can buy. And it is quite a bit of money. But surely you knew that already."

"Not really," said Virginia. "At least not until today."

Wadena picked up the pitcher and refilled their glasses. "Do you think these things just happen? That they aren't planned? How do you suppose that Clayton got the idea he needed a wife, that he had even a frog's hair of a chance in politics. You may not be aware, Virginia, but my family is very influential in an organization that has connections to Clayton. They—we—have had an eye on Clayton for a long time. This has all been very well planned. Roland will vote for me. He knows his position depends on it. And the same goes for Jocelyn Hind Crowley. But Clayton sometimes gets distracted. Like a horse that has been let loose without his blinders. You may have cocktails with him, but make no mistake. I will marry Clayton Claiborne. And I will help guide his future. You know the men think they make the decisions, but we do hold the power."

"But he likes me. I can tell," said Virginia. "You didn't count on me."

"Oh, there is always one or two like you in every mix. You know you never really stood a chance. Even before what just happened downstairs. Don't think that you are fooling anyone. Virginia Blankenship, my ass." She paused. "Yes, I may be loud and vulgar and crass as a tin spittoon, but that's because I can afford to be. I'm the real deal, sweetie. I am named for General Wade Hampton. I have Southern aristocracy on both sides of my family. You may prance around down there like the Queen of Sheba, but I know the score with you. That's what I came to the kitchen to tell you. That I would blow the whistle on you unless you dropped out."

"You have no proof."

"I have enough. The rest will be easy enough to find out," she said. "But there is no need now, is there?"

"I don't know what you mean," said Virginia.

"You and the nigger downstairs. Tell me, is he the girl's father?"

Virginia put her drink on the table and returned her hand underneath the jacket, where it touched the cool metal of Butcher's knife.

"No," she said resolutely. "You have it figured all wrong."

# 9

# boudin noir /
# blood pudding . . .

"I have to leave now," Butcher said to Mona. "Come with me. But you have to decide this now, because there is no time."

"She told you that if I came back, she would tell me."

"But that was before." Butcher finished buttoning his shirt. The uniform trousers lay discarded in a heap on the bed near his open suitcase. "The man who owns that hotel is Klan—crazy. I'm not waiting around for him to get wind of me. I've seen them cut a man's pecker off for less."

"Then you're a coward to leave her," said the girl.

Butcher grabbed her hard by both arms, pulling her to him. "She will do what she needs. She may be packing a bag as hard as she can right now herself. Or maybe she has already run—left us both to fend for ourselves. She knows there isn't anything she can do. And there isn't a goddam thing I can do to help her either." He relaxed his grip but still held her. "I have some money. Enough that I can make a life for you. A good life. There isn't anything I would like more than that. But I have to go. You said you wanted to be free of her. I am giving you the chance."

"It wouldn't be of any use," she said, breaking free from his grip. "It would always be between us."

Butcher unwrapped some cash he pulled from his pocket. "Then you will need this. I am heading south, to New Orleans. If you want to find me, come there."

She held the money in her fist. "Just let me hear from her what she has to say. Let her know that I am going to be okay. Where I will be in case . . ."

"It's not possible."

"Mr. Butcher, she is all I have ever known. I need to say good-bye to her. And then I will go with you. I will be with you."

Butcher knew then that he could not leave her. That he would take her back to the hotel. No matter what the cost.

He put on his suit coat and carried his satchel with him as they walked from the boarding house to the hotel. Butcher anticipated every passing glance, but no one noticed them or seemed to care as they walked in the back entrance and onto the service elevator. The hallway on the fifth floor where her room was located was empty, but Butcher did not think it a good sign that Virginia's door was ajar. Perhaps she wanted to leave it open in case Mona returned, he told himself. Perhaps that was it and nothing more.

Virginia had changed from her dress and sat in semidarkness in the chair by the window in her dressing gown, a ring of light from the floor lamp lapping at her feet. Butcher was struck once more by the paleness, the luminescence of her skin. She seemed to him almost a sprite, a fairy from an illustration. If she saw them or heard them, she paid them no mind. She sat stone still, his knife in her lap, waiting—if not for them, then for someone.

Finally, Mona broke the silence. "Ma'am. It's Mona. I have come back. Mr. Butcher brought me back to you."

Virginia did not look at either of them. "He shouldn't have," she said. "You should not be here."

Mona fell at Virginia's feet on her knees. "Please, ma'am," she said. "He told me you would give me my answer. Do that and then I will leave you if you want, but I have to know."

"Which is the answer that will drive you away from me?" asked Virginia.

"Is that what you want—to drive me away?" asked Mona.

"What I want," said Virginia. "I have wanted nothing else since you were born. You have been a curse in my life. Every day, every hour—a burden that I could not shed. Until today, and I thought that I had lost you. Then I wanted you here with me forever. Know this, Mona. If you come back, things will be no different than they are now, no different from how they have ever been. You will be my maid. There will never be anything more than that between the two of us. If you leave, then know that I am a mother who would turn her own daughter into her slave. Know that and be done with me."

Mona reached to put her head in Virginia's lap, but Virginia would not have it. She pushed the girl aside and stood to face Butcher. "Take her from me. I give her to you. Which is more than you would have done for me," she said. "I should scream, scream as loud as I can, and let them come and find you here. That would serve you right. Serve you right for selling me out." She pulled the note Butcher had written from the pocket of her dressing gown. "You would have given them this. Betrayed me with this."

"No, ma'am," he said. "I only wanted to make sure I got what was owed to me."

"Then take the girl. That is your payment. You are paid in full." She looked down at Mona, crumpled on the floor, weeping. Her face softened for a moment. "Things are different now. Go away from here. They cannot find you here. Go to New Orleans or St. Louis or to San Francisco. I will send you money to take care of her. It is only for a year. Just until the contract is up with Mystic White."

Butcher did not quite know what to say. "You can't win this thing, Miss Virginia," he said. "Not after that woman saw us together downstairs. She will tell what she saw."

"Wadena is dead," said Virginia. "She won't be telling anything to anyone."

"Miss Virginia," said Butcher.

"You are right, though. She said she would tell Clayton Claiborne everything if I didn't withdraw. If I didn't leave. But where would I go, George? Back to Fayetteville? There is no way I could ever just walk away from this—this chance." She spoke as if naming the steps in a recipe back to him. "And so, when she asked for my decision, I walked over to her and stabbed her in the heart." She opened her hand to reveal his knife and laughed scornfully. "Deep in the heart of Dixie."

"Miss Virginia," he said, "please tell me that you are lying to me." Though he knew she was not. "There's no way you can get away with this."

"But there is," she said. "They will not suspect me. No one saw me go to her room. No one saw me leave. And when they look for her killer, George, they will look for you."

Butcher felt the skin on his arms and neck turn to gooseflesh. "What have you done?" he asked. He tried to keep his voice even, tried to keep his fear from breaking through.

"I left the jacket to your uniform in the room. That is when I found this," she said, holding the note in front of her. "Wadena Chastain is dead. And you have no power over me now, George Butcher. I am going to be *The Lady in the White Hat*. I have earned that money. They will take my picture. I will work for that smarmy man for the next year peddling his flour. Then I will leave and become whatever I choose to be after that. Take the girl if she wants you. I am free of you both. Go before I scream and they find you here. It's more of a chance than you were willing to give me."

"You have chiseled my name on a gravestone," he said. "I never did anything but ask you to help me a bit. I was never anything but kind to you. And now you do this to me. Why do you want to do that to me, Miss Virginia?"

"You have become expendable," she said. "Now go. Or I will scream. Do not think I won't."

However, before she could follow through on her threat, Butcher grabbed her and pulled her face close to his, so close that he might have kissed her. But he did not kiss her. Instead, he wrapped his hands around her neck and as he began to squeeze, he could feel her windpipe slowly collapse under the pressure. Her breath came in short, rasping wheezes, and her face bloomed bright red, almost purple. She dropped the knife, dropped the letter, and fought at the air with her hands trying to grab hold of him, kicked him furiously as he lifted her off the ground attempting to stop the inevitable. Nothing she could do now could harm him. He looked square into her eyes. He wanted to watch her die. Wanted to feel her neck snap like a chicken's when you wrung its head from its body.

There was a sudden cold fire in his shoulder—a burning deep down near his spine like he had been stung by a hornet. He tried to hold on to Miss Virginia, but the pain bit him again and he dropped her hard on the floor, trying to take hold of whatever was worrying him. When he reached up behind his head, he was surprised to find the hilt of his knife lodged there. He grabbed at the knife and pulled it out with a single motion, turning to see who had attacked him. The blade swung out in front of him.

This is the scene that would haunt Butcher for many years to come. What if he had not resisted, but just accepted the blade in his back? What if he had not turned to confront her? What if she had not been standing so close? There was a flash of memory— Johnson Everetts and a honky-tonk just outside of Wilmington and a tall woman in a black dress—just as the knife slid across Mona's throat, slicing a small pink crescent from one side to the other.

She did not scream—could not scream—but merely regarded him with the sad, knowing eyes of a dead animal. He had seen this look before, as a boy on the morning after the first hard frost of the year—slaughtering day—when they would tie the hogs up by their hindquarters, string them up into the air so they could slit their throats in order to catch the blood that his mam would then boil down and make into sausage. Boudin noir, Laurent had called it. The animals would shriek in fear, powerless to free themselves until the swift silence brought on by the stroke of the blade. And then came the blood—a curtain of blood cascading down the front of her dress, pooling at her feet, seeping out to swallow him in it as well. Butcher caught her as she collapsed, her head lolling backward like a marionette. He held her, slipped to the floor so they sat in the ever-growing circle of dark red—hot like fire. Absolute as the pitch-black of a grave.

Virginia howled. Low, guttural, primitive. The sound seemed to Butcher to come from someplace far away, a feeble scratched wail, a yowling like a concertina being crushed. Still, it was enough to bring people to the room, and in a matter of minutes, the night clerk, the police, Clayton Claiborne himself were crowded around them to observe the hideous tableau. At first, the policeman did not want to step into the blood, but Claiborne cursed at him, and so he came over and kicked the knife out of Butcher's reach. Then he and another policeman pulled Butcher up by his arms, handcuffed him, and led him out of the room. As he left, Butcher turned to see Claiborne wrap an arm around Virginia's shoulder, a bloodstained piece of notepaper held tight in his other hand.

# 10

They did not hang Butcher, despite the fact he was convicted of the murder of two women and the attempted murder of a third. In fact, at his sentencing trial, Miss Virginia—now Mrs. Clayton Claiborne II, took the stand to plead for his life, told the judge that as a Christian, she prayed that mercy be granted him. In the years after he was sentenced, Butcher wondered whether this was a kindness from her because she knew that would be what Mona would have expected—forgiveness for what had happened, for their plan that had gone so terribly wrong. Other times, he wondered whether she wanted him merely to live out his life imprisoned like herself.

The murders were big news in the paper for the next year, until Margaret Mitchell's book about the South was published, and a fictional Atlanta became the focus of the nation. After that, only the curious stayed at the Plantation House Hotel, and it rapidly fell into disrepute, replaced by the more upstanding Georgia Terrace just around the corner. In fact, by the time the movie of *Gone with the Wind* premiered in the city, only journalists from second-rate newspapers dared stay there.

Butcher did not work in the kitchen at the Georgia State Prison, even after he had been there for more than twenty years and was too old to do the hard labor imposed on prisoners. Food had lost its taste, its texture, its beauty for him. He could have been served cardboard or sawdust or sand for all he cared about it. The early days were rough for sure—he was beaten more than once, sometimes for no reason, sometimes by people who told him he should never have dared put his hands on Wadena Chastain. He never fought back, would have welcomed it if they had bashed his skull in.

But he didn't die. And after a while, he decided if he wasn't going to die, that if they weren't going to kill him, then he might as well live—wanted to see if he could hang on longer than her. Did not want to give her the pleasure of his death if that is why she had sent him there. He read snippets about her through the years, about the sale of the Plantation House Hotel, read about Claiborne's failed attempts to win an office in the Senate, read about the publishing of each new Miss Virginia cookbook.

And then one day, there it was. On the front page of the *Journal*: "The Passing of a Lady" under a picture of Virginia as an old woman. Inside, there was nearly a full page detailing the story of her life—how she, as a young widow, won a baking contest in the 1930s, how she had married the owner of Mystic White Flour and served as its representative even after she sold the company when her husband died, how she had over time become a symbol of all that was gracious and true and gentle about Southern womanhood. They even included a short piece written by Jocelyn Hind Crowley, who had known Virginia ever since those early days and had written her official biography: *The Lady in the Mirror.* She wrote in glowing terms of Miss Virginia, not just in regard to her dozen cookbooks, which had influenced a generation of Southern women and homemakers, but about the woman herself who she claimed was the epitome of style and charm. Jocelyn Hind Crowley also detailed how, after the death of Clayton Claiborne II, Virginia sponsored cooking competitions for girls throughout the South that awarded college scholarships for winners and runners-up. In the days before integration, she even funded scholarships for colored girls. When Jocelyn Hind Crowley had written about this in Miss Virginia's biography, she said Miss Virginia had told her, "Some things can never be made right, but we must each attempt to do our part."

Surrounding the page was an assortment of pictures taken from various Mystic White flour campaigns with Virginia in an ever-advancing array of extravagant white hats. But it was the first picture that drew Butcher's eye. A grainy picture of her taken all the way back in 1935, when Virginia wore a white straw hat, the crown formed of interwoven strips of satin ribbon. Butcher cut the picture out and taped it to the wall next to an old advertisement that he had pasted there years before. And every day from then until he died, they were the first things he saw each morning, the last things before he closed his eyes. They reminded him of the price paid for dreaming.

# The Brambles

# . . . 1 . . .

Freddie Bramble tips the cup of steaming coffee into her saucer to cool the first sips, making sure not to spill any drops on the cloth Jewel has laid out for supper. Though Mr. Odom's bus is not due until after 4 PM, Jewel has already set the table. *Too early*, thinks Freddie. In fact, the vase of pink peonies and antirrhinum have already begun to wilt a bit. But that is Jewel's way. Always in a rush. Always in a hurry to get to what comes next. The next task. The next meal. It is commonplace that she will announce what is for lunch while they are finishing breakfast, what is to be made for supper while they are eating the noon meal.

"It doesn't hurt to plan," says Jewel. Freddie agrees, but knows too often Jewel gets caught up in the whirlwind of her own campaigns and forgets to pay attention to the details right in front of her. Like the flowers. Freddie would have left them in the icebox in the container of water they came in from the florist, then taken them out just before they went to fetch Mr. Odom. That way they would still be fresh. Now, they will be lucky if the tablecloth isn't littered with petals by the time dinner is served.

She lifts the saucer to her lips and sips the sharp, bitter coffee. "I hope you don't do that in front of company," Jewel chastises her whenever she catches her holding the saucer to her lips. "It is so common." Freddie doesn't care. At forty-eight, she is old enough to drink her morning coffee the way she likes. Saucer first, followed by the remainder in the cup. It takes patience. It centers her for the day. She likes how the delicate pattern of intertwined chrysanthemums, dogwood blossoms, hyacinth, and geraniums appears like magic when she drains the black liquid from the bottom of the saucer—a mystical garden buried beneath a murky swamp.

The cup and saucer are two of her prize possessions, purchased years ago when she and Jewel were on a trip to Charleston. She had seen the set in the window of an antique store on King Street and knew instantly it was something she wanted. The saleswoman, who tried to impress them with her genealogy—as if it made working as a sales clerk in a store somehow more respectable—was reluctant to show her the cup, which came with a matching teapot and twin cup and saucer. Freddie wondered at first if the woman thought she couldn't afford it, but knew she was dressed respectably enough. Still, she couldn't help but notice how the saleswoman hesitated, warning Freddie that it was Chinese porcelain, hovering over her as Freddie held the cup in her short, thick fingers.

"Look at you. You can't even get your finger through the hole in the handle," mocked Jewel. "Talk about a bull in a china shop." The saleswoman couldn't resist a snicker, which only made Freddie more determined to have it. She knew it wasn't her dress or her hat that had caused the saleswoman concern. It was Freddie herself. A bull in a china shop.

As she sets the saucer back onto the table and lifts the steaming cup to her lips, the sugary tang of a Miss Virginia lemon curd pound cake fills the house. Jewel has planned an elaborate dinner for Mr. Odom's first night. *Too fussy,* Freddie thinks for someone she has never met in person. However, she knows Jewel wants to—needs to—make a good impression on Mr. Odom. Nine years Freddie's junior, Jewel is not young, though she jokes that she plans to "be like Jack Benny and stay thirty-nine forever." It is apparent to Freddie that while she may act like a girl, Jewel is rapidly losing all vestiges of youth. Her hips have widened, her bosom has gone slack. Her hair has begun to go gray, though she covers it up with a blond rinse from the beauty parlor. She wears too much rouge to give a blush to her cheeks. The makeup has begun to crack in the crevices around her eyes. Freddie thinks it a sad game and wonders if the only person Jewel is trying to fool is herself. She isn't young. She is plain as a paper sack. She has a tendency to prattle on about the most trivial things. None of which is a quality men desire in a wife. And since Mr. Odom is coming all the way from Athens, Georgia, with the prospect of marriage, it would be disappointing to discover that she couldn't cook. So, Freddie forgives her the meal and the opportunity to show off—roast pork and mashed sweet potatoes. And the Miss Virginia pound cake. She knows Jewel is merely doing what she thinks she must to hold up her end of the bargain.

They have been cleaning for days in anticipation of Mr. Odom, oiling the heavy dark furniture, ironing linens, polishing silver. These are not tasks that Freddie minds, however, for the results are so immediate and gratifying. Now, as the cool, late-winter sun filters through the lace curtains in the dining room and across the foyer in the parlor, the house has a soft luster, a satisfying glow to it. Freddie enjoys the morning light on the front side of the house. In the summer, she will take her coffee out on the veranda that circles the entire house like a wide brim on a hat. From here, as she sits in her rocker, she can survey a good, wide expanse of the property—seventy-eight acres in all—planted mainly in tobacco, cotton, and corn. She likes to walk the fields, loves the order of the rows. Many mornings, she will pull on her brogans, a pair of men's khaki workpants, and an overshirt as she inspects nature's progress. She would have enjoyed walking on a bright blue morning such as this, but the brogans have been put away in safekeeping in expectation of Mr. Odom's arrival. As Jewel reminds her, they have to project the correct image for him.

Freddie knows that will not be a problem. If he is not impressed with her or with Jewel, he is certain to be impressed by the house and the farm. It is a beautiful home, one of the best, most stately in the whole town of Morris. The house itself is now over a hundred years old, built back before the Civil War. Though not as grandiose as some of the plantation homes she has seen in Charleston or

Georgetown counties, Freddie knows it is nonetheless a striking example of Antebellum architecture with its deep porches and balconies, its broad columns posted like sentries along the front—a rarity for this part of the low country. She and Jewel have lived here twenty years, since 1933, when they bought the house and farm at auction. The previous owner, grandson of Milford Deegan, who had built the house, had not been much of a farmer or businessman, and gone belly-up almost immediately when the Depression hit. That in itself wasn't unusual, but the young Mr. Deegan must have taken it worse than most, for rather than seeing how he could get out from under the pile of debt with which he had saddled himself and his young wife, he decided it was easier simply to hang himself in the barn. His wife, who they said found him when he didn't come in for the noon meal when she called, walked into town straightaway and told the sheriff that she needed someone to come out to "help him down." She buried him in the family plot, a small, fenced area barely visible from the porch. She had selected a double tombstone—one side with his name and BELOVED HUSBAND inscribed underneath; her name on the other, along with an engraving that read DEVOTED WIFE. The only thing left blank was the day of her death. After the funeral, she fell into a stupor, until relatives had her put away in the State Hospital to help end the gossip and speculation. She had died there, Freddie supposed, lost, forgotten, so devoted to her husband that it drove her mad.

"Out of sight—out of her mind" is what the real-estate agent told them when they had driven down to look at the farm. The house had already fallen into a bit of disrepair, and the fields lay fallow except for those a few tenant farmers laid claim to, figuring they had as much right to plant on a dead man's land as not. No one wanted to buy the place because of its unpleasant history—not that people were buying much of anything in those days, but Jewel had come into her inheritance from her first husband, Mr. T. L. Landry, and they needed to put some distance between themselves and Rockingham, where Mr. Landry's death had brought its own share of unpleasantness. So, with hard cash in hand, Freddie was able to negotiate a deal that was a bargain, even in Depression-era real estate, and the house and the farm, located on the outskirts of Morris, became their new home. Over time, the town forgot the dead young farmer and his institutionalized widow. In fact, they forgot about the Deegans altogether. And the farm became known as Bramble Farm.

Many in the town think of the two sisters as spinsters, even though both have been married—in fact, Jewel has been married twice. It may be because no man has ever lived on the farm with them in the twenty years they have owned it. It may be because they both prefer to use their family name since their married names might carry a degree of recognition, infamy, even scandal. In Rockingham, Jewel's first husband, Mr. Landry, a man twice her age when they married, suffered a horrific accident when a meat grinder that someone had carelessly stored on one of the overhead shelves in the kitchen fell and cracked his skull open. He lingered for several miserable days in a delirium, but finally died from what the doctor determined was an internal brain hemorrhage. His life insurance policy left Jewel with just over $50,000. When Jewel had married her second husband in 1938, Mr. Arthur Potts, she had moved with him to his home in Charleston until he succumbed to a tragic fall from a ladder while he was hanging Japanese lanterns for a party to honor a visit from Freddie. Mr. Potts had left Jewel almost exactly the same amount in his insurance.

Freddie's marriage was the briefest of all. It had lasted only a couple of months—to a young officer she had corresponded with in the VA hospital in Washington, D.C., where he had been shipped after losing a leg in the Allied invasion of Italy. At Jewel's insistence, she traveled to Washington to meet Lt. Jonas Calder, where they were wed while he was a patient in the convalescent hospital. She can still remember the shock on his face when he first saw her. She had not lied to him about her age in the letters, told him that she was a "mature woman," so he could not accuse her of deceit. However, when he had asked her for a photograph, she denied the request, told him that theirs was to be a "spiritual bond, not dependent on physical appearance or ability." She had meant to shame him—after all, what could a middle-aged man with only one leg hope to offer any self-respecting woman—and he relented. Yet, seeing him in person for the first time, she could sense his keen disappointment not only in her age, but in her bulk, her distinctly unfeminine appearance. Still, he didn't turn her away. So, every day she would go to visit him and they would discuss the events in the paper, play dominos or gin rummy when he wasn't practicing walking with his crutches. And slowly, a friendship built up between them, and he confessed that many marriages had probably begun from less.

Unfortunately, on the train ride to meet his family in Birmingham, Alabama, Lt. Calder somehow managed to slip beneath the connecting carriages of the train, severing his remaining leg. It was a freakish mishap, and by the time the train had stopped, he had bled to death on the tracks. In addition to his insurance policy, Freddie was also awarded a generous settlement from the railroad and a widow's pension from the U.S. Army because Lt. Calder had been a disabled war veteran. His family in Birmingham contested the disbursements, but since she was his widow and there was no will, there was little they could do. His death was deemed a terrible tragedy. The money was Freddie's money. She did, however, pay for the funeral and agreed to have his body shipped to Birmingham for burial. Lt. Calder's mother had called her horrible names, had refused to let her attend the burial, said she would as soon spit on her as look at her, but took the money just the same. Freddie knew she would.

Jewel taunted Freddie that she was the only bride to have survived marriage without so much as a "diddle," but Freddie minded the teasing even less than the slurs vented on her by Lt. Calder's mother. What she couldn't erase was the sound as he called to her just as he fell from the train. He had been walking in front of her on their way back from the dining car to their compartment when she—with only the slightest brush of the toe of her shoe—kicked his crutch out from underneath him. She knew he didn't see her do it, was ignorant to the fact that this had been the plan all along, just as it had been with Mr. Landy and Mr. Potts, that they should die so she and Jewel could inherit their money, but just as he fell, he called her name: "Freddie." And that was all. Then he was off the platform, disappearing into the night. But sometimes in her room, when everything is silent except for the trains passing through town, just before she drifts off to sleep, she can still hear him. That sudden gasp of horror as the world gives way beneath him, his crutch flying away into the darkness, and the desperate, hopeful plea, "Freddie."

She met Jonas Calder the same way Jewel had met Arthur Potts and T. L. Landry. The same way Jewel has met Mr. Odom—through the personal advertisements, though Freddie would have to agree with Jewel that it has become increasingly difficult for a respectable woman of means to use the personals. In fact, when Jewel had met Mr. Landry, many women were so bold as to send notices to matrimonial bureaus. Freddie thought that too direct. Advertisements in newspapers were perfectly upright and proper, but much more discreet. However, many newspapers dropped the practice over the years, and when they had found Mr. Odom, they had been forced to use a romance magazine called *Heart's Desire*. Jewel had discovered the ads while waiting to have her hair done one afternoon at Lurdelle's Beauty Clip. When Freddie had come to fetch her, she rushed breathless out of the shop to tell her about it. But, as was typical with Jewel, she forgot to bring a copy of the magazine with her.

The very next day they had driven the hour or so to Florence to buy the magazine in a local drug store. And when they had written the ad, they had driven back to Florence to mail the letter placing the ad. They had also opened a post office box there for one year. Jewel was too nervous to do any of this, worried what someone might think when she presented the magazine for purchase or filled out the slip requesting the post office box. Freddie, on the other hand, told herself she did not care, that they made the magazine to be sold, so why not? And women had just as much right to open a post office box as anyone. Besides, that is why they had come to Florence. It was a world away from Morris, and if letters addressed to Jewel had shown up in their mailbox at home, they both knew there would be talk.

If Jewel was hesitant in the placing of the ad, she was just as adamant in her suggestions about what it should say:

> Personal—Comely widow who owns profitable farm desires to make the acquaintance of a reputable mature gentleman with a view to joining fortunes. No replies by letter will be considered unless the sender is willing to follow an answer with a personal visit.
> No triflers, please.

They had been through this before, and they knew what they were looking for.

They had received a reasonable share of responses, many pathetic and needy, some overtly sexual. All of those were immediately discarded without reply. But there were a handful of keepers as well, those from men who exhibited a certain degree of opportunism, men who declared themselves to be in reasonable health, boasted they enjoyed a modest amount of success, but who also were quick to make mention that they were not seeking any financial security. The men who offered nothing in return but themselves—as the prize. The men who Freddie knew supposed she and Jewel were somehow weak, somehow stupid enough, they would be content with their presence and nothing more. Freddie knew the surest way to determine the liar is to find the man quickest to tell you he isn't lying. But there was one more criteria that winnowed the field: those men who declared themselves to be without any known relations—those men who were absolutely alone.

Some, including Mr. Odom, had included a photograph as well. Freddie said that Jewel shouldn't be concerned with looks, but Jewel countered that she was going to be the one lifting her nightdress, and while she didn't expect a movie star, she would prefer Joseph Cotten to Raymond Massey when the time came. They had narrowed the field by location, did not want to encourage anyone who might have been from too far a distance—in case the initial meeting did not go well and they had to send him away. Mr. Odom was from Athens, Georgia, which was not even a full day's bus ride.

In the photo he had sent, he was wearing a suit and tie, looking directly into the camera, smiling broadly. He had a good head of hair and his teeth looked to be his own. Solid. A man of substance. Confident. Jewel told Freddie she imagined it had been taken for a directory of members for the Rotary or Chamber of Commerce. Freddie thinks the smile forced, his jaw held too tight, his eyes just shy of puffiness. A man impressed with himself. He reminds her of their own father, though she would never mention this to Jewel.

It suits their plan that Mr. Odom holds himself in high esteem, will expect to be taken care of. It is a weakness easily exploited. Jewel will pamper him, fix him bacon every morning for breakfast if he wants. They will comply just as they have with their other husbands and do what is required. Back in Rockingham, Mr. Landry knew himself to be getting older. His mother had passed away, and he did not like living alone. He was eager to have a young woman like Jewel to tend his house, cook his meals, wash his clothes for him just as his mother had. As for Mr. Arthur Potts, there had been some unsavory talk among the better families of Charleston that he was wont to keep the company of too many young men. With Jewel in the house, the rumors subsided.

And Lt. Calder had wanted, needed a nursemaid to assist him on his return to Birmingham. In her letters, Freddie described how she had taken over the household at eighteen when her mother had died bearing a stillborn son. She had helped to nurse her own father through a lengthy illness until his death, all the while help- ing to raise her younger sister. She did not tell him that she reviled her father, that he had kept her prisoner for a decade after her mother's death, shamed her into staying to care for him. She did not tell him that her father had called her an atrocity, an outrage of womanhood, barely adequate to fetch his meals and carry his bed- pan. She did not tell Lt. Calder that she had smothered her father in his sleep.

For all of his hatefulness and cruelty, her father had left behind a substantial bit of insurance. It had been purchased before her mother had died, undoubtedly to provide for any son who would bear his name if he should not be alive to do so. She and Jewel and her dead mother were afterthoughts, but beneficiaries just the same. Her father had done more for them in death than he had ever managed to do while he was alive—a most remarkable lesson, she thought. Marriage and childbearing had killed her mother. Her father reminded her constantly that a woman was unfit for anything else, that marriage was all she and her sister could ever hope for. As much as she hated to admit it, what he said seemed true enough. All around her she saw women indentured in marriages willing to work for the barest of necessities. If she and Jewel had to be wives, then she decided they would enter into it on their own terms and be rewarded handsomely for the privilege.

Freddie doesn't think of the killings as criminal, any more than slaughtering hogs is murder. Merely a matter of financial necessity. Killing her father had liberated her. She knew she could not live inside the lines that had been painted for her, and financial independence meant that even if people thought her odd, they would give her a wide berth. She had not thought beyond Mr. Landry, had assumed her father's legacy combined with his would carry them for a long time. But Jewel likes nice things, has expensive tastes, likes to flaunt the fact they have money. Freddie would have been content to live modestly on the farm, but Jewel seemed to always crave more, whined and pleaded until Freddie acquiesced to Mr. Potts. She had even agreed to court Lt. Calder herself, when Jewel told her that she couldn't always be the one being married off "like a prize cow." That should have been enough, Freddie thinks. But enough is never sufficient for Jewel.

"One more," she tells Freddie. "Think of it as our retirement plan. We will be able to travel to Europe. Or winter in Florida. This will be the last one. I promise. Besides, in a few years, I would have to pay them to propose."

Freddie doesn't know if it is the money or the attention Jewel craves most. And before Freddie has a chance to make up her mind, Jewel forces her hand, tells Freddie that she has promised five thousand dollars to Christ the Shepherd Methodist Church for their new stained-glass window.

"Are you crazy?" Freddie roars when Jewel gives her the news. "It will make people suspicious to give a gift like that."

"Pish!" says Jewel. "I am merely doing what is expected of us.

The other part will not happen for months and months. No one will ever connect the two." And, as she always seemed to do when it came to doing what Jewel wanted her to do, Freddie relents.

Freddie hears Jewel's footsteps overhead in the bathroom, so she knows she is free to wash her cup and saucer and put them away without any interference or bother from her sister. Jewel knows "Freddie's china," as she refers to it, are off limits to her, since she chipped the teapot and broke the other matching cup and saucer outright nearly as soon as they got them home. Jewel claimed both were an accident, but Freddie has never been sure. Certainly Jewel is careless—she is continually misplacing things, forgetting appointments. But Freddie knows her sister well enough to know she is also selfish and possessive. Jewel would never begrudge her a fair share, but would never allow her nothing more than that. They had fought over the tea set when they left the shop on King Street. Jewel claimed it was an indulgence bought to impress a saleswoman. And Freddie could not deny the claim. Still, that did not stop her from wanting it—and she was not surprised when pieces of the set turned up chipped or broken.

It is shortly after three when they collect themselves and are ready to go. Most likely, Mr. Odom's bus will have arrived by the time they get to Florence. Undoubtedly it would be easier to meet him at the bus station or train depot in Morris, but they do not want to attract attention in case things do not go well. Jewel is in full flutter. She has not been able to find her pocketbook, then her handkerchief, her compact. She checks again and again to make sure the stove has been turned off, fearful she will ruin dinner. She complains that her girdle is cutting off circulation to her legs.

"It will be a fine how-to-do when I just collapse in a heap in the parking lot," she says, but Freddie pays her little mind, knowing the chatter is just nerves. Jewel is like the radio—something that you keep on for the noise. Something you notice only when it goes silent. Fortunately, she will soon have Mr. Odom to focus on, and Freddie will be able to retreat into the background for a while.

Freddie's braid is pinned so tightly that it is giving her a headache. If it were left to her, she would just cut it all off. She tried that once, but the results were disastrous. When Jewel had returned from Mr. Potts's funeral, she was horrified to discover that Freddie had cut her own hair, or as Jewel described it, "scalped herself." She immediately made an appointment at Lurdelle's, where they had trimmed and combed, permed and styled her till her scalped burned. Jewel was pleased with the results, but Freddie felt like a show dog that had been groomed within an inch of its life. She washed as much of the beauty parlor as she could out of her hair, but the permanent wave only frizzed so that she looked like a woman in a cartoon who has been shocked by electricity. In the weeks after, until her hair relaxed and began to grow back, Jewel did not speak to her, only pointing her finger with an exclamation: "Bzzzzpft!" Since then, Freddie has not cut her hair again, keeps it at an acceptable length for braiding. Jewel combs out her hair for her after Freddie washes it and then weaves the hair into a respectable bun. Freddie doesn't complain, knows the persistent nagging Jewel will subject her to if she does not submit. And so she sits and lets her braid her hair while she sings some song she has heard on the radio or some hymn that has been sung in church. And while she braids, Freddie pinches herself, squeezing the flesh on the inside of her wrist as tight as she can to keep from screaming.

Jewel instructs Freddie on how fast to drive, where to turn, where to park. She says she wishes she had thought to bring a snack for the ride home.

"Peanuts would have been nice," she says. "I should have roasted some."

"They would only make a mess in the car," Freddie reminds her. "And it would spoil the lovely supper you have made."

As they make their way inside the bus terminal, it is clear to Freddie that they are late. There are not many people waiting, the benches are mostly empty. It is easy to recognize Mr. Odom, though Freddie can see at a glance that the picture he submitted to them was taken years ago. He still has a shock of pumpkin-colored hair, but his temples are entirely white. And he has gained a fair amount of weight. He looks to be well over 200 pounds to Freddie, a fact only emphasized by his suit, which is several sizes too small. He has unfastened his shirt collar and loosened his tie to give him some breathing room. He reminds her of a suitcase in a comedy film, one that is filled to overflowing so that bits of fabric hang out all around. She wonders if Jewel is disappointed.

But it is not Mr. Odom's appearance that commands her focus. She is not surprised that his form does not match his photograph. She has expected some deceit. After all, she and Jewel have not put all their cards on the table either. What does command her attention, however, is the fact that sitting next to him is a dark-haired woman. Not a woman, really. A girl. A young, beautiful girl. Mr. Odom has brought a companion.

# . . . 2 . . .

Freddie is happy to concentrate on her driving. It means she is not required to talk but can take the time to process this wrinkle in their plans. Mr. Odom forgoes the more spacious front seat, insists that he and Jewel sit together in the backseat where they exchange pleasantries, mostly a recitation of facts from their letters. He apologizes profusely for the girl, whose name is Isabelle, who Mr. Odom says is his stepdaughter.

"I wasn't trying to keep her a secret," he says as they load his valises into the car. It is obvious from the amount of luggage that he has most likely brought everything he has with him. He has come to stay awhile. The girl, on the other hand, has but a small suitcase—merely passing through. Mr. Odom continues, "It is a complicated situation. And I did not know until just a couple of days before I was to leave on this trip that Isabelle would be joining me. I tried to call long distance, but it just rang and rang."

"That phone," says Jewel. "It never works right. I think there must be something wrong in the lines."

Freddie thinks about the phone in the front parlor, which she had disconnected well over a year ago after she had been confronted by Jack Haines one afternoon when she had driven to order feed and fertilizer at Standard's Farm Supply.

"I don't mean to interfere, Miss Winifred," he said. "But you need to do something about her. Your sister. She listens in on other people's conversations. It is not becoming. My wife says she can hear her snort when she thinks something is funny."

Freddie had threatened to have the phone taken out, but Jewel had cried and complained that everyone would think they couldn't afford it. "I will change," she promised. But Freddie knew better, so she had solved the problem by taking the kitchen shears and cutting the cord.

"Prove it," she replied. Now it sits mute on the table in the front parlor as a reminder and a rebuke to Jewel.

The conversation between Jewel and Mr. Odom dulls to a murmur as he confides things to Jewel that he obviously doesn't want Freddie or the girl to hear. Freddie thinks about challenging him but knows he is staking a claim for Jewel, strengthening a bond. She can ignore them for now—she knows that Jewel will tell her everything when they are alone together at home. Now, she can concentrate on the drive and also study the girl, Isabelle, who sits still as stone on the seat next to her. Isabelle wears a simple blue dress buttoned at the neck. Her hair is lustrous and dark, her skin smooth, bone white. Freddie imagines for a moment that she is carrying home a statue that they have purchased at auction—the statue of a young maiden. And then there are Isabelle's eyes. A shade of blue that Freddie is hard-pressed to describe: the color of the Mediterranean in a picture from the *National Geographic*, the noon sky in summer? Then she has it. They are the same deep blue of the flowers painted on her teacup. A hyacinth barely bloomed. When they were introduced at the bus station, Isabelle looked directly into Freddie's eyes, and Freddie was immediately transfixed by them, by her.

As the familiar road unfolds before her in the evening sun, she is keenly aware that Isabelle has scooted close against the passenger door, too close, her fingers clenched on the handle. Freddie wonders if she were to fling herself out of the car, would she shatter into pieces like marble?

"Have you locked the door?" she asks.

Isabelle says nothing but turns her head slightly. Her eyes are wet, filled with sadness.

"The door," Freddie repeats. "You should make sure it is locked. I would hate to go around one of these bends and lose you by the side of the road."

"I suppose," says Isabelle. She takes her hand off the handle and reaches up to press the button down.

"Now I've got you prisoner," Freddie jokes, and smiles to try and reassure her.

"Yes, a prisoner," she says as she begins to cry. Tears fall in a silent stream down her face. Jewel and Mr. Odom are caught up in their conversation and do not notice. Freddie fears if she speaks to her ask what is the matter, it will alert Jewel, so she contemplates what lies ahead.

When they arrive home, there is first the issue of sleeping arrangements and where to put everyone. Jewel has given up her room to Mr. Odom and taken the small guest room next to Freddie. Though she has fixed the room to her fancy, she insists that Isabelle take that room and she has Mr. Odom and Freddie carry the fainting couch from her sewing room into Freddie's bedroom, announcing she will sleep on that. For now. Mr. Odom smiles in hopeful expectation.

"It isn't any trouble at all," she says as she carries an armful of clothes from the highboy. "Naturally, Freddie has taken the largest bedroom in the house for herself—an older sister's prerogative she tells me, so we will have room to spare. Besides, Freddie and I haven't shared a room since we were girls. It will be great fun. An adventure."

"And you will have a proper chaperone as well," adds Mr. Odom. Jewel laughs at the innuendo, but when she closes the door, she throws the clothes into a pile on the bed and collapses in a heap beside them, running her hands up through her hair.

"This is a fine mess," she says. "I nearly fainted when I saw that he had brought—her."

"Hush," warns Freddie. "They will hear you."

"What does it matter? Of course, they will have to leave. This will never work. I wonder if I should just tell him straight out or wait a day or two. I don't think I can keep up the pretense of interest. And sleeping on that torture device. I will ruin my back." She points to the fainting couch.

Freddie knows that Jewel is fishing, hoping she will offer to share her bed or give it up outright to her during Mr. Odom's and Isabelle's stay. "What did he say to you? Who is she? Why is she here?"

Jewel kicks off her shoes and massages the bottom of her left foot. "He says she is his stepdaughter. His dead wife's child. I knew he was a widower. He never mentioned children."

"But he said he didn't know until just a day or two ago that she would be coming. How is that?" Freddie doesn't like that Jewel is so casual in this space, wishes she would at least sit on the fainting couch instead of the bed.

"She had been gone for months. He had no idea where she was. Evidently she had run off with a boy." Jewel pauses. When Freddie doesn't say anything, Jewel continues. "Do the math, numbskull. She's pregnant. And when the boy found out about the baby, he sent her home. I guess it speaks well of Mr. Odom's character that he didn't just pitch her out. He is absolutely bewildered by this. I feel sorry for him. I really do. I think he is only trying to do the right thing. But, of course, this can never work."

"How do you mean?"

"I don't think he will stay without her, and we are not opening a home for unwed mothers here."

Freddie thinks about Isabelle's fingers on the door, poised to leap. A baby growing inside her. She remembers her tears. How alone, how frightened she must be.

"Jewel," she says. "Perhaps we should not rush to judgment here. We can still proceed with our plan for Mr. Odom."

"Did you not hear what I said? He won't stay without her—I know it. And I won't—I can't have her here. What are people going to think? To say? Have you forgotten that I am *Chairwoman* of the Stained Glass Committee? I have a position. Those women at church look up to me. Besides, we know even less about her than we do about him. That baby could come out with eyes slanted as a Chinaman's or skin browner than a hickory nut. It will cause a scandal. And we do not need to draw any attention to ourselves that we don't have to. I am just shocked at you."

Freddie has not forgotten that Jewel is Chairwoman of the Stained Glass Committee, and she knows the mention of it is an attempt to draw her into a quarrel. Otherwise, she would not bring up the stained glass window, the committee, or the women of the church. Freddie wants to say that the women of Christ the Shepherd Methodist Church do not look up to Jewel. That no one with more sense than a chicken looks up to Jewel. She has been made chairwoman of the committee solely because of the size of the donation she has promised them. However, Freddie does not want to open that can of worms now, so she does not take the bait. Instead, she tries to soothe Jewel's nerves. She motions to the fainting couch.

"Why don't you come over here and stretch out. You will be more comfortable, I know. I can make you something to drink."

"I need to get dinner together," Jewel remembers. But she does as Freddie directs and reclines on the couch.

"Just consider this," Freddie says, leaning against the corner of her four-poster bed so she faces Jewel. "If Mr. Odom goes away, we are back to square one. You and I both know he was the only real contender in the whole lot. We will have to start all over. You would have to withdraw the offer of the donation."

Jewel's eyes fly open wide. "I could never. It would make me a laughingstock."

"Then, we are agreed that Mr. Odom is our man. And the fact that she is pregnant doesn't really mean anything to what we are doing. Did he tell you how far along she is?"

Jewel snorts. "Goodness, no. He is much too polite to say that. He never even said the word *pregnant*. Told me she was 'in the family way.' But you can't tell by looking at her, so I would guess no more than three or four months at tops."

"And does she plan to keep the baby?"

"No. I mean, how could she? She is so young. He said she had not even graduated from high school. She dropped out during her last term."

"We can help her, then. If she wants to give the baby up, we can arrange for that. She will be gone before our business with Mr. Odom is concluded."

"Our business is with him," Jewel retorts. "She is an unnecessary complication."

"Jewel, it is obvious to me that she doesn't want to be here. That she would be anyplace else if that were possible. Evidently, Mr. Odom is the only person she has that she can go to. We are going to—to alter that. I think we can afford to show a bit of compassion here."

"I suppose you have a point. But what will we tell people?"

"Why do we have to tell them anything? No one ever comes here except Mr. Ray and his work crew. We can take her to a doctor in Whiteville. Or Florence. My guess is that she is not especially eager to be stared at by the women of Morris if she can avoid it. Or we can make something up. Perhaps she has a husband. Off in the army. People will believe what we tell them. You know that."

"Yes, Donna Johnson has a niece in just that condition."

Freddie smiles. "Or so she says."

Jewel laughs in agreement. "So she says."

Freddie encourages Jewel to rest for a few minutes, tells her she is going to light fires in both the parlor and the dining room. "Not too many fires left in the season, and it is just cool enough," she says. "Soon it will be spring. And it will make the house more inviting I think. More welcoming for our guests." Jewel promises to be down in a few minutes to begin the final dinner preparations.

Freddy is happy that it was so easy for her to convince Jewel to let the girl stay, thankful that Jewel did not press her any further on her reasons for wanting to let her stay. How could she tell her what she does not understand herself? Only that now Isabelle is here, she doesn't want her to leave. Freddie pauses on the upstairs landing. She can hear Mr. Odom rumbling around in his room, the soft thud of a dresser being closed—claiming his territory. On the other hand, outside Isabelle's door, it is silent. She pictures the girl inside, unpacking the pitiful suitcase she has brought with her.

Freddie stands still as she can, trying to hear any movement on the other side of the closed door, but there is no sound, and she concludes the girl must be resting. Freddie has been dreading Mr. Odom's arrival, but discovers she is suddenly happier now than she has been in a long time. Happier than she can ever recall for that matter. *I am your prisoner,* she thinks as she descends the stairs.

# . . . 3 . . .

As the weeks progress, two facts emerge: Freddie disdains Mr. Odom as much as she regards Isabelle. Mr. Odom is excessive in his flattery toward Jewel. Meals are not just good or even excellent, they are "delectable and delicious." But he is also extremely officious and overbearing. He does not like having to ask Freddie for anything. They have gone round with each other about the car.

"I am perfectly capable of driving your Dodge, Miss Winifred," he informs her one morning. "And I have in my possession a valid Georgia driver's license. I can show it to you if you wish."

"If you wanted to drive a car, then you should have brought one" is Freddie's reply, which brings on a litany of excuses and defenses. His lamentations, Freddie has begun to think of them. Business deals that went bust through no fault of his own. Associates who had maligned or mistreated or deceived him. Errors in judgment, but only made in the cause of being too trusting, too loyal, too eager to help someone. It doesn't change the situation, however. When all is said and done, they both know he doesn't have a pot to piss in. He will do what she and Jewel tell him to do. For now. He has the expectation that once he is married to Jewel, things will change.

Yet Freddie has acquiesced to some demands Jewel makes on his behalf—the need for new suits, for example. Jewel simply bursts out with it one night at dinner. "Conrad, everything you own is either out of style or too small or both. It is a disgrace. I am ashamed to be seen with you in public." Freddie is not surprised at her sister or the abruptness of her remark, but she can see that Jewel has wounded his pride calling attention to a defect.

"I am sorry, milady, if my appearance does not please thee," he says, attempting to make light.

Jewel does not recognize his protest, already caught up in a plan. "Now, Freddie is like you. She doesn't give a whit about fashion. If I need her to look presentable, I have to pick out her clothes. Practically have to dress her."

"That is not true," says Freddie, but Jewel ignores her as well.

"I think we need to get you some new suits. Some shirts as well."

"I shall be the first groom to have a trousseau," he says.

"It is a good idea, but we should not overlook Isabelle," Freddie interjects. "She will need some new clothes as well—as things progress."

"Yes, I can see that your clothes are binding you. They can't be comfortable," says Jewel.

"I don't mind. I don't want maternity clothes."

"Don't be rude, girl," Mr. Odom commands. "It is never polite to refuse a gift." As he speaks, biscuit crumbs tumble from his mouth.

"You may not want them, but you will definitely need them," Jewel reminds her. "We can put some elastic on your waistbands for now and I will pick up fabric and a Butterick. I can make you some smock tops. They will do you for around the house. What is your favorite color?"

"I don't know," says Isabelle.

Before she thinks, Freddie blurts, "Blue. For her eyes."

Mr. Odom adds, "But we should get some pink as well. Don't want to stack the deck."

Isabelle blushes, but Freddie is not sure which remark has embarrassed her. She is relieved when Jewel nods and says, "Yes, blue is a good choice for you."

And so it is decided. Jewel has concocted a story for Mr. Odom's existence, their courtship, tells the women at Lurdelle's that she received a letter from her "long-lost beau out of the blue." Isabelle's story is easy enough to weave into the fabric of the tale, and if anyone in town is shocked that Jewel is soon engaged to Mr. Odom, they do not demonstrate it. The ladies of her Stained Glass Committee even arrange coffee and coconut cake to be served at the regular monthly meeting held in early June just before Jewel departs with Mr. Odom for Savannah, where they are to be wed by a justice of the peace and spend a brief honeymoon touring historic sights.

Freddie has also become aware that Mr. Odom drinks, something she and Jewel discuss at night in their room before they go to sleep. He is never drunk, but on some evenings when he comes to dinner, he is noticeably wobbly and talkative. Freddie suspects that he has packed away a couple of bottles in his suitcase. They do not normally have wine with dinner, but Jewel has offered him a bourbon several evenings. He never declines the offer. Freddie also suspects this is why he wants to drive the car. So he can seek out a Red Dot store, replenish his supply. She does not mind the drinking, though she does hate the way he carries on. Story after story about people and places meaningless to her. Still, if he does drink, it may make things easier down the road when it is time for him to be disposed of. Drunks have accidents. Drunks fall down. She encourages Jewel to bring some bourbon back with them when they travel to Savannah.

Freddie is also troubled by, annoyed by his treatment of Isabelle. He watches her. Jewel tells her that he says he is afraid she will run off again. Afraid she could even try to harm herself. She thinks it admirable of him in such a difficult circumstance, but Freddie is not as sure. He does not act like a father should. He is often dismissive of Isabelle, calling out orders like she is a waitress in a diner: "Girl, bring me and Miss Jewel some fresh coffee. This one has gone cold." Freddie can see Jewel is more than happy to have someone, anyone, fetch for her, and therefore does not intervene. When Freddie reminds him that Isabelle is pregnant, his retort is, "She will need to move quick once she has a youngin' to chase." And then there are the times she catches him just looking at Isabelle, his gaze lingering, or his hand placed over hers as a gesture of thanks. He is expansive in his assertions of adoration of her, especially when he has been drinking. On some nights, he allows himself to be overcome and weeps openly while Jewel serves dessert and coffee.

"A lovely thing she is," he says, waving his arm toward Isabelle. "And so like her mother. I do no disrespect to you, dear Jewel, to speak of her. She was my wife. And I loved her. I am not ashamed. And when I look at Isabelle, it is her dear mother I see. How I failed her. How I have failed them both. But you know that I love you, sweet Isabelle. Love you more than I can say."

Isabelle sucks on her bottom lip when he talks like this, and Freddie speculates on what history has passed between them. She wonders if Isabelle can feel his gaze, notices how she pulls away from him when he reaches out to her, avoids him whenever possible. Yet she returned to him. Was she that desperate that Mr. Odom is the desirable alternative?

Jewel leaves casseroles and chicken salad for Freddie and Isabelle to eat while they are in Savannah. Jewel wanted to depart from Morris in broad daylight from the train station so everyone can see. Freddie knows she wants the ladies from her committee to see her boarding the train in her new suit, with her orchid corsage, and her fiancé. The train routes are not compatible with their schedule, however, and they are forced to drive to Florence, so there is no opportunity for Jewel to show off for her friends. Mr. Odom sulks for most of the drive. Freddie believes he has half expected her to relinquish the car for the trip. And then what? Walk to town? He is presumptuous beyond belief, and Jewel scolds her to be in a better mood as they say good-bye at the station.

"Goodness, Freddie. Don't send us off under a rain cloud." Jewel is nervous, she knows. This is where things will change for her. It is one thing to have a suitor, another to have a husband. However, she assures Freddie she does not mind the intimate parts that will soon follow.

"In my opinion, people make more of it than they should," she says. "Not really worth the bother or the messiness." Still, in the past week, she has been like a hummingbird, flitting from one activity to the next. Freddie has left her alone, let her pack and repack, cook, clean, and babble as she needs. Freddie takes care of other business, has a heart-to-heart talk one morning with Mr. Odom.

"I will just come out and say it," she says when Jewel takes the remaining breakfast plates into the kitchen to wash. "We should talk about financial matters." She has waited for a morning where he is slightly hung over, more manageable. He fidgets like a schoolboy, searching for a reply. She does not wait for him to find one.

"It is my observation that you have . . . limited assets."

"I have thought my good character to be a virtue," he says. He pushes his chair back from the table and stands to emphasize his point. He is a big man, once muscular, probably considered to be attractive to many women, Freddie thinks. He knows he cannot charm her, so he stands over her. He reminds Freddie of a gorilla, wonders if he will beat on his chest for emphasis.

"Yes, but when this marriage occurs, Mr. Odom, my sister's property and investments become yours as well. Since her property and investments involve me, I think it only fair to make sure we are protected." She gestures to the chair. "Please sit. I only wish to speak with you about the future. It is not an insult to make provisions."

"I can assure you, Miss Winifred, that I have only the most honorable intentions with your sister. I think I have made that apparent."

"I am not here to wound you, Mr. Odom. The marriage will be what it is. I imagine that you and Jewel will live here. This has been her home—our home—for twenty years."

"Yes. Yes, I would imagine that we would stay. It is beautiful. And I hope that you would stay here with us if that is what concerns you."

Freddie is tempted to laugh out loud, realizes he thinks she is asking permission to stay in her own home. "Thank you, Mr. Odom," she says. "That is so kind. Now, let's talk about what arrangements need to be made." And with that, she lays out for Mr. Odom his future in the house, his role in their affairs. She can see in his eyes as looks ahead—imagining the rest of his days spent like a fat basset hound sprawled on a soft pillow. She talks about Jewel's will.

"I leave everything to her, and she to me, which I think is only fair. But she will want to provide for you. She has arranged to take out a life insurance policy on herself. You would be her beneficiary."

"Yes," he says. "That is very kind of her. To be so generous. It was difficult when my wife—my first wife passed."

"And do you have insurance on yourself, Mr. Odom?"

He tells here he does not.

"But you should," she insists. "Absolutely."

Freddie arranges to have Deland Coombs, the insurance representative, come by to sign the papers two days before they leave for Savannah. He is happy to make the drive, with the promise of two policies. Jewel is not pleased that Mr. Odom has stipulated he wants to leave a portion of the policy "just in case" to Isabelle. Jewel has calculated the loss she will incur and complained mightily to Freddie, but Freddie appeases her by having Leland Combs up the amount on the whole policy to compensate. When they sign the policies, they make it a festive occasion. Jewel serves pecan shortbreads and tea. Mr. Odom makes a toast to "long and happy lives."

On the drive back to Morris, Freddie jokes to Isabelle about how quiet the car is without them, how glad she is to have things "back to normal." The drive has become a habit for Freddie and Isabelle since McCloud's Hospital and the doctor who will deliver her are both in Florence. Freddie insisted on that, arranged with Mr. Odom to pay for the expenses from her own accounts. She assures him that no one, not Jewel, not Isabelle, needs to know. When he hesitates, seems reluctant to accept anything from her—especially something without Jewel's knowledge—Freddie reminds him of his advice to Isabelle, that it is "rude to refuse a gift." Mr. Odom even makes the first trip with them to see the doctor, making a show to Jewel that he needs to get everything in order. Freddie has withdrawn money from her savings account and gives it to him for the doctor, tells him to bring her the receipt and the projected costs for the doctor's care and the hospital. She will pay those as they need to be paid.

Mr. Odom does not go to the doctor with them after the first visit. Isabelle tells him that there is no need for him to be there. Freddie does not insist, is happy not to have him along for the ride, but when she parks the car at the doctor's office, Isabelle tells her that she wants to go in alone.

"There is no reason," she says, turning on the seat to angle toward Freddie. Her hair is pulled back, tied with a sky blue ribbon to match the smock Jewel has made for her. When Isabelle looks at her like this, Freddie finds it difficult to breathe, like she has swallowed all the air in the car. She struggles to roll down the window. "And it is not that I don't appreciate what you are doing. But this is something I must do."

"But I want you to know . . ." Freddie stammers. "I want you to know that you can count on me if you need."

"I will remember that." And then she is out of the car, up the steps, into the building. Freddie spends the better part of an hour walking in and out of shops on Evans Street, then checks back to see if Isabelle has come out, if she is waiting by the car, but she is not. After fifteen minutes, Freddie begins to worry, wonders if she should go inside to check on her. It is another fifteen minutes before she can bring herself to go into the office.

The waiting room bustles with women—most are pregnant, their large, round bellies on proud display. They chatter loudly, competitively comparing complaints. Several small children sit on the floor, playing with a puzzle. An old woman, sitting with a woman who resembles her closely, holds a small baby—her grandchild, Freddie assumes. Most of the women pay Freddie no notice, but the old woman eyes her cautiously. Freddie feels awkward, like a giant crammed into a dollhouse. This is not a world in which she belongs. She stands frozen in the doorway until the old woman points at a partitioned glass on the other side of the room. When she knocks on the glass, the office receptionist slides back the window over her desk and Freddie gives her Isabelle's name. The woman checks a large ledger and tells Freddie that Isabelle finished with her appointment and left over half an hour earlier. Freddie apologizes, tells the woman she is there to pick her up, take her home, she is sure she must have just missed her. "Probably looking in a store." But on the inside, she is panicked. She remembers what Jewel told her—Mr. Odom's fear that Isabelle would run off again. Has she bolted?

As she walks back to the car, she contemplates how she will explain this to Jewel. To Mr. Odom. She knows she cannot just stand by the car and wait. She has to do something, try to find her. She sets back off toward Evans Street. Just as she rounds the corner, she sees her, hurrying down the steps of the post office. Isabelle throws up her hand in a meager wave. Freddie wants to shake her for alarming her so, but Isabelle looks sad, tired, anxious.

"You shouldn't just leave without telling me where you are going," Freddie says. "It wasn't polite. You frightened me."

Isabelle stops. "Why would you care?"

"I told you before that I wanted you to know that you can count on me. I meant that."

"Are you going to tell them?"

"What is there to tell?"

Isabelle gives her a queer look, as if deciding whether or not to trust Freddie.

"Nothing, I guess. Nothing at all. I came for a walk, that's all."

Freddie wants to tell her she knows this is not true, that she knows she has come to mail a letter to someone. The boy? She wants to tell her that she will help her, will be her friend, but does not, cannot find the right words. Instead, she offers to buy Isabelle a soda from the drugstore she has passed. This becomes part of their ritual when they visit the doctor's each month for a checkup. Freddie no longer walks around, but waits patiently where she can keep an eye on the door. Then, after Isabelle's appointment, they stop for a treat. A soda. A hot dog. A portable record player. Several albums by Isabelle's favorite singers: Patti Page, Jo Stafford, Perry Como. Jewel scoffs at the gifts, asks Freddie what she thinks she is doing, but Freddie doesn't listen. While Jewel drones on, she can conjure the excitement on Isabelle's face searching through the record bin to find an album.

"I love this one," she squeals, and though Freddie has no understanding of which singer is which, she is pleased she can make Isabelle smile.

On the day they drop Jewel and Mr. Odom off at the train station, Freddie suggests they don't head home but go out for dinner.

"Why should we have to eat one of those casseroles when they will be eating in a restaurant?"

"But they are getting married," Isabelle reminds her. "It is a special day for them."

"Well, it is a special day for us as well," says Freddie. "I imagine we must be related in some way or another. By marriage. If they can celebrate, so should we."

They stop at a roadside café for barbeque, fried chicken, home-made peach pie. When Freddie crawls into bed that night, the same feeling she had on the stairs the first day Isabelle arrived floods over her. She recollects Isabelle laughing as they ate, her lips pursed as she studied the little jukebox at the table, selecting which songs she wanted to play, how she curled up in the passenger seat next to her like a small child and slept on the way home. Freddie remembers watching the moon rise in the distance as she followed the familiar road, and as she dozes off, she smiles to think how the moonlight streaming in on her also finds its way to Isabelle sleeping just down the hall.

Freddie wakes early, when the world slumbers in twilight. The house is so still that she strains to try to hear a sound, but nothing returns to her. She makes her bed, pulling the spread to make sure it is even all around. When she is finished, she inhales quickly, knowing it is time to dress. Knowing that what she wants to do, plans to do has been forbidden by Jewel. It is a risk. She knows she would not dare this if Jewel was here. Jewel would not allow it, call it unseemly. But Jewel is not here. There is no one to see. And Isabelle will not wake for an hour or more. She goes to the dresser and pulls out her men's trousers, the overshirt, her brogans. They are like friends discarded, lost—now returned. She goes downstairs, makes her coffee, sits on the front porch until the sun crests the horizon, then walks out into the fields.

She has not attempted the walk since Mr. Odom and Isabelle arrived. She has watched from the porch while the foreman they have hired to tend the farm for them and his workers plowed and planted the field crops, only coming down to confer with him before and after the work was completed.

"Winter wasn't too hard," Mr. Ray had told her. "So if we don't have that dry spell like we did last summer, I expect we can get a pretty good yield on the tobacco. And if cotton holds true to last year, we should be near three-quarters bale per acre." They had talked about the acres planted in soybeans, a new crop for Freddie, one that Mr. Ray tells her will probably do better than corn. She doesn't care. She will not give up planting corn even if it is not as reliable as cotton, less profitable than soybeans.

Freddie walks up and down the rows, marveling at the precision of the order. The cool spring mornings have given way to summer's thick, moist air. Looking out over the field, it is as if she is standing waist deep in a green sea. She wishes that the world could stay just as it is at this moment. The sun warm on her face. Jewel and Mr. Odom far away in Savannah. Isabelle and her unborn baby sleeping soundly upstairs. She thinks about how the world will change by the time it is ready to harvest, when the crops have grown so tall that she will not be able to see over them.

When Freddie returns to the house, she removes her heavy shoes, partly because she does not wish to track any telltale signs of dirt into Jewel's kitchen, partly because she wants to be as quiet as possible, change into her familiar dress before Isabelle wakes. However, as she steps inside the back door, Isabelle sits at the kitchen table in her nightgown, spreading Jewel's homemade fig preserves onto a piece of toast. When she sees Freddie, she says only, "I was hungry. When I didn't see you downstairs, I made myself something to eat."

"I was going to cook some eggs. I can make you some as well."

"Yes, that would be good. I would like that."

Freddie moves toward the door to the hall, the stairs, her room. "I just need to get dressed."

Isabelle wipes a bit of preserves from the corner of her mouth. "You look plenty dressed to me. No need to change on my account."

"It's just that Jewel doesn't like me to look like this," she says.

Isabelle shakes her head. "Well, then we just won't tell her, will we?"

She quickly turns away so Isabelle will not see the flush in her cheeks, the tears in her eyes. Freddie wants to weep, wants to fall on the floor at Isabelle's feet, thank her for this gift. Instead, she pulls some bacon and a bowl of eggs from the refrigerator, fumbles for a pan.

"You know," Isabelle continues, "you and your sister are nothing alike."

Freddie laughs. "No, not really."

"I don't see why she wanted to marry him," Isabelle says.

Freddie stops, looks at her. "What do you mean?" she asks.

"Him. My stepfather. I don't know why she would want to marry him. You two seem to do perfectly fine here on your own."

"Jewel is made to be someone's wife," says Freddie as she unwraps the bacon, sets several slices in the pan, adjusts the burner to low to render the fat. "I think she needs more company than I can provide her."

"Well, she has sure picked herself a winner. A gold-plated chump! He was a real jerk to my mom before she got sick. And then he acted like she was an angel sent from heaven."

Freddie wants again to ask Isabelle why she has returned to him, but says instead, "It isn't my business. If they are happy, then who's to say?"

"I guess," says Isabelle. She pauses for a moment. "Have you ever been married?"

Freddie over cracks the egg, so some of the shell goes into the pan. "Yes," she says, surprised by her own response. "He died. Does it surprise you? That I was married?"

"A bit. I was thinking you seemed like someone who . . . who was different. I always thought that I wanted to get married. Now, with all that has happened, I don't know. I don't know."

"Well," says Freddie. "There is time for that. That is still down the road. Now, let's just tell ourselves today we aren't going to worry about what is to come tomorrow. It will get here soon enough on its own."

Jewel and Mr. Odom are gone for five days. One day traveling each way, with three days for the ceremony and sightseeing. Jewel says that any less will make it seem too much like "running off" rather than a planned elopement. Freddie is content to have them out of the house. She tries to make each day an adventure for Isabelle, for herself. One afternoon, they drive into town to see a Doris Day picture, *By the Light of the Silvery Moon*; one evening Freddie announces they will have breakfast for dinner and serves them both big plates of pancakes, fried eggs, and sausages. Isabelle enjoys the movie, likes the attention—she can tell, but she can't help but think that something works beneath the surface as well. One afternoon she happens upon her in the front parlor fiddling with the phone. The girl jumps when she sees Freddie.

"I noticed that it never rings," Isabelle says. "I thought it might be broken."

"Not broken," replies Freddie. "It was a nuisance, so I cut the cord."

"Wow! You must have been pretty mad."

"Yes," Freddie admits. "Pretty mad. Was there someone you wanted to call?"

"No, no one." But even as Isabelle returns the phone to the cradle and walks out of the parlor, Freddie knows they both recognize she is lying.

The day before Jewel and Mr. Odom return home, Freddie asks Isabelle to choose what she wants to do for the day.

"Anything?"

"Of course," says Freddie.

"I have never seen the ocean . . . if that isn't too much, I would like to go to the shore."

"It's not far," Freddie assures her. "We can be there for lunch. Take a walk on the beach. Put our feet in the water."

"I won't look funny if I am not wearing a bathing suit?"

"No," Freddie says. "We can roll our pants legs up. And I will find someplace that isn't crowded. Who wants that anyway?"

It is a bright, brilliant day, though the clouds on the horizon promise a late-afternoon thunderstorm. Freddie packs an old spread so they will have a place to sit on the sand, and after they park along a stretch of road without too many cars, they both take off their shoes and she helps Isabelle over the sand dunes to the beach itself. The sand is hot, but it doesn't burn—still, the dark, wet sand at the water's edge is a welcome comfort when they reach it.

Isabelle giggles with delight as the waves crash in front of them. "I knew it was enormous," she says. "But who could imagine?"

Freddie agrees with her that it is an amazing sight.

"I wish I could swim," says Isabelle. "I would swim as far out as I could till I couldn't even see the land. Till there was nothing else. Just me and the water all around me."

Freddie thinks about the feeling she gets when she stands swallowed up in the middle of the corn field. "Yes, that would be grand."

"And then I would drown," says Isabelle. "Sink to the bottom of the ocean and be forgotten."

Freddie laughs, but realizes that Isabelle isn't joking. "Why would you want to do that? Isabelle. Honey. You have so much in front of you. The baby."

Isabelle's face darkens like the distant clouds on the horizon. She turns away, her back to the ocean. "I don't want this baby. I never have wanted it. I hate it. I want it to die. I wish that I would die, too."

"No. No, you mustn't talk like that." Freddie is unnerved, doesn't know what to do. She wants to pet Isabelle, like you would pet an animal to comfort it, but cannot bring herself to touch her. Isabelle wraps her arms around herself, hugging herself tightly, hangs her head, and begins to cry. It is the same crying that she saw in the car, the same crying she has heard sometimes when Isabelle is alone in her room.

"I know you must be afraid," she said. "I am here to help you through this. We are all here to help you. Jewel. Mr. Odom. You don't have to be scared."

"Him!" spits Isabelle. "Him. Why do you think I ran away?"

"I thought there was a boy. I thought the two of you ran away together."

"There was no boy," says Isabelle. "That is a lie that he concocted to make himself look good. There was no boy. I ran away to get out of that house—to get away from him. My stepfather."

## . . . 4 . . .

Freddie has come to the conclusion that killing Mr. Odom is more than just a necessary part of a plan. It is justice. And she has begun to look forward to it.

Isabelle doesn't speak to Freddie the whole ride back into Morris, sits with her face turned to the open window, as if searching for something she expects to fly by at any moment. As she starts up the stairs, she turns to Freddie. "I know you meant well." And then she is gone, up to her room.

Jewel and Mr. Odom return the next morning, and in the two months that follow, the house, which normally feels large and rambling to Freddie, becomes as closed and confined as a sharecropper's cabin. She can count on one hand the times she has been alone with Isabelle, and then only for just a moment. If she invites Isabelle to drive to town, then Jewel remembers that she needs to fetch something at the Winn Dixie. If she sees Isabelle sitting in the front porch swing and joins her, Mr. Odom will appear like a mosquito at sunset before she has time to settle into a rocker. Most of the time, however, Isabelle secludes herself in her room. They have missed Isabelle's last two doctor's visits—postponed because Isabelle complains she doesn't feel up to travel. Freddie protests to Jewel that someone should insist she go, but Jewel chides Freddie as a worrisome nag.

"It is her decision," says Jewel. "I can't say I would want to get jostled all the way to Florence and back in this heat if I could avoid it." Freddie understands that with her swollen, ripening belly and the heat, Isabelle has to be uncomfortable. And scared. She thinks about the waiting room full of noisy, clucking women. How hard that would be for Isabelle.

She has not spoken to Jewel about what Isabelle told her on the beach, just like she has never spoken to her about seeing Isabelle come out of the post office all those months ago, just like she would never tell about her trying to use the phone. She feels loyal to Isabelle in a way that she has never felt with anyone, particularly Jewel. She understands Isabelle's loneliness, her isolation. There is someone out there whom she thinks of—someone whom she has written to, someone she has tried to call. The worry of it all has worn her down, Freddie thinks. Perhaps that is why Isabelle has been so poorly. The baby—which she will not discuss. A boy who has abandoned her when she needs him most. However, Isabelle was adamant there was no boy, and Freddie believes her.

The first parts of the pregnancy seemed to be a breeze for her. She was never sick, seldom complained. But since her last doctor's visit, as the time for her delivery approaches, she has changed. Her color is off, her cheeks flushed. She has headaches. She is listless. Has little appetite. In fact, Jewel has taken to preparing meals for her on a tray when she doesn't want to come down. She likes grits. She tolerates chicken and dumplings. Freddie thinks she would live off scrambled eggs and toast with Jewel's fig preserves if given the choice in the matter.

Freddie offers to take the trays, but Jewel will not allow it. "She is in my charge now," she says. "You tend to the outside chores. I will tend to the inside ones." Freddie agrees, happy enough that at least it won't be Mr. Odom who is caring for her. Nevertheless, she often finds herself hovering around the door whenever Jewel comes out, hoping for a word, perhaps an invitation to step inside. One afternoon, she starts when she sees a bloody cloth in Jewel's hand. Freddie asks if Isabelle is okay. Should they take her to the doctor?

"It is perfectly normal," says Jewel. "I was talking about it with Betty Robinson after church. Isabelle is spotting. Betty says it is not unusual at all. Just bed rest and she will be fine."

Freddie asks what expertise Betty Robinson has in such matters, but Jewel shoos her away. "She knows more than you do, that's for sure. Now, go on. Stop hanging around here. I don't know what has gotten into you. If you want to make yourself useful, go catch that rat I saw running off from the henhouse this morning."

Freddie tells Jewel she must be mistaken. "That rooster isn't going to tolerate any vermin around those brood hens."

"I know a rat when I see one. I don't want to go in one morning and get bit. Just put out some bait."

When Freddie goes to the barn later, she is surprised to see the box of Dairyland is nearly empty. It has been a while since she has used it. She doesn't much care for poison, but she figures if you are going to poison a rat, Dairyland is about as painless as it comes. She goes that afternoon and buys a new box at Standard's. She also goes into the drugstore to find a magazine for Isabelle, tries to imagine something that she would enjoy reading. She can find nothing except for *Good Housekeeping* or *My Home*. These would not make Isabelle feel better. She buys her a Milky Way bar instead, and for herself a Coca-Cola, which she drinks on the way home. She stops at the end of the driveway to gather the mail—it will avoid the walk in the sun later. She parks the car, puts the sack with the Dairyland up on a shelf. Is it accidental or providence, she asks herself later, that she just happens to notice the letter addressed to Isabelle. How strange to see her name there in print. Isabelle Odom. Her name the same as his. There is no return address. She puts the letter into the pocket of her dress, lingers for a minute in the barn, considering what to do. She knows instinctively that she cannot tell Jewel about this—to tell her would be just as good as handing the letter directly to Mr. Odom.

Later, after lunch, she asks Mr. Odom to join her to spread the pellets for the rats. He protests—he doesn't have gloves, will have to change, isn't sure he would be much help—but follows her out to the barn.

"Don't worry," she tells him. "I am not going to ask you to work."

"It's not that I am not willing to . . ."

"I just didn't want to speak in front of Jewel. I was thinking that you and Jewel might enjoy an evening out together. What, with you being newly wed and everything. It can't be much fun to be stuck here with me all the time."

She watches him roll the idea around. He wants to drive the car. Not be chauffeured around like a guest. Would enjoy a night out on the town.

"I don't know that Jewel will want to leave Isabelle," he says. "What if . . ."

"The baby isn't due for two weeks. Besides, you are only going to be gone for the evening. Jewel is gone to church for that long or more when she goes to Lurdelle's or to her committee meeting. It is barely an hour down to Myrtle Beach. You could get some fried oysters. Walk on the boardwalk."

"Yes," he says. "What a nice idea. But I think Jewel has already begun dinner preparations. You heard her at lunch. Roast chicken. Fried okra."

"Then tomorrow. It will give her something to plan for besides our next meal."

He ambles back toward the house to tell Jewel. Freddie touches the letter to make sure it is still there, knowing that tomorrow night she will be alone with Isabelle. The heat in the barn nearly makes her swoon. She pulls on her sunhat and begins her chores.

Freddie knows Jewel is suspicious of her as Jewel and Mr. Odom drive off the next afternoon. Freddie doesn't care. This is not something that involves her. She has even managed to keep the Milky Way bar a secret, hidden at the back of the freezer. Jewel tells her they will be home early. She has left a cucumber salad in the Frigidaire and a cold plate of chicken. Isabelle has been fed. She is resting. There is no need to disturb her.

Yes. Yes. Yes, says Freddie. Once the car disappears down the road, she waits as long as she can and then takes the candy bar to Isabelle. She knocks gently on the door in case Isabelle is sleeping, but Isabelle calls her in straightaway. She is lying on her bed, on top of the covers, propped up by pillows. There is a small fan on the highboy that oscillates the air back and forth in the room. Freddie notices that Isabelle's hair is pulled back into a loose ponytail, her neck damp with perspiration. Freddie leaves the door open to get some breeze in the room. It seems to Freddie that Isabelle's belly is even larger than she can recall.

"You never come see me," Isabelle says.

"Jewel is worse than a prison guard," Freddie replies. "She tells me I shouldn't make a nuisance of myself. That you need your rest."

"I don't know why she has me in solitary confinement. She won't even let me go downstairs. She is so bossy."

"It's just easier to do what she says sometimes. Else she will just go on about it until you end up doing what she wants just so she will shut up. I think Mr. Odom has learned that already."

"He won't stand for it too much longer. You wait. They will have a fight sometime when she tells him what to do and he just tells her to go suck an egg."

Freddie laughs. "I think I could enjoy that. It's been an adjustment for everyone to be here together. Takes some getting used to."

Freddie asks how Isabelle has been feeling, if the heat and the humidity are wearing her down, asks if she has packed a bag yet for the hospital. She does not mention the bleeding, does not want to embarrass her, frighten her to think that it mattered enough for Jewel to mention it. She gives her the Milky Way, still cold from the freezer. "I like them frozen like that," she tells Isabelle. "Especially when it is so hot. Otherwise, they just melt."

Isabelle breaks off a bit and shares it with Freddie.

"And I brought you this as well," she says, pulling the envelope from her pocket. She holds it flat in her hand as she offers it to Isabelle. "It came for you yesterday. I figure whomever you wrote to all those months ago must finally have written you back."

She can see Isabelle's hand shake as she reaches out for the letter as if she is handing her a sacred relic, a charm. She studies it for a moment, as if to make certain that it is real and she is truly holding it, that it is not an apparition. She does not make a move to open it. After a moment Freddie backs away from the bed.

"I will let you have some time to yourself," she says.

"Thank you," says Isabelle, but Freddie knows she means more than just the offer to leave her alone.

The sun has begun to cast long shadows of evening before Freddie returns. She has not turned on any lights downstairs, letting the house cool as dusk settles over the farm. It is dark upstairs as well when she climbs the staircase, and as she stands at the top of the landing, she can hear Isabelle playing a song on the record player. When it ends, she picks up the needle and begins it again. Freddie walks to her room. It takes a moment to discern Isabelle's silhouette obscured amongst the gloom. Isabelle makes no indication that she sees Freddie.

"Listen to this," she says softly. A mournful guitar strums a tune. A woman begins to sing:

> *I went to your wedding*
> *Although I was dreading*
> *The thought of losing you.*
> *The organ was playing,*
> *My poor heart kept saying,*
> *"My dreams, my dreams are through.*

"She's getting married," she says, turning toward Freddie.

"The girl in the song?" Freddie asks.

Isabelle looks at her funny, as if surprised she does not understand. "Yes, her too. My friend Alice, though. She is the one I meant."

"Is that who the letter is from?"

"No," says Isabelle. "It is from her mother. Alice asked her to send it to me so I would know."

Freddie knows this news has made her terribly sad, and Isabelle's mood frightens her. She is the same as when they stood on the beach. Absent. She thinks to turn on the light but does not, afraid a sudden burst of light would startle her like it would a skittish animal. She walks over to her. She stands so close that she can smell the powder on Isabelle's neck. She wants to place her hand on Isabelle's shoulder—to comfort her. She does not. Isabelle begins to sing along with the music:

> *You came down the aisle, wearing a smile*
> *A vision of loveliness*
> *I uttered a sigh, and then whispered good-bye*
> *Good-bye to my happiness.*

"Why are people so cruel?" she asks.

Freddie thinks suddenly of Lt. Calder, of the men whom she and Jewel have killed, the ruse that has brought Isabelle to this house. "Perhaps I am not the best person to ask. Each of us has our own share of brutalities to answer for. Our own selfishness. Our own greed."

"Not Alice," says Isabelle. "Not Alice."

The song has reached its end, and a snappy pop melody fills the room. Isabelle grabs the arm of the record player so abruptly there is a scratch as she picks it up and returns it to where she wants.

"What do you notice about this song?" she asks.

"I am not good at music," says Freddie. "It's sad. It's a sad song." She knows Isabelle is reaching out to her, but feels lost, helpless. "I can't say. I don't even know who it is singing."

"It's Patti Page. But that isn't important. That isn't what I am asking you. What do you hear?"

Freddie listens closely to the music, finds the story hidden in the words.

"Someone she knows is getting married. Someone she loves very much. And she feels like her life is over."

"Yes," says Isabelle. "But there is more."

Freddie listens intently, but she cannot hear what it is that Isabelle wants her to hear. She can feel the night on her arms, her legs, like it has reached in and swallowed them up inside it. She and Isabelle have disappeared into nothing—there is only the music. Their disembodied voices.

"I don't know," she says. "I don't know."

"She is singing to the bride," says Isabelle. "The groom doesn't walk down the aisle. Whoever heard a groom described as a 'vision of loveliness.' She is singing to the bride."

And then, suddenly, Isabelle's head is pressed against Freddie's chest, Freddie's arms wrapped around her. Isabelle begins to cry, and Freddie pulls her closer, close enough she imagines she can feel the baby in Isabelle's belly kicking between them. She reaches up to stroke Isabelle's head. The ribbon falls to the floor.

"There. There. Sweetie. Don't you worry. Everything will work out. Just you wait. Now, why don't you tell me everything?"

And Isabelle does.

Later, when she is alone in the kitchen, after Isabelle has cried herself to exhaustion, Freddie repeats the promises she has made to Isabelle, the confidences of her own that she has shared with her.

Isabelle has changed to her nightdress, washed her face. In the soft yellow glow from the small table lamp by the bed, Freddie can see her eyes are swollen from the tears. Freddie turns the covers down for her.

"What would you say if I told you that Mr. Odom was going to be leaving here very soon?"

Isabelle sighs as she scoots down into the bed.

"I would say 'good riddance.' But he isn't going anywhere as long as there is free room and board for him here."

"I wouldn't count on that," says Freddie. "And after he is gone, I want you to know that you can stay here for as long as you need. As long as you want."

"But what about your sister? Would she allow this?"

"You don't have to worry about her. We are in agreement on the matter of Mr. Odom."

"I had no idea." Isabelle smiles. "I would sure like to see the expression on his face when you tell him."

"Yes," says Freddie. "I am certain he will be surprised."

Freddie is still sitting at the kitchen table with her half-eaten

plate of cold chicken and cucumber salad in front of her when
Jewel and Mr. Odom return.

"My goodness," says Jewel. "Are you just now eating dinner?"

"I forgot," says Freddie. "I sat on the front porch watching the
sunset and I guess I just lost the time."

Jewel laughs. "You would lose your head if it wasn't attached."
Freddie can see that Jewel doesn't believe her excuse, but she
doesn't care. Things like that don't matter anymore.

## ...5...

"Good Lord Almighty!" squawks Jewel the next morning when Freddie enters the kitchen wearing her work pants, overshirt, and boots. "You could have given me some warning." Freddie doesn't speak to her, just goes to the cupboard, takes out her cup and saucer, pours herself some coffee, and leans against the counter.

"When you have her breakfast ready," she says, "I will take it up to her. And put a couple of pieces of bacon on a plate for me while you're at it, if you please."

Jewel turns from the stove. She looks to speak, but Freddie stops her.

"I wasn't putting that up for a vote."

Mr. Odom has stopped reading the paper and sits slack-jawed, staring at her. She tips the saucer of coffee to her lips, drains it in a long gulp.

"Jewel doesn't like for me to drink my coffee out of the saucer. Says it makes me look common."

"If you are trying to shock me," says Mr. Odom, "you will need to do more than drink coffee from a saucer. Or dress in men's trousers."

"Well, the way I see it, someone has to wear the pants in the family. I figured it might as well be me."

Mr. Odom puts the paper down. "Miss Winifred, I think you are trying to pick a fight with me."

"Not a fight, sir. And please do call me Freddie. It is what I prefer."

Jewel puts a plate on the tray. "It's grits and scrambled eggs. I made them the way she likes them. A piece of toast. Some preserves. I hope that will meet with your approval."

Freddie smiles. "Jewel, you make a good wife. Yes, you do. Don't you agree, Mr. Odom?"

She tops up her coffee and sets it on the tray. She finishes it sitting in the white wicker rocker near the window of Isabelle's bedroom while Isabelle picks at her breakfast.

"You need to eat it all," she tells her.

"Everything just tastes so salty," Isabelle complains. "It makes me thirsty."

"I will tell Jewel to make you a pitcher of lemonade. That should be nice on a hot day." Freddie puts her cup and saucer back on the tray. "Now, Isabelle. I want you to promise me something."

"Yes, what?"

"Just remember everything we talked about last night. Just remember that I told you I would make him go away from here."

"Yes."

"Well, it may take some convincing. So, you just stay up here. Play your records. And by this time tomorrow . . ."

Isabelle nods. "Do what you must. You don't need my consent. He is a miserable bastard, and I will be glad to be shed of him."

Freddie takes her hand in hers, squeezes it. "Then I will see you—afterward."

It takes no effort to draw Mr. Odom into the barn. Freddie merely says she has something she needs to discuss. Undoubtedly, she imagines he must think she has another treat in store. Take the car again, why don't you? The surprise, however, comes when she knocks him hard up side of his head with the ax handle she has purchased from Standard's for just this moment. It doesn't knock him out like a conk on the head does in the movies, but it does bring him to his knees. He instinctively brings his hand up to his

temple, stunned, searching to see if there is blood. This delay pro-
vides her a moment to wrap the rope suspended from the pulley
overhead around him, underneath his arms, cinched tightly behind. Easy as trussing a bird.

She pulls him to his feet, and then, just for good measure, hoists
him so that he is forced to stand tiptoed.

"Holy shit!" he mutters. "Have you lost your mind?" He bel-
lows for Jewel.

"If you think she is going to come and help you, I'm afraid you
are going to be disappointed," she tells him. "This is a working
farm, Mr. Odom. I am sure you have noticed that, though I can't
see that you have actually contributed much in the way of labor."

He starts to speak, but she prods him with the handle. "No,
don't, please," she says. "The time for you to lend your support
will come, rest assured."

He shouts again for Jewel. This time, Freddie hits him with the
end of the handle. "Ugh!" he grunts. "You crazy bitch. I will—"

Freddie hits him again. "You aren't going to do anything. To
me. To anyone. As I was saying, this is a working farm. Everything
here serves a purpose. We raise crops, and we make a profit on
them. We raise hogs, and then we slaughter those hogs in the autumn to sell. And we will turn a profit on you as well, Mr. Odom."

She has his attention. He looks at her wide-eyed. "Please don't
hurt me," he says.

Freddie laughs. "My plan, Mr. Odom, is to kill you. How much
pain you suffer depends on you."

"Oh, Jesus God. I am a sinner, but I don't deserve this," he
cries. "Jewel! Jooo-el!" The rope catches him tight up under his
arms, so that his elbows are thrust up and out above his shoulders.
His breath comes in short gasps. "I never did a thing to you.
Never. You have no right to treat me this way."

"I am astounded by the audacity," she says. It is oppressively
hot in the barn. Sweat drips down the back of her neck. She takes
out a kerchief and wipes her face, dries her palms. "The sheer
nerve it must take just to be you. To get up every day and just
be—you. Tell me now, if Jewel had come to you with the same pit-

tance that you brought to us, would you have thought that a fair deal?"

"I told you, I have had setbacks, misfortunes. I was limited in my options. I could not travel and leave the girl."

"Yes, I have heard them all, Mr. Odom. Answer my question."

"No," he says. "I would not have considered it a fair deal. But I never claimed to be anything that I am not. Now, please, if you—if Jewel—if my being here is a cause for distress, I will leave. I will leave today, and you will never see me again."

"And would you want to drive the car? Or would you expect someone to take you to the train, to buy you your ticket, perhaps pack you a sack lunch?"

"Goddammit. I don't know what you want from me."

"The truth is, Mr. Odom, you are worth your weight in gold to me. I may just buy myself a tractor with the profit I will make off you. I could use a new tractor."

"I don't know what you want," he repeats.

"What I want is for you to take responsibility. Own up—be a man," Freddie says, resting the handle on her shoulder. "Now, tell me about the girl."

"Isabelle? What do you want with her?"

"I want to know what you did to her."

"Do to her? I did nothing to her. Anyone who says I have not been a good father to her is a liar. A goddamn liar. I may not have been able to give her much, but I have provided the best I could." Freddie notices that his shirt has bunched up around his middle. She pokes him with the tip of the handle and watches as it sinks into his slack belly. "Tell me about Isabelle. Tell me how you provided for her. Tell me about the baby."

"Fuck you!" he sputters. "I know what you are, Miss Freddie Bramble. Your sister and I talk about you at night in the dark. I know about you."

She swings hard, catches him on his left side, just under his ribs. She can feel the bone splinter as she hits. He screams. "Why are you doing this? I never did hurt you. I never did hurt anyone."

"Tell me about Isabelle. Tell me about the baby." She pauses for a moment and steps closer to him, close enough to whisper. "Tell me about Alice."

Panic floods his eyes and he kicks out at her. She steps away as he loses his footing and spins around like a ham dangling in the smokehouse.

"Vile. Unspeakable. Disgusting things they are. You all are. Her and that girl. That Alice. Has she come around here?"

"No, her parents have married her off to a boy from their church. Her mother sent Isabelle a letter. Said Alice had begged her to send it so Isabelle would know what had happened to her. Wouldn't think she had just abandoned her. Said she only agreed to get married if she saw her put it in the mail."

"God will punish you," he says.

Freddie ignores him. "So Alice is gone. A wife. And Isabelle?"

He begins to cry. "I raised that girl after her mama passed. I didn't have to do that. I could have left. She's no relation to me."

Freddie aims for his left knee. There is a loud bang, like a pistol firing as it shatters. A dark stain runs down the front of Mr. Odom's pants.

"Now she sits up there with your baby inside her, sadder than anyone should ever be. You did that to her. You should have let her go. Instead, you raped her. You raped her again and again. Lay on her and sweated and grunted and stuck yourself inside her. You made her pregnant with your baby. Her nothing more than a child herself. And not just a child. She was your child. You should have protected her. She had no one else."

"I meant to make her right," he sobs. "I only meant to make her right. I thought if she knew a man, I could make her right. I never meant for the other. Jesus as my witness I never meant for the other to happen."

"You did it because you could do it. There was no one to answer to. You could do it and no one—especially her—had the power to stop you."

"You don't understand," he says. "I only wanted to save her— from herself."

"Enough," says Freddie. "I can't stand any more." She steps around behind him, raises the handle, and brings it down full force on the back of his head. His skull caves in under the impact, the ax handle leaving a small, channeled indentation down the center. He goes limp and sags lifeless in the harness.

"You are a lying piece of shit," she says as she leans the handle up against the wall. Freddie fetches the wheelbarrow from the corner and rolls it over to where Mr. Odom hangs. She positions it behind him and then untethers the rope, letting him drop. His head flops back, mouth agape. It is easier to cut the rope than try to untie it—she will only lose a few feet at most, so she uses a large pair of garden sheers to slice through it. She coils the rope and hangs it back where it belongs, hoists the handles of the wheelbarrow, and rolls Mr. Odom's body to the house.

Jewel stands on the steps leading to the kitchen, wringing a dishtowel between her hands. "You should have told me, Freddie. You should have given me some warning what you were planning."

"What did you want, Jewel? Would you have cooked him a better breakfast if you had known? Fried some country ham instead of bacon this morning?"

"I have a say in this as well. You are putting me in a position I do not choose to be in."

"I couldn't trust you not to tell him," says Freddie. "You talk too much. He said you had plenty of talks with him when you were alone. Talks about private matters."

"I don't know what you mean," says Jewel. "I am just saying it wasn't up to you to decide this. The girl is here."

"I don't think she will care. Where is Isabelle?"

"Probably hiding in her room. I have never heard such sounds before—when you were out in the barn with him. She is bound to have heard them as well. She will know, and she will want to know why."

"She already knows why," says Freddie. "Now, unless you want him to start swelling up out here in the sun like a dead possum by the side of the road, I need you to help me."

Freddie instructs Jewel to hold the screen door for her. She then leans over Mr. Odom and lifts him up onto her shoulder, carrying him as if he were a sack of feed. She is strong. She does not struggle with the weight. She controls her breath and marches purpose-fully up the steps into the house, in through the kitchen, and up the stairs. When she reaches the landing, she turns and heaves Mr. Odom's body headfirst down the stairs so that he tumbles down like a broken toy all the way to the bottom.

She looks down the hall. Isabelle's door is closed.

"Get the bourbon," she says to Jewel, who has crept into the front hall.

"He won't have drunk any," Jewel reminds her. "They will be able to tell."

"You need to just be quiet and let me tend to this," says Freddie as she pours some onto his shirt. "They will just need to smell it on him. He had been drinking. And he fell down the stairs. It is that simple."

"We were supposed to wait until after the baby," says Jewel. "I thought the girl would be gone long before any of this. She should not be here for this."

Freddie takes a swig of the bourbon to steady herself. She caps the bottle and hands it to Jewel to return to its proper place. "She is here, though. And she is going to stay here. With us. With me."

Freddie begins to climb back up the stairs as Jewel calls out after her. "I have a say in these things, Freddie. We had an agreement."

"We can sort out the details later," Freddie says. "I have to get changed so I can drive into town and get the sheriff. I told Isabelle you would make her a pitcher of lemonade. Why don't you do that? That should help keep you occupied. Make extra. I am sure Joe Parks will want a cool drink as well. I won't be gone long—an hour. Maybe two if he isn't in his office."

"A pitcher of lemonade. And a dead man at the foot of the stairs."

"Then just go sit on the front porch and wait. Or go to your room. Or go stand out in the middle of the road. I don't care. Just please shut up till somebody asks you for your opinion."

Jewel storms out onto the porch, the screen door slamming be-hind her.

Freddie runs some cool water in the sink, washes herself. Her braid has come loose, and she wonders if she should have Jewel redo it. She decides against it. Before she heads downstairs, she goes to Isabelle's door.

She knocks gently and opens the door. Isabelle is on the bed, lying on her side, her knees pulled up, her face to the wall. Freddie can tell she is hurting.

Freddie walks over to her and touches her on the shoulder. Isabelle is clammy from the heat. The girl doesn't move.

"It was the only way," says Freddie. "It was the only way to be rid of him. Your new life starts today. And I promise you, you will never be sad again—as long as I have a say in it." She leans over and kisses Isabelle on the head.

Jewel is still sitting on the front porch, rocking fiercely. She determinedly ignores Freddie.

"We will get the details of everything worked out when I get home," she says. "We just have to get through this next bit and then we can work out the rest. Who is to say, Jewel? Perhaps we can all just be happy. Wouldn't that be nice?"

"You don't have the right just to decide these things, Freddie. You have put me in a bad position here."

"Well, it is too late now to turn back."

"Yes, I guess you're right there. You best be going so you can get back here. I don't want this to go on forever."

Freddie takes her time driving to town. Joe Parks isn't in his office. The secretary says he has gone to get a haircut and should be back in half a hour. She does not ask Freddie why she needs him, does not offer to call the barber shop, so Freddie tells her not to interrupt whatever it is she is doing that is so blasted important and she will just go look for him herself. She finds him exactly where the secretary said he would be, sitting in the barber chair. Several men, some of whom she recognizes from Standard's, sit around— waiting, reading magazines, joking with each other. They stop immediately when she walks in, eye her with suspicion. Women are not often here.

Harold King, the owner of the shop, speaks to her. "Miss Bramble, is there anything I can do for you?"

"Sheriff Parks," she says. "You need to come out to the farm. There has been an accident. My sister's husband has fallen down the stairs."

"Did you call the ambulance?"

"There wasn't any need. He broke his neck. He is dead."

It takes a minute for Harold King to get the paper collar off from around the sheriff's neck. Joe Parks stands up, his hair half cut. He walks with Freddie back to his office, tells the secretary where he is going, asks her to call the hospital, have an ambulance sent out to the Bramble farm.

"He doesn't need an ambulance," Freddie reminds him. "He needs an undertaker. He is dead. I am certain of it. He had been drinking."

"They will need to examine the body," he says. "Then they can release him to the funeral home. It is just the process we have to follow. Are you able to drive yourself, or do you wish to ride with me?"

"I can drive myself," says Freddie. "He was Jewel's husband. She is the one to grieve him, not I."

She follows the sheriff back to the farm. Thunderheads loom large in the east. There will be a storm before sunset, she is certain of it. As they pull into the driveway, she looks up to Isabelle's room, sees the curtains lifting with the breeze. Then, as she steps from the car, she notices Jewel at the top of the front steps, her hands waving over her head like a madwoman. She shrieks incoherently. No, not a shriek. A howl. A caterwaul. But it is not the sounds that Jewel makes that freeze Freddie. It is the blood. Blood on Jewel's apron. Blood on her hands and arms and legs. Blood streaks on her face.

Isabelle's blood.

## . . . 6 . . .

Freddie tips a cup of steaming coffee into her saucer. It has been a week now that Isabelle has been dead, three days since they buried her and Mr. Odom and the stillborn baby. They buried them all in the family plot next to the Deegans. Jewel wanted to bury Isabelle with the baby, but Freddie would not allow it. She does, however, consent to a double headstone so that Jewel will leave her alone about the matter. Sitting on the porch, she can see the graves outlined by a wrought-iron fence from her rocker. Freddie tells Mr. Webb from the funeral home that due to the circumstances, they require only a graveside interment. Nothing at the church. Nothing at the funeral home. Jewel's preacher conducts the service—reluctantly, Freddie thinks. He doesn't know them, refers to Isabelle as Miss Odom. Miss Odom and her father. He does not mention the baby except in a passing reference to "all the young angels You have called home." A few of the women from Jewel's committee attend and serve supper afterward. Freddie wonders if they have drawn straws.

She thinks about Isabelle lying cold in the ground. She would not let Jewel bury her in a maternity smock. She bought a new dress. A blue summer dress that she gives to Mr. Webb. In the coffin, he had washed the blood off her face, out of her hair. She did not look sad as she slept there, her hair tied in a ribbon. Freddie had wanted to give her something, a keepsake to take with her, to keep her company, to let her know she would be missed. There was nothing of hers that she could think to give that would matter to Isabelle—no memento to mark an occasion, a bond between them. She decided to put in the record Isabelle had played for her. Jewel ridicules her for it, tells her it is pure folly. Freddie thinks about the young Mrs. Deegan who simply sat down after finding her husband hanging in the barn. Thinks about the sadness that rooted her to the ground, sealed her tongue forever. Freddie understands this now, understands why Mrs. Deegan had her own tombstone inscribed as well the day her husband was buried.

It did storm the night that Isabelle died, just as Freddie had thought. She knows now that whenever the wind picks up and there is the breath of dampness in the air, a rumble of thunder on the horizon, she will revisit that night.

The images pop in her head on a continual loop. Jewel collapsing in the sheriff's arms. The harsh overhead light in Isabelle's room. Isabelle in a pool of blood on the bed. Her baby, a girl, puddled between her legs. *Abruption*, the doctor had called it. The dislodging of the placenta before birth. The baby followed the placenta out instead of the other way round. It had drowned in its own blood and, for good measure, killed Isabelle in the process. No one is there to give the baby a name. Freddie wonders if Isabelle would have named her Alice? She can think of no other name. She imagines the headstone with both their names and the writings on the Deegans' tomb: BELOVED, DEVOTED.

She and Jewel are not speaking, are avoiding each other as best they can. She knows that Jewel imagines she holds her responsible for Isabelle's death, and she tries to resist the urge, but cannot. The doctor said it was all a terrible, tragic calamity. A lamentation. No way to see it coming. Perhaps. Freddie thinks, trying to convince herself that what she believes cannot—could not—be true. But she has lived with Jewel too long, and there is a dread that rattles around her head like a pebble at the bottom of an empty milk pail. Jewel. Jewel. Jewel.

"The phone," Jewel screamed at her, at the sheriff, at the ambulance driver when he arrived. "I couldn't call. I couldn't call.

And she just started to bleed. To bleed and bleed. There was no way to stop it. I never knew there could be so much blood." Jewel shrieked again until Freddie forced her to sit down. She brought her a wet cloth from the kitchen and gave it to her so she could wipe her face. Poured her a sip of bourbon from Mr. Odom's bottle in the kitchen. Freddie sat on the porch beside her. Jewel quieted, but continued to sob. Each broken catch of breath sounded to Freddie like the snap of a whip. She could not cry.

Mr. Odom's body at the bottom of the steps was more a nuisance than of interest to those who arrived at the house. In fact, the ambulance driver and his attendant moved him out onto the front porch and covered him with a cloth to get him out of the way. They were all more concerned with Isabelle. She could not merely be moved out of the way, covered with a sheet. The sheriff used his radio to call back to his office. They sent out someone to clean up inside the house. They sent the undertaker. And the coroner. And the newspaper. It was dawn before they were gone. The sheriff told Freddie that he had asked for someone to come out and check on the phone. He told her they will talk after the funeral. She and Jewel went into the house, silent not only in the new morning, but stilled now by death as well. They washed. They changed clothes. They waited for what comes next.

It does not seem like a week to Freddie. It seems to have been a moment ago. An eternity caught inside a flash of lightning from the storm. In that week, she had things to keep her focused. And Jewel had the women from her church to occupy and distract her. Now, Isabelle and Mr. Odom and Baby Alice are buried. Freddie thinks about the young Mrs. Deegan. She wonders what comes next.

Freddie hears the creak of the screen door. Jewel lowers herself with a sigh into the chair next to Freddie.

"I thought I might join you," she says. "Have my coffee before I begin cooking breakfast. Is there anything you want in particular?"

"Nothing I have a mind for. Just whatever you make for yourself will do."

"I was thinking we might drive over to the Belks in Florence this afternoon. I need to get new linens for my bedroom. We could have lunch out. Eat at the Skyview if you want. I know you like their hot dogs, and you won't have to dress up."

Freddie imagines she would prefer being trapped inside a locked box with a nest of stinging wasps than to spend the day trapped with Jewel in a car listening to her incessant babbling. "Not today, Jewel. I will take you some other day. Not today."

"I need to get new linens," Jewel insists. "Those were ruined."

"It's not like we will be having guests. It won't hurt to let the bed stay unmade another night or two."

"Except that I don't want to do that. I like things the way I like them. I want to get back to my life."

Freddie thinks for a moment what that means. Her life. Their life. Her and Jewel morning after morning, meal upon meal, day unto day."

"I have boxed up all of his things. Hers too. There isn't much. We can give them to the Goodwill. Someone could benefit from them I'm sure."

"No."

"We can't keep them, Freddie. What use do we have for his suits or those homemade smocks? And when you think about it, we didn't even really know them. And it will be good to get back to some sense of normalcy," says Jewel.

"I knew her," says Freddie.

"What?"

"I knew her. And I will not allow you to simply box her up and dispose of her like she was yesterday's newspaper."

"The sooner we put all of this behind us the better."

Freddie pauses. *What if I am not ready to put this behind me? What if I can never put this behind me?* Instead, she says, "I hope you don't mind, but I really don't care for company right now. I was enjoying sitting here alone. With my thoughts."

"And what if I do mind?"

Freddie lifts her gaze, puzzled. "I am not sure what you mean."

"Where does that leave me, Freddie? You, with your thoughts. And me. Just left."

"I don't mean it to be rude, Jewel, but I just can't. Not right now." She sinks back into her chair.

Jewel stands. "Well, I guess that settles that. Blame me if you will . . ."

"That is not what I said."

"But it is what you meant. You have decided. Just like you always do."

"I don't know what you want from me," Freddie says, her voice rising. "Just leave me be."

"At least he was decent company," says Jewel. "It was pleasant to have someone to talk to that paid me more attention than if I was a fence post."

"He was a shit-hole bastard is what he was," says Freddie. "And don't try to tell me any differently. I am glad he is dead. I am glad I killed him."

"Likewise," says Jewel.

"What do you mean by that?" asks Freddie.

"It means what it means," says Jewel.

"You are talking about the girl, aren't you? You don't have sense enough to know what you are saying."

"I know that she played you as a fool."

"You shut the hell up."

"Or what? Or what, Freddie?"

Freddie clasps her hands and presses her thumbs against her temples. "Jesus, Jewel. You are giving me a headache."

"Because all you do is think. You are not pleasant to be with, Freddie Bramble. You are not good company."

"Is that what he said about me?" Freddie asks.

"I don't think either of you cared for the other very much. That much was plain."

"But you liked him."

"You don't understand. I liked having *someone*. Someone besides you to cook for. Someone to tell me that I looked nice. Someone to talk about with my friends."

"So, go and call your goddamn friends," says Freddie. "You have your phone back. Call them and talk. Talk about whatever pleases you till your tongue falls out of your head. I don't care. Just please leave me alone."

"So you can sit and brood about that girl."

"Yes."

"It is your fault she is dead. We should have sent her away when she came. You should have done as I asked."

"I know."

"If you sent her away, none of this would have happened."

"Why do you say that?" asks Freddie.

"Because. If you had listened to me, if you had done what I asked, this could have been avoided. It is your fault that she is dead. I know you blame me. But you bear the responsibility for this. You had no right to put me through that."

"I don't blame you."

Jewel sips from her cup. "I woke up this morning and do you know what I was thinking about?"

"Who knows, Jewel? Who cares? New linens for your bed."

"I was thinking about Mr. Landry. And Mr. Potts."

Freddie is surprised to hear their names. It has been years since Jewel has mentioned either of them.

"I guess that would be only natural," she says. "With all the commotion, it is bound to set your mind on the past. I think sometimes about Lt. Calder. How he survived the war only to die on the train coming home from the hospital."

"No," says Jewel. "I wasn't thinking about their deaths. I was thinking about if they had lived. I could have made a life with Mr. Landry. I was happy enough with Mr. Potts as well."

"Then why didn't you?"

"You know why."

"Jewel, please don't pursue this. Nothing good will come from it."

"I didn't stay with them because I could never leave you."

"That's not so," says Freddie. "I am perfectly capable of taking care of myself."

"Sure, you can fry an egg when you are hungry and wash your drawers when they are dirty. But remember how you cut your hair when I was living in Charleston. How long would it have been before you made a complete spectacle of yourself?"

"If you were living in Charleston, then you never would have known. You didn't stay with Mr. Landry or Mr. Potts or Mr. Odom, for that matter, because you are a greedy, greedy woman who couldn't wait to get her hands on their money."

"I didn't stay with them because I am loyal to you. I have always been loyal—to you! Only you. Why can't you see that? Appreciate what I do for you?"

"Because you drive me crazy. You are always at me. At me. I would appreciate if you just left me be. Please."

"When Papa . . . died . . . I didn't say anything because I knew how he had treated you. I thought perhaps it was fair."

"Are you saying this has all been my doing?"

"No, I am saying I have always chosen you—over Papa. Over Mr. Landry. Over Mr. Potts. Over Conrad."

"So what? What do you want from me?"

"I want you to listen to me! That is what I am saying. Listen to me! You think you are so smart, that you have it all figured out. You didn't even tell me that it was the day you had arranged to remove Conrad. You just decided. And that was that. Why didn't you tell me? You didn't have that right. We were in this together. I did everything I was asked to do, but you didn't trust me enough not to tell me."

"No," says Freddie. "I didn't."

"I hate you," says Jewel. "For that. And for the thousand hurts you inflict on me every day. For thinking that living here with you is enough for me—for anyone. Did you think that you could just eliminate Conrad and that I would allow you to keep her here? Just because you had a mind to. I know that is what you were thinking. I know that is what you had planned. And you thought that you would just decide to do it and I would agree."

"Yes," says Freddie. "I wanted her to stay here—with me."

"You would choose her."

"Yes. Yes, I would choose her."

"Then I am glad she is dead. I am glad I killed her," Jewel says, smoothing out her apron. "You are not the only one who can decide these things."

"No," says Freddie. "She died in childbirth. A terrible tragedy, but no one's fault." She knows, however, even as she speaks that what she says is a deceit, knows that what Jewel says is true. Has known it from the moment she saw Jewel on the steps covered in Isabelle's blood. To hear it, though, to have it become real made her fear the sky will crack and the sun rising over them will fall from the heavens and that the night stars will pour down around them, that she will come unrooted from the earth itself and float away into oblivion. It cannot be. It cannot be.

"All it took was a jab," Jewel says, balling up her fist. "To her belly. I hated that little slut. And to think you would imagine you could . . . Never! A jab. And then . . ."

"You are a lying bitch. I will never forgive you this!"

"I killed her. As sure as I am standing here. By myself. I planned it. Day by day. No one knew. Not even you. Hell, you even went to the store to buy me some Dairyland. A little bit in her grits. In her eggs. In her fig preserves. Just enough so that when it was time for the baby, she would have bled out. Easy as that. Over and done with. But you would not wait for that. You forced my hand."

"No," says Freddie. "It isn't true. It cannot be true. If I thought it was true, I would sell my share of the farm and leave here forever, and you can talk yourself to death, you stupid, vain cow."

"Believe me or not," says Jewel. "She is still dead and buried."

"Why are you telling me this? Don't you know that I could do worse to you than what I did to him?"

"I am not afraid of you. Any more than you should be afraid of me."

"Why didn't you just kill me as well? Then you and Mr. Odom could have lived here without any bother. I wouldn't be here to spoil it for you."

"You don't understand at all. We had an agreement, Freddie. You are my sister—and we had an agreement between us. I was prepared—am prepared—to honor that. I cannot confess to understand what it was you felt for that girl, but it did not fit into our plans. Just like I knew that I could not keep Conrad here forever. But there is no way I could allow you to have her here."

"Allow me?"

Jewel reaches over and picks up the teacup and saucer, holding them out in her hands. "Allow you. Just like I allow you to drink from this stupid cup every morning. This damned saucer." She leans over close to Freddie, the cup and saucer between them. "You know, every morning I get up and I want to smash these precious pieces of yours to bits."

"They don't bother you," says Freddie. "They have nothing to do with you."

"I hate them. I hate them simply because you love them so much. I hate them because they mean something to you. Something that belongs only to you. But I do not smash them. I allow you to drink your coffee out of the goddamn saucer like a field hand every morning. I allow you to put on your work pants and your work boots and your men's shirt and stomp around the field. Because you are my sister and we made an agreement that this would be our life together. But you cannot change that agreement without my consent." She raises her left hand, which holds the saucer, as if to toss it against the wall. "Do you understand me?"

A sharp knife cuts behind Freddie's eyes and she winces with the pain. Her ears ring with faraway bells. Bees bite at her fingertips and toes.

"Do you understand me?"

"Yes," Freddie cries. "Yes, I understand. What I don't understand is why people can be so cruel."

"To get what we want," replies Jewel. "To endure the atrocities that life thrusts upon us. Now, I am going to make breakfast. I will call you when it is ready. Then we are going to drive into Florence and I am going to shop for new linens. And when I am done, we will have lunch at the Skyview. And then we will come home." She puts the cup and saucer on the table next to Freddie. Freddie ponders them for a moment; forgotten objects from a museum they seem to her.

Freddie climbs out of her chair with difficulty. She cannot breathe. The sunlight scorches her eyes and the ringing in her ears has turned to a shrill, piercing alarm. She lumbers down the stairs and across the yard with only one thought in her mind—to throw herself onto Isabelle's grave, to beg her forgiveness. For bringing her here. For wanting her to stay. For thinking that things could be different.

But she does not even make it to the edge of the yard before the ground melts beneath her and swallows her like a molten green lake. The grass fills her mouth. She feels the pulse of the sunlight in her veins. She watches sideways as an ant crawls up her arm. When she tries to shake it off, she discovers she has turned to stone.

## . . . 7 . . .

Freddie lives for twelve years after her stroke, dying in 1965. Jewel does not move her to a rest home as many would have done, but keeps her at the house, hiring a full-time nurse to attend to her. Accommodations have to be made, of course. There is no way to carry her from one level to the next, so Freddie's bedroom is moved downstairs into what had been the dining room. Jewel takes over the larger bedroom for herself. The nurse sleeps in the room where Isabelle had died.

The stroke leaves Freddie paralyzed completely on her left side. If she can speak, no one knows, since she does not. If she is able to see, to understand, no one can tell since she does not respond. The nurse tells her friends that Jewel is a dutiful, doting sister. She insists on feeding Freddie at every meal, talking to her in soft, soothing tones. And in the morning, she makes her coffee for her, and after the nurse has wheeled Freddie to her resting spot in the parlor or the kitchen or the porch, Jewel brings it to her and holds the mug—which reads, WORLD'S BEST SISTER—to Freddie's lips until she has finished every drop.

The nurse drives Jewel wherever she needs to go—to Lurdelle's, to church, to her committee meetings. Jewel also has Mr. Ray's work crew construct a ramp from the kitchen steps so the nurse can push Freddie to the car so she can accompany them on their outings.

One such event is the dedication of the Bramble window at the Christ the Shepherd Methodist Church. The women of the Stained Glass Committee put forth a petition to name the window in honor of Jewel and her family since she has experienced more hardship than a good Christian should have to. As an expression of her appreciation for this gesture, Jewel increases her donation by $2500. Jewel gives the nurse some money to buy a new dress for the dedication ceremony, and on the day, the nurse wheels Freddie down to the front of the church so she can sit next to Jewel, who has the place of honor in the front pew.

There is a great celebration in her honor, and a covered dish dinner afterward in the reception hall. During the dedication, the preacher says many kind things about Jewel, about her willingness to help those in need. He makes special mention of her kindness in tending to her infirm sister, and those sitting close enough swear they can see a tear flow down Freddie's cheek.

Jewel lives for over twenty years after Freddie's death, dying in 1987. By then, she has sold off nearly all the land to a developer who plans to build a country club and golf course residences for people in Morris. He even consents to calling the development Bramble Estates, so people will know it had been part of the farm. As for the house, she gifts that to the State Historical Society with the provision they maintain the house and grounds for visitors.

But for all her good works and donations, Jewel cannot fend off the punishing march of age, and she ultimately has to be taken to a private nursing home in Florence, when she is found by her caretaker one morning wandering without her nightgown out on the highway. When she is coherent, Jewel tells everyone that she hates the place, hates the food, wants to go home. In her less lucid moments, she weeps for Freddie, a name that means nothing to the people at the nursing home, who assume Freddie must be the name of a dead husband or child.

When she dies, Jewel is returned to the Bramble Farm, as it is known by everyone in the low country of South Carolina. Most of her friends from Christ the Shepherd Methodist Church have died or are in nursing homes themselves, and she is buried next to Freddie in a simple ceremony attended only by the funeral home staff. Her tombstone is identical to Freddie's, with only her name and dates of birth and death to mark the difference. And there they lie, side by side, to this very day.

# Sandra and the Snake Handlers

... 1 ...

Before Carson's death, if you had asked Sandra to explain how the universe worked, she might have told you that we are all connected in the mind of God, each of us to one another, not in a way that you can see really, but more like the way you can trace the outline of a shape using the stars. See, there is a fish. There, balanced scales. It took imagination and faith to believe. And not simply that we are connected to each other, but to everything—to ourselves. So that if you could somehow manage to draw your finger from one event in her life to another, you could sketch the outline of her being—see how she fit into the whole scheme of things. However, if you were to ask her the same question after Carson's death, she would probably have told you to go fuck yourself—or that you better learn that God loved no one, no thing, and His creation was nothing more than a festering puncture in the empty sky, waiting to swallow us whole. So was she changed by her husband's death.

It was staggering really, the way Carson's death caught Sandra totally off her guard. Sure, she understood that people died—she wasn't a nitwit after all—she had studied to become a LPN before she married, and even worked at a nursing home. And since Carson would have been sixty-two the next month, they had attended plenty of funerals for men younger than he. Still, the reality of his death was stunning, like the hailstorm that came without warning and destroyed her hydrangea bushes last August. People had called that freakish, a caprice of nature. Carson's death, they told her, was God's will. Take your pick. She couldn't see any difference between the two.

The way it happened was like this. It was the year after Hurricane Floyd and all the terrible flooding that followed. Sandra and Carson had not evacuated. They never did. She always had plenty of canned goods in the pantry, and there was a generator in the garage if the power went out. They had lived long enough along the coast to know what to do, how to prepare. They had weathered plenty of storms together: Diana and Hugo. They both remembered Hazel as well, though Sandra was still a young girl and lived with her family in the mountains when that storm had struck. Still, this was different. Floyd was a slow-moving storm, so there was plenty of time to anticipate and prepare. At church on the Sunday before, there had been plenty of talk about when and where the storm might come ashore. A group of men agreed to meet on Tuesday to board up the Bramble stained glass window if the storm's course hadn't changed. Helen Hobbs said she would host a group for a vigil to "pray the worst of it up the coast." Sandra thought that seemed mean-spirited and petty—why should they benefit from someone else's misery? She did not want to believe that God worked like that. But that had been before.

On The Weather Channel, Floyd covered a space the size of Texas, and what no one predicted was the torrential, unrelenting rain. It began early on a Thursday morning, the sky deep and terrible, trembling with wind and thunder. For hours they sat as the rain began—hard, fierce, angry. She imagined Noah's family sitting in the ark, waiting for the skies to open and wash away the sins of the world. How hard that rain must have been. How long that rain must have lasted. But she knew what Noah and his family had lived through could have been no more awful than this—it was as if God Himself was pelting the earth. It came in waves, hard sheets of water blowing sideways through the trees. They had covered all the windows with plywood, and when the power failed just after noon, they sat in the gray twilight, Carson fiddling the dials of the transistor radio to get the latest updates. Often there was a snap of a tree limb cracking away from the trunk; occasionally, the crash of a whole tree coming down. What they couldn't see were the tree trunks that had uprooted themselves and lodged in the drainage pipes next to the highway so that the rushing water could not pass through. It didn't take long for the water to begin to rise. Higher and higher it came, over the roads, over the driveways, up into the yard. When Carson opened the door to get a glimpse and cast the flashlight over the front yard, it was as if their house sat marooned in the middle of a giant murky lake. Off in the distance, Sandra could see her patio furniture drifting away in the dark.

It was three days before they could leave the house. Even after the rain stopped, it took a long time for the water to recede. When they finally ventured out, they discovered cushions and chairs and couches washed up along the sides of the road like debris from a shipwreck. Sandra would never forget the dead pigs—swollen and bleached along the creek bank near the house. The news told them to boil all the water and to be careful and watch for snakes. There was a story that one woman had found a nest of moccasins living in her oven when she returned from evacuating. The thought of snakes terrified Sandra.

Carson had hugged her and told her that once again God had spared them. There was damage, but nothing they couldn't repair. They were luckier than so many others. How wrong he was.

The men from FEMA and the State Department of Transportation, officious sorts with large bellies slung over ill-fitting pants, men consumed by their new sense of importance, came by to tell them that they needed to widen their drainage ditch—so that the next time there was a storm, the water could flow more easily. Sandra knew that was just so much nonsense—when there was that much water, it did not matter how large the hole was for it to go into, it would still overflow and flood. They left measurements with Carson and told him the backhoe would be around in a week or two.

When the backhoe arrived, it dug a trench that was nearly seven feet deep at least and as wide as it was deep. Sandra never minded the new ditch. In fact, it gave her an odd sense of security to have the separation from their house and the highway. It reminded her of a moat, like in the stories of castles and knights. But Carson wasn't pleased one bit. He said it was a scar on the land. That it ruined their property value. "Might as well be living in a trailer with a bunch of tires painted white to mark the driveway. That damn thing is good for only one thing—a pit for every piece of trash to dump their cans and bottles." So, he hired a second-year student in turf management from the community college to come over and instruct him how to blend the ditch into the landscape. Which he did. It took another backhoe and two extra workmen a solid day to even out the ditch so that it became a part of the total fabric of the place, and Carson was pleased with the result. But the incline was still steep and the ditch was over six feet deep at its center.

The day of the accident, a Saturday, Carson was out riding his Toro Lawn Master just like he did every weekend. He was deeply proud of their home and the four and a half acres surrounding it. He had spent the better part of the year restoring and improving the house and the yard after the hurricane so that what damage had been done had been erased. Shaded by pecan and dogwood trees, the house itself was a modest, three-bedroom brick ranch, set back from Highway 905 at the end of a long gravel driveway. Flowering shrubs and plants rotated in the beds along its border— azaleas and agapanthus in the spring and summer, mums and pansies in the fall, purple-frilled ornamental cabbages in the winter. Sandra would have preferred to have lived in Bramble Estates, where you had neighbors close by, but Carson said there were too many rules there, and he didn't want anyone telling him what he could do with his own land. They had plenty of room out back for a vegetable garden as well, and Carson kept the portion of the property that was lawn manicured like an enormous putting green.

He was mowing out near Highway 905, which ran in front of the house, and doing long, lazy sweeps in and out of the new gully. When she stood on the front porch, Sandra could watch him ride the mower down the slope—he would disappear from sight as if the earth were swallowing him and the mower whole, only to reappear in a different spot with a wave of his hat like an explorer just returned from a trip to the earth's core.

But on that Saturday, as Carson angled in and out of the trench, he spied a beer bottle in his path, thrown there undoubtedly by some of the redneck teenagers at the high school who had nothing better to do than get drunk and destroy property or litter. So he stopped the mower, climbed off, and deposited the bottle into the Hefty bag he kept on hand just for such purposes. The problem came when Carson went to get back on the mower. He had parked parallel, so that his wheels were running in the same direction as the embankment rather than against it. As Carson got back onto the mower, the whole thing just tumbled over on top of him, like a child going head over yonders on a tricycle.

He didn't even come to the house straightaway. Sandra hadn't been watching him at that moment. She had been inside, happy as a clam, ignorant as a goose, re-creating a recipe from Miss Virginia's *South of the Rio Grande*, a Mexicana chicken casserole to take to a potluck dinner at church. If she had been watching, she would have called 911, she told herself later, and things might have been different. But she hadn't been watching, and so he righted the mower, climbed on, and finished his work. When he finally did come up to the house, he told her what had happened, that he felt like a durn fool for making such a stupid, careless mistake, and said he had a terrible stiff neck and a pain in his shoulder, could she please put some Deep Heat rub on it. He adamantly refused to go to the doctor.

"Doctors are for when you are sick," he said, "and I am not sick. I've just pulled something is all." But on the Tuesday following, when he wasn't feeling any better, he relented and made an appointment to see the chiropractor in Morris. She fussed and fumed, saying he needed a real doctor just this once, but Carson believed that a little poking and prodding of his muscles and a good quick snap of his neck was all he needed to make him 100% again.

She had never understood Carson's fascination with chiropractory ("chiro-quackery," she called it), but she figured it probably had something to do with his downright fear of needles. She had seen him go white as a sheet and keel over at a Red Cross Blood Drive once, and if there was ever a medical show on with an operation or where they were giving a shot to someone, he would change the channel quick as a wink or hurry off to the kitchen for a glass of water. He said having regular spinal adjustments was all he needed to keep fit, and she had to admit, they seemed to work for him. Carson was a strapping, healthy man—full-chested, muscular, with big arms and a thick coating of hair across his upper torso and stomach. She let him go to the chiropractor.

The night after his appointment he told her he felt better but complained of a slight headache and said his vision was fuzzy. He didn't eat all the dinner she had made for him—salmon croquettes with cucumber-dill sauce—and went to bed before the late news. The TV picture was hard to focus on, he said, and it was making him nauseous to look at it.

The next morning during his bowel movement, he fell off the toilet onto the bathroom floor. This time she did call 911, but it was no use. They told her at the hospital Carson had an embolism in his shoulder area, which had most likely been dislodged by the chiropractic adjustment. The strain of trying to move his bowels threw the blood clot to his brain—he was dead before he hit the floor.

She never realized how much she depended on Carson, how empty her life was without him. Sandra felt utterly lost and abandoned. This was not the way things were supposed to go. She had put in her time, lived a good, upstanding life—in her opinion, the sums did not balance out.

In the days and weeks after the funeral, anger propelled her. It was her only fuel. She was angry at the chiropractor for his negligence. She was angry at the attorney for telling her that she had no legal recourse against the chiropractor. She was angry for how her friends hovered around her when she wanted to be left alone with her grief and for how they neglected her when she needed the comfort of their company. She was angry at Carson for being so set in his ways. Angry at herself for all the things she had not done for him. But most of all she was angry at God. She had served God all her life, attended church regularly, been recording secretary for the Women's Society of Christian Service for three years in a row, and always contributed to any bake sale to raise funds for the youth group or for mission work. It was not fair that she be repaid like this.

One night, she rolled the Toro Lawn Master from the tool shed Carson had built adjoining the garage. She could not bring herself to sit on the mower and drive it, and it took nearly all her strength to push it out behind the house to the edge of the vegetable garden. If anyone could have seen her as they drove past on Highway 905, she reckoned they would have thought her mad, rushing around in her nightclothes in the middle of the night, barefoot, her hair uncombed, unkempt. She soaked the mower with gasoline and, standing back, flicked a lighted match in its direction. That was all that was needed. The mower ignited with a *whumpf*, and as she shielded her face from the heat of the blaze, she looked to the dark, moonless sky. She thought how in India and other, non-Christian countries, wives would often throw themselves onto the blazing funeral pyre. Whereas once she would have thought such an act to be irrational or uncivilized, now it did not seem entirely without logic or merit to her.

"You wanted a sacrifice," she said. "Here is your burning altar, you son of a bitch." She left the mower smoldering in the back-yard, unconcerned if it burned the garden or the yard or the whole damn house as far as she cared. The next morning, when Peggy Adcock called to say she and her husband, Donald, had seen what they thought was a fire coming from the direction of her house, was she okay, Sandra told her to mind her own damn business, to take care of her husband, and to leave her alone.

The hardest thing to get used to was cooking for one. It broke her heart just to think of having to halve the recipes that she made every night for Carson and herself—Meatloaf Surprise, chicken divan, stuffed flank steak. She could not bear to do it. Even worse was the concept of leftovers. Packing his uneaten portion into Tupperware for the following night. That made it seem to her that Carson was away on some interminable business trip—while she was left behind, dutifully stockpiling food, always waiting, waiting, waiting for his return.

She finally settled on sandwiches. She could make herself a

sandwich and there was nothing left over. Nothing wasted. Nothing in excess. It was a perfect meal made for one—a widow's meal. She ate them for nearly every meal except breakfast, when she would have toast instead.

The yard began to grow up around the house. The vegetables they had planted in the garden, she left rotting on the vines. Weeds choked the flowers in their beds. She could not sleep, and spent days in her nightdress, wandering through the house or sitting vacant in front of the TV, flipping the channels between the Home Shopping Network or infomercials for exercise equipment or get-rich-quick real-estate schemes. One afternoon, Sandra took the duct tape from Carson's workbench and sealed off the spare rooms in the house—rooms she did not use regularly, rooms she felt she no longer needed. She removed all reminders of her past life, souvenirs and photos from the mantel and hallway—framed snaps of her and Carson when they had vacationed in Flat Rock or Cypress Gardens—and placed them in the rooms like artifacts into a crypt. When she was done and nearly all the duct tape used up, only the kitchen and the den and her bedroom remained opened. She had considered shutting off the bedroom as well since she no longer slept in her bed, but the bathroom was in there, as were her clothes.

She did not answer the calls left for her on the answering machine by the church ladies. Finally, she turned off the machine and just let the phone ring itself to exhaustion. One day she heard a car in the driveway. She peeked through the curtains. It was the young, pimply-faced minister who had been assigned to their congregation. He had preached Carson's funeral and she hated him for it. She did not answer the door. He stood for a long time in the doorway, first ringing the door bell, then knocking, then ringing again. Finally, Sandra decided he wasn't going to leave, and opened the door.

He seemed startled by her. "We haven't seen you at services for a long while and we—I was wondering—hoping you are all right."

"You've seen me," said Sandra. "Now go away." She closed the door in his face.

She wrote a letter to the church and told them to cancel her membership. It was as easy as stopping a magazine subscription. She started driving into Myrtle Beach for her groceries. It took longer, but she did not have to encounter anyone she knew. Friends from the past whose lives had continued on their merry ways. The TV became her only friend, her companion. She had it on continuously—it did not matter what was on, as long as there was sound, voices.

She learned by heart the names of the soap characters and the intricacies of their dilemmas as if they were her own blood kin: would Brooke sleep with Tad, would Natalie's evil twin leave Ashley imprisoned in the basement, would Summer tell Adam the baby was not his but his brother Jason's. She became an expert on retail prices for major brand-name items, and would curse and yell at the contestants on *The Price Is Right* when their stupidity cost them the grand prize. "Everyone knows the large-size Armor All is more expensive than a single-serve can of Dinty Moore Beef Stew. You stupid bastard. I could leave here right now and go out and buy two cans of Dinty Moore *and* a loaf of bread for what you say it costs. You didn't deserve the maple bedroom suite. I'm glad you lost everything. That should teach you, you sorry asshole."

As the late summer turned to fall and fall fell into winter, her life with Carson became a vague memory—like the photographs she had stuck away in the drawers of the bureau in the sealed-off room, left to yellow, turn brittle, decay. She wondered if it would have been better if she had died as well.

Then, on the second Sunday in January, a cold, steel-gray day, the strangest thing occurred. Sundays were always hard for Sandra because there weren't any soaps or game shows. TV was filled during the day with public service programs, news commentaries, sports events, and religious services. Sundays interrupted her routine, made her uneasy, agitated. On that Sunday she was standing in the kitchen making herself a bacon and egg salad sandwich, using the remote to scan the airwaves for company. She had breezed past two old coots talking about politics, a black-and-white western movie, and a children's show with a talking hippo, when she suddenly heard Carson's voice. She halted dead in her tracks. "And I tell you, brethren, the du-hay of the La-hord shall ca-hum!" She stopped chopping the sweet pickle for the egg salad, wiped her hands on a dish towel, and went to see what Carson was doing on TV. Sandra squinted her eyes. It wasn't Carson, not really, she knew, but it could have been him when he was younger or perhaps his brother if he had had one.

There on the picture tube stood a handsome, clean-shaven man in his early thirties wearing a white shirt with the sleeves rolled up to reveal muscular forearms, his striped tie loosened and collar button undone so his chest hair popped out of the top of his shirt. He waved a floppy leather-bound Bible in one hand and pointed his other hand directly at her. Sandra was mesmerized as he disclosed the untold glories of heaven and the ferocious perils of hell. The way he described them sounded like he had visited both firsthand. Heaven was endless green pastures and golden streets. Hell was fiery lakes and mountains of molten lava. If he had been selling tickets to either place, Sandra would have bought one just to see for herself.

This wasn't some scrawny pale preacher. This was a man—a real man, strong and self-assured—a farmer or laborer who had taken up the call. As he preached, striding around the platform, pounding the podium for emphasis, his dark, wavy hair, which he had slicked back, became disheveled and fell across his forehead almost covering his left eye. He smoothed it back without notice.

That gesture. That confidence. Sandra stood transfixed.

She felt hot and dreamy as his words poured out of the television over her. It was then she realized she was touching herself—down there. She was shocked to become conscious of it—she had always left those matters to Carson. But she didn't stop. Instead, she pulled her nightdress up and waved her privates at the preacher. He waved his finger back at her. She spread her legs wide so he could see. The camera zoomed in on the preacher for a close-up shot. She pulled her fingers from inside and brought them to her mouth to taste the delicate saltiness of herself. The preacher closed his eyes, tilting his head back toward heaven. His smile was ecstatic. He began to pray softly, earnestly.

Sandra stuck her fingers back in deeper, harder.

"Come to Jesus today," he crooned.

"Yes," said Sandra. "To Jesus. Come to Jesus."

Her knees gave way beneath her and she slumped down onto the braided rug in front of the TV. She held herself—her body felt electrified, on fire. In the background, she heard an announcer invite her to join Reverend Shep Waters next Sunday morning, same time, same station. Sandra looked up from the floor, hoping to catch another glimpse of the preacher, but it was too late. Shep was already gone and she was alone again. The emptiness roared within her.

It took a long while before Sandra got up from the floor. She felt as if she were waking from a fever dream or some sort of drugged sleep. She threw the sandwich she had made into trash. She felt queasy, as if she was going to vomit. She showered—turning the water on as hot as she could stand, using the cloth to scrub her skin till it was red, nearly raw. She toweled off with her back to the mirror. She did not think she could stand to face herself.

How could she have done such a thing? She was nearly sixty years old and she had never ever done anything like that in her life. Even when she was a girl, she never dreamed that it was something a woman could do—would do—to herself. Yet, coupled with the shame was another sensation—deeper, and more troubling to her, the almost delicious feeling that she had been outrageous, that she had crossed a boundary of some sort. If her women's circle at church knew what she had done, they would have been shocked by her behavior, mortified.

She resolved that it was an aberration, something brought on by the shock of Carson's death. It would never happen again. She would not allow it. To ensure this, she decided that the next Sunday, when she knew Shep Waters would be preaching, she would take a long walk around the house and the property. But when she woke on Sunday, it was storming fiercely outside and a walk was out of the question. Another of God's cruel jokes on her, she thought. Then, without realizing it, she found herself bathed, perfumed, her hair combed, makeup applied, dressed in a pale blue satin peignoir, one she kept tucked in the rose-scented drawer of her dresser that held her special lingerie.

As the hour approached for Shep's arrival, she fluffed the pillows on the couch and made sure there were no sandwich crumbs on the rug. Instinctively, she knew everything needed to be just right.

And then he was on the air. She watched intently as the announcer introduced the *Hour of Praise and Worship* brought to her by the Shep Waters International Evangelical Ministries. There was singing and Bible reading, and during much of the first part of the hour, Shep was merely a peripheral figure, though there were video clips of him at various rallies and crusades. He was always dressed the same: dark slacks, white shirt and tie, and the effect was unfailing—he always looked rugged and intensely masculine, as if he had just come from closing up a hardware store or checking to see if there was enough feed for the livestock or doing some other sort of men's business.

Sitting in the maple rocker Carson had bought for her at Christmas three years ago, she tried to resist the urges she felt, wanting to merely listen as Shep preached. There was no harm in that, she told herself. She had not gone to church in over ten months; maybe there was something she could gain from the sermon. But before she knew it, her nightgown was hiked up around her waist so that she could finger herself as he talked. Her touch was light at first, like a feather duster, but as the sermon progressed it became more intense—searching deeper, probing.

The address lasted nearly twenty minutes and even though it was freezing cold outside, Sandra was perspiring heavily as he reached the end, when he gave the altar call. She wept as those on TV crowded around Shep to have him touch them, pray for them. She could almost feel his gentle caress as he laid his hands on them. She untied the top of her gown so Shep could see her breasts. He opened his arms to her and she got down on her knees in front of the TV to kiss his image on the screen. "You must pray every day," he implored. "You must pray every day and you must read the Word every day so that God will stamp it in your heart."

"Yes, I will," she said. "Every day. I promise." The static from the TV tickled her bare skin and her climax was even more ferocious than the week prior. She let herself lie back in the golden glow of the moment. She felt alive. She felt loved.

And then he was gone again. Sandra thought she would die knowing it would be another week before she could see him again. Even worse was the understanding that what had happened was no accident, no aberration. That what had occurred last week and then again today would take place next Sunday as well. And she felt helpless to control what was happening. It was as if a force greater than herself compelled her.

It was then that Sandra got the strangest idea. Perhaps Carson's death was not an accident after all. Perhaps it had been Divine Intervention. Carson's death. Then the appearance of Shep Waters like Moses and the burning bush. What else could it be? Moses had been tending sheep when God called him to lead the people of Israel out of Egypt. When Moses had doubted his ability, Jehovah had replied: "I AM WHAT I AM." Yes, God was God, and He had somehow decided He needed Sandra for something—something so important that she needed to be free to follow His instructions. Ruth and Naomi had been widows. Yes. And God had used them to do great things. All that had come before had been a part of God's plan for her. The hurricane. Carson's accident. It was all necessary, like the flood that cleansed the world for Noah. Now she was free—no more women's circle at church, no more potluck suppers. She had been chosen. Like Mary, she could feel the Spirit of God move up inside her like a warm hand. Why else had she been free to touch herself, to open herself up like never before. There could be no other explanation for it. She just had not been able to see it before.

Sandra lifted herself from the floor, ignoring her peignoir that hung carelessly about her waist, and raced to the front bedroom. She ripped the duct tape off the door frame with the zeal of an archeologist unearthing an ancient tomb, looking for hidden treasure. Once inside, she pillaged through the piles of things she had crammed into the space. Finally, she retrieved the heavy, gilt-edged Bible that her mother had given to her and Carson as a wedding gift.

Sandra didn't even bother to reseal the room—what was the point now? She couldn't be bothered shutting out the past anymore. The past had no bearing on her now. Now she had purpose.

She was reborn. Her destiny lay with Shep Waters. She wasn't sure how or why just yet, but she knew.

She managed to read from Genesis through to Numbers the first night, and by the time Shep arrived the next Sunday, she was almost to the New Testament. She would read and reread passages, making soft, cooing sounds to herself, as she sought to understand the great mysteries held within the words. "Oooh, yes! Ah! I see. Ummm. So there you have it." When Shep preached the next Sunday, Sandra didn't even bother to dress. She stood naked in the den in front of the TV, singing with the congregation, shouting "Hallelujah" or "Amen" when he said something that was particularly exciting—one hand holding the Bible, the other free to do its business.

Though she had no clothes on, it had still taken her the longest time to make herself ready. The preparations had started on Thursday, when she had gone shopping for food. Sandra scoured the cosmetics counter at the Eckerd's drugstore, searching for just the right shades of blush, powder, eye shadow, and lipstick. She was enthralled by the names on the tiny tubes: Scarlet Interlude, Passion's Kiss, Flaming Desire. On Saturday night before rolling her hair, she washed it and gave it a cream rinse, then used Lady Clairol to brighten the dusty gray-blond bits. The next morning, Sunday, or Shep-day as she had begun to think of it, she tweezed her eyebrows and used pencil to give them a dramatic arch, then took nearly an hour with her eyeliner and shadow. Sandra had never worn much makeup—Carson didn't care for it, but she knew Shep would want her to look like his goddess. When she was done, her face was a dramatic palate of lavender around her eyes, pink across the tops of her cheeks, and blood crimson on her mouth.

It continued in this way for weeks, perhaps months, for time ceased to exist for Sandra. There was only one day each week for her. Every other day was a leading up to or a falling away from. Sunday nights were the worst, with so long before the next time, but she would steel herself with prayer and Bible study. She subscribed to the publications put out by the ministry and sent money to help pay for the work that he did—their work. She ordered elegant costume jewelry and naughty negligees from the hostesses on the Home Shopping Network. She studied the characters on the soaps, the ones closer to her age, to see how they presented themselves, made themselves attractive, alluring. She knew the time would come when this would be important for her.

Then, one Sunday as she lay on the floor relishing the glorious tremors that shook her body after Shep had entreated her to surrender to Christ, she heard something too wonderful to even believe. As the announcer listed the locations for a series of crusades, he said, "And we invite all our friends in the Carolinas to join us for a week of revival at the Greensboro Coliseum." Sandra jumped up to write down the details—*as if she could forget them!* Carson had taken her to the ACC basketball tournament in Greensboro years before. He had won tickets in an office pool, so they made a weekend of it, staying in a motel near the Coliseum. Greensboro was less than four hours away. She could drive there easily—to meet Shep. Who would be waiting for her.

## ... 2 ...

On the night before she left for the meetings in Greensboro—*four of them—four!*—where Shep would be preaching—*in person!*—Sandra laid out all her clothes on the bed before gently packing them into the suitcase. Running her hand over the soft, luxurious fabrics reminded her of another night so long ago when she had packed her bag to go on a honeymoon. *Another night so similar in its anticipation, its possibility.* Tonight, everything was organized to the most minute detail so that each night her appearance would be totally coordinated: jewelry, shoes, handbags, lingerie. It was vital to make a good impression.

The first night of the crusade she would wear her cream lamb's wool suit with matching cowl neck insert—*guaranteed to make her the center of attention!* That particular item had also been available in jade and rust, but Sandra felt those colors too harsh for her first appearance. The following night she had selected a violet velour pantsuit set with a pewter-colored paisley tunic. *Casual with a flair of sophistication!* This would be followed on the third night by a maroon mohair skirt topped with a sequined sweater accented by a faux fur shawl collar. *For those who understand true style and elegance!* For the final night of the crusade, she chose a Diane Von Furstenberg silk fringed animal print ensemble. *Daring and dramatic!* That particular item had not arrived until two days before Sandra had been scheduled to leave for Greensboro, and she was nearly frantic with worry that something had happened to it in shipping. When the UPS delivery man pulled into the driveway, she let out a shout of praise to God for His goodness to her.

The morning of her departure, Sandra cleaned out the refrigerator, unplugged all the appliances, and resealed all the rooms in the house including her bedroom. Just before she closed the door on the house for the last time, she thought of something she needed, wanted to give to Shep. In the cedar chest in the den were all of Carson's things—his important papers, deeds, policies, stock certificates. It was where she had put his wedding ring when she had returned from the funeral. As Sandra unearthed the documents and relics of the past, Carson's smell came flooding over her like a presence. *So long ago!* She tried to picture him in her mind, but could never see him wholly—he remained a fragment in her vision like a puzzle piece. Next to the box with his ring was Carson's gun. She had forgotten it was there, but now that she had found it, she knew she could not leave it behind. Carson had too often warned her about the dangers of a woman traveling alone. She made sure it was loaded and put it into her handbag along with the wedding ring.

Sandra checked into the Ramada Inn on the bypass outside of Greensboro shortly before two in the afternoon. After hanging all her clothes and setting her shoes in a neat row, she drove to find the Coliseum. She did not want to take any chances that she might get lost that night. As she rounded the corner where the map showed her to go, Sandra let out a small yelp. There it was. Right where it should be. She pulled the car over quickly to the nearest spot the traffic would allow, got out, and walked onto the grass in front of the dome-shaped building where a huge marquee proclaimed for all the world: TONIGHT! IN PERSON! SHEP WATERS! Sandra soaked the majesty of the sight into her being for as long as she could bear—*so close!*—then got back into her car and returned to the motel. It was time to make herself ready.

When Sandra arrived back that evening, the sky hung behind the auditorium like a blanket striped in alternating lines of pink and blue. *A baby's blanket!* The air was still hot and moist from the afternoon sun, but a cool breeze waved gently over the crowd that had gathered. Sandra was amazed by their number. The parking lot was nearly half full; several church busses lined the side of the building, and many groups were laying out covered dishes for supper. Pretending to have been separated from her friends, Sandra determinedly worked her way up through the throng till she was almost at the front of the line. Then, when the doors were opened, she was safely swept inside the auditorium in a crush of people so no one noticed her deceit. Once past the turnstiles, the crowd thinned as people made their way to their seats and she was free to do as she pleased.

Souvenir stands had been set up and Sandra purchased a cassette tape, *Shep's Songbook: Favorite Hymns of Shep Waters*. There were hawkers selling Ten Commandments bookmarks and black velvet paintings of the Last Supper and Jesus praying in the Garden of Gethsemane, but they were not officially sanctioned by the ministry and did not bear Shep's logo on them. Sandra would have nothing to do with them.

The Coliseum was large enough to host the circus and Ice Capades once every year, and those first in line pushed for the good seats nearest the stage. The balconies had been closed off, and downstairs large blocks were reserved for churches and for youth groups and people in wheelchairs.

Sandra quickly chose a seat on the end of a row about halfway back. She knew from the TV that Shep often went out into the crowd that far. If he did so tonight, he would come up along this path. She was certain of it.

She let her eyes scan the auditorium. Behind the stage, itself banked in rows of pink, yellow, and white gladiolus, hovered a banner: WINNING THE WORLD FOR JESUS ONE HEART AT A TIME. There was a piano and room for musicians and a choir. And in the center was the pulpit where Shep himself would stand.

In front of Sandra sat a pregnant woman in a smock decorated with pictures of traffic signs. She reminded Sandra of the instruction manual for the Department of Motor Vehicles. "It's not that I need saving," the woman said to no one in particular, "but I have heard of demons possessing babies in the womb, so you can never be too careful." A choir in purple and gold robes filed past with a clanging of tambourines on their way to the stage.

To her left, Sandra noticed a small-framed woman who sat with a young child, obviously her daughter. Sandra noticed the woman wore no wedding ring. They reminded Sandra of the mother-daughter detergent ads in the supermarket. Both wore black stretch pants held down by stirrup-like loops that ran underneath their heels, both had on shiny black knit tops outlined in silver thread, and both wore their hair long down their back and cut short in the front with bangs. The child would have looked exactly like a miniature version of her mamma except that Sandra observed one of the child's eyes was bright blue, the other a murky yellow-green. *Trash. Common trash*, thought Sandra.

"Jasmine is a singer," said the woman. "She has been on the radio with the Swing-Low Symphony." Sandra watched the child color a drawing of Jesus and the Samaritan Woman at the Well in a picture book. In the picture, Jesus sat on the edge of the well, his hands outstretched to the woman, who held a large clay pot, which the child had colored purple.

"That's a pretty picture," said Sandra.

Jasmine did not answer but glared at her with the malformed green eye as if she were abominable, contemptible, base.

"I want her to sing for Reverend Shep," continued the mamma. It had never occurred to Sandra that other women might have a desire for Shep's attention. She wasn't sure what to do about this unforeseen situation, but she knew the woman in her tacky Target outfit, reeking of Jungle Gardenia, would not stand in her way. She would not allow it.

Sandra smiled pleasantly at Jasmine's mamma. "I guess it doesn't matter about her eye then—since people can't see her on the radio."

"Her eye is a gift from the Lord," said the woman.

Sandra laughed. "That's one gift I would have thought about re-turning."

"You're a . . ." the woman spat, but Sandra ignored her, focusing on the child instead.

"Do you know what the picture you're coloring is about?"

Jasmine eyed her warily.

"The woman has come to get some water for her house—that's the way they did it in Bible days. They all went to the center of town to get water. But Jesus knew the woman had a secret—that she was living with a man, but they weren't married." Then, she shifted gears. "Tell me, Jasmine, do you sing for your daddy at home?"

Jasmine didn't speak but looked at her mamma with her one good eye for what to do, what to say. Sandra knew she had struck a blow. Jasmine's mamma shifted uneasily in her seat. "Her daddy and me ain't together," she said. "I knew him before I was born again. Jesus washes away all our past. Makes us new again."

"That He does," said Sandra.

"I'm hungry," said the child.

"I told you to eat before you left the house," replied her mother. "I told you there wasn't going to be any treats—not unless you sing real pretty."

"I don't want to sing. I want some chicken nuggets."

Quick as a breath, Jasmine's mamma had her flat-soled shoe in her hand and struck the child hard across the tops of her legs with it. The shoe left behind a whitish dust-colored mark on Jasmine, almost as if she had been stepped on. Jasmine did not flinch at the blow, but silently dropped tears onto her coloring book so Jesus faded into a picture of a leper. "As the Bible says," Jasmine's mamma confided to Sandra, as if to impress her with her parenting skills, "spare the rod and you get a spoiled brat."

The crusade service began in the way a play opens—lights dimmed and several colored spotlights raked the stage with their beams finally converging to a single circle of white light. Sandra never saw Shep make his entrance. He just appeared as if by magic in the center of the circle of light.

"Sit up now and look pretty," Jasmine's mamma told her daughter. "Maybe Reverend Shep will notice you and ask you to come on stage and sing."

Sandra let out a noticeable snort of indignation. "I thought this was to be a worship service," she said, "not a talent show."

"And the Bible says not to hide your talents under a bushel neither," replied the woman.

"Is that him?" asked Jasmine, quietly.

"Who else do you think it would be?" her mamma answered.

"He looks like a TV star," sighed Jasmine.

"As handsome as Elvis," agreed her mamma.

"He is a man of God, called to preach the gospel," chided Sandra, throwing a stern look at both females.

But Jasmine was right. He did look like a TV star. Sandra could feel her breath becoming short and shallow at the very sight of him. Shep stood statue-like for a moment with his head bowed, his floppy, leather Bible clasped in front of him. So close she could see the freshly pressed crease in his trousers. His broad shoulders were relaxed like those of a warrior poised in the moments before battle. The light danced off the locks of his hair, so dark it was blue-black. Raising his eyes to encompass the entire audience, he spoke in a voice rich and smooth as heavy cream.

"Let all those here tonight who love Jesus raise their right hand," he commanded.

Everyone who could, did. Sandra's freshly painted nails reached as high as she could point them.

"Now, let everyone who expects a miracle tonight, raise their left hand." Again, in a congregational "Simon Says," everyone raised their left hand.

"Praise Jesus!" exclaimed Shep, and with an auditorium full of upward-stretched arms, he began to pray.

When he was finished, Shep welcomed everyone to the meeting and introduced a short, ruddy-faced man who Sandra knew was the song leader, Brother Toby. Shep retired to the wings. The choir was on their feet in a flurry of tambourines, starting to sway back and forth even before Brother Toby named the first hymn.

" 'We're Marching to Zion,' " he said.

Jasmine's mamma tried to pick up on the alto part in the song, but only managed to stay off-key. Jasmine, with a voice like a honking horn, held her own against her mamma, wailing as if she were trying to reach the ears of Shep offstage with her solo.

When they were done, Sandra leaned across the child, close to Jasmine's mamma. "I don't know how to say this, but your little girl screeches instead of sings," she said.

"Who made you an expert?" the woman hissed.

"Reverend Shep Waters and I are very intimate friends. I know what he likes—what his tastes are. He wouldn't like you or your little girl. You don't cut the mustard."

"Says you! You've been on my ass ever since you sat down here. I could take you out right now and kick the crap out of you—what do you say to that? That would show you who cuts the mustard." The woman bounced lightly on her toes as if ready for a fight.

Sandra turned so she faced the woman squarely. "Threaten me again and I will have the ushers escort you and your daughter out." *By your ratty, over-dyed hair if necessary!* "I am just trying to save you embarrassment." *You no-talent, worthless piece of white trash.* "Jesus may wash away our sins, but sometimes He leaves a little reminder, if you know what I mean." She let her gaze drift down to Jasmine and then back to Jasmine's mamma. "Pastor Waters would not be impressed." She gave the woman a long, cold stare to let her know she meant business.

Jasmine's mamma's face scrunched up as if she was deciding whether to cry or take a swing at Sandra. Finally, she reached and grabbed Jasmine by the arm. "We're going home," she said.

"But it hasn't finished yet," Jasmine pleaded.

Jasmine's mamma gripped the child harder, so tightly you could see where her fingers imprinted in the flesh. "Shut up, will you? We're leaving now!" With that she pushed past Sandra and disappeared up the aisle.

With her foe thus vanquished, Sandra was able to focus fully on the service.

After several hymns, none of which Sandra noted was on her cassette, and the collection that was taken up by a group of Boy Scouts passing around jumbo-sized popcorn boxes covered in aluminum foil, Shep reappeared.

He read from the book of Daniel and from the Book of Revelation. Sandra followed closely in her own Bible, though she now knew the verses by heart. She studied the Bible intently for hours each day and had lost count on how many times she had read the entire thing. To be honest, she had only read it through from cover to cover that first time, but she wasn't telling. After that she had given up on what seemed to her to be the boring parts and focused instead on the books that Shep liked to preach from. She had become proficient in the teachings of the Old Testament prophets, the Gospels, the Acts of the Apostles, the letters of Paul, and the Book of Revelation. Shep's sermon that night was taken from both Daniel and Revelation as he foretold of the coming Apocalypse.

"Reading the book of Daniel," he said, "is like reading tomorrow's headlines in the newspaper. The only question is when we get to the obituary section, which column will you be listed in? Those going to Heaven or those bound for Hell?"

"Amen, brother," answered the crowd.

*Cling, clang,* echoed the tambourines.

Sweat glistened on Shep's forearms and he mopped his wide brow with a linen handkerchief. *Now that was a souvenir!* she thought. *A linen hankie covered in Shep scent!* The fierce light revealed the faintest trace of a beard on his handsome face. *He probably had to shave twice a day. How would that stubble feel raking her cheek? As he sang hymns in her ear?*

Sandra thought for a moment she might have to leave the auditorium. She had considered this possibility—that things might be too much for her and she might have to excuse herself to the ladies' room. She was prepared to do that, but then, there was an intervention, another step in her transformation. Shep gave the invitation to accept Christ as Savior.

Sandra was among the first to stand and she walked unsteadily to the makeshift railing that had been constructed around the bottom of the stage. As Shep pleaded with the crowd for their eternal souls, Sandra knelt at the railing, letting her body take over, giving herself over to the glories of redemption in Jesus.

Wave after wave of rapture shook her, though she kept her hands clasped tightly on the rail in front of her. Several times she was tempted to release the railing, to let her hands roam free, to rip through the layer of cream-colored lamb's wool, down to the red lace undergarment, and beyond. Each time she resisted the temptation.

Shep jumped from the stage and began to touch the crowd that

had gathered with her at the barrier. Light poured from his fingertips as he drew near to her, and she could feel the heat from his
palms as he laid his hands upon her head. There was a familiar tin-
gling between her legs and she knew that even without touching
herself she was going to come. She could feel Shep entering her
just as the Holy Spirit had entered Mary. "Oh, Glory! Jesus!" she
cried. Her tongue flicked against her teeth and across her lips in
ecstasy. She felt as if she was about to swoon.

"Hallelujah!" she heard Shep cry.

"Praise God!" she shouted, her eyes rolling back in her head.

"We are going to Glory tonight!"

*In cream-colored lamb's wool and red lace panties!*

That night, back in her motel room, Sandra was almost in de-
spair. To have been so close—to have been touched by him. And
now, to be so totally, so utterly alone. This was worse than when
Carson had died, worse than the days after she had first seen Shep
on TV—and those times had been horrible, too painful almost to
bear as she recalled the ache that had eaten at her insides like a
cancer.

In the motel, she reread the passages Shep had preached on,
trying to recapture all the beautiful sights and sounds of the auditorium in her mind, trying to relive the moment of ecstasy when
he had touched her, but it was no use. It was gone like a mist in the
morning sun.

And so the pattern continued for the next two nights, which
she called Violet and Maroon after her ensembles. Each afternoon she would spend hours preparing herself, then make her
way to the Coliseum, choosing a place on an aisle not too far back
so that if Shep came into the crowd, he would be able to walk past
her. Each night she would follow along with his sermon topics:
"The Wages of Sin" on Violet, "The Mark of the Beast" on Maroon. Each night she would answer Shep's invitation to join him at
the altar. Each night she would feel the power rush through her
body as Shep's hand brushed over her. Each night she wept tears
of rapture and joy; then as the crowd dispersed and Shep disappeared into the recesses of the stage with Brother Toby, she would

collect her things and return to the isolation of her motel room, desolate, inconsolable.

On the afternoon of the fourth night, which she called Safari, she wrote Shep a letter. Actually, she wrote him four letters, or four drafts of the same letter. It had to be just right. The first version was seventeen pages long, and explained everything that she had gone through, how she had come to feel a special connection to him, be devoted to him. But something told her not to send that one, that she needed to keep things simple and straightforward— if she wanted to get the results she wanted. So the final draft was short, less than a page. Sandra forced herself to concentrate in order to keep her hand from shaking when she thought of the possibility that his hand might be holding this very page. The note read:

> *Reverend Waters,*
>
> *I am writing to you because you have saved my life!!!*
>
> *I watch you <u>every</u> Sunday morning on TV. I have supported your ministry with both my prayers and with my tithe for some time now. It has been my great joy to have been fortunate enough to attend all the meetings here in person, and I have been truly blessed by your teaching.*
>
> *I would like to make a <u>generous</u> <u>donation</u> to your efforts. I have written the check but will only give it to you in person. I have some personal matters that I would like to discuss with you as well and would appreciate some time to go over these with you.*
>
> *I am at the Ramada Inn. Room 211.*
> *<u>Tonight Only!</u>*
> *Yours in Christ Jesus who died on the cross for our sins,*
>
> *Sandra (Mrs. Carson) Maxwell*
>
> *P.S. This is on the up-and-up.*

Sandra scented the pastel-colored paper with perfume and sealed it in a matching envelope. She ordered a chicken club sandwich from the restaurant at the motel and afterward took a nap. When she woke and showered, her preparations took even longer than normal, so when she got to the auditorium, people were already going inside. She was panicked she might lose her prime spot, but by a miracle—Shout *Hallelujah!*—her aisle seat was still vacant.

The opening parts of the service were now a familiar ritual to her. First came the welcome, then songs (she had still not heard one of the songs from her cassette and would surely have to speak to Shep about that), then a prayer, more songs, a personal testimony (usually from a recovered drunk or convict), Bible reading, more prayer, the offering, and finally, the choir's special anthem. All this was the prelude to Shep's sermon and his invitation to join him at the altar in prayer. That was when she planned to give him the note.

As Shep took the stage for his sermon, Sandra could see angels in white robes standing around him. He gave off an aura of blue-white light tinged with purple, and his presence was so fierce she could almost smell him from where she sat. He had his shirt-sleeves rolled up. This usually didn't happen until he was well into his sermon. She knew he meant business tonight.

"Brothers and sisters in Christ—this evening I am not going to give you a sermon. I am not going to try and convert you to become a soldier in the army of God. No, we have talked for three nights about why Jesus Christ is Lord and Master of the Universe, and if you still don't believe that, then I guess you are just going to hell."

There was laughter among the devout and a smattering of "Amens" from the crowd. Sandra rattled her Shep Waters Tambourine, which she purchased the second night—Violet.

"No, tonight I am going to talk to you about the gifts of the Spirit. The Bible says the Holy Spirit will manifest itself to those who believe. It doesn't say it will make you feel good—it says it will give you Power. Do I hear an 'Amen' on that?"

More "Amens."

"Power. And I am not talking about the power of a V-8 engine or a jet engine or even a rocket engine. I am talking about the Power of God himself. I am tired of namby-pamby religion. The Apostle Paul tells us that we can expect to heal people, to work miracles, to drive out evil spirits—demons, to speak in tongues, to prophesy."

The crowd was firing up—Shep's words sizzled like drops of water in a hot pan. He wiped his face with his handkerchief.

"Now, I am not a particularly smart man. I am certainly not a very well-educated man. But I do know that either what the Bible says is true or it isn't. And do you know how I know?"

He paused as the throng hushed in anticipation of his answer.

"I know because I have seen it! I have heard it! I have lived it! Glory Hallelujah!"

"Glory be to God!" called Sandra. A heavyset man in a dark blue suit and red necktie danced beside her in the aisle.

"When I was a boy," continued Shep, "my mamma took me to church every time they opened the door. And I bless her sweet memory, now she has passed on to be with Jesus, that she brought me up to love the Lord. Can I get an 'Amen' on that, brothers and sisters?"

He got it.

"Now, the church we went to was not one where they were concerned with being dignified."

Shep pulled himself up into an exaggerated pose, scrunching his face in his impression of a stuck-up clergyman. "Dignified" came out through his nose—high-pitched and whiny. The crowd stomped in agreement.

"Because it wasn't dignified when Jesus was hanging naked on the cross, I can tell you that. When he shed his blood that day on Calvary. No sirree, brother, they humbled him so that God Himself could glorify him in Heaven. So that the Father could lift up the Son."

Sandra let the tambourine brush against the front of her blouse. She could feel her nipples hard and erect beneath the silk.

"I don't know how many of you know where I come from, but it was a tiny place, not even a town, just a speck on the map—Pison River Gap—and the church we went to—Mt. Pisgah Holiness Tabernacle—was a way up in the mountains. It was just a worn-out, rickety, one-room church, but that didn't matter because it was a Holy Ghost Church. We would raise the roof off that old building sometimes as people got filled with the spirit. And I saw healings, and I heard people speaking in tongues. . . ."

From around the auditorium came a smattering of clicking, guttural sounds as the true Holy Ghosters rose up and began to speak in tongues.

"And I knew that the Power of the Almighty was not a theory, like that theory they try to corrupt the minds of our children with these days, the theory of evolution." Shep paused, realizing he was about to shift sermons in midstream. He gave a boyish grin. "But we can save the theory of evolution for another time. Tonight we are talking about the evidence of the Holy Spirit!"

The audience shouted its approval.

"Now, we had a man in our church, Brother Hiram, who I reckon was about as old as Methuselah himself."

The group gave a generous laugh.

"Brother Hiram couldn't come to church each week because he lived even farther out of town than most of us, but we knew when he would come, it would be a special day. Because when Brother Hiram came to church, he would bring the snakes."

Sandra tried to picture this old man, creeping down the side of mountain with a burlap bag filled with snakes. She didn't like the image. She hated snakes. Once, she had had to kill one in the garden and as she hacked at it with the hoe, each severed segment writhing at her feet, she had screamed in anguish like she was being hacked to pieces herself.

"Brother Hiram would bring the snakes and we would claim the Scripture that whoever believes shall not perish by the serpent nor by poison."

Sandra noticed he pronounced the word in the mountain way: "pie-sin."

"And the serpent had no power. We would hold those snakes like they were kittens, and even though they had the fangs of a viper, they did not harm us. And do you know why? Because when God is walking beside you, the Devil gets stomped on."

Events began to unfold around Sandra like a children's pop-up book, each more fascinating, more wondrous, more bizarre than the last. A woman several rows down sprawled full-length into the aisle jumping and shaking as the Spirit overcame her. A young man in the wheelchair section jumped up and ran out toward the lobby, healed. Behind her, Sandra heard a voice announce, "My daughter just got an anointing in the hospital. I can feel it. She won't need the operation. I'm going to go take her home tonight. Praise God!"

*Praise God.*

When Sandra focused again on the stage, she saw Brother Toby walking out from the side of the stage holding a brown cloth sack. As he clutched the top tightly, she could see the twisting and turning going underneath the surface. She knew at once that Brother Toby had brought Shep his snakes.

Shep did a little dance on the stage, a rapid *tap! tap! tap!* with each foot and then a hop. He reminded her of a young boy on Christmas morning eagerly waiting to unwrap the last toy, his favorite.

"I think Brother Toby has brought us a surprise. Something to show the power of the Lord! Do you want to see it?"

The crowd roared as one. "YES!"

*No!* thought Sandra. *I do not want to see this. Not this.* This is not what she had come for—she was elegantly dressed, for God's sake! She wanted the spectacle and the colored lights—the beauty of Shep's voice—the softness of his touch. Snakes were low, vile.

But Shep already had the snake in his hands. It dangled before him—long, fat, slimy. Shep held it up so the audience could see. "This snake could kill me," he said, "but it won't. And you know why? Because Jesus won't let it!"

"Praise be to Jesus!"

Shep walked to the edge of the stage. Sandra knew that tonight was the night she had been waiting for all week—when Shep would descend into the crowd.

He took his time as he made his way up and down the rows near the stage, stopping, praying with one or another, swaying back and forth with the crowd like a tree momentarily caught by a breeze, distracted; then he would hold the snake high over his head and turn round and round like a whirlwind before setting off again. His golden white light shot at her now like arrows, like lightning. It was too much. She clamped her eyes closed. But she could feel him coming closer. Closer. Closer. Then he was there beside her. "Sister."

She lifted her head and opened her eyes. The brightness of Shep shone down upon her. He held the horrible serpent in front of him with his right hand—so long that it almost touched the floor. He extended his left to her as an invitation.

"Is there anything you want tonight, sister?" he asked.

Her throat was dry, parched. Her voice cracked as she tried to speak. "I love you," she said. "I brought you a letter." She thrust the envelope out toward him. He took it and in that instant when their hands touched, Sandra knew the snake was watching her. She could feel its cold, dead eyes turn down toward her, searching her thoughts, her heart. It opened its mouth wide so she could see the fine points of its fangs.

"I love you, too," said Shep as he slipped the note into his pocket.

The snake squirmed in Shep's hands trying to jump free. Sandra heard herself scream; then she fainted.

When Sandra came to, she was lying on a cot in a cordoned-off area in the lobby of the auditorium. It had been set up for those who had been overcome during the services and was staffed by two female volunteers, both LPNs. They had taken Sandra's blood pressure, which was low, and when she woke they offered her a can of orange juice and a dry chocolate chip cookie in case her sugar was also below normal. Sandra's head ached, and she could feel a small knot rising on the right side of her forehead. She could taste blood in her mouth, and the inside of her cheek felt like ragged meat where she had gnawed it.

The three of them were alone in the makeshift room, but Sandra could hear people walking by on the other side of the screen. She knew the services were over. She wanted to leave here, Shep might be waiting for her at the motel. The recovery room seemed too small for herself and the two attendants. They sucked up all the air in the room and Sandra was afraid she might faint again. Lying on the cot, looking up at them as they hovered over her, Sandra imagined the women were dirigibles or inflatable floats like the ones in the Macy's Thanksgiving Parade. Sandra figured that the hostesses on the Home Shopping Network would recommend they buy the stretch knit fabrics in sizes L-3X. *For those who don't want to sacrifice fashion sense for comfort!* They wore tags pinned to their blue polyester smock tops that showed both their name and their church affiliation. Betty Church of God of Prophecy spoke first.

"You got a powerful knock on your noggin there," she said. "You will have a bump there for a while."

"How are you feeling now?" asked Aurelia Calvary Baptist.

"Woozy," said Sandra.

"They said the Lord just jumped down and slayed you in the spirit," said Betty.

"There was a snake. I thought it was going to bite me. It seemed to know me."

"That was just the Devil trying to get at you when the Spirit was coming on you, honey," said Betty. "They said you spoke in tongues."

"I don't remember it," said Sandra.

"Not important that you remember it," said Aurelia. "God remembers."

And so does the snake, thought Sandra.

When Sandra got back to the motel, she discovered she had ripped the hem out of her pants so one leg was frayed like the skin of wounded beast. Her makeup was smeared, and the reflection looking back at her from the mirror was of another woman, another face, distorted, bizarre. Her hair was wild and uncombed, and she had lost one of her earrings. She tried to repair the damage while listening for Shep to arrive. She wanted to take a shower but did not, fearing she might not hear his knock. So she just stripped to her black foundation garments and sponged the sour sweat off her body, which stuck to her like a poultice. When she was done, she put on her best robe—midnight lace—and waited. Finally, some-time after the clock said 3 AM she fell asleep on top of the covers, propped up by the pillows.

When she slept she dreamed that Shep and the snake were one in the same. That when Shep stood naked in front of her, the snake was where his penis was supposed to be. The snake hissed and curled around her like a boa constrictor, wrapping her from head to toe in its embrace, squeezing so tightly that she felt bones crushing, the breath being squashed in her lungs. Shep smiled his best smile and asked if there was anything she wanted. She tried to ask for help, to tell him that she was dying, but the words that came out were in a language she did not understand.

When she awoke it was daylight. She realized Shep had not come.

Sandra showered, washed her hair, but did not set it or even blow it dry. She left it tangled and clumped to do as it pleased. It seemed futile. She packed her suitcase, the new clothes now dull and drab. She knew she would never wear them again. She thought about the long drive back to her house, which struck her more like a tomb than a home. She did not think she could bear to go back. Then she remembered the gun in her handbag. She got it out, held it, studied it. She thought how painless it would be—like the bump on her head really. Had she felt that when she hit the floor? No. It was only afterward when she woke up that the pain set in. This would be just like that, except there would be no after.

She knew not to take too long, that too much thought would de-stroy that part of her that was acting on instinct, on impulse. She knew the best way was to simply put the gun in her mouth, like a child sucking its thumb, and pull the trigger. Pointing it at the side of the head was clumsy—often people did not die right away like that if they died at all. She had seen a report on *Hard Copy* where a teenager had survived a gunshot wound to his temple with the bullet still lodged smack in the center of his brain. They had inter-viewed him. He had trouble coordinating his eyes and his speech was slightly slurred, but he still functioned well enough to show the camera an X-ray. He then pointed to his head, and said, "In there," like the bullet was a key to a door he had forgotten how to open. No, she reckoned putting the gun to the side of the head was used only for dramatic effect in the movies. Putting it any-where else except inside the mouth where the shot would lift her brain up through the top of her skull might only result in injury, disfigurement, or disability.

So, that was decided. In the mouth. Quick. One. Two. Three. And then it would be over.

There was a knock at the door. Sandra thought the maids were probably coming to clean the room. She smiled to herself. Just give me a minute and then you'll really have something to clean up.

Two more knocks. Then a voice. "Mrs. Maxwell, are you still there?"

She knew that voice. It was as familiar to her as her own heart-beat. It was Shep. Sandra laid the gun gently on top of the dresser and unlocked the door.

There, he stood. Shep Waters. Her Shep.

"Mrs. Maxwell?"

"Yes, I prefer Sandra." She squinted her eyes against the morn-ing sun. She moved so he blocked the light from her, so that she stood in his shadow. As her eyes readjusted, his silhouette loomed over her, framed against the bright open sky.

"I went to check on you at the infirmary last night after the ser-vice," he said. "I wanted to make sure you were all right. But they told me you had left."

"I wanted to get home. I was expecting someone," she said.

"How are you feeling now?" She noticed he wasn't wearing his blue slacks and white shirt and necktie. Instead, he had on a pair of old jeans and a pullover shirt that fit him too tight across the chest and around his arms. She could smell a mixture of aftershave and deodorant soap. It was the way Carson would smell when he had just showered and was ready to go to town.

"My head hurts some. Would you like to come in?"

"The Lord must have given you a powerful whack," he said. "I was afraid you might have a concussion." She closed the door be-hind him and slipped the security bolt into place. "I prayed for you last night when I couldn't find you, and then this morning when I was packing up, I found the note you left me." He pulled the envelope from his back pocket and held it out toward her. The note was creased where it had been folded over and casually stuffed into his pocket. The note she had so carefully crafted, delicately perfumed, sealed with a kiss. She imagined her scent mingled with his just as Mary Magdalene's did with Jesus' when she washed the Lord's grimy feet with her tears, dried them with her hair.

Sandra studied him. Now that he was up close, away from the auditorium, Shep didn't put off any light like before. He seemed oddly human. She wondered if he had brought the snake with him. She thought of her dream and how Shep and the snake were one. She imagined he could have it hidden, wrapped around his waist, or maybe bunched up in his crotch, ready to spring out at her like a Jack in the box.

"I won't keep you," he said. "I just wanted to see if you were okay. And in the note . . ."

"Yes," said Sandra, trying to recall what she had said in it.

"You wrote that you wanted to make a donation."

"A donation," Sandra repeated.

"You said you had written a check."

"The note also said one night only. Did you read that part?"

"God's work knows no season, no time," he said. "And the Lord has put it on your heart to help us. That is what we are here to do, isn't it? Serve the Lord and help each other out? You said you wanted to talk to me about some personal things. What can I do for you, Sister Sandra? What is on your heart? What is it you need?"

Sandra thought of all she longed to tell him. How lonely she had been when Carson had died, how Shep had saved her life, had given her purpose. How she wanted him to take her in his arms, to lay her across the bed, to shower her body with his kisses, to melt into her. Then she remembered the snake. How the snake had been attached to Shep. That instead of caressing her, stroking her, Shep only wanted to feed her to the snake. She picked up the gun from the dresser and pointed it at Shep.

"I know why you've come here," she said. "God showed me

the snake. Showed me how you planned to use it against me. To hurt me."

"I am not here to hurt you," he said. She could see that he was lying. She could see the snake twist and turn down his pants leg.

"I need you to take off your pants," she said.

His face flushed with color. "Sister," he said, "we shouldn't even joke like that."

"I'm pointing a gun at you," she replied. "And I'm not joking. Take off your pants. I want you to show me."

"I am a married man," he said. "I have a wife at home in Sumter—we are going to have a baby in four months."

His voice had lost its confidence, its edge. He sounded like a schoolboy. She was struck how young he had become in the daytime. Shep. With his beautiful wife and bouncing baby on the way. "You should have thought about that before," she said. "Take your pants off—now."

"No, ma'am," he said. "I won't do that. You can keep your money if you want. I am going to leave here. I got the shield of God protecting me. You can't hurt me." With that, he turned toward the door.

The first bullet blew a chunk off his shoulder and spun him around hard like a puppet on a string. The second bullet hit him just above his left eye and his whole face seemed to crumble behind it, as if it were chasing the bullet to a secret, faraway place. Standing over him as he lay on the floor, Sandra held the gun tightly, hand shaking as she undid his trousers, ready to kill the serpent. But it was not there. She searched frantically for it on her hands and knees throughout the room, but it was no use. The snake had eluded her, escaped.

Sandra picked up the note from where it had fallen and tucked it into her suitcase along with the gun. A thick, gloomy stain spread across the plush pile carpet. She understood if Shep had waited only a few minutes it would have been her blood instead of his. God's hand, however, had intervened, saved her. But for what? If she was ordained to kill the snake, she had failed. The snake was still loose.

Stepping over Shep like she would a pile of soiled, rumpled laundry, Sandra placed the DO NOT DISTURB sign on the outside knob of the motel room door. No one had even come outside to see what the noise was, probably thought the gunshot only the backfiring of a redneck's car. She walked calmly down the steps— *a single woman with a suitcase, nothing more*—then got into her car and drove away.

## . . . 3 . . .

What was next? She had to plan carefully. Without a plan the only other option seemed uncontrollable, unending screaming. She had killed Shep Waters, shot him, left him lying on the floor of the Ramada Inn in a pool of his own blood. People would not understand that she was acting as God's instrument. They would hold her responsible. In a movie this is where she would start to run, take it on the lam. She imagined herself like Janet Leigh in *Psycho*, after she had taken the $40,000, tainted in her black slip, a shady lady. Wary. Watchful.

So she began to drive and drive and drive. On the way out of Greensboro, she stopped at a bank and withdrew most of the cash from her savings account. She told them her husband had suffered a stroke (she even had Carson's ring to show them as evidence). She told them he did not believe in using credit cards. That much was true. Carson had ingrained in her the merits of cash-only transactions, which is how she had paid the Ramada Inn. No credit card to trace her. Just her last name and an initial on the registration slip. Her address was a rural box number. And as usual, she had not remembered her license plate number so she had left that space blank. She wondered briefly if it all had not been a foreshadowing. *God works in mysterious ways His wonders to perform.* They let her

withdraw the money with no questions. The teller had even pat-
ted her on the arm and said she would pray for her.

As she drove, she imagined herself poised high above the car
watching as it zigzagged a cobweb of highways and back roads.
When she stopped to sleep, she ignored the major chain motor inns
along the highway and stayed only in the second best motels—lost,
lonely places on the outskirts of town. In those places they did not
request ID, and cash in advance was always appreciated by the
weary desk clerk who she was sure pocketed the money and tore
up the registration. Even so, she was careful not to give herself
away and concocted exotic aliases for herself, names like Marion or
Delores or Yvonne. None seemed to suit her fancy, though. Each
day she felt Sandra fade away just a tiny bit more.

Time moved like sunlight through water. She was aware of it
only when she would catch the glimpse of a clock tower on a bank
or when the news would announce three o'clock or six o'clock.
Music distracted her and she would turn the radio on only for brief
intervals when she thought about it, wondering if there was some
news of Shep. It was on the third or fourth day when she finally
heard the report that a popular television evangelist had been
found shot to death in a motel room. They gave no details. They
did not mention her name.

That night, when she had stopped driving, she listened to the TV
news at 6:00 and at 10:00 and again at 11:00. Each time the report
was roughly the same. A bleached-out video showed the Ramada
Inn now festooned with yellow police tape across the parking lot,
then an interview with the manager, pictures of Shep preaching, a
wedding photo of him with the wife. Police were not sure why he
was at the motel. He had left Brother Toby that morning and said
nothing about going there. Brother Toby thought Shep had
headed back straightaway to his wife in Sumter. No, he did not
think sex or drugs were involved. Shep Waters was a good man, he
loved the Lord. He loved his wife. Whoever had done this was a
crazy person. Maybe a Satanist trying to stop the work of God that
could never be stopped. *Hallelujah!*

She thought about Shep as he lay on the floor of the motel
room, how he must have looked when they found him, his hand-

some face now pulp. She took out the note she had written to him, the note he had brought with him to the motel. Speckles of dark red flecked the pink paper like dried, crumbled rose petals. Clasping it like a sacred relic, she held it to her nose where she could still smell his aftershave impregnating the paper that she had scented with her own fragrance. The two smells intertwined—Old Spice meets L'Air du Temps.

That night she dreamed of Shep again. In the dream, he was hosting a show on the Home Shopping Network wearing a tight, shiny snakeskin suit; but when she looked a second time as he stepped through the TV screen, she couldn't tell if it was truly a suit or simply his flesh. She only managed to view him with a quick backward glance, over her shoulder as she ran away from him. Then in front of her loomed a mountain, tall and craggy, dense with vegetation. She was trying to climb it wearing only her undergarments and high heels, and she could hear the stones chip beneath her shoes with loud cracks like limbs of trees breaking off. She would slip and scrape her skin against the boulders as she tried to scurry up over them, inching her way toward the top. When she looked down to check her wounds she was amazed to see she wasn't bleeding. Instead, the rocks had merely loosened large translucent pieces of her flesh that lay scattered behind her like tissue paper.

What was at the top of the mountain she did not know. But she was desperate to get there, to reach it. She was acutely aware that the snake could hide in the small spaces between the rocks, ready to spring out at her at any time. And she knew she was making too much noise. It would only alert him to her—and there was no place to hide a weapon, dressed as she was. She felt absolutely vulnerable. She knew if she encountered the snake she would have to wrestle it, hold it in her hands and strangle it. Or it would kill her. Then as she pulled herself up over the top of one of the rocks, she saw it tangled and knotted with dozens, hundreds of other snakes, a kingdom of vipers. His kingdom. The snakes twisted and writhed, interlocked in a slow, solemn dance. She knew that they were mating, except as they copulated, the smaller snakes somehow merged, melded with the king. She watched helplessly as one by one they disappeared, as he grew larger and more hideous. Finally, when all the other snakes had been consumed, he rose up from the rock, towering over her, and struck.

When she woke, the room was deep with shadows. Sandra ripped open drawers, dumped her suitcase into the middle of the room, searching desperately for the snake, to make sure it wasn't there. When she could not find it, she read in her Bible, she prostrated herself on the carpet in prayer, she pulled at her hair in hope for relief. But there was none. What was the dream trying to tell her? She was afraid to go back to sleep—afraid that the snake might return. She kept a vigilant watch all night.

Then in the morning, before she left to begin driving, she saw another TV news report about Shep. They showed everything she had already seen, but this time they highlighted parts of the state with stars showing where Shep had been born, where he had been killed. They interviewed a male cousin who looked remotely like Shep and who still lived there in Shep's home town, Pison River Gap. High in the mountains where Shep had learned to love the Lord. Where Shep had told of old Brother Hiram who kept the snakes and brought them to church. Looking at the TV screen as the name blazed yellow on the emerald green map, Sandra knew that God was calling her there—to Pison River Gap.

It was early when she arrived. The morning sun had just cleared the crest of the highest ridge when she passed the Pison River Gap Chamber of Commerce welcome sign. A black wreath hung from the top of the sign.

Pison River Gap reminded Sandra of her own hometown, and the similarity saddened her. In her mind it seemed every town on her journey had become a composite, each main street virtually interchangeable with the next—a homogenized blend. Wal-Mart, Kentucky Fried Chicken, Hardee's hamburgers, one, two, or three banks depending on the size and wealth of the population, the same rule governing both the number and denomination of churches. Though she had been driving for what felt like forever, where she had arrived seemed almost exactly like where she had left.

She stopped at the Huddle House for breakfast. She was too early for the regular coffee crowd, and the few construction workers who allowed themselves the luxury of a full breakfast instead of a drive-through sausage biscuit were just clearing out. She had the place almost to herself. Sandra chose a booth in the rear and rummaged for a paper to see if there was any more news. The local paper, a weekly, had run a special edition that was little more than a memorial to Shep. *The Asheville Citizen Times*, however, featured the story on the bottom half of the front page. The details were still vague, but the investigators said they were following a strong lead. They were not revealing anything till they could be more definite, but they felt they would certainly solve the case and bring the murderer to justice. Sandra's stomach tightened at the word. *Murderer.* Did that mean they thought it was a man? Wouldn't they have said *murderess* if they were looking for a woman? Or was murderer just generic enough to make her relax until the net had dropped over her and she was caught in its snare.

"It breaks my heart." Sandra looked up to the waitress, Darlene: small framed, pink polyester, tight gray perm. Run-of-the-mill hash house. Sandra took her to be well past fifty. She wondered what sad story had brought this woman to this point in her life. She was too old to be slinging pancakes and eggs, how her feet must ache at the end of each day while her derelict husband drank up all the tips at home sitting on his redneck ass.

"Yes, it's tragic. I'll have the Number Three, eggs over hard, bacon crisp, white toast, and coffee." She did not want to engage this Darlene in conversation.

"He was from here, you know."

"Yes, I heard that."

"He used to come in here when he was a boy. He worked at Dobson's Tire till he got the call to preach." Sandra pictured Shep, sweaty in his coveralls, hands grimy, making an old engine purr. "I never was one for the religion myself. At least that type—you know, the Pentecostal. Church is fine for Sunday, but everything in moderation is my motto. What brings you to Pison River Gap?"

"I'm just passing through."

Darlene's expression darkened quickly like a cloud crossing by the sun. "Pardon me for being rude, ma'am, but not many people just pass through Pison River Gap. You're usually either coming or leaving. You're not a reporter, are you?" she asked. "There's been people snooping around trying to get dirt on Shep—since they found him in a motel and him with a pregnant wife and everything. But I know he was a good boy—a good man."

"I'm not a reporter," Sandra replied. "I did know him, though. We had planned to work together—Shep had persuaded me to join his ministry full-time, before this happened."

"Then why ain't you at the funeral? That's going to be tomorrow—down in Sumter. Half the town left here yesterday to get there." "Yesterday" came out like "Yas-tiddy." Darlene was mountain born and bred.

Sandra cut her off quickly. "Jesus said, 'Let the dead bury the dead.' My work is here."

"And what work is that?" Darlene made no attempt to move. Sandra knew country folk well enough to understand what this meant. Darlene didn't trust her—she wanted an explanation. Sandra tried to think quickly, confabulate a story. She did not want to call undue attention to herself.

"The saddest thing that could come from this is that Shep's ministry would not continue, don't you agree?"

Darlene did not answer.

"I worked with Shep handling the finances for the ministry. As you can well imagine, there was quite a lot of money. It was a huge responsibility. Shep relied on me tremendously. Now, that money must be used in a good way."

"Why not just give it to his wife and baby? That would make sense to me."

"There is plenty of insurance for that, I can assure you. Shep provided well for his family, but we aren't allowed to give it to her anyway. The government is very strict—money collected for religious purposes can only be used for those purposes." She saw by Darlene's expression that she had made an inroad, so she added, "That is covered under article twelve, section nineteen of the federal tax code."

"Damn government."

"Render unto Caesar," said Sandra. "It is my job to make sure the money is distributed as Shep would have wanted."

"You going to give it to a church, then?"

"In a way. We will set up a fund for families who need help here in Shep's hometown. He would have wanted that. We will call it the Shep Waters Memorial Fund. One of the churches will distribute it."

"I hope you ain't planning to give it to the Methodists. They will just use it for a beautification project or something." Sandra knew the idea of free money had hooked Darlene. "Who did you say could get hold of this fund? My daughter and her kids need help something terrible. Her littlest one, Edgar, has a short leg, so there is always money going for special shoes. . . ."

Sandra interrupted before she got the whole sorry tale. "We will make an announcement in the paper," she said. "And I am sure your daughter would be just the kind of person we would want to help."

"My husband has been out of work with a displaced hip. . . ."

"It will be in the paper." Sandra smiled. "But for the moment, Darlene. I hope you don't mind if I call you by name. For the moment, we need to keep this pretty quiet. I don't want to call any attention to myself while I am here. I just want to get the ball rolling."

"Sure, I understand."

"But if you write down your last name and your daughter's name, I will pass them along so they get special attention."

"Thank you, Mrs. . . ."

"Just call me Lucille. My last name is a tongue-twister, so everyone just calls me Lucille." She liked the way it sounded. It fit. Then she added, "By the way, I need to get directions to Mt. Pisgah Holiness Tabernacle. That is where Shep said he attended church."

"It's about twenty miles up the old Rosman highway. It's a ways off the main road. I can draw you a map if you want."

"I would appreciate that."

"And I didn't mean anything bad about the Pentecostals earlier. Lord knows I'll be speaking in tongues if it means some extra cash."

Darlene floated off to place her order, spending the imminent windfall in her mind, Sandra was sure. When she returned with breakfast, she gave Sandra a detailed map to Mt. Pisgah Holiness, and both her name and her daughter's printed in heavy block letters. Sandra chuckled to herself. She liked this deceit. It was easy. And it seemed to suit this new woman she was becoming, this Lucille. She noticed also Darlene had managed to secure two extra slices of bacon for her on the order—*Prime the pump, you greedy hillbilly,* she thought. *Prime the pump.*

The turnoff was a two-rut road that twisted up the side of the mountain, the kind of road you don't want to meet anyone coming in the opposite direction. Sandra would not have taken it had it not been for the small realtor's sign that had been repainted and stuck into the ground at the entrance: MT. PISGAH HOLINESS TABERNACLE and an arrow pointing the way.

Up and up she drove as if ascending into the clouds. The air was thick with the smell of an oncoming storm, and wild azaleas dotted the mountainside with fiery bursts of brilliant orange. Dogwoods hung heavy with blooms. The dense woods and underbrush appeared to her impenetrable, ancient, primordial.

Finally, she reached a clearing where a small-framed building, weather-beaten and in sore need of repainting, stood built up on cinder blocks. There was no steeple, no stained glass—she doubted even if there was electricity or running water. She removed her purse with the gun and the money inside from under her seat and wrapped the strap around her arm. Sandra did not bother to lock her car as she got out and approached the building. When she climbed the steps, she discovered the front door was not fastened, but she did not enter the tabernacle. It was as if there was an invisible line she dared not cross. Standing at the entrance, she noticed folding chairs arranged neatly in rows on either side of the room, creating a center aisle that led to a small lectern. There was an upright piano in the far right corner, and hanging on the back wall was a handmade cross, two rough-hewn tree limbs still covered in bark, lashed together with leather bands. Several milk-glass globes hung on chains from the ceiling. There was power here after all.

"I made that cross myself."

Sandra jumped as a man walked up the steps behind her. Turning to face him, she recognized him as the man from the TV—Shep's cousin.

"It's made from the trunks of two dogwood trees. Did you ever hear how the dogwood came to look like it does?"

"No," said Sandra.

The resemblance to Shep was stronger in person. He was almost the same height and weight, though he looked older, more world-weary, and had begun to go slack in the belly some—probably from too much beer. But his hair was dark and shiny like Shep's, combed back like Shep's, and his eyes were just as piercing.

"They say that the dogwood tree used to stand taller and more proud than any oak tree or elm," he said, "and that when they went to find something to crucify Jesus, they naturally chose the biggest, strongest tree they could think of. Well, the dogwood was so sad that it had been used to kill the Son of God that it shriveled right up and its branches became gnarled like an old woman's hands. And its flowers—that's why each one is in the shape of a cross with a little red stain on the petals—like a drop of blood, to show us that Christ died for our sins."

"That's a lovely story," said Sandra.

"Ain't no story," Shep's cousin said. "It's a fact. Whatch you doin' up here?"

"I was looking for someone. I came because of Shep Waters. He told me this is where he went to church."

"Shep was my cousin. My name is Claude. Claude Earl Waters."

"I know," said Sandra. "I saw you on TV."

A sly smile slid across Claude's face. "Didja now? Saw me on TV? You ain't from the TV, are you?"

"No," said Sandra.

"I live just down from here. I was listening to the news when I heard you driving up—they said the police had a suspect. Closing in fast. I thought it might have been another reporter wanting an interview."

"I'm not a reporter."

"You look like you could have been on TV, though."

"No, I have never been on TV. I was a friend of Shep's." She did not like this man. He frightened her.

"Well, any friend of Shep's . . . as they say. What can I do you for . . ."

"Lucille."

"That's a purty name. Lucille. Do folks call you Lucy for short? I love Lucy." He laughed at his joke.

"It's Lucille."

"Well, Lucy Lucille, what brings you all the way up to the mountaintop? Shep's funeral is down in Sumter."

"I know."

"You knew Shep, then?"

"Yes, he helped me through a difficult time."

"I would've gone to the funeral, but Cousin Shep and I didn't exactly see eye to eye on a lot of things. I don't think anybody will miss me not being there. Why aren't you there?"

"Shep told me about Brother Hiram. He said I should go and see him. That he was a holy man."

"You're looking for Old Hiram Poole? Shep told you to come and see him?"

"Yes. Did he go to Sumter?"

Claude let out a snort. "Not unless today is Judgment Day and the dead in Christ have risen. Old Hiram has been dead for pretty nigh on six or seven years now."

Sandra's hopes fell at the news of Hiram's death. And her lie had been a stupid, clumsy one—easily exposed.

"What did you need to see Hiram about any-hoo?"

"I wanted him to help with me with something."

"I can't imagine Hiram could have helped anybody with much of anything. He lived off by himself, never really took to people, just come down the mountain long enough to sell some home brew or bring his snakes to a meeting. He was dead three weeks before anybody even thought to go looking for him. It might have been longer, but I got a powerful thirst one night and went up to where he lived. Figured it was easier to walk up the mountain drunk than to try and drive down it to town. When I got to

Hiram's, there he was sitting at the dinner table, dead as a rock. Had the durn dinner fork still in his hand. But dead just the same." He paused to let the effect sink in. "Now, you don't look like the type of lady who would drive up here for white lightning. You sure you aren't from the TV."

"I'm sure," said Sandra.

"Well, I don't know. You just look awful familiar to me—if you know what I mean." His smile was like a dirty joke.

Sandra stared at him hard. "I have absolutely no idea what you're talking about."

Suddenly the sky opened and the rain poured down on them. Claude pushed opened the door to the church wide for her but seemed to sense her resistance to stepping inside.

"I got my trailer just down yonder," he said. "If you want to come over, maybe I could help you with whatever Shep sent you to see Hiram about."

"I don't know."

"Or you can stand out here and get drowned. Suit yourself."

"I don't know."

"What don't you know? What do you think, Miss Lucy, that I am going to take you down to my trailer so I can have my way with you? Well, in case you haven't noticed, we are purty much past hollering distance from anything—if I meant you any harm, I reckon I would have already made that known."

He walked off down toward a path in the brush. The rain was so heavy he was almost lost to her, even at a short distance. He turned as he reached the edge of the wood and called as he would to a dog or a petulant child. "Come on, now. I'm not going to beg you. But don't you worry, Miss Lucy Lucille, I'll hook you up with whatever you're looking to find. You can count on that."

Sandra closed the door of the church behind her, then walked into the blinding rain, obediently following Claude Earl into the woods.

The trailer was, in fact, a camper, sloped at both ends so the only place you could stand up straight was in the center—the part with the kitchenette and bathroom. In the front section, which was the living/eating area or the rear, which she knew would be Claude's bedroom, it was necessary to stoop to prevent hitting your head. Sandra felt like she was inside an egg.

"Make yourself to home," said Claude as he cracked open the top to a Bud longneck. The trailer reeked of stale cigarette smoke, moldy food, and alcohol. "Do you want something to drink? Don't got no tea or coffee. Just sodi pop and beer." He took a swig from his drink and smacked his lips. "Ain't nothing quite so good as the taste of a cold one from a bottle. Never did like drinking beer from a can. Gives it a different taste."

"I'm fine," said Sandra.

"Yes, you are that, but do you need anything to drink?" Claude smiled at her, and took another swallow.

"No, thank you," said Sandra.

"This rain won't last too long," said Claude, leaning over past her to look out the window. The trailer rocked beneath his weight. "We get a shower most every afternoon. Keeps things cool in the evening." As he got close, she could tell he had not bathed in days. His clothes smelled musty, rank. He leaned himself up against the counter and propped his boot on the seat opposite her. "So now, I guess we got us some bidness to take care of."

Sandra held her purse tight against her. She would fight him if he tried to take it. If he attempted to rob or rape her.

"What is it that brought you here, Miss Lucy Belle?"

"I told you Shep sent me to see—"

"And a bigger crock of horseshit I never heard neither! Let's get one thing straight here. You don't want to play coy with me—it's not to your advantage. All it's gonna do is cost you time and piss me off. My motto is, 'Honesty is always the best policy.' You understand? Now why don't we start again?"

"I don't know."

"You keep saying that, Miss Lucy Lou. That you don't know. Just what is it you don't fuckin' know?"

Claude was not stupid like the waitress. It would not be easy to deceive him—and if she were caught out again, there could be trouble. She decided to confront him head-on. "I don't know if I can trust you," she said.

Claude Earl laughed, "And visi versi. For all I know you are just some crazy woman here to do me harm. But I guess them's the breaks. 'Cause I figure we both have something the other one wants. So, I do for you, you do for me."

"And then I can go. You won't try to stop me?"

"You found me, remember. Why would I want to keep you here, Miss Lucy? I got no reason—unless, of course, I decide to tie you to a tree and cut your titties off so I can keep 'em in the frigerator and watch 'em jiggle on a plate like Jell-O."

Sandra gasped.

Claude chuckled. "Now, don't get your drawers in a knot. I'm just funning with you. If I want pussy, I don't have to get it at knifepoint, you can best believe that." He put his hand on his pants leg and pulled his trousers taut, revealing the outline of his penis. "And I don't mean to be disrespectful to you, but you're old enough to be my mamma. Not that she wadn't a good piece of pussy, my mamma." He stared at her hard, trying to scare her, but Sandra drew strength from it. He was playing a game with her. She couldn't let him roll over her this way. She would not. She had come here for a purpose. She had a mission. She would not be denied.

"Okay, you're right. I do want something from you."

"That's better."

"There is a snake."

"A snake?"

"Yes." Sandra began to shake. "I think I might have that beer if you don't mind." Claude finished his with a huge gulp and opened two more. It was cold in her throat, dark and mellow. "I don't quite know where to begin."

"You said Shep sent you."

"Shep saved me."

"Jesus saves," said Claude. "Moses invests."

"I can't tell you if you interrupt me. It's hard enough to think as it is in here. It's suffocating. And it stinks. You stink."

Claude slid open a window set into the door of the camper shell. "I guess pig shit don't smell to a pig," he said.

"I wasn't trying to be rude," replied Sandra. "So many things have happened. I haven't slept in over a day. I drove all last night to get here."

"Where did you come from?"

"That's not important. I came here because God led me to come here. I thought it was to see Hiram."

"Because he was the one with the snakes."

"I saw the snake. It knew me."

"For real? I seen plenty of snakes in my time, but never one who recognized me on sight. How is that possible? Or were you smoking some wacky weed? Tell me the truth now. Don't bullshit a bullshitter."

Sandra reached for the words that tumbled in her head like socks in a dryer. "My husband died. I served God all my life and then my husband died. It was very unexpected. They told me it was God's will. If that was true, then I thought, what has all this been for? It makes no difference. God is not good."

Claude lifted his beer as if toasting. "Fuck you, God! Goddamn you to hell. You motherfuckin' bastard."

"I lost my faith." She paused. Her voice cracked and she fought back the urge to cry. She would not cry in front of this man. And if he tried to hurt her, she would shoot him. She would take the gun out of her purse and shoot him. She knew she was capable of it. "But then Shep came into my life—and he reminded me of my husband. Not really, but he had an air about him."

"Shep was an anointed instrument of the Almighty," said Claude. She noticed there was not a trace of irony or sarcasm in his voice. "He wasn't always a holy man. Him and me—we was raised up here on this mountain. His daddy and my daddy was brothers. Shep and me were close enough to the same age that we just naturally took to running with each other—like dogs from the same litter. Folks even used to think we was brothers."

"There is a resemblance."

"We even got saved at the same time. Only I guess mine didn't take. Shep believed, but I could see the cracks in the plaster. Ain't no prayer meeting on Sunday morning I found that could compare to the hell I could raise on Saturday night."

"Shep showed me a way out. And then I saw the snake. Or rather it saw me."

"Where was this?"

"In Greensboro."

"Where Shep got killed?"

"Yes."

He clenched his mouth closed tightly and sighed. "But why?"

"I don't know. That's what I came here to find out."

He took a long moment, as if considering her case. "I can find your snake," he said. "People up here love to use 'em at the tabernacle for church. Makes 'em feel powerful, righteous. They dance around with 'em down in the service, and when they are done, they say they have been purified."

"Yes," said Sandra.

"After Hiram died I sort of inherited the franchise. You should know, though, I don't work for free and I don't do nobody favors."

"I can pay you."

"I figured that—otherwise you'd be heading down the mountain by now with my boot up your dainty Lucy Belle ass."

"How much will it cost?"

"What are you willing to pay?"

"Anything."

"Everything you have?"

She nodded her head. She knew there was no other way.

"Okay, then. I'll go and fetch you what you want. The rain is letting up and there's a place where they will come to catch the afternoon sun."

"Do you want me to come with you?"

He was suddenly deferential. "No, ma'am, not now. You stay here and get yourself ready. Do what you need. Pray, read Scripture. It would probably be best if you take off your face, though?"

"My face?"

He drew a circle around his own face with his finger. "You know, your makeup. A snake is sensitive to that sort of thing."

"I'd like to take a bath."

"I don't think there's time for that. Besides, probably best not to anyhow. Use a sweet-smelling soap and it's just gonna get him riled up. And I don't reckon you would enjoy the facilities too much." He handed her a roll of paper towels. "You can wipe yourself down at the sink if you want. And take off your jewelry too. I don't care what you do with it. I don't want it. Don't want nothing I have to barter—cash in hand is the way to go I say. But be plain and solemn when I come back to get you. This is serious bidness."

"I understand."

Claude shut the door behind him and she waited to hear if he had locked her in, but there was no click. She was free to go. She knew that it did not matter to him if she stayed or left.

Getting up from her seat, her legs felt wobbly. She was afraid they might not support her as she walked unsteadily to the sink. Leaning over the stained basin, she made a cup with her hands and ran the water from the tap, splashing her face with the coolness. She moistened a paper towel and wiped her face, then her neck. She undid her blouse and took it off. She unhooked her bra and removed it, and wiped herself clean under her arms and across the tops of her shoulder. She did not care if Claude came in now and saw her standing half dressed in the trailer, did not care if he was watching her from outside through the window. What did she have to lose now? She had come this far. There was no turning back. When she was finished, she put her blouse on, but not her bra. It was the deep purple one, the one she had worn the second night of the crusade in Greensboro—the night she called Violet. She put the bra into her purse, rearranging the contents so it was tucked in underneath the money and the gun. She removed her pearl stud earrings and wedding band and the gold cross she wore around her neck, and dropped them in as well—as if they were no more than loose change.

From the kitchenette, Sandra could see straight into Claude's room. She walked backed toward the space. The curtains were open and she could see outside that the storm was over. Sunlight now poured through the trees, steam rising off the damp earth. The room was cramped, barely larger than a closet. Claude's bed was little more than a box built underneath the window. She could see the distinct outline of his body on the dirty, unwashed sheets. The walls were covered in pin-ups, naked women who sat grinning, their legs opened wide to the camera. A small TV was mounted in the corner and on the shelf underneath it she noticed Claude's collection of videos—obscene titles like *Cuntalicious* and *Backdoor Bangers*. But those were just the store-bought ones. There was also a row of black plastic video containers with homemade labels written in a childish scrawl—*Robin, Nov. 2. Kim, April 13. Tina and Annette, June 19.* She tried not to imagine what sinister things Claude had recorded on those tapes for his pleasure, but wondered if soon there would be a new box with her name on it.

She heard the door to the trailer open. She turned, buttoning her blouse. Claude stood at the entrance to the trailer, his hand wrapped around a burlap sack. The sack hung heavy by his side, pulsating with a slow, steady rhythm.

"It's time," he said. Then again, "It's time."

Claude led her along a path through the woods to a series of low rocks formed into natural steps that opened onto a single, large, smooth slab of granite. As they stepped out onto the rock from underneath the canopy of trees, blue sky materialized before her, around her. They were on top of the mountain. In the distance, far away she could see the dark green hills and valleys as the landscape fell away from her to the horizon. Her spirits were lifted by the majesty, the beauty. *I will lift up mine eyes unto the hills, from whence cometh my strength*, she said in a whisper. But when she looked down, she stopped short. What she had at first thought were branches littering the surface of the stone she realized now were, in fact, snakes. Dozens, hundreds of them roiling in the heat of the sun on the warm rock after the storm.

"I can't," she said.

"Can't what?" asked Claude.

"I can't do this. The snakes. They will devour me."

"It just a bunch of black snakes, maybe a garter snake or two. They won't bite."

"I can't."

"Stand here, then," he said impatiently, "and hold this. I'll be right back." He handed her the burlap sack and disappeared down the path.

Sandra remembered as a girl holding a sack of kittens for her granddaddy. They had walked down from the house through the pasture to the creek and he had given it to her to hold as he went off into the woods to pee he had said. She remembered how she could feel the kittens inside, hear their soft mews as they squirmed and wriggled in the bottom of the bag. When Granddaddy had returned from the woods, he carried with him a medium-sized stone that he placed into the sack and then knotted. In a flash he pitched the sack into the creek where it immediately sank. Sandra remembered the horror she felt, how she had run wailing back to her grandmother. Her granddaddy had said it was never too early to learn about how things are. She did not want to know what those things were.

Now she felt that was what her whole life had become—looking into the bottom of the darkness to see what lived there, slithering, struggling to become free.

When Claude returned, he held a length of rough rope in his hand. She stepped back from the path as he strode past. When he got onto the rock, he unfurled the rope, took out a long, sharp hunting knife, and cut a long piece of it off. He then lay the rope down so that it made a circle. When he was finished, he waved at her with a single motion, meaning for her to join him. Seeing her hesitate, he said, "A snake won't crawl acrost a rope. Stand in this circle and you'll be safe. Stay where you are and the least thing that will happen is you'll get poison oak all over you."

She had no choice but to believe him. Sandra held the sack far in front of her as she followed him onto the rock, joining him inside the magic circle. In her mind's eye she could see as the other snakes stopped what they were doing and gathered around to observe the ceremony. She handed the sack to Claude and waited to see what came next.

"Do you have any verses you want to say?" he asked.

"No," said Sandra.

"When you hold him, talk to him or sing to him. He'll like that.

You can hold him up high or down low—you can even dance around with him if you want as long as you hold both the head and the tail. That's important, 'cause if you let either end get away, he'll try to turn on you. The tail is as bad as the head. He'll wrap it around you and squeeze till you forget what's what trying to shake him off. Then he'll bite you for sure. When you're done, you can just tell me and I will take him. Okay?"

"Okay."

"Now, where's my money?"

Sandra opened her purse. She removed the roll of bills and handed them over to Claude. He stuffed them into his pocket without so much as a glance. She looked down at the gun.

"You won't need that," he said. "I don't reckon you're a good enough shot to hit a snake on the run. And I know you wouldn't try to shoot me." He pointed the knife toward her. "Or if you did, I'd have you gutted like a speckled trout before either of us hit the ground. We clear on that?"

Sandra nodded. She closed her purse and put it down at the edge of the circle.

He put the sack down on the ground in front of her.

"Now, you step back a little, 'cause when he comes out, he is gonna be a little pissed off. Just stand real still and let me grab him. . . ." He untied a loop of twine from the top of the sack and turned it upside down. A copperhead, no more than three, maybe four feet long and about the same circumference as Sandra's wrist spilled out. Sandra covered her face, but even with her eyes closed she could still see glimpses through her fingers in the same way a child watches a horror movie. The snake glided over the surface of the rock toward the edge of the circle, hooking the ground with its belly and then contracting its muscles like a rolling spring in an effort to escape; but before it could, Claude's boot came down on it just behind its head. The snake arched up, but Claude caught the tail with his left hand, stretching it out like a fisherman measuring his catch. "I could have gotcha a timber rattler if I had known you was coming. They's a little harder to find. Will this one do you?"

Sandra felt as if she might vomit. But she would not give herself over to that. She had come too far. She would do this. She would hold the snake, she would look into its eyes and then she would kill it. And be free. When she brought her hands down from her face, Claude was standing directly in front of her, facing her with the snake held toward her in his outstretched arms. Sandra reached to take the snake from him.

She put her left hand just behind the snake's triangular-shaped head, which was crowned by a rusty-colored patch on the top like molten metal. Bands of dark brown shaped into an hourglass pattern ran down its bronzed back to a greenish yellow tip that was the tail. She thought suddenly of Jasmine and her murky eye. She grasped the snake's tail with her right hand and as Claude released the whole weight of it to her, she could feel its muscles ripple the length of its stout body.

The snake felt dry, smoother than she had imagined—not slimy in the least. The underbelly was a light creamy color, and she could also distinguish a dark streak running from each eye to the angle of the jaw. Using her hand, she squeezed the snake's neck so that it opened its mouth. She could see the two fangs, folded back against the top. The snake was quiet, letting her study it. It did not appear threatening to her like when Shep had held it. Or when it had come to her in the dream. Now it seemed docile, even frightened of her as it waited for her to finish. She watched as the lens closed over the elliptical eyes. She held the snake to her face so she might possess its mystical gaze.

"I know who you are."

Sandra's meditation was broken.

Claude repeated, "I know who you are, Miss Lucy Lucy Lou. I known it all along. Ever since you got here. Your name is Sandra Maxwell. And you are the woman who kilt Shep."

Sandra turned her head slightly. The snake followed in mirror image. "I tolt you I was watching the TV when you come here. They had a special report on the news about you. They showed your picture."

"It was an accident," said Sandra. She could feel the snake become restless in her grip.

"I reckon the po-lice have a different idea on that. They're calling it murder plain and simple," said Claude.

"I am an instrument of God," she told him. She doubted that the snake could kill Claude, but it would immobilize him while she escaped. "This is my destiny. I have sacrificed everything to be here. I will not be denied." She released her left hand from the snake's head so that she could throw it at him. As she did, she could see the deep pits on the sides of the head tense, feel the snake puff up, become rigid, as it inhaled the moist air. Its fangs swung downward in position for biting and as she released the snake, Sandra closed her eyes and shouted, *"Hallelujah!"* With a single swift motion it struck.

There was no pain, only a slight prickle of discomfort. Sandra instinctively brought her hand to her heart. When she opened her eyes, the snake hung from her breast like a talisman. She cupped its head tenderly with her other hand and pressed the snake close, as if suckling it. When it had released its venom into her, she let the snake drop to the ground and watched as it recoiled, prepared to strike again if necessary. As she gazed in amazement, the snake's head magically detached from its body—then she realized that Claude had thrown the knife, severing the serpent in two. Sandra turned to thank Claude, but as she did, the ground rushed up to meet her and she fell hard, hitting her head against the surface of the rock. It felt as if she were laying her head on a pillow.

Her body stiffened in a hard spasm and Sandra gnawed her tongue, filling her mouth with blood. Her eyes rolled back into her head as if in a spell. As sound and sight ceased for her, Sandra thought of Carson and the music the water made splattering on the tiles when he would shower in the morning, the smell of the breakfast as she cooked bacon for them, the way his calloused hands grew tender in the night when he touched her. She saw her home, before all this had happened to her, restored to her now forever with the dogwoods and agapanthus in bloom at the end of the driveway stretching before her like eternity. Shep stood there waving to her, shining brightly, his wounds all healed from the gunshots. The snake was there, too, had always been there, she realized, and as she took it all in she could feel her heart explode in the wonder and the joy that comes from understanding. She felt herself escape through the two pinpricks above her heart, flowing out into the grass, the water, the air.

She became light.

Claude looked down to where Sandra lay, the snake curled at her feet like a servant. He took the sack and gathered up a half dozen or so snakes from the ones remaining on the rock. He needed to dispose of her as quickly as possible. No telling when someone would come snooping around for her. He would turn the snakes loose in the car with her as he rolled it over the edge. Then if there was an investigation, the authorities would assume that they had gotten in and bitten her after the crash. It could work. It had the ring of truth to it. After all, stranger things have been known to happen.

# M.R. Vale

*After,* when the police ask Lonnie about the time he and I first met, what they will really want to know is about the first time we had sex. That's okay because it would be the time Lonnie would re-member as being when we met. It's not the truth, but it is what he would recall. Sex is like that for most men. It has a way of holding events in place in their memory like a thumbtack.

I also understand that Lonnie would know if he told them about that time, it could cast me in a bad light. Possibly portray me as a predator even. I want to believe he would not intentionally paint me with the broad brush of guilt, but he would want to make ab-solutely sure he, himself, wasn't smeared with it—and if that meant slopping some suspicion onto my shoulders, then so be it.

So he would tell them how I invited him—he may even say I lured him if he was thinking quickly—to the back of the store when he came to drop my van off after servicing it and then ever so matter-of-factly offered him money to show me his private parts. Which is true. I did offer him five dollars to show me his dick. Ten if he made it get hard. Which he did. He is proud of his pecker, as he likes to call it, and he likes to show it off. I've seen the way he looks when he takes it out, cupping it gently in his hand. He ad-mires it. He expects others to do the same. I don't blame him. I've seen plenty of dicks in my day up close and personal, and his is one of the finest. Fat and plump like a sausage even when it is hanging limp. But if that is what you're waiting for, sordid tales of me in bathroom stalls, waiting for whomever to stick his whatever through a glory hole in the partition, then I'm afraid you're going to be disappointed. My purpose is to dispel just those notions—that I am some perverse perverted pervert straight out of Edgar Allan Poe with a dash of John Rechy thrown in for good measure. Just take my word for it when I say I know what I am talking about when it comes to men and their Don Johnsons.

Then Lonnie would tell them how I gave him another ten to let me touch it. We're up to twenty-five dollars, in case you are keeping count. I doubt he would add that I didn't have to pay him extra to jerk him off. Once I had it in my hand, it wasn't too difficult to finish the task. A little spit and a few firm pulls. But I knew not to try any more than that. I knew he wouldn't have let me. Still, he didn't object at that point. In fact, I would describe him as a willing accomplice, but I doubt if the authorities would see it like that or that Lonnie would tell it that way.

I can imagine how Sheriff Plummer would respond to that salacious tidbit. Me holding Lonnie's hard, thick pecker in my hand in the back of my shop three short blocks from Main Street where anyone could have walked in at any time. Plummer would press for details, would love hearing about Lonnie's dick, how big it gets, would have asked to see it if he could have gotten away with it in the pursuit of evidence. But Plummer's interest in cock is not necessarily because he is homosexual—I wouldn't know about that. I've had my suspicions, mind you, but until I get the "mother may I" go-ahead, I don't take that giant step. I once had a good ole boy chase me halfway around the woods at Pine Grove Lake with a tire iron because I offered to finish him off when he was sitting in his truck playing with himself. But that's another story. My feeling is that Plummer's curiosity would stem from the fact I doubt the good sheriff has seen his own prick in the last dozen years with that huge corn-fed gut of his hanging down like it does. Besides, big, fat men inevitably have no dick. Like I said, I've seen enough to know.

There is even a rumor afoot that I sucked Lonnie off in an

empty baptismal pool of one of the Baptist churches. That salacious chitchat is especially hurtful since there are three Baptist churches in town, and a blow job in the sanctuary would make me seem both degenerate and unrepentant at the very least. However, it does make me smile to myself to imagine Joanne Jackson leading all the good Baptist women of the town and organizing committees to get down on their knees to Clorox those pools clean of the stench of sacrilegious man-on-man sex.

But the time in the back of the shop wasn't the first time I met Lonnie. No, the first time was late one Friday afternoon toward the beginning of last spring when the afternoon breeze still carried the promise of a cool evening. I remember I was driving by JB's garage, having just delivered all the flowers to the Presbyterian church for a wedding there the next day. If I am to be thorough in my accounting of this, I should add, as a footnote, that while deemed acceptable to choose the flowers with the mother of the bride, arrange them, deliver them to the church, I am never asked to the church for the wedding or the funeral or the baptism, never asked to the reception or the receiving for a slice of cake or a glass of fruit punch. That is the way here and I accept it. Once in a great while they might send a picture of the "lovely arrangement" enclosed with the check to let me know I helped to "make their special day truly special." But like I said, that's the way it is and I always accepted it—happy to stay on my side of the fence. Solitary confinement, so to speak. Until I met Lonnie.

The afternoon I met him I was on the way home from the Presbyterian church. Lonnie was changing the gas prices on the metal sign out front of the garage, fumbling with the numbers. He had the prices turned back to front, so that hi-test was two dollars and eighty-three cents instead of thirty-eight. He looked befuddled, innocent like a child putting together an alphabet puzzle where there were too many letters. To be totally truthful (which is my aim here), his T-shirt was torn under his left arm so that when he reached up there was a good glimpse of his armpit, the matted hair on his chest, his nipple, but that is not what struck me. It was not merely carnal lust that drew me to him. There are plenty of men who would have welcomed me and my soft, luscious mouth, anytime, anywhere. So don't think of me as desperate. What drew me to him was that confusion, that childlike innocence, that helplessness.

That is the image I would ask that you keep, for it is the image I hold even after all that has happened. It is the one of the Lonnie who existed in some faraway time and place. The ideal Lonnie.

Do you believe in love at first sight? In fate? In destiny? No, then you will pass all of this off as some ranting of a giddy queen eager for a one-off with a grimy mechanic in a torn T-shirt. But I swear to you when I saw Lonnie, I knew that he was my future. I don't believe there was any way I could have resisted it—him. Even if I had wanted to. I knew at that instant that he and I were linked in some special, inevitable way.

I pulled into the garage and saw Joe Boggs, the owner, told him I needed to have a service on the delivery van. This was nothing unusual, though I usually had my mechanical work done midweek since weekends were busy with deliveries. To cover myself, I told him that I thought something was wrong with the fuel line or the carburetor. I told him I heard a dreadful sort of *ping-ping* when I got to around thirty miles per hour, and I was afraid the engine was just going to blow up and leave me stranded by the side of the road with a van full of flowers. This was, of course, a lie, but I knew Joe wouldn't test it, would only change the oil, squirt some grease onto the springs and axle as he always did. My experience has shown mechanics hold homosexuals in general contempt, tolerate them even less than they do women in a garage. He would figure I was just being flighty, not knowing a carburetor from a candy bar. But business was business. And Joe Boggs is as greedy as they come.

I told him I would leave the van in the morning, but had a very busy day at the shop and didn't think I would get back before he closed. Which posed a real dilemma since I had to deliver the flowers for Sunday service to First Methodist, St. John of God Episcopal, and the Church of God of Prophecy where he was a member. Could he have someone drop it off for me when they closed at two on Saturday afternoon? Joe didn't want to, didn't want to be seen as too comfy cozy with me. But in a small town, it is almost impossible to say no to such a request—even a bigot like Joe Boggs would not want to be perceived as rude. So I knew he would say yes, even if he didn't want to, especially since if he didn't comply, there would be no flowers for his church on Sunday morning. How would he explain the lack of a mixed bouquet to his wife and fellow church members, not to mention the God of Prophecy. I knew it was a slight he wouldn't be willing to risk. I also knew he would pawn the task off to someone else.

"I guess I can have Lon run it over when we close. He's staying out your way."

"That would be so helpful." I smiled. By this time Lon—Lonnie—had walked back in the small, cluttered office of the garage. His smell—no, not smell, his scent—sweat, mixed with dirt and grease—almost overwhelmed me. But I refused to look at him. Knew that if I did, I would give myself away by some involuntary, trembling glance or smile—that he and Joe Boggs would know the truth about what I felt.

"Lon, I'm going to have you take Mr. Vale's van over to him tomorrow when we get done."

Lon shrugged a consent as he sized me up. At 5'6", and a svelte 135 pounds, I am sure he considered me nothing more than a puny runt. And if he noticed them at all, the highlights in my nutmeg-tinted hair, my gold dangle belt, my teal Ralph Lauren Polo shirt would have been similarly dismissed with a single thought—fag. But I didn't care. I am a butterfly. I am a work of art. I make beauty wherever I am. A flaming scarlet silk purse can never become a sow's ear, my dears, and I for one have never seen any good reason to try; besides, the stage was set. Lon was coming to my shop.

The next afternoon, instead of just zipping up and walking out like so many other men would do (and have done!), Lon walked back into the main part of the shop, checking out the lay of the land. Perhaps he felt the connection as well, I told myself. As he strolled casually among my displays I thought how Roman women would pour their tears into tiny urns as their husbands left for battle, to commemorate their love, their loss, their yearning, their suffering. Looking back now, I should have preserved that moment, used a vial to immortalize his milky spunk, his essence—and my love, my loss, my desire, my pain. Instead, I swabbed my hands with a Wet and Wipe, and tossed it into the trash can.

"This where you stay?" he asked.

I have learned you can always tell someone's breeding by the questions they ask—or more to the point, the way they ask questions. Rednecks and white trash always refer to their home as *where they're stayin'*, as if we are all a part of a communal caravan.

"Yes," I told him. "I have lived here since I was a boy."

"And this is yourn?"

"You mean the house—yes, I own it."

"Who-ea," he said. "I don't think I ever met nobody who owned a house outright. You must be a right rich little fella."

"I have no complaints."

"And all this from putting flowers together in a jar."

"A vase. Or an arrangement. But floral design is a highly respected trade. And I have been nationally certified."

If he was impressed by this, he didn't show it.

"Where's your mamma and diddy?"

"Mother died when I was twenty-seven—my father was never around. What about you?"

"Ain't got no kin . . . at least none that will claim me." His face darkened, and I knew there was more here.

"Would you like a beer?" I asked. I had stocked my refrigerator with longnecks.

"Sure. I guess. Whatever's going."

When I brought the beer, I found him out on the back porch, sitting on the steps in the long shadows of the afternoon sun, leaning back against the rail. Male models work frantically to affect the effortlessness of that pose, that off-handed, casual, relaxed masculinity.

*I'll buy you things*, I wanted to tell him. *If you will only come and stay here and let me look at you in this light, let me touch your face, your skin. I will worship you like the god that you are. And I will do whatever you ask me to.*

But I didn't say that—I didn't have to. Lonnie already knew that I belonged to him.

If my life is ever made into a movie—and yes, I do imagine that it will be now since the word on the street is producers are already clamoring for the rights—the next few months would be a montage, the part of the movie shot in a golden glow where lovers skip playfully through fields of flowers, pausing only to sip wine from each other's lips or loll playfully in front of the fire. A conversation that begins on the beach at sunrise in spring dissolves into a candlelit discussion over dinner in autumn. A touch on the hand across the breakfast table concludes with a final caress before the sheets billow in the breeze as a background for their lovemaking. I hope that is the way it is shot. It is the way it should be shot.

In reality, Lon would come by once every three or four days after he got off from work at the garage. He would appear without warning at my back door, like he stumbled upon my house by accident. Or had been sleepwalking in a dream. We both knew why he was there, of course, even though we always pretended that the sex just happened. It was like when I used to buy weed from Drexel Smith before he burned up his trailer cooking methamphetamine and got sent to prison. I would only see Drexel a few times each year like the change of season, and when I would go to see him, I would always have an excuse for showing up, like we were friends or something. That he was more than just a dope peddler. We would pretend to have a conversation—the drugs would be an afterthought. "Oh, by the way, do you have an ounce you could sell me? Thanks so much. Sorry, I have to run." If I am to tell it all, I would have to say that Lonnie was like that with me. There were no golden sunsets or claret-filled goblets—and very little talk.

So to the director and the scriptwriter, if you want to show how it was, write it like this: Lon would show up at my back door like I said, ask if I had anything to drink—he knew, of course, that I kept beer in the fridge for him—then after knocking back a couple he would ask to use the toilet. Generally, he would leave the door open, and when he was finished peeing, I knew he was ready for me to make my move.

"Looks like you could use some help there," or "Why don't you let me take care of that for you." And so we fell into a rhythm, a pattern—like a real couple. When I got more comfortable, I would push the boundaries: "It's pretty hot—you're welcome to take a shower if you want. I think I might have a pair of jeans and a shirt that would fit you"—since *I ordered them especially for you.* Slowly, slowly, slowly our courtship progressed from me blowing him in the bathroom with his jeans and boxers down around his ankles. Soon, he would arrive, drink his beer (after helping himself), take a shower (without asking), and leave his dirty clothes for me to launder. While he would shower, I would make him a sandwich (bologna and olive loaf with mayonnaise were his favorites) or heat up something I had made for dinner the night before (meatloaf, pot roast, chicken—no casseroles) because I knew he would be hungry later. After covering his plate of food and leaving it on the table in the kitchen, I would stand outside the bathroom—waiting, watching. Soon, he would step out of the shower, naked, glistening like a seal pup, dry off, and comb his hair. Sometimes, he would shave. I will confide that he loved my toiletry products—the lotions, colognes, the hair tonics. He would liberally douse himself with whatever; slick back his blue-black hair so that it shined like wet ink. He would pat the remaining wetness from his chest or along his shoulders and saunter nonchalantly past me into my bedroom where he knew his fresh clothes would be laid out for him. That was my cue. I would find him reclined on the bed, waiting. And I would kneel between his legs, the soft heaviness of his balls beckoning me to the tower of his manhood. And so you do not have to wonder, I will answer the question for you. No, I never once undressed, never once touched myself, never once asked Lonnie to touch me or hold me or regard me in any way beyond what he did. And I would pleasure him, and he would give himself to me, and in those soft, quiet moments, even though there was no golden sunset, or claret-filled goblet, or romantic conversation, it was perfection. It was life like it is in the movies.

# . . . 2 . . .

You have undoubtedly formed opinions about me. Certainly enough has been written. And *Nancy Grace*, good Lord, she has featured stories about us almost every night. You must have seen her—how she gets positively googly-eyed when she recounts some of the more sordid rumors: "We hear from the owner of the Peach Bottom Motel, a Mr. Rex Galloway, that Flowers and Vale never left the room after they bought a chicken bucket from a local drive-through, so are we to *assume* that they *slept* in the *actual room* with the *body* of the *murdered boy*—Sammy Hutchens?" True, Nancy, we did not leave the room. Lonnie invited Sammy back to the motel with the promise of money, drugs, sex, and a bucket of fried chicken. Then Lonnie fucked him, broke his neck, and ate the chicken while watching reruns of *Cops*. And yes, we slept in the room with the body of the murdered boy. Get someone to tell you about the smell sometime. It isn't something you forget easily. Now, thanks to the free publicity, Mr. Galloway and his wife are giving tours at the motel—the "Death Room," as they call it, has been cordoned off with red velvet ropes borrowed from the local mini-plex. A real trailer-trash version of an estate tour if you ask me.

But I am hoping you, dear friend, will keep an open mind. And though this is not an apology, I never did intend for things to turn out like they did, had no inkling that the night in the motel was going to end up like it did. I could only see as far as what Lonnie was asking me to do. Believe that or not—it's the truth. Good purpose can have the same horrific results as bad. I loved Lonnie. Wanted only to please him. And if we can never know the impact, then should we not be judged solely on our intent? If a blind man, reaching for the light switch, breaks a vase, then is it really his fault? But, you say, why would he need to turn the lights on anyway? So, let me give you an example a little closer to home.

There was a woman who worked for my mother and me after Mother had her first stroke—a woman very near my mother's age, but of lesser circumstance. Her name was Lois Bell. She came three days a week and did the chores that I did not have time (or the inclination) for. She vacuumed and dusted, polished silver, washed and ironed. If nothing else, Mrs. Bell was worth every cent we paid her just to iron. She could put a pleat in a trouser leg or a point on a collar like nobody's business. If truth be told, she wasn't really very good at much else. She was also addicted to the soap operas on CBS—*As the World Turns, Guiding Light,* in particular. She had watched them all her life, she said. For her, it was like spending time with friends, and she could recount in great detail the minute miseries of each of the characters. "Now that one, Abigail, is a sweet girl, really, though, she has had her share of trouble. She was one of them Amish people and was hard of hearing, so she left so she could have an operation and be normal, but then Roy attacked her and put her in a coma. When she came to, she shot him dead, and even though she didn't go to jail, I think she still suffers from the incident. Why she ever got involved with that Roy, I just don't know. He was bad business from the get-go."

The other, newer shows like *The Young and the Restless* and *The Bold and the Beautiful* were too brass, too brazen for her—which I interpreted as too sexy—and she would have nothing to do with them or the afternoon talk shows where people sang their perversions and woes to the world. I wonder what Mrs. Bell would have thought about Nancy Grace's commentary on me. I can see her standing at the ironing board, pressing down on a freshly starched pleat. "Nancy, you have to believe me when I tell you he was a nice boy, really. Devoted to his mamma, and could put flowers together like nobody's business. About all the other, I wouldn't know." She liked to watch her shows while she ironed. She also liked to chew ice and kept a small bowl on the end of the ironing board, cracking ice cube after ice cube with her back teeth, sucking the cold, melted slush down with a slurp. It drove Mother crazy.

But there was one problem. Mrs. Bell didn't drive. Which meant that someone always had to fetch or deliver her from where she was coming to where she needed to go. So two years after the stroke, when Mother finally admitted that she would not be driving again, she thought it would be a kind gesture to offer the Rambler to Mrs. Bell. So we did. Mother even paid for Mrs. Bell to go to driving school. Mrs. Bell was overjoyed. A car meant she wouldn't have to depend on her daughter for rides. And she could go to church on Wednesday evenings without having to wonder if she would have to take the bus home after at night. Then on Christmas Eve, as Mrs. Bell was on her way to church for the Nativity Play and song service, she hit a strip of black ice out on Highway 905. Went sideways smack into a telephone pole and was killed instantly. Mother was distraught, said that if she had not provided her with the means, then Mrs. Bell might not have been killed. I only thought that it was oddly appropriate that Mrs. Bell had been killed by ice, and it was not until later that I understood what Mother had felt.

You see, I killed my own son.

Now before you run off and call Nancy Grace and start hollering, "He's got another one," Byung Hun Lee was not really my child. You should know by now that I could never, would never do such a thing. I adopted him from the back of a magazine.

It was Mother's *Better Homes and Gardens,* to be specific. You know the type of thing—one of those ads sponsored by a relief agency to foster a child. The picture of the smudged toddler with a shy, raggedy smile and innocent, imploring eyes. *For less than twenty dollars a month you could make a difference in this child's life.* The child in the ad was not my child, of course. But I did clip out the coupon, write a check, and mail it in. In a few short weeks I received a very official-looking packet decorated with the authorized seal of the charity containing all the information on the child who was depending on me to make a difference: Byung Hun Lee, an eight-year-old South Korean with much the same expression as the child in the magazine. I wondered if someone had pinched them just prior to the photo being snapped. I had heard of such things happening. A letter explained to me that Byung lived with his mother on the outskirts of Daegu in the central part of the country. They had exceptionally limited resources. My money would allow him to go to school instead of working with her full-time in a tailor's shop. While he would still help out on Saturdays and after school, my support would provide books, a school uniform, and a hot meal every day. They also informed me that Byung himself would write to me once a month. I was ecstatic.

Because the letters had to be translated from Korean, it took several months to receive the first one. It read:

> *Dear kind sir,*
> *Because of you my life is very different now. I am able to learn new things like mathematicals and reading. You do not know me, but I will work hard to make you proud of me. My mother is very grateful for your generousness.*
>
> > *With respect and admirance,*
> > *Byung Hun Lee*

I figured they must have had an older student in the school learning English translate the letters as an exercise. It would appear even charity isn't beyond exploitation. Included with the translation was the actual letter from Byung—a nearly transparent piece of light blue paper, the tiny foreign symbols scratched in his tentative child's script. A treasure. I commandeered one of Mother's old stationary boxes and stored his letter—a record of what I imagined would be a long and rewarding relationship. And for a time, it was. Each month I received a letter: *Dear kind sir, most generous benefactor* . . . Byung was doing well in school. He hoped one day that he might open a shop like his uncle who lived far away in

Pusan. He enjoyed playing tops with his friends. He could also run very fast. But was sure not to play tag when he was wearing his uniform.

And then one day—almost a year from when I first clipped the coupon in *Better Homes and Gardens*—I received another official letter from the agency: Byung was dead, they told me. Drowned while on a trip to visit relatives. So sad, so sorry, would I like to replace him with another deserving child? I wrote back that a child was not a light bulb or a defective radio part and they could go and fuck themselves. I did not want a replacement.

But someone forgot to inform the translator. After all, he probably still needed the practice, and who had time to sort out a letter from a dead boy? And because of the time delay, Byung's letters continued to reach me for three months after the news of his death—strange, sad songs from my ghost child.

> *Dear kind sir, most generous friend,*
> *I am reading better now. And on my last*
> *examination I received superior markings in equations.*

In the last letter, Byung wrote of his plans when school would be out for the term.

> *My uncle has invited me to visit him in Pusan. I*
> *will take the train there by myself. It will take all day to*
> *make the trip, and it is the first time I will ever see the*
> *ocean. My uncle has promised to teach me to swim. You*
> *have made my life full beyond measure, benevolent*
> *mister. I am in your debt always.*

Guilt overwhelmed me. If it had not been for me, he would have been working in the tailor's shop, unable to afford the luxury of a vacation. What had I done? What was my part in the death of this small boy who only depended on me for a hot meal and tuition?

After that, I began to dream of Byung. The dream was always the same. I would run through the rail station looking for his train, but inevitably I was unable to find it—my feet would become heavy, my legs turned to jelly, the rail platform would move away from me in a mist. But always, always in the instant just before I awoke I was able to see Byung sitting in the railroad car, his shining face framed in the window. And when I would awake from the dream, I could still see him—so absolutely alive—so impossibly dead. What would have happened if I had ever caught the train? Would I pull Byung from the moving train? Would I tell Sammy not to come back to the motel? Would I beg him to take the money that Lonnie had offered him and run far, far away? Or would I only inform him how sorry I was that things had turned out so badly?

And even more troubling perhaps, I wondered if, as the train began to heave from the station that day, did the slow, soft pull of the engine's wheels call to Byung like the dark depths of the ocean? Did he know? Did he blame me?

Or was he clueless as a cow—like the murdered boy Sammy Hutchens, he was doomed—Sammy, who thanked Lonnie for buying extra-crispy chicken because it was his favorite, who was reaching for the chicken, his back to Lonnie, so that I could see Lonnie standing behind him. And then the moment. Lonnie's massive hands gripping Sammy's head in that relentless grasp. Lonnie commanding me not to look away. "You need to appreciate this," he growled. I could see the confusion that turned to fear and then to hatred and finally to understanding as Lonnie held Sammy's head in his hands, lifting it up and away from Sammy's shoulders, twisting it around back and forth, front to back so the bones in Sammy's neck began to creak, and the gurgle in Sammy's throat became a sad, high-pitched whine. Until the bones, unable to stand the strain, began to splinter and the only sound was a low, guttural sigh that was Sammy's final breath. "Now you know," Lonnie said. "Now you know, and you'll believe what I tell you."

Dear Byung, my dead son, did you recognize death when it came for you? Were you afraid? Did you understand what it meant to die? And did you blame me for it? Or, as the wheels slipped from the platform toward the inescapability of the ocean, did you simply close your eyes, and whisper, "Thank you, kind sir. Generous friend. Benevolent benefactor. Father."

# . . . 3 . . .

But enough of this. It is killing you came for and killing you shall have. So, how about this: It wasn't until Roger Simmons's head splattered across the marble fireplace—bone and brain embedded in Laverne Simmons's antique fire screen—that I believed Lonnie actually intended to kill him. Even though Lonnie told Roger he was going to die and Roger seemed to believe what he told him. *But you see, your honor, I just thought we were going there to scare him. To frighten him so that he wouldn't speak to anyone about Lonnie or me.*

I realize now how ridiculous that sounds. Of course Lonnie intended to kill him. There was only one way for Lonnie to be sure that Roger would never expose him. Roger's death was as inevitable as the evening tide.

Roger Simmons worked in Morris as an insurance representative for as long as I can remember. He was a few years older than I, but we both went to the Thomas Drayton High School where Roger played fullback for the Generals and was All-State during his senior year. He received a scholarship to play football for Wofford, though he was sidelined permanently in his sophomore year with a knee injury, and when he received his Bachelor of Science in Business, he returned to Morris, unlike most who had the opportunity to leave. He said it was his home, that there was nothing he needed anywhere else that he couldn't have in Morris. He promptly married his high-school sweetheart, Laverne Taylor, and they opened Simmons Independent Insurance agency. He was the salesman and operating executive; she worked in the office as the accountant and secretary. That is how I first got to know Roger and Laverne. He was Mother's insurance agent. Roger and I had also become intimate friends—occasional lovers—over the course of twenty years.

In a town like Morris, it doesn't take a great deal to distinguish yourself, but Roger and Laverne were definitely stars—the upper crust of society. They built an elaborate, but tasteful four-bedroom, white brick ranch house at the entrance to Bramble Estates, just down from the landmark and named for it. Bramble Estates was also home to the country club and golf course, where Roger and Laverne hosted ice-cream socials for the Methodist youth group from church, pig pickin's for high-school fund-raisers, elegant cocktail parties during golf tournament weekends. Laverne was known for her parties—from down-home, laid-back, serve-yourself buffets to lavish, sophisticated affairs with delicate hors d'oeuvres that she had found in *Southern Living* or *Better Homes and Gardens* or in one of her collection of Miss Virginia cookbooks. Laverne was a natural hostess, had been awarded third place in the Miss Virginia Homemaking Competition, a statewide contest for high-school girls to promote "excellence in the domestic arts." She had flair. She had organization. She knew what she wanted. All earmarks of a great compère. Why, even when she was in high school and won the third place prize for a coconut cake recipe, she had not squandered her winnings, but had used her prize money to attend a secretarial school where she learned typing, shorthand, and double-entry bookkeeping. From the get-go, she made sure her plans were interwoven with Roger's.

As a client, Laverne was a dream. Not like some of the women in town who think chrysanthemums are the height of elegance. She would bring pictures from magazines of arrangements she had seen, consult with me on which colors would help to lighten or soften the ambience, and I would deliver crystal bowls filled full of floating camellias, or grand Oriental vases crowded with calla or Asian lilies, or small woven baskets of mixed spring flowers—peonies, hyacinth, sweet peas—depending on her theme. A day or two after the event, Roger would regularly bring me a sampling from the menu that had not been eaten by the guests, sometimes accompanied with a note of thanks from Laverne.

Now that Roger is dead, nostalgia for the years we were friends overwhelms me. Perhaps this is what hell is like. To feel the pain and regret for what was, for what never was, for what might have been. Certainly, I was very fond of Roger. He had been our insurance agent—Mother's insurance agent, to be more specific—and after her stroke, he was a wizard sorting out the hospital bills. He even pursued the disability claim in the rider. It was sometime later that I ran into Roger at the state park one afternoon. It was surprising, but when I think back on it, I don't know that it was all that unexpected. He had all the earmarks for "gay": He dressed well (even after he gained the weight), he knew the flowers in the shop by name ("M.R., that is a beautiful shade of pink on those anthurium—almost a fuchsia."), and he was devoted to opera. He would bring a cassette just to play a new recording of a favorite aria. So when I met him in the state park that afternoon, I followed him into the bushes and helped him to accomplish what he had come for; then afterward, he asked if I wanted to walk along a trail and talk.

"Aren't you afraid you will be seen by someone you know?" I asked.

"I know you," he replied.

"Someone besides me."

"If they are here, then we are probably here for the same reason. Wouldn't you suppose? Besides, it goes on more than you think."

I couldn't argue with him there.

Roger was the only other homosexual I knew who lived in Morris—that is, unless you counted Drexel Smith. But Drexel was a trailer-trash gay, good only for scoring some weed. I never trusted Drexel, always thought he short-changed me when I bought grass from him. Not because he didn't like me. No, that didn't matter. Drexel aroused my suspicions, seemed just the type of person who wanted to get something over on you so he could feel superior. But on a deeper level, I was a little scared of Drexel. It wasn't that he was that physically intimidating, though he was tall and taut, with lean, sleek muscles covered in swirling ribbons of green and yellow, red and blue tattoo art. He had arrived in Morris as if dropped from the sky, living in a trailer off Highway 905. The trailer had been the home of my previous drug dealer, Miss Annabeth Owensby, who served drinks to truckers and local shit-kickers at the Spooky Angel Lounge. I had met Miss Annabeth when she came to buy flowers.

"I just can't abide those tacky little supermarket arrangements," she said. I think you can tell a great deal about a person from the types of flowers they like. Mother's favorite flower was the calla, which means "magnificent beauty." Annabeth was fond of anemones— the flower of the forsaken. I would make sure I always had some on hand when I could get them, and every other week, she would stop in for a loose bouquet. One afternoon, she said she was short on cash and wondered if I would take something in trade, so she offered me up a joint. After that, I would stop in to visit and pick up a bag or she would drop off some weed for me when she picked up her flowers. It was all so very convenient. We would swap stories about the men in our lives (she had many more than I), and she would bemoan her frailty for troublemakers.

"But the dangerous ones are so sexy," I reminded her.

"And therein lies the heartache," she said, passing me the remainder of a joint.

Then, when I went to visit her one afternoon, all of a sudden she was gone, disappeared, and in her place was Drexel. He studied me contemptuously as I stood at the bottom of the cement steps leading up to the trailer. When I inquired after Annabeth, he said simply that she had "moved on."

"Oh," I said. "Do you know where she might have moved or if she might be coming back?" It troubled me that Annabeth's car was sitting in front of the trailer, but I didn't question Drexel. I didn't know what her relationship with him had been, what arrangements they had made.

"Do you see a fortune-teller's sign hanging out here? No? Then I reckon I don't know where she's gone. I only knew her a little spell and she said she had bidness to attend to out of state. So, what you want with her?" Then, pointing to my truck, she said, "You bringing her flowers?"

"No." I tried to think of something to say, but like most rednecks, Drexel had worked it out as soon as he had laid eyes on me.

"Then I reckon you must be one of her customers. How much you need?"

"A half. An ounce if you have it."

And that was that.

Drexel walked back into the trailer, and I scurried up the steps behind him, forgetting about Annabeth and her abandoned Chrysler. I won't say I was shocked to see the copies of *Honcho* and *Mandate*, which lay strewn over the coffee table and piled carelessly on the floor, with some of his favorite centerfolds taped or thumbtacked to the wall. What surprised me was that he was so blatant in his disregard. I knew I wouldn't have been the only of Annabeth's former customers to come calling, and it was as if he was daring whoever set foot in the trailer to challenge him about his sexual desires. Drexel would not want to trade flowers for weed.

Roger, on the other hand, was a man of means; but even more than that, he was a good man. Over the years that I knew Roger, I grew to appreciate his robust laugh, his kind eyes, his thoughtful gestures. There was, however, a sense of sadness to him that I wonder if he would have been able to explain if I asked him about it. He and Laverne never had children. When he would talk to me about their life together, he would explain that Laverne never really liked, as he put it, "the bedroom stuff." I never knew if he sought me out for sexual release or just for companionship. Many times, especially after Laverne became ill and when he had gained all his weight, he would forget to even unzip his britches. We would just talk about something that struck him as funny, or a bit of gossip that he had overheard and knew I would enjoy, or a cruise that he and Laverne were preparing to take when she recovered.

Yes, Roger Simmons was a fat man. The knee injury from college gave him an excuse not to exercise, and the years of double old-fashioneds every evening followed by one of Laverne's generous meals took their toll. He was always big, but when he was young, he could carry the weight. But as muscle turned to fat, his waistline grew round as Tweedledee's, his barrel chest became bloated and droopy, and the flesh under his chin puffed out so much that his neck sagged down enough to cover the top of his tie and shirt collar.

It was during one of those visits that he told me about Laverne's cancer. Of course I had already heard about it from a customer in the shop. The whole town was abuzz with Laverne's illness, but I didn't let Roger know that I had heard. He needed to tell me himself. He cried when he spoke of how they had discovered the lump, and how the doctor had removed both breasts as a precaution, but that he said the cancer was already in the lymph system, so it was only a matter of time before it spread to liver, bone, lungs, brain. In fact, it took Laverne nearly two years to die, two years to shrink from a tall, vivacious, full-figured woman to a withered sack of rotting flesh and bone. I will admit I didn't go over too much toward the end, but I did take her flowers two or three times over the course of her decline, and once made a pimento cheese-ham casserole when she had gotten out of the hospital after chemotherapy. I was shocked by her appearance, and not just the fluffy, peach-colored Eva Gabor wig that sat perched on her head like a dead Pomeranian, or the fact that she had plied makeup heavily on her cheeks and around her eyes to disguise her gauntness. Laverne had always been broad-shouldered and big bosomed with a broad, round bottom. Some large women resemble eggs with legs, but Laverne was statuesque, uninhibited by and unafraid of her size and shape. She was fond of bold colors—sapphire blues and magentas, emerald greens, canary yellows. Even when she was sick, she had on an animal-print bed jacket that hung on her like a pillowcase. She reminded me of the craft projects that women around town were so fond of making in autumn. They would take a bale of straw, top it with a pumpkin and a pot of mums from Wal-Mart, and lean a homemade scarecrow wearing one of Grandma's old dresses or Grandpa's trousers, bowtie, and braces. Laverne looked like one of those scarecrow women. A sad, worn-out craft project. When I came into the room, she propped up on one of her elbows and made me show her the casserole. When she saw what I had brought for her and Roger, she said, "I see you've been reading your Miss Virginia's cookbook."

I knew that it touched Laverne that I had thought to use a Miss Virginia recipe. "It was one of Mother's," I replied.

"Which one?"

"*Tried and True Southern*, I think."

"That's one of her best. I used to serve the layered salad to my women's circle from the church when they would come for lunch. It was always a hit," she said.

"Did you ever meet her?" I asked.

"Miss Virginia? No, she was much too old and ill to travel when I won the scholarship. I think she died the year after. I did get a card with her name on it and her signature, though. I saved it. I will show it to you the next time you come."

"I heard she was a drinker."

"Well, you never know a person's life unless you are on the inside of it. But speaking of the scholarship, I do have something for you."

"An autographed Miss Virginia."

"Nothing so extravagant I'm afraid." She handed me a small, unwrapped gift box. "But I did get this at the reception when I received my prize."

I opened the box. Inside was a delicate, ornately decorated teacup and saucer. I lifted it out to examine the intricate pattern of flowers: pink chrysanthemums, white dogwood blossoms, red geraniums, deep blue hyacinth.

"It's lovely," I said.

"I don't know that it is worth much," she said. "But I thought you would enjoy it. I think it must have belonged to Miss Winifred Bramble. Her sister gave it to me."

"Now there was a horror," I said, and Laverne laughed with me.

"The reception was held out at the Bramble Farm. All the ladies from town were there. It was very fancy. Mama had bought me a new dress, of course. I had my hair pulled back with a ribbon. Miss Jewel was there. It was before she was taken away, but she must have been in her dotage because she thought I was someone she knew from years and years before. And then, she went into the kitchen and came back with this. She said, 'Freddie would have wanted you to have this.' I tried to refuse, but she insisted."

"It's an antique," I said.

"But aren't we all?" Laverne said. "Yes, like I said, I doubt that it is worth anything, but I have kept it all these years just the same. I thought that you might enjoy it—because of the flowers."

"Yes," I said. "I will certainly treasure it."

Then she said something very curious. "You know, M.R., that Roger will be lost when I am gone."

I thought about lying and saying she wasn't going anywhere but a cruise to the Caribbean when she recuperated and got her hair grown in again, but knew I couldn't. "You will be missed by many people," I said.

"He will have the worst of it, though." She took a moment, then continued. "He will need friends. I hope that you will be a friend to him."

"I will do my best, Laverne," I promised. I meant it, too. In another time, another place, I might have courted Roger after her death. I won't say that a home at the entrance to the country club, cruises to the Caribbean, and hosting parties for the local elite were not without their appeal. He and I were certainly compatible, even if I didn't find him desirable. That isn't unlike a great many couples who live long and happy lives together. However, by the time Laverne passed, I had taken up with Lonnie, was consumed with him day and night, so Roger Simmons's happiness wasn't the uppermost of my concerns. As a tribute to Laverne, however, I did some of my best work for her funeral spray—a blanket of ivory and lavender roses with just a touch of Lunaria for drama. Christ the Shepherd Methodist church was packed for her service, and when I saw Roger at the front, he did indeed look like a man lost in the mist, unsure of his footing, as if the landscape of the world had come unstable, unfixed, unglued. I stood at the back with the gentlemen from Haywood Family Mortuary Services while Roger was guided to his seat by Laverne's sister and her husband. He reminded me of an untethered dirigible, pilotless—left to the generosity of those below to hold the ropes and guide him to safety. On the way out of the church, he saw me and smiled—a faraway, vacant cast to his eyes. I realized he was either taking pills or had been drinking.

It was only a few weeks before my suspicions were confirmed. He showed up at the shop to thank me for the funeral flowers, and I could smell the bourbon on him. It didn't take him long, however, to get to the real purpose of the visit.

"What do you say, M.R., that you and me go on a trip somewhere. Close up the shop for a few weeks and we can go down to Key West. Get a bungalow. Cut loose. Waste away in Margaritaville."

"It's not a good time for me to leave, Roger," I said. "I have clients—and homecoming is just around the corner. I will have corsages to make for the queen and her court."

"Fuck fucking homecoming. They can go over to Whiteville to get their fucking corsages."

"Roger, it doesn't work like that. If you want to go to Key West, then go. There will be many people down there who would be happy to spend time with you—to have you buy them a drink, take them to dinner if you are lonely."

"But you are my friend, M.R.—it wouldn't be the same."

"People would talk. It would be a scandal. It would ruin your business."

"I don't give a shit about what people might say. I have lived my whole life doing what I was supposed to do. I was a big kid, so I played football. I don't even like football. I married Laverne because she was the first girl who ever let me kiss her. And everyone in town said we were made for each other."

"You had a good life with her, Roger. You know that."

"I'm not saying I didn't. I just wonder whose life I've been living all this time, because it sure as hell doesn't seem like mine. When I married Laverne, it was a different time. Men married women. So what if I fooled around with the boys in the locker room—it was just boys having fun. And then it was the same thing at Wofford in the fraternity. But I married Laverne because it was what I was supposed to do. And you know what, M.R.—she knew about the men. She told me at the end that I needed to find someone who could make me happy. I told her that she was the only girl for me and would always be. You know what she said to that?"

"No."

"She said, 'I didn't say it had to be a woman.' She knew. She knew all the time."

If only I had said *yes* to him then. If I had said, "Let me pack a bag and we will drive all night till we get to Key West. We will raise hell and drink rainbow-colored cocktails till we pass out. I will give you dollar bills to stuff into the underpants of dancing boys." But Roger Simmons was a fat man, and I did not desire him. I had a young, strong mechanic who came to me when he wanted, and I was crazy for the very idea of him, crazy that if I was out of town (even to comfort an old friend) that it might disrupt, destroy my connection to Lonnie. I was selfish that way. I thought, *Roger, you have made your bed. Now you must lie in it. You took all the sweetness that life has to give, the golden fruit, and now you must pay the piper. This is my chance to have what you have had, and I will not let you take that from me.*

So, I sent Roger home that day alone, and when Lonnie showed up at my house late in the evening, I did not even give him time to take a shower before I pulled his pants off and laid him back on the bed. When I was done, there was a big oil stain on the sheet from his clothes. Black, treacherous, unrepentant.

It wasn't long before people in town began to talk about Roger and the change in him. People noticed that he was drinking more. He often wouldn't return to the office after lunch at the country club. Some days he did not open the office at all. Clients began to complain their affairs were not being tended to. There was a rumor that he had been pulled over for driving while intoxicated, but only given a warning when the officer saw who it was and understood Roger's situation. There were times at night when the phone would ring and I was sure it was Roger, but I never answered. Then, one night, he showed up at my back door. It was early December, and he had a small gift for me: a bottle of Kahlúa. It was unexpected and alarming, not just because he had never done anything like that before—he typically dropped by the shop during business hours—

but because Lonnie was there, and Roger saw him, and he made the fatal mistake of recognizing Lonnie.

Lonnie was eating dinner at the kitchen table, wearing only a pair of boxers and a T-shirt, when I heard Roger's knock on the screen door. Lonnie looked over his shoulder as if to say *what the fuck is this nonsense*, and I knew I had best keep whoever it was out of the house, and since the back porch separated the kitchen from the yard, I thought I might be able to do just that. But I had forgotten to latch the screen door that night when Lonnie came over, and before I could get to the porch, Roger was already lumbering inside.

Roger wasn't stupid, and it didn't take him long to figure out the "what's what" of the situation.

"Oh," he said, handing me the package. "I thought you might want to have a drink in honor of the season. But I see you are previously engaged."

Lonnie didn't say anything, didn't acknowledge Roger's existence.

"Roger," I said, trying to step in between the two of them and back Roger out the door. "Why don't you come by the shop tomorrow and we can talk. You shouldn't just walk in people's houses unannounced."

"No, I guess not," he said. I saw that he was embarrassed, humiliated by his intrusion.

"So, tomorrow then . . ."

And then, ever so slightly, the light came into his eyes. I knew what was coming but could not stop it.

"I know you," he said. "You work down at Joe Boggs's place. I've seen you there. Lon—that's your name, right? I'm Roger. Roger Simmons." Roger extended his hand to Lonnie.

Lon scooted his chair back so hard that I thought the legs would dig into the linoleum. "Well, I really don't know who you are, mister, and you are interrupting my supper, so if you have half a brain, you will get the fuck out of here right now before I smash your face in."

I could see that Lonnie had scared Roger, who didn't need to be told twice to leave. "I'm sorry, M.R., I didn't mean to intrude. I just . . ."

I turned Roger out the door and eased him down the steps. "Now, you run along," I told him. "And you forget that you even came over here tonight. And I will call you tomorrow."

The night was black without even the sound of a cricket to lift the darkness as Roger pulled out of the driveway. When I walked back into the house, Lonnie was standing with the door to the refrigerator open pulling a beer from the shelf, his back to me. I went to clear his plate from the table, but he stepped out, blocking my way.

"I guess you and me need to have us a talk," he said.

I scraped what was left on his plate into the trash, dropped the plate into the sink, and sat down at the table to prepare myself for what was about to come.

It was well after dark when we pulled around to the back of Roger's house. A small sliver of a new moon hovered far overhead, and there was a chill in the air that accented the Christmas displays on the homes we passed on the drive over. Perhaps it was just nerves, but every Santa, every Frosty, every Wise Man seemed more clearly articulated, more brightly illuminated. In contrast, I couldn't help but notice the entrance to Roger and Laverne's house was unadorned with even so much as a wreath or sprig of holly.

I had called Roger that afternoon as promised and arranged to meet with him later that night. I told him that I had a white poinsettia for his living room, and I told him that we would have a good long visit. What I didn't tell him was how Lonnie had questioned me on so many details about Roger. Some of them were expected. Did Roger live alone? *Yes.* Did people know he was a queer? *No.* Some of them frightened me. How close was the next house? *Maybe a quarter mile away.* Did Roger keep money at the house? *I didn't know.* Did Roger own a gun? *Probably.* Most everyone in town owned a gun. Even my mother had had a small pistol that she kept next to the bed beside her Bible. "Jesus can only help you so much," she would say.

Roger responded immediately to my knock, turning on lights as he ambled to the back door through the darkened kitchen. When he saw Lonnie standing behind me, his face turned from anticipation to apprehension, and as he ushered us into the house, I could see he had some chips and dip open on the counter. It struck me as woefully sad, suddenly, that he would have gone to any trouble in preparing for my visit. Roger was dressed in his robe and pajama bottoms, his soft, pink flesh framed against the blue satin lapels of the robe. I wondered if he had meant that as a tease. If he had, it wouldn't have done the trick. There are few things more unattractive to me than the piggish flesh of a fat man. Hairy men can get away with a few extra pounds. Hairless men look like swollen hot dogs steamed too long.

"I'm afraid I am pitifully underdressed," he said. "M.R. didn't tell me he was bringing a friend. I can offer you a drink if you want. I usually drink bourbon." Roger gestured toward the liquor cabinet, an antique sideboard that Laverne had had refurbished as a bar.

Lonnie nodded. "Bourbon will do for me."

I shook my head. Liquor was the last thing I wanted.

We took our places, Roger and I on the couch like awkward teenagers on a blind date, Lonnie leaning against the fireplace. He had showered for the longest time when he arrived at my house, refusing any offer of sex, refusing dinner as well, saying he would eat later. He had groomed himself meticulously, scrubbing all the dirt from his cuticles and from underneath his nails. Lonnie wore a pair of jeans that I had bought for him and his tight-fitting "Far from Finished" Dale Earnhardt T-shirt. His hair shimmered in the lamplight of Roger's living room, and when I glanced at Roger, I could see that he was trying hard not to stare too intently at Lonnie. But I could also see that Lonnie was posing, posturing for him, wanting Roger to look. I recognized this stance—it was the same way Lonnie had moved about in the shop the first afternoon. I realized, a sudden sickening in my stomach, that he was posing for Roger. Was this some attempt to seduce him? Roger seemed just as confused as I. After what seemed an eternity of awkward silence, Roger offered the snacks we had seen in the kitchen.

"I ain't hungry," Lonnie said, "but you go ahead and eat if you want, M.R. I was thinking that Roger here might show me around the house."

"I guess. If you want," Roger replied. He appeared hesitant of what to do next.

"I do," said Lonnie. "Since you want to be in my bidness so much, I thought it might be a good idea for me to see what all you'ens is up to. M.R., you can stay here."

Roger rose from the couch, a bit unsteady on his feet. I wondered how much he had had to drink before our arrival or if it was just his nerves. "Where do you want to begin the tour?" he asked, a thin smile on his lips.

"Bedroom will do," said Lonnie. And with that, Roger led Lonnie out of the living room and down the carpeted hallway. I could hear the bedroom door close, and I was left alone with only the ghostly footprints in the thick pile of the carpet, like a shadow in damp sand. I decided to have a drink after all and poured myself a tumbler of straight bourbon. I thought about tiptoeing down the hall to see if I could hear what was going on in Roger's bedroom, but decided against it. Lonnie had told me to stay put, and put I needed to stay.

There are few things I hate more than a closed door. What lives behind it exists only in the imagination, and I tried hard not to envision what was happening back there. There were a few heavy thumps like furniture being moved. Was that a slap? A punch? Was he hitting him? Beating him? As bad as that idea was, it was actually a relief, since my chief fear was that Lonnie had taken Roger to the bedroom to make love. But how could he? It would make no sense. Or did he plan to have sex with Roger and then hold that knowledge over him as a way to blackmail him? Or even worse, would he expect me to share him with Roger?

I tried to divert my thoughts by studying the living room. For Laverne, decorating meant covering every square inch of space with a picture, a fabric, a flounce. She had used a neutral back-

drop—plush, Saxony beige carpet, off-white, satin-on-twill brocade for furniture upholstery. She had accented the room with gilt
frames and shining brass lamps, and over the fireplace hung the
requisite family portrait: an oil painting of Laverne and Roger re-
produced from a photo they had taken for the Methodist Church
Directory. Laverne told me how she had seen it advertised on
Home Shopping. All she had to do was send in the photo and the
size painting she wanted and "Zap!" she had an original piece of
art. Of course, it was all done by a computer, but still, it was totally
customized. I looked at how the painting had washed age and care
from their faces, and instead of a photographer's backdrop, the
painter had placed them in a rose-covered arbor. Even the flowers
were golden yellow and a soft white light radiated from behind
them. A hummingbird hovered over Laverne's shoulder as if ready
to burst into a spirited rendition of "Zip-a-Dee-Doo-Dah." I wondered if Laverne had made those choices as part of the custom job,
and what other locations were available? What if I were to have a
photo of Lonnie taken with me and then made into a painting?
Could we escape together to a courtyard in Italy or a dew-covered
meadow by a stream? Would we sit together under an arbor bathed
in light?

I traced a pattern with my fingers along the edge of the sumptu-
ous cushion, as if trying to decipher a secret Braille message embedded in the fabric. I could feel fear rise in my stomach, dark bile
mixing with the bourbon, leaving a sour taste in my mouth. I had
drunk too much too quickly, but I knew that was not the reason for
my sick stomach. I was terrified of what was going on behind the
closed door to Roger's room. Were those grunts, groans, muffled
sobs? Or was that merely my imagining? What if I were to burst in
on them—what then? What if they were making love? What if
Lonnie was holding Roger in his arms? Kissing him? Caressing
him? Things that had never been available to me. What if Lonnie
preferred Roger? And then I had a very bad thought—where I had
been afraid that Lonnie would hurt Roger, I was now afraid that he
might not. I was afraid that he might throw me over. And I could
not allow that to happen.

I sat there, watching the ice melt in the bottom of my glass, try-ing to imagine life without Lonnie, how I would beg him not to toss me out, that I would do anything he wanted me to do—*just don't leave me*—when I heard the door to the bedroom open and Roger and Lonnie's footsteps in the hall. I was hesitant to look up at them, afraid that something would show in my face when I saw them together. Roger came in first. He was still wearing his robe, though I noticed he no longer had on the bottoms of his pajamas or his bedroom slippers—he was bare-legged, barefooted. *He wasn't wearing pants—what did that mean?* But there was also something else that was different. It took me a moment to realize that Roger was wearing lipstick and rouge and powder. I almost burst out laughing until I saw that Lonnie had a gun pointed at Roger's back. I would swear that Roger had been crying, but now he just looked like a man who was in shock. I thought of Laverne and her cartoonish face that day I had brought her the casserole.

"You sit here in the chair," Lonnie said, gesturing to one of the wingbacks flanking the fireplace. Roger didn't say anything but did as he was commanded. "M.R., here, you hold the gun." And with that, Lonnie handed the pistol over to me. "Keep it pointed at him, and if he tries to run, shoot the son of a bitch. I will be back after I talk to a man about a horse." When he had gone, all I wanted to do was ask Roger if he had had sex with Lonnie, had seen him naked, had touched his dick, but I was afraid if he said *yes*, I would fire a bullet straight into his heart.

Roger spoke instead. "M.R., what kind of crazy shit have you got yourself tangled up with."

I wanted to say that I wasn't the one tangled up, sitting in my house looking like Baby Jane, but all I said was, "I don't know what you mean."

"This man of yours. He's crazy mean and dangerous. What do you know about him?"

I couldn't really tell Roger that I knew practically nothing about Lonnie. From the first day he had stepped foot in my shop till now. I knew he liked Sun Drop better than Coke. I knew he liked fried chicken better than baked, I knew he like his balls sucked rather than licked, but that was about it. What I said was, "He doesn't talk much. And he's never been hurtful to me."

"Give him time, and then God help you." Roger paused for a moment. "He said he was going to kill me."

My stomach lurched. "He doesn't mean that. He's just trying to scare you," I said. *See, dear friend, I didn't know for certain that Roger was about to die. Or perhaps the truth of it is, I didn't want to believe it.*

"Actually, I think he does mean it. But you know what, I'm not scared. Maybe I am too tired and worn-out to be scared."

I thought of the two years when Laverne was sick, how Roger had nursed her and cared for her.

"I worked my whole life doing what people told me was the right thing to do, and what did it come to? Laverne rotting in a box—taken much too early. Is this all that is left of her, of me and her, of us?" He gestured around the living room. "Good ole Roger and Laverne. The bedrock of the community. If they only knew."

"But at least you have had this," I said. Then something I had not ever even dared utter: "I can have that with Lonnie."

"Jesus, M.R., if you believe that, then you are a fool. You think you are going to settle down with him and live here in Morris and live happily ever after? He wants something from you. He will get it from you, too, by the sounds of it—or take it from you, and then he will be done with you. Do you know he wanted to know about my cash accounts, and where the title to the cars were, and if Laverne had any jewelry? Why would he want to know those things if he didn't plan to hurt me? How will you be able to build a life on that? Are you that desperate for love?"

"Don't lecture me about love," I barked. "You have had a life. You have had love. I have never had . . ." I didn't finish my thought because Lonnie walked back into the room. I wondered how much he had heard of the conversation.

"So, ladies, what's been going on without me?" he asked. When neither of us responded, he continued. "I thought Roger might want to show off his outfit for you, M.R. Go on there, sir, show M.R. your fancy dress-up."

Roger didn't say anything, but stood and untied the sash to his robe and opened it wide to reveal what was underneath. He wore what must have been some of Laverne's old lingerie—bra and panties. Even though Laverne had been a large woman, they were still hideously too small for him, and cut into the folds of his flesh like he had been wound too tightly in Ace bandages. If it was meant to shame him, humiliate him, Roger did not show it. Something had happened to Roger. He had crossed over. Whatever was coming was just the final step. I tried to avoid his stare.

"Isn't he purty?" said Lonnie. "As purty as a picture?"

"Why are you doing this?" I asked. "Is it really necessary?"

"I have my reasons," Lonnie said, "and don't you concern yourself with them or you will find out . . ." His voice trailed off. "I have my reasons. Ain't nobody going to talk about me. Ain't nobody going to be in my bidness that I don't want. You should know that, M.R., and if you don't, you best learn it quick smart. Now, gimme the gun."

I did as he asked.

"I have a request," said Roger.

"And what would that be, your highness?"

"I would like to have some music."

"I don't go in for no hymns or no church bullshit," said Lonnie.

"No," said Roger. "Just a bit of music. If you are intent on doing what you said, then please, at least let me have that. Some last bit of something that belongs just to me."

"You better not be trying to get one over," said Lonnie.

"No, I'm not trying to trick you." And before Lonnie could stop him, Roger was loading a CD into the player. He took a moment to find the track that he wanted, then settled back into the chair, closing his eyes. Music filled the room, the sad, beautiful, mournful song of a woman.

"What is this?" I asked.

"Violetta. *La Traviata.* Act Three. 'Addio del Passato—So Closes My Sad Story.' "

> *All hope is dead!*
> *Farewell, happy dreams of by-gone days;*
> *And may God pardon and make me his own!*

*Ah, all is over,*
*All is over now.*

And with that, Lonnie walked over to Roger and fired a bullet straight into his head.

I have felt badly that one of the last things that I ever said to Roger was untrue. It occurred to me in the same instant I heard the explosion from the gun that I *had* known love once. Even though it only lasted a short while. Deep, pure, real love. I was a very young man. And with the echo of the blast ringing in my ears, my thoughts ricocheted back to him. His name was César.

I had gone to New York for a floral design show, and to take the test to receive my certified floral designer qualification. It is very prestigious indeed to be able to put those initials behind your name: M.R. Vale, CFD. It is like being a doctor or a professor—it denotes expertise. Mother had treated me to the trip as a way for me to celebrate my new life, though she feared that I'd find my way into the world outside Morris. She had every right to fear. I was determined to leave at the first opportunity. César provided that opportunity, but that was not why I loved him.

The design show and convention was held over a three-day period with a gala reception on the closing night to honor those awarded CFD status and to honor winners of various floral design competitions. The conference also featured sessions on such useful topics as *How to Grow Your Business* and *Falling into Spring: Staying Ahead of the Season.* But they held little interest for me. My focus was to pass my exam and receive my accreditation. In one grueling four-hour practical examination, I would have to prepare and present arrangements from a variety of categories including Sympathy Design, Centerpiece, Wedding, Corsage, and Duplicate. In the last category we would have to reproduce an arrangement from a picture so if we had a call from a florist in another city who had a customer who wanted the Mother's Helper FTD arrangement, I would be able to reproduce it faithfully. To be honest, I doubted any florist from any other city would ever have a customer wanting to send flowers to anyone in Morris, but once I moved on, well, who knew what requests I might get.

Mother had arranged for me to spend five nights in New York, so I arrived the day before the conference began to sightsee, and I planned to stay on the Sunday following the Saturday night gala so I could go to a matinee of *A Chorus Line*. I had the album and knew all the songs by heart, and even though I knew the original cast would have long ago left the show, I didn't care. It was Broadway. "Kiss my ass good-bye, and point me toward tomorrow!"

After I had taken the Grey Line tour of the city, I wandered down to Columbus Circle to the New York Coliseum where the conference would be held. Even though the conference was not scheduled to begin until the next day, the place buzzed with exhibitors setting up displays and contestants arranging flowers for the competitions. I was studying one of the entries in the Japanese flower arrangements competition when I met César. He was just completing an arrangement of tulips, narcissus, iris, and lilies in a shallow black bowl. The card identified it as a Moribana arrangement, and I looked in my index of terms to see what that meant. In my experience I had done only ovals, or domes, or fans—nothing so exotic as this. As I was looking in my index of flower terms, I noticed him—or rather I noticed him looking at me. He smiled, and when he finished, he came over to me.

"You like?" he asked.

"It's beautiful," I said. "I've never seen anything like it."

"I'm not talking about the flowers, sugar," he said, his smile spreading across his face. "Do you like me?" And with that, he stepped back, pointed a toe, and fanned his hand out—*ta-da!* I wasn't quite sure what to say. I knew that I was gay, had been called *sissy* and *pansy* all my life, but my only sexual experience had been masturbating over the models in the underwear section of the Sears catalog. This was the first time a man had ever actually spoken to me like that. I mean, he knew. He saw me and he knew, and even more, he wanted me. I wish I could say that I played hard to get, that I was all *fiddledeedee* with him. But the truth is, I was ripe for the picking and César knew it.

So, without so much as a "May I buy you a drink?" César packed up his tools and whisked me back to his apartment on MacDougal Street in Greenwich Village. I felt like a character in one of Mother's Harlequin novels. The virgin set loose in the big city, seduced on his very first day. Everything was happening so quickly it nearly took my breath away. We stopped at a small grocery on the corner and bought fruit and cheese and two bottles of Chablis. "One for now. One for later," he said. His apartment was everything I imagined a New York apartment to be: tiny, old, eclectic. César had draped off the bedroom area with a swooping sheer fabric in metallic gold, alternating with layers of purple and maroon. It was like being inside the tent of an Arabian sheik. César was small framed like me, and after pouring the wine, he lay me back on a paisley printed velvet bedspread and began stroking my face, kissing me softly on the neck and on my temple. He was dark complexioned, with soft brown eyes, and he smelled sweet like lilac mixed with cherry blossom.

The charm of his scent mixed with the wine was enough to make me swoon. I was inside a dream. And so César made love to me all afternoon and into the evening. Afterward, he ordered Chinese take-away, and we sat naked in bed cross-legged eating egg rolls and fried rice.

"I cannot believe your parents named you Malcolm," he said. "It is too grim. No, no, no. It doesn't suit you, sugar."

"It was a family name. My mother's grandfather was Malcolm."

"It makes you sound like an undertaker. Malcolm Vale. It isn't a name for a florist. *César*, that is a name for a florist, but that is taken already," he said, bowing his head. "What is your middle name?"

"Rex."

César erupted in laughter. "Someone has played a nasty trick on you, my sweet sugar. Malcolm Rex. Ha. Ha." And he began to laugh deeply. "It will never do." And then he thought for a moment. "M.R.—M.R. Vale. It is very dignified. People will call you Mister, but your friends know you as M.R. Who knows, perhaps you will become more famous than Mr. Blackwell."

"And what will you call me?" I asked.

"I will call you Sweet Sugar."

There is no way to elucidate love, to justify its madness. I can't explain it any better than to say I fell hopelessly in love with César. I didn't know how it would happen, but I knew that my whole life would be spent loving him from that moment forward. I had no way to understand that our love would not even survive the weekend.

The next morning, César escorted me to the conference. I told him I needed to go back to the hotel for a change of clothes, but he would not hear of it. He selected some things from his closet—a pair of tight jeans with a Gap T-Shirt. I had planned to wear pleated slacks and a tie for my four-hour arranging examination. It was the same outfit I had worn to graduation a couple of years earlier, and I wanted to look professional.

"You are going to be working for four hours in a room full of queens. Pack yourself into these jeans and they will remember you. Make their little Jack in a Pulpit stand up." And he flicked his little finger up into the air. Then with a flourish, he tied a fuchsia-colored silk scarf around his neck. "Seriously, you are so serious. Look at me. I am a butterfly. I am a work of art. I make beauty wherever I am. And I know what is what in this world. If you go in there looking like Mr. Malcolm Rex, a hillbilly rube, they will mock you, and no matter how good your flowers are, they will not like them. You have to show them you know how to play the game. Put it back on them, M.R. Vale. Dare them not to like you, and they will think you are a bitch, but they will know you are one of us."

It may sound odd, but I understood what he meant. All my life I had stood outside the circle, looking into the groups. Here was someone, like me, someone I was in love with, who was showing me how to step inside the ring. I would have worn stilettos if he had told me to. So, at the registration table, I had them change my name tag from Malcolm Vale to M.R. Vale. When the woman at the table sniped that the card had been processed to match my application, I did not apologize or make an excuse. I simply said, "It's a mistake. And you need to do your job and fix it."

And so for the next two days, we went to the conference, César attending the workshops, me creating casket sprays, bridal posies, and holiday centerpieces. And we would find each other at the breaks for coffee or to go to lunch. Once, he was waiting for me as I exited from the exam room, pulling me close and whispering in my ear as he leaned in for a kiss. "Oh my man, I love him so." Just like in the song. And we would walk along the aisles of booths at the close of the day critiquing the flowers entered into the contests, me telling him about my own arrangements. César had a sophisticated eye, and he would point out to me how the subtleties of color in a gladiola lifted a pyramid or how height and volume of a crescent had been distorted by peacock feathers. "It looks like a fan for a stripper. No, no no." Sneaking a peek inside the room where my own arrangements were housed, he returned with positive but constructive criticism. "You have the ability, you are very talented, my sweet, but you lack confidence. That will come in time. I will teach you."

In the evenings when we would get back to the neighborhood, he would hold my hand as we walked down the street to a restaurant or bar. It wasn't unusual to see men walking arm and arm, but it was new for me. It was if I had suddenly gained substance, become visible. We went shopping for shoes, pants, shirts, even underwear. Gone suddenly were my schoolboy briefs as César introduced me to a world of silk and Lycra. "Does the queen keep her crown in a cotton sack? No, so do not keep your jewels there either." He showed me inside his small shop, named simply *César's*. "I am the star. It is my name I want them to remember," he said.

On my third night with him, he made dinner in the apartment, chicken and rice, and then we lay in bed late into the night intertwined in each other, unable, unwilling to sleep, the sounds of the street creeping up through the windows. It was then he suggested that I come to New York. "Where you live is nothing but rednecks and shit-kickers. They will never let you be who you are. And you know that. You couldn't get me there on a dare. Here you can bloom like the rare and exotic flower that you are." I would like to say that I resisted, that I was levelheaded as a judge, and said, "But we just met two days ago. What do we really know about each other? What guarantees are you offering me? And you know nothing of where I live—the kindness of neighbors, or the quiet of a summer evening sitting on the front porch, or the buzz of a covered dish supper." But I said none of those things because I knew what César said was true, if not in whole, at least in part, so I simply said, "Yes, yes, yes."

I have promised to be true in the telling of this tale, dear friend, so I will tell you that I allowed César to have intercourse with me. Oh, I can hear you now—*intercourse*, how very delicate. What you mean to say is he fucked you. Yes, César fucked me, or rather we fucked each other, but there are times when a physical act becomes transcendent. That was perhaps the only time in my life that I have ever made love to anyone. As César began to push inside me, I let out a small cry. "Sometimes love hurts just a little bit, sugar. Breathe out—*one, two, three*, like that. And say, 'I love you so much, I do this for you.' And then the pain will go away."

So I breathed out—*one, two, three*, and repeated the words, losing myself in his eyes. And he was right. The pain went away.

The next morning the announcement of who had received certification and the scores for their arrangements were posted on an easel outside the room where we had worked. I had scored in the upper 10% of the group and was given a distinction. César had received an honorable mention for his Moribana arrangement. He suggested we celebrate with a picnic in Central Park, but I told him that I absolutely must return to my hotel. "I haven't even spent one night there. Besides, my suit is there, and my good shoes, and I want to wear them to the gala tonight."

"A suit. You will look like a revival preacher."

In truth, I planned to shop for a new shirt and tie—perhaps even an ascot or scarf—but I wanted to surprise him. "You can call for me there. We will have a date."

"What time do you wish me to call for you on this date, my sweet?"

"The gala begins at eight. Come at seven."

"I cannot wait that long. I will die." He held his hands over his heart as if pained and pouted his lips.

"Seven. And then we will go to the gala."

"And you will never leave me ever again?"

"Never."

"Then, until tonight," he said, removing the apricot-colored scarf from his neck and tying it around mine. "*Te tengo en mi corazón mi amor.* I will hold you in my heart, my love."

I walked the blocks back to my hotel alone, wrapped in the

warm glow of love, rehearsing how I was going to tell my mother that I was not coming home. She would be surprised, shocked, hurt, but she would understand. I would make her understand. However, Mother had her own surprise waiting for me.

When I walked into the lobby of the hotel to retrieve my key, the clerk gave me a funny look before handing me a stack of messages. "Someone has been trying to contact you since late yesterday. They say it is urgent for you to get in touch immediately." As I boarded the elevator and rode to my room, I tried to fathom why Mother's doctor would be calling me in New York. Surely this was not a good thing.

My suspicions were correct. When I called the number on the message sheet, Dr. Everett answered almost immediately. "Malcolm, where the hell have you been? Not that it matters right now, but you need to know your mother has had a stroke."

"Is she going to die?" I asked.

"No, I don't think so," he said. "But it is very serious. She has paralysis and some speech loss, but those may be able to come back some with rehabilitation. She wants you here. She needs you here. This is going to be a long, hard road for her—for the both of you. You need to come home right away. She is awake and asking for you." Then a final exasperated, "Where the hell were you? I have been calling since yesterday afternoon."

"Out," I said. "I have been out."

"I can only imagine," the doctor replied. I could sense the condemnation in his voice.

"Yes, well, I will get the next plane home," I said.

"That would be a good thing."

"And Dr. Everett," I added, "please don't call me Malcolm. I go by M.R."

"Whatever," said the doctor. "Just get your tail home."

In the movies, there is always the scene where the jilted lover waits—whether in the bustling train station, the empty town square, or the noisy hotel lobby. In my scenario, I imagined César waiting in the hotel lobby for me that night holding a single rose in his hand as a token of his love, what he said when the hotel clerk would have told him I checked out without leaving any message, wondering if he went to the closing night party looking for me, tried to envision him dropping the rose in the gutter. Or did he press its petals in between pages of a book? I played it so many different ways in my head. I did not have the courage to call him, the courtesy to even leave him a message. Besides, what could I say, "Mother is ill. Must leave. I'll keep you posted." I knew that when I boarded the plane for home, I was closing the chapter on César once and for all. I could not leave any trace of myself for him, could not give myself any hope for return. It would have been impossible to leave if I had. So, I took my suitcase (which had never been unpacked), had the doorman hail a taxi for me, and returned to Morris.

I am not sure what happened to César. I did try to contact him once after Mother had died and I was really down in the dumps. I thought I would tell him that I was free now to leave, to return to New York, to him. I don't know that I expected him to forgive me, to want me to come back, but that shred of hope was all I had at the time. However, the directory assistance operator said she had no listing for a César's in New York City. I knew that César would never leave New York, and it crossed my mind that perhaps he had succumbed to the gay plague that was sweeping the big cities at the time, but decided that the operator had just not been able to locate the number. I did not try anymore after that. But the things that César gave to me, I have kept forever. He was right—customers do call me Mister Vale, and after all these years, I doubt if anyone ever remembers my given name. I wear a scarf every day around my neck just like he did, tied in the same way he tied it that afternoon. But even more, I live by his philosophy, so all the rednecks and shit-kickers and born-again bitches who come into my shop every day cannot touch me or hurt me because I am a butterfly. I am a work of art. I make beauty wherever I am. And I know what is what in this world. *Te tengo en mi corazón mi amor.*

Lonnie followed me into the house after we parked the van. I tried hard not to remember how the left half of Roger's head had lifted away from rest of his face like a shard of glass splintering off a shattered vase. His eyes had opened at the sound of the explosion in his ear, and as his head fell back against the white brocade of the wingback, it seemed as if he had thought of one last thing he wanted to ask. "Why?"

That was the question burning in my head as well. Why did it have to turn out like this? Surely there could have been another way. I warmed a plate of food for Lonnie, who seemed to have no difficulty eating. In fact, his appetite was as hearty as ever. When he was done, he leaned back in his chair and motioned for me to sit. He took a swig of his beer, and said, "We got some things to figure out."

I sat down at the table. Perhaps he would explain it to me, give me some insight that would help me to understand.

Instead, he said, "I don't think I can be coming around here anymore."

"But why? Roger is gone. He won't tell anyone."

"This is a small town. There is bound to be some talk."

"Not from me," I said. "I swear I have never mentioned you to anyone."

"But from someone. Someone will see me coming here or leaving. And I don't want anyone talking about me like that. You got to understand. Ain't no one can know about me and you. Can't no one see me here or know about me and you."

I was suddenly angry for Lonnie, sad for the shame he must feel, wanted to protect him.

"Men have . . . special friendships with other men," I said. "There is no reason to be afraid or ashamed."

He turned his head sharply toward me, his eye burning. "Don't you think I don't know that? I been around enough to know what's what. When I was—before I was old enough to be on my own, I lived in a place, a place where they put boys like me."

"A foster home?"

"Foster homes is for those that can get taken in. Or shows potential for getting placed somewhere. Where I was is where they put boys who nobody wants or who has done stuff so they needs to be looked after."

"A group home."

"Yeah," he sneered. "If that's what you want to call it. Birchwood Boys Home. About the only good thing it did for me was help get me ready for living on the inside."

I didn't ask what he meant by this because I knew he meant prison.

"In those places, there are men like you there that do for other men. But sometimes there are men who do for each other, but it ain't nobody's bidness but their own what they do. When I was a boy, I had me a friend. He was about my age. Well, some of the boys talked about us. Said things. Called us queers. It didn't bother him any, but I fought the ones who said it. Told them if they ever said it again, I would cut off their peckers and make them suck their own dicks. But that didn't stop some of them. So I had to show them that I meant bidness."

"What happened to your friend?" I asked.

"He had to go away," he said.

I wanted to ask where, how long, but knew it wasn't allowed, that Lonnie would never tell me more than that. But who had been this friend?

He took a swig of his beer before continuing. "That friend of yours, Roger—he was like those boys at Birchwood. He needed to know what was what."

No, I wanted to say. You're wrong, Lonnie. Roger was kind and caring and sweet and tender. He was sad and lonely. He only wanted friendship and affection. He didn't need to be killed. But I didn't say anything.

"Anyhow, it don't really matter now, does it? There's only one way to make sure somebody don't talk. Otherwise they has something on you and can use it. Now, the way I see it, M.R., is that you and me is in this thing together. It wasn't my fault that your friend invited himself over here. He was the one to blame. And you should have stopped him from intruding into where he didn't belong. But what's done is done, and now we need to put that behind us."

"But surely there is a way," I said. "We can be careful. We can go to Whiteville. I will get a room there for you to stay."

"No," he said. "That won't do. Besides, now I got to know that you have my side in this." I tried to look deep into his eyes, to see what kind of hurt could be housed there, but he looked at me hard and cold, and I knew that if he did not trust me, I would soon discover what Roger had said was true. Lonnie did not plan ahead—or so I believed then. He only acted according to what was required in any given situation.

"You don't have to worry about me," I said.

Lonnie thought for a moment. "Maybe if I was to come over and work for you a bit. Like that first time I came over here was to bring you the van. Didn't nobody give a whistle about that."

"But the van only needed to be serviced," I said. "And you can't work in the shop."

"No, I reckon not," he said. "But I could drive the van for you. You have to take the flowers out to people sometimes, don't you?"

"Yes," I said. "I do a great many deliveries—to churches, to the funeral home, to the hospital. But I don't need anyone to drive me, and I have never employed a driver before. It would look odd to people."

Lonnie thought again. "But if you couldn't drive yourself."

He waited for the full implication of this to sink in.

"What's to say if you had an injury and couldn't drive? You could call over to JB's and ask him to see if there was anyone could make deliveries for you. And then when I was to come in and out of here every day, I would be coming through the front door and nobody would wonder why."

I heard him talking, but my mind had shuddered, stalled at the word *injury*. What exactly did Lonnie have in mind for me?

"Besides," he said, "the way I figure it is you would be demonstrating your loyalty to me. My friend was the only one who I ever knew was loyal to me."

"I am loyal to you, Lon," I said. I didn't know what he had planned, but it couldn't be worse than losing him.

"Well, I guess you're going to get a chance to prove that then, aren't you? You know, it wasn't my fault that things went the way they did tonight. You was careless. You was the sloppy one. And look what come from it. So, now we are linked, and I need you to show me that you is on my side. Or else I am going to leave here and never come back. And if I ever hear any talk about me that you said, then I can tell you . . ."

"Lonnie, I will never say anything to anyone about you, about us, about tonight."

"Then you need to prove that to me. I'm gonna give you a chance to prove that to me. Why don't you wash up here and give me a minute. Then we will see how loyal you really are." He pushed away from the table and was out the door, into the black. I scraped what was left from his plate, washed and dried the dish, and placed it back in the cabinet, my hands shaking so terribly that I thought I would chip the plate. Just as I was finishing, Lonnie called to me from the porch. I wondered if he had been there, watching me. In the dark night it took a moment for me to see that he was holding a stick of some sort in his right hand, but an oddly shaped stick. Or perhaps not a stick at all, but a crowbar.

"When I was on the inside," he said, "there was a fella who wanted to get out of work detail, so he said the best way to lay off was to have a broke leg. Said a broke leg would heal, wasn't like getting shot or stabbed, but it would lay him off for a while."

"What are you intending, Lonnie?"

"You need to prove to me that you got my side, that you want me here."

"I want you here more than anything."

"Then sit here on the step. You can tell people you was coming out the back door and tripped."

He made it sound so logical. A broken leg was so much more easily mended than a gunshot wound or a gash from a knife. "Where will you . . . ?"

"The bottom's easier than the top. And you is pretty skinny to begin with."

I lowered myself to the step.

"I won't say it won't hurt," he said. "But don't holler out. Someone might hear. And when I leave, you can get yourself into the house to call the doctor. Or else wait for someone to find you in the morning. Are you ready then?"

"Yes, I'm ready."

And as he swung the crowbar back over his head in a high arc, I thought how easy it would be for him to bring it crashing down on my head, smashing my skull. Then he would never have to worry about me saying anything to anyone. That what had happened tonight would disappear with me. But I knew deep inside that Lonnie didn't want to bash my brains in. At least not yet. He wasn't done with me. There was more to come.

And as the crowbar began its descent, I remembered what César had said to me all those years before: "Sometimes love hurts just a little bit, sugar. Breathe out—one, two, three, like that. And say, 'I love you so much, I do this for you.'" *I do this for you.*

# . . . 4 . . .

People had to order flowers for Roger's funeral from Tabor City and Mullens. I remember that Joanne Jackson was actually snippy with me on the phone when I told her that I wasn't taking orders.

"But, Mr. Vale," she said. "I do think it is important to make a nice impression considering the circumstances."

"I don't know that you have heard, but I have a broken leg. I can't stand."

"Yes, I did hear. But you are supposed to be a professional. You could always sit on a stool while you worked if you really wanted to."

I hung up and took a pain pill. Yes, I could probably have sat and put some flowers in a vase for her, perhaps I could even have balanced on my crutches long enough to put together a spray, but it didn't seem appropriate. Roger was dead. I had watched him die. Besides, I knew that Joanne Jackson was a gossip and what she really wanted was the inside scoop. Not that she would have suspected I had any involvement with Roger's death—what she was interested in were the "circumstances," which certainly had caused a stir in town. Though the police were quick to rule his death a suicide, there was no note, and so speculation and rumor were like a wildfire in a dry cornfield. The most generous in town speculated that Laverne's long illness and death had simply driven him crazy, and the holidays had proved to be too much. The evidence was clear. He had been drinking heavily for months, not acting himself. If only someone had taken the time to help him. A heavy helping of grits and guilt to serve along with the Christmas ham.

The more vicious were interested in the sordid nature of his death. Roger was found wearing bra and panties with half his head splattered all over Laverne's off-white living room. Surely that all meant *something!* Was Roger a homo? Was he a transvestite? Perhaps he was engaged in some sort of Satan worship or maybe even a sex game. After all, there were two cocktail glasses, washed and left to dry in the dish rack, and a half-eaten plate of cheese and crackers. Who has guests over for drinks and snacks before blowing his brains out? The autopsy also said he had had anal sex shortly before his death. I remembered the whimpers, the grunts, the groans coming from behind the closed door to Roger's room. I tried not to think about what that had meant.

And then there was the matter of Laverne's jewelry and her car. Her sister said some of her earrings and a necklace were missing, and Laverne's Cadillac was gone from the garage. She said the jewelry were pieces that had been promised to her personally by Laverne. I wasn't sure whether Laverne's sister was due to inherit the jewelry, but I was pretty sure she would know exactly how much loot there was and where it was kept. As for the car, Laverne had been dead and buried for some time, so no one had seen her car or even thought if Roger had gotten rid of it. To most, Laverne's sister was just a greedy grave robber, willing to steal the pennies off her sister's eyes. However, I suspected she might have been on to something.

The funeral was held quietly with only Lorraine's sister and her husband attending. Roger's family had died off years before, and even though he had sponsored a generation of Little League teams and while half the town had attended his barbecues and golf events for the country club, no one wanted to be seen standing at his graveside. It would be as if they were complicit in his hidden decadence.

The whole thing was very depressing—certainly Roger deserved better than he got, but that wasn't what had me down. Lonnie had not come around the shop since the night of my "accident," which meant that I had spent the holidays alone. All the plans I had made for a romantic Christmas Eve together, the stocking stuffers I had stashed away for him, the bottle of real imported champagne I had purchased for a New Year's Eve toast—all for naught. I was missing him like a crazy person—just to see him, I told myself, would be enough. But I knew that was a lie. I wanted to touch him. To feel him. To taste him. But it was impossible, I knew. I had a home health care provider for the first week I was home, a heavy-set LPN who went about her duties with an unrepressed contempt for me that she masked with only the slightest hint of professional pleasantries and Southern propriety. I chalked it up to her having to work for a homosexual during the celebration of Christ's birth. Whenever I would wake from a nap, I could hear the religious broadcasting station playing in the living room, evangelicals trumpeting the end of days and the spiritual defilement that had become America. I figured she saw me as a part of that wilderness, a leper for her to tend to in order to gain stature in the kingdom beyond. *I will wash your clothes now, and fix you a sandwich, and by the way it's too bad how you are going to burn in hell for eternity.* But I was a good patient—a model patient. I wanted to recover as quickly as possible. The sooner I was able to maneuver on my own without her help, the sooner I would be able to reopen the shop and hire Lonnie.

The day before the doctor gave me the all clear, I called Joe Boggs and told him of my predicament.

"I am able to get around the house, but with this cast on my leg, I am going to need someone to make deliveries. Is there someone at the shop who might want to work a couple of evenings—I don't want to impose on you, but I need to get back to my church deliveries."

Joe hesitated a moment. "I'm not sure." I knew he was squeamish about sending one of his men over to me—goodness knows what I might expose them to.

"I thought business might be slow now after the first of the year. If you would just ask. Maybe someone could use some extra money. I'm happy to give you a finder's fee as a courtesy as well. I can donate some flowers to the sanctuary in honor of whomever you choose."

There was a hesitation as I knew he was considering the offer. "My mamma's birthday is coming up in a few weeks."

"Perfect," I said. "I am happy to do an arrangement for her if you can find me a driver. I will call you tomorrow to see if anyone is interested." If the thought of free flowers weren't enough to close the deal, I knew that last comment would at least get him to ask—he knew I would pester him until he did.

When I called the next morning, Joe told me that several people had been interested in the job, but in the end, it had been decided that Lon would come over to see what I needed if that was okay by me. He also told me that I should know up front that Lon had been in a little trouble with the law, had spent some time in prison, but that he was conscientious and dependable. "Just don't expect him to say too much. He's a quiet one."

I assured Joe that would be fine with me, but secretly my heart was dancing—no, not just dancing, it was Fred Astaire in a tuxedo tapping up a marble staircase, tipping his hat. It was smiling like Gene Kelly. It was singing like Mario Lanza.

*Someone else*—one or more of the other workers—had shown interest in the job. How had Lonnie reacted? Did he bully them into submission, stare them down? Or did he say, "He belongs to me." I wanted to ask Joe Boggs for more information, but was afraid to show too much interest. After all, it was only a delivery driver that I was after. And if there had been a confrontation, I knew Lonnie would never speak to me about it. But still, it was better than a scene from a Hollywood musical or a romantic opera. Lonnie had fended off the other candidates—repelled these other suitors, if you please, in order to keep me all to himself.

I arranged with Joe that Lonnie would work for me two evenings a week and on Saturday afternoons when they closed the garage at noon. What I didn't tell Joe was I had decided that I would ride with him when he was making the deliveries; if anyone asked, I could tell them I was merely showing Lonnie all the regular stops I delivered to. The truth was I just wanted to be with him. And not only with him, but we were in public together. Driving around Morris as big as life for everyone to see. And when we finished our deliveries, we went home—together. I want you to know the next few weeks were like a heavenly honeymoon for me. Lonnie would arrive at the store, walking in the front door like he owned the place. No one cared. I ordered him a shirt with the Vale's Floral Design logo stitched on the front and his name embroidered directly below on the shirt pocket—our names close enough they were almost joined. And I was happy with that. I began to think that this was going to be how life might be. I thought of the hundreds of ways I would express my gratitude, my appreciation, my affection, my . . . *love* to him.

Yes, I loved Lonnie. But therein lies the curse of love. It feeds you, but it also consumes you. As my love grew for Lonnie, it only left me emptier, more lonely. It isn't enough to be the lover, to cast all your affection out like feed seed to hungry chickens. Love must come back—César had shown me that. My life with Lonnie had a pattern, a certain routine, but I felt as if I walked behind him in his shadow. I cooked for him, washed and ironed his clothes, gave him cash for his work, and blew him whenever he would allow. Still, I wondered sometimes if he ever even noticed me. It began to weigh on me more and more every day. I wanted to matter to him. He was my whole world. Could he not see that? What I needed, what I wanted, what I desired more than anything was to know that Lon wanted me, needed me, desired me as well. In short, I wanted Lonnie to love me back.

If the truth be told, the more I did for Lonnie the less I seemed to matter to him, or even worse, the more I seemed to irritate him. When I would approach him with the offer of sex, he would brush me off. He grew ill-tempered if his shirt wasn't pressed to his satisfaction or if dinner wasn't to his liking. Then, if I didn't have cash to spare between "paydays," I began to notice cash disappearing from the store. I knew he was taking it, but there wasn't anything I could say about it. I began to suspect, wonder if his attention was drifting. It didn't help that he insisted I stop accompanying him on the deliveries.

"I don't need you watching over me every minute," he said.

And so, I stayed at home and waited for him to return, his shirt ironed, his dinner warm in the oven. And like so many stories of this type, there was one night when he didn't come home. I worried at first that he might have been in an accident, but I knew if he had, the police would have called me since the van was registered in my name. I told myself that he needed some time to be alone, that it was okay. Then I sulked. Then I cried. Then I wrapped his dinner up and put it in the fridge and went to bed. I was used to waiting for Lonnie. I had spent many nights when he did not come over or in the weeks after Roger's death when he could not come over. But this was different somehow. In those long, still nights, I had imagined that he wanted to be with me. But now, I could not pretend. He wanted to be somewhere else. And with every stray headlight I would rouse, thinking finally he had come home to me. I don't know when I finally fell asleep, but when I awoke the next morning the van was back in the driveway and everything was back to normal. Then it happened again. And again.

Finally, one Saturday afternoon in mid-February, just after Valentine's Day, things came to a head. A piece of toast overcooked, who will control the TV remote, whose turn it is to take out the trash: Like so many squabbles that escalate into a full-blown quarrel, ours began when Lonnie complained about the lunch I made for him.

"With as much fucking money as you have, you think I could get something besides baloney."

"But you like baloney."

"I like *The Dukes of Hazzard*. Doesn't mean I want to watch it all goddam day."

"I am happy to make whatever you want. You should know that. Just tell me what you want."

I could see the wheels clicking in his head, like tumblers in a lock turning over. This wasn't about baloney. He wanted to ask me for something—and not a tuna or roast beef sandwich.

"What is it, Lon? Is there something you want me to give to you?"

He laughed. "Whatcha got in mind, M.R.? You gonna get me a puppy?"

I stopped short. "I just want you to be happy. What would that take?"

"I don't know," he said. "I'm getting tired of driving that piece of shit van of yours. Goddamn, there ain't even a decent radio in it. And I can't smoke in it."

"It would mask the scent of the flowers. Besides, I haven't even paid all the bills for the hospital yet."

"Shit, M.R. I see the money that comes in here. And what kind of expenses do you have? With all the money that comes through this place, you must be stashing money away. You own this house outright, don't you?"

"Yes, you know I do," I said. "But . . ."

"Yes, but," he mocked, making a face at me like a child who doesn't want to eat his dinner. "I don't want a car. If a car was all I wanted, I know how I can get me one."

"Then what?"

"You don't understand. I ain't never had nothing except what I could fit into a box," he said.

"It's not a sin to be poor."

"Why don't you try it sometime, then?"

"Lonnie, I am not a rich man."

"But you own a house. You ain't got no expenses except for yourself and whatever little thing you think you might want to give me. And what happens to this place when you're gone?"

"I don't know," I said. "I've never really thought about it. Perhaps I will sell it and set up a scholarship at the community college."

"Hah! You act like you want me to be here, but you're the one who says how much I can have. You get to be the one who decides. And when you're gone, you're gonna give all this to somebody who don't even know you. Somebody you don't know. Why do you get to decide that? Why do you get to be the boss here?"

I had no reply for that.

"What is it you want? A car? When I get the hospital bills paid, we can go look."

"I told you I don't want a goddamn car." His chair flung backward across the floor as he stood up and headed to the door. I hobbled behind him, but by the time I caught him, he was already at the van loaded with the flowers to take to the churches for Sunday services

"Then what?"

"I think we need to be partners here. That way I would know you was on my side and wasn't just going to turn me out. That you was loyal."

*I let you break my leg,* I wanted to scream. *I stood by and watched you shoot my dearest friend in the head. Doesn't that count for something?* I was trying not to think of what Roger had said to me: "He wants something from you. He will get it from you, too . . . or take it from you, and then he will be done with you."

He closed the door on the van. "You just think about it. You just think about what could keep me coming back here to be with the likes of you."

I must say, that wounded my vanity. I knew I should just walk back in the house, let things settle, but I was deep in the white water, paddling with all my might. "So, since you don't want to be with the likes of me," I said, "I guess that means you will be keeping the van tonight."

He didn't say a thing, just turned and backhanded me across the face so that I fell backward into the azalea bushes along the front of the shop.

"Where I go ain't none of your bidness," he said. "Besides, you can't drive it, so if you ain't using it, then why shouldn't I? I make the deliveries in this pile of shit, and if it weren't for me it probably wouldn't even run. I don't need the grief. So you better watch it—if I wanted, I could just say you go and do all this yourself. Would you like that? No, I bet you wouldn't. I should be able to get something back out of it for myself."

I thought about mentioning all the food, the clothes, the money that he had "gotten back," but lying on the ground has a way of changing your perspective. So, I merely helped myself to my feet and walked back inside. I heard the motor start. Gravel flew as he sped out of the driveway. I hoped he would at least make the deliveries that were scheduled. I had a professional reputation to think of after all. I attempted to occupy myself with the notion that churches would be flowerless the next morning and how the congregations would react, but I knew it was only a game to keep my mind from settling on what was really wanting to claw its way into the center of my brain. I went to sleep that night for the first time hoping that Lonnie would not return.

## . . . 5 . . .

I spent Sunday afternoon fielding calls from the local churches trying to explain why they had no flowers. I blamed the pain medica-
tion, said that I had been unable to work, should have called, so
sorry. As might be expected, the Baptists were the most unsympa-
thetic.

"We had an agreement, Mr. Vale. Do I need to remind you? Our
members expect flowers on Sunday morning. Especially in the
winter. It brightens the sanctuary. You should know, the early worship service was ruined because of it—ruined. Dot Owens went
home during Sunday school and brought in a potted plant just so
we would have something to put on the altar for color. It wasn't
right."

"I am so sorry," I said. I did not want to have another fight. I just
wanted to be left alone. "I will do whatever it takes to make it up."

"What you can do is never let it happen again." And then the
click of the phone.

In my experience, despite their unbending belief in eternal
green pastures and streets of gold, Baptists are a pretty angry lot.

Neither Lonnie nor the van showed up on Sunday, and I
thought about reporting it stolen, but I knew that would just
sound foolish since Lonnie had been driving the van all over the
county for months. The same was true on Monday, and I decided

not to open the shop. Joe Boggs had called early in the morning to see if I had any knowledge of where Lon might be. Lon wasn't now just gone from me, he was gone all together, and I made my-self sick with worry. There was no way I could bear to deal with the likes of Joanne Jackson or any flowerless Baptists who might want to pay me a visit.

I started a hundred chores and abandoned them almost as soon as I had begun, unable to focus my attention on anything except *Where is Lonnie? When is Lonnie coming back? Will Lonnie come back?* Then, about midafternoon, when I was lying down to rest, I heard a car pull into the driveway. I knew by the crunch of the tires on the gravel that it wasn't the delivery van, and I almost didn't go to the door when they knocked. But when Lon called out, "Hey, M.R.—you in there?" I sprang from the bed as quickly as my bro-ken leg allowed. When I answered that I was coming, I could hear Lonnie whispering to someone. He wasn't alone.

I opened the back door to the porch and was astonished to see Lonnie standing with his arm draped over the shoulder of none other than Drexel Smith. From the looks of them, it had been a hard weekend. I wasn't sure if they were drunk or high; the neck and armpits of Lonnie's shirt were ringed with sweat, and his pupils were large black dots in his brown eyes. Drexel shifted his weight from one leg to the next dancing to his own internal rhythms. He chewed on his fingernail as if scared of how I would react to him standing at my back door.

"What was you doing sleeping in the middle of the day?" asked Lon, as he walked past me into the kitchen and opened the fridge, taking out two beers.

"Not sleeping. Resting," I said.

"You sure you wasn't pounding the pud," said Drexel, holding his right hand at his crotch and shaking his wrist back and forth.

Lonnie uncapped the longnecks and handed one to Drexel. "M.R., you remember Drexel here, dontcha?"

"Sure he remembers me."

"Yes, I remember you, Drexel. What I didn't know was that you had gotten out of prison. I thought you were gone away for three years."

"Well, you know how that works. It was my first offense and they labeled me with manufacturing instead of possession because of the fire. But because most of the evidence burned up, they couldn't stick it to me very hard. Plus, I 'accepted responsibility for my wrongdoing and sought out drug rehabilitation on the inside.'" At the last comment, Drexel put his hands together like a penitent. But he seemed unable to stop himself from talking. "Yessirree, I was a fucking model prisoner. I been back a couple of months now," he continued. "I bought me a camper van and parked it out where the trailer burned up. You should see it. There's still just a pile of burned-out shit sitting there. No one even hauled it off. And as long as the lot was empty, I figured I might as well settle back in for as long as I needed to be here."

"So, you're not back for good, then," I said. I didn't know whether this was a good sign or a bad one.

"Hell no," Drexel hooted. "We plan to get shed of this place as soon as we can."

"Shut up, Drex," Lon interrupted. "You're on one of your talking jags and just spilling over like a plugged-up toilet." Lonnie drained his beer in a gulp, then reached in the fridge for more. "M.R., why don't we step into your parlor where we can all relax a bit. Me and Drex got something to talk over with you."

I had turned Mother's old bedroom into a den so I could have a place just to watch TV. It ran along the side of the house, and as we entered, I couldn't help but notice the nearly new Cadillac they had driven. I wondered whether they had traded the van for a new car but knew that was impossible. Besides, the car looked familiar to me. It took a moment for me to realize that it was Laverne's missing car. I can tell you this, it did not give me comfort to know that Drexel and Lonnie had sequestered the car—probably out at Annabeth's abandoned lot, waiting until they were ready. For what, I could only imagine. This meant that they had not just run into one another or recently met. Roger had been dead for over a month—they had known each other before his death. This had been planned.

I dropped to the couch, wondering what Lonnie had in store for me. Would he bring out the tire iron again, or would he just shoot me and be done with it like he had Roger? He sat in the recliner where I had serviced him so many evenings; but instead of putting his hands behind his head, he leaned over to make sure he had my full attention. It wasn't typical for Lonnie to be so intimately engaged, and I wondered whether he was trying to help me relax or if he wanted to intimidate me. Either way, he had my complete consideration. Meanwhile, Drexel stood in the doorway doing his own private jitterbug.

"M.R., you remember the talk me and you had the other day."

"Yes," I said. "Very well."

"You remember that you was wanting to know what you could do as a favor to me for helping you out around here."

"That's not quite the way I remember it," I said.

Lon sat back and sighed. "Well, whatever," he said. "I seem to recall there was some discussion about what you could do for me."

"Yes, you know I only want to make you happy. But this frightens me. I am not sure what you want. Or what it means when you show up to the house—not alone."

"It means he may have other friends besides you," chirped Drexel. "Me and Lonnie known each other a long time. Longer than you. I known him before we was together on the inside even."

Lon held his finger up in warning. "I told you, Drex. Stop running your mouth. Let me talk to M.R. here."

Drexel leaned against the doorjamb and sulked.

"Anyways," Lonnie continued, "I was thinking about your offer of what you could do to help me out, and I thought about all what you got here that don't belong to nobody else but you. And so I thought maybe it was about time you and me became partners."

To be honest, there was one fleeting moment when I wished that what he meant by partners was that he wanted only to use my store as a place to sell drugs, that I would launder money for him, let him use the van to make deliveries, but even as I considered that, I knew it was not even a remote option. *Crash, bam, boom. Would he break my neck, throw me down the cellar steps, blow my head all over the shop window?*

"Partners. In the business."

"Yeah, me and you. You can make the flowers and I can deliver them. And we can split the profits."

It couldn't be that simple I knew, so I followed the trail to see where it would lead. As it turned out, the path was a short one with a cliff not too far beyond. "Of course, we would have to have an agreement, so it would be legal and everything."

"A contract, you mean."

"Yeah, but just one that we could write out together that would say we were partners. We wouldn't need to go to no lawyer or anything. Just sign it and date it and it would be an agreement."

"And what would I be agreeing to?" I asked.

"Like I said, that we would be partners here in the business. In everything. Like the house and everything."

*Crash. Bam. Boom.* It became crystalline clear. It wasn't the business Lonnie was interested in. It was more than just wiping out the bank account. It was also the house. In the same way Drexel had acquired Annabeth's trailer, Lonnie wanted to acquire the house. I watched Lonnie's eyes dart back and forth across my face so quickly that it appeared as if they were vibrating. I wondered how it would feel to die.

"So, what do you say, M.R.—you think you could see your way into cutting me in?"

"Lon, this is a conversation we should have in private."

"I told you I known him even before you did," Drexel declared.

I looked at Lonnie as hard as I could. "Is he a part of this?" I asked.

"I'm here, ain't I?" Drexel held his arms wide as if I might not have noticed him before.

"I told you to keep quiet!" Lonnie shouted. "I am handling this."

"Lonnie, you will not get away with this. Do you think I don't know what you will do if I open my bank account to you, sign my business, my house over to you?" I turned my attention to Drexel. "I'm not like Annabeth Owensby. People in town know who I am. They would be suspicious."

Drexel sneered. "They wasn't so interested in your friend when he bit it. And he was a lot more popular than you are."

"And then what?" I asked.

"Surely you two don't plan to set up house here and run the store?"

Drexel let out a belly laugh. "Can't you see it, Lon? You can pick the flowers and I will put 'em in the jars."

"They're called vases," I said. I wanted to add *you moron*, but knew the thread was extraordinarily thin, and I was dangling with no safety net. They hadn't just come in and killed me. They could have done that, but they knew they needed my signature on a document that gave Lonnie ownership of my life.

"Whatever," said Drexel. "I told you we're getting shed of this place."

"So, what do you say?" asked Lonnie.

"No, Lonnie. I say no. No. No. No." I could hear my voice pitching up and I knew he could hear the panic and fear.

"You know I can make you do what I want," he said.

"Are you saying you can hurt me?" I pointed at my bandaged foot. "We both know that is true. And I also know that no matter what I do you're going to hurt me, so might as well get it over. Besides, how would you explain bruises and more broken bones when the police ask you to explain my signature? I have lived here all my life. I wouldn't just disappear. You will need a body, and it better look natural because the spotlight will turn on you both. There is some money, probably not as much in the account as you think."

"Nearly forty thousand last time I looked," he said.

He had been looking at my bank receipts. What else did he know? I took a gulp and kept talking. "That would only get you so far. It will take time to sell all of this. You can't think there won't be questions."

Lonnie and Drexel exchanged a look. I wasn't sure what it meant. Was I making sense to them? Lonnie stood, motioned Drexel toward the kitchen. "M.R., you sit for a moment. I need to talk to Drex. And don't try nothing stupid like trying to run away. You know we'll just catch you."

"Why are you doing this?" My voice trembled and I struggled not to break down.

"It's bidness," he said. "Bidness. And I plan to get what's coming to me."

I could hear them talking in hushed voices from the kitchen. I was happy to think that I had thrown a wrench into their plans, bought myself some time. If I had known what was to come, I would have asked them where to sign. Offered to have the document notarized for them. But I didn't know what was to come. I only knew I was scared and didn't want to die. Winter shadows were beginning to fall across the room, and I wondered what would happen if I managed to escape and hop down the street on my good leg screaming bloody murder. Would they arrest Lonnie and Drexel Smith? Would they both come back one night and finish what they had begun? Besides, Lonnie was right. It was a long way to the front door, which was locked and bolted. I would never make it outside before Lonnie grabbed me.

In a few minutes, Lonnie and Drexel returned to the den. "We're gonna take us a ride, M.R.," said Lonnie. "You got to know I am serious here."

"I'm not doubting that," I said. "But I am just as serious."

Drexel plopped down on the couch, obviously preparing to stay while we 'went for a ride,' but Lonnie would have none of it. "Have some sense, Drex. You can't be here. Whatcha gonna do? Sit here in the dark? What if somebody sees you here? Besides, you got some cooking to do. I'm going to drop you off at your place. M.R. and me will get this figured out on our own."

Drexel pouted, but complied. And with that, we piled into Laverne's Cadillac like three good mates off for an evening out and drove away. I didn't bother to lock the door behind me.

$\dots 6 \dots$

Before we left Drexel at the camper, he and Lonnie packed a pipe and smoked some drugs—an awful-smelling concoction like burned plastic that had been soaked in cat piss. Drexel made sure Lonnie had some extra for the road, and we took off together. So many times I had imagined Lonnie and I traveling, perhaps to Charleston or Savannah for a weekend of sightseeing. Instead, when we hit the interstate, we turned northwest toward Florence and Columbia. After about an hour, Lonnie pulled off at a truck stop, smoked some more from his pipe, and then roamed around to some of the parked rigs, peddling drugs to the truckers. While he went from truck to truck, I watched the usual assortment of men— young, old, married, ugly—as they entered and departed the Gentlemen's Agreement Adult Bookstore and Video Lounge next door. In the past, I would have been excited to be in such a place, wondering at the prospects and opportunities inside. Now, it only depressed me and seemed a pathetic waste of time to see the stream of traffic in and out its doors. It didn't take Lonnie long to earn what he needed, and after another short drive down one of the back roads flanking the freeway, he deposited me at the Peach Bottom Motel, which promised free cable TV for only $39 a night. I say deposited me because once we were in the room, Lonnie tied me to a chair and taped my mouth. He knew I would run if given the chance, and he was right. My mind was working frantically trying to find a way out.

Before he left, he gave me another chance to give him access to the bank accounts, to sign the business over to him. "This is gonna happen, M.R. You gotta believe me when I tell you that. Now, if you sign the paper, maybe you and I can make us a deal that Drex doesn't have to be a part of." I merely shook my head. "Have it your way, then," he said, turning the TV on. He turned the volume up loud enough to cover up any attempts I might make to call for help, but not so loud that the manager would come knocking to tell me to turn it down. "Don't want trouble," he said. And with that, he disappeared through the doorway, bolting the lock as he went.

He wasn't gone long, maybe half an hour or so, when I heard the key in the door and some laughing just outside. When the door flung open, Lonnie was carrying a twelve-pack of beer and literally fell into the room—the only thing that kept him from hitting the floor was the fact that a youngish man, a boy really, was holding the back of Lonnie's belt in his right hand. Under his left arm, he clutched a bucket of chicken.

They were drunk as sailors, and the young man laughed as Lonnie broke free from his grasp and landed on the bed. "Damn, man, you almost made me spill this durn chicken all over the floor."

"You drop it and I'll kick your ass," said Lonnie. He smiled large as he rolled over on the bed and pulled a beer from the box. I had seen this look before. "Now, lock the door and drop your pants."

The boy, tall and gangly with a shock of reddish brown hair, turned to put the food on the table, his free hand already undoing his belt. He stopped abruptly when he noticed me.

"What the fuck, man? You didn't say nothing about somebody else."

"Don't mind him," said Lonnie. "He's just here to watch."

"I don't know. What's the matter with him? Why's he all tied up like that?"

"Ain't nothing the matter with him. He likes that."

The boy studied me up and down and broke into a shaggy grin.

"I saw that in a magazine. But I never seen it in real life. What's he do?"

"He does what I tell him to do," said Lonnie. "He'll suck you if I tell him to. You want him to suck you while you suck me?"

"I don't know," said the boy. "He's kind of old—I thought it was just gonna be you and me."

"Yeah, well, he's gonna be here, and he's gonna watch everything we do, so if you want him to suck you off, tell me and I will untie his mouth. He sucks good."

"What's his name?" the boy asked.

"What the fuck do you care what his name is," said Lonnie, lying back on the bed. He had his pants off and the bulge of his dick pressed up through his boxers. "His name is 'Mister' to you. So when you get done socializing, come over here and get down to bidness."

"Howdy, Mister Mister," said the boy, saluting me. "My name is Sammy. Sammy Hutchens. Proud to meet you."

Sammy stripped down naked except for his socks, and he and Lonnie smoked more from Lonnie's pipe. Then, for what seemed like an eternity, he and Lonnie fucked on the bed not three feet from me. It was as if I had been brought there to record the deed, and if ever I attempted to look away, Lonnie would kick a foot in my direction or curse at me until he had my attention. The drugs gave Lonnie an animal zeal, and he fucked Sammy Hutchens hard and long. Where I had only been permitted to touch Lonnie below the waist, these two wrestled in front of me with abandon, their hands exploring, clutching, stroking, their mouths and tongues licking, sucking, devouring. For all this time I had only wanted Lonnie to notice me, but now I tried to will myself invisible. *Let me just evaporate into mist,* I prayed. *Just let me disappear.*

When they were done, Sammy asked if he could take a shower. Lonnie shrugged his approval, and Sammy scurried into the bathroom, light and steam pouring out from the open door. Lonnie lit a cigarette and opened a beer and came over to me, untying the gag from my mouth.

"Why do you do this to me?" I asked. "Is this what you want . . . to show me how little I mean to you?"

Lonnie flexed and stretched, running a hand through that jet-black hair of his. The hair on his chest was damp with sweat, his cock still plump from sex. Even then, I wanted him, would have forgiven him all the injustice if he had untied me, and said, "Yes, that is what I wanted."

But as Sammy emerged from the bathroom, a towel wrapped around his boyish hips, I could see that Lonnie was not done with either of us. And as Sammy stepped around me, he opened the bucket of chicken, and said, "Hey, little mister. We got extra crispy. It's my favorite. Lon bought it special just for me."

And then the moment. Lonnie's massive hands gripped Sammy's head in that relentless grasp. At first Sammy thought it was more sex play and laughed. Lonnie commanded me to not look away. "You need to appreciate this," he growled. I could then see the confusion that turned to fear and then to hatred and finally to understanding as Lonnie held Sammy's head in his hands, lifting it up and away from Sammy's shoulders, twisting it around back and forth, front to back, so the bones in Sammy's neck began to creak and the gurgle in Sammy's throat became a sad, high-pitched whine. Until the bones unable to stand the strain began to splinter and the only sound was a low, guttural sigh that was Sammy's final breath. "Now you know," Lonnie said. "Now you know and you'll believe what I tell you."

Sammy shit all over the floor as he died, and Lonnie dropped him in a heap so that he lay stretched out in front of the door like a barricade, his broken neck tilting his head so that it crooked up against the door. Lonnie took the chicken off the table and sat back on the bed. "This is your fault," he said. "None of this had to happen except you wouldn't do like I asked. Now, can you and me come to an understanding, or do I need to fetch me another young-in' in here? I can stack 'em up like firewood, M.R. It don't mean nothing to me."

"Take me home," I said. "And I will give you whatever you want."

"I'm too fucked up to drive now," he said. "I think I'm gonna crash for a spell. We can set out in the morning." Then he walked over to me, untied me, and said, "I expect you may need to use the toilet. Then we can get some rest and head back to Morris early in the morning. We got a busy day in front of us." With that, he turned on the TV and started flicking channels on the free cable TV until he found what he wanted to watch. I stood up slowly, moving ever so gingerly around the dead body that had been Sammy Hutchens to the bathroom. There was no window, and the air was still thick with moisture from Sammy's shower. I splashed water on my face, relieved my bladder, and came back into the bedroom. I sat on the other bed, waiting for Lonnie to go to sleep, but knowing there was no way I could touch Sammy to move him out of the way in order to leave. I was trapped here. Lonnie knew that. There was a phone, but whom could I call for help? Who was to say that I wasn't a part of this whole thing, had helped Lonnie to lure this boy to the motel for a sex game gone bad? So I sat and I waited until it was morning and time for us to leave.

There are churches in Europe—*ossuaries*, they are called— where the bones of the dead are stacked in decorative arrangements around the sides of the church. A pile of skulls used to make a cross. Femurs, fibulas, humeri, and ulnas mounded into pale, moon-colored mosaics so the joints resemble a peacock, a shell, a martyr's rose. In the San Bernardino alle Ossa, the decapitated skulls of the damned sit in a silent row at the rear to oversee all that passes in front of them: the endless eternal parade of baptisms, communions, weddings, funerals. Perhaps that is what hell is: the knowledge that life is there in front of you, but you are unable to participate. In the silence of the motel room, I saw myself as a severed skull, watching the parade of life that had passed through my shop, unable to touch it, to feel its texture. That is why Lonnie had chosen me. He and Drexel knew that I lived only on the fringe of life, and that when they wiped me away, it would be as insignificant as a speck of sand washed from the shore. A house cannot blame the tornado for the wind that blows it down. A tree cannot blame the fire that consumes it. A rabbit cannot blame the wolf. Lonnie was right. This had been my fault. If I had not refused him, then Sammy would still be alive. I also knew that he had a taste for killing. That whatever bond existed between him and Drexel would lead to this scene or one like it: a dead boy in a corner, an innocent man's head blown off, a lonely waitress dumped in a field. I also knew that it had to end—with me.

I woke Lonnie up just after it was light. I recognized that it was important for us to get away from the motel before the other customers began to stir with the new day. It took a few moments for him to realize where he was, and when he saw Sammy's body stretched out across the floor, all he could say was, "Oh, yeah."

He showered, and after he was dressed, he pulled the body into the far corner of the room so that it was not the first thing the maid would see when she walked in. As we left, I tried not to look at the nightstand separating the beds. I hoped Lonnie did not see me looking.

He bought sausage biscuits at a drive-through window and we drove back to Morris in silence, a couple whose vacation had ended badly. The morning chill persisted, unwilling to give way to the cool winter sun. I looked out the window at the wax myrtle, the red bay trees, the scrub pines streaming past my window. In a month, these desolate lowlands would be full of green, new plants fighting for survival. As Lonnie would say, it wasn't anything personal, it was only business.

Arriving back in Morris, I was struck with a sudden sense of longing and loss for all the years I had spent here. Wanda's Main Street Cafe was open for business, and as we drove past, I could see some of the businessmen having their eggs and bacon and coffee, ready to start the work day. Shirley Cooper was turning the sign on the front of the bank to open for business. But I also saw Simmons Independent Insurance agency, empty of all the office furnishings, only the sign painted on the front window to remind the town of what it had once been, that there had been life inside. It would be the same with me, I suspected. Everything that I had valued so much, taken so much pride in, everything that I had given my life to build was now going to be wiped away like scribblings on a chalkboard.

Lonnie pulled to the back of the driveway, as far from the street as possible. He came around to help me out of the car, and I was struck by his newfound decorousness. The house felt cold and still inside, and I turned the light on in the kitchen to bring some life back into it—it reminded me too much of a tomb. I offered to make Lonnie coffee, but he declined.

"So," I said. "I guess then we just need to get down to business."

"Probably best."

"I'm going to write out a paper here that will give you access to all my accounts," I said, "and will make you an equal partner in my business. That way, you will have the right to sell anything you see fit to sell. What will you do with it all?"

"I don't know," he said. "Drex and me got an idea that we can go out West to learn to drive long haul trucks. If you got a record, you can still get a license to drive."

"Even if you have been convicted for drugs?" I asked.

"No, not for that. But Drex says he knows a man who can give him some papers. Or, if we can't do that, then he might just use your . . ." His words trailed off and Lonnie hung his head, as if embarrassed by his admission. I wondered which one of us he was trying to protect.

"Drex will use my identity," I said. "I see. A trucker. How very butch of me." I offered a feeble smile and directed Lonnie to the front of the house. "I keep my letterhead and business accounts in the shop, but you know that already. We will need to go in there to write the contract."

As Lonnie followed me into the shop, I remembered the afternoon so many months before where I had shown him the house, the shop, hoping to impress him with my affluence. Had he been scouting me even then? Had Drexel told him about me in prison, that I was an easy mark? Was my inviting him to the house to seduce him merely a coincidence in a plan where I was not the player but the one being played? If that was true, and I knew that it was, I felt that my heart could burst with sadness, that if I began to cry for the level of this deception that had been thrust upon me, that I could not cry hard enough or long enough and that I would surely split in two from grief. I was now not only prepared to die, I welcomed it.

I wrote out the paper for Lonnie but did not sign it straightaway.

I told Lonnie that since the paper would not be legal unless it was notarized, he would have to take it to the bank. I called Shirley and told her to expect him.

"I know this is all a bit unusual," I told her, "but I have been in a bad way ever since my accident. I am going to take a long vacation. I am certainly overdue for one. Lon and a friend will handle things here for me."

"Whatever you say, Mr. Vale," she said. "Tell him to bring the signed paper over in the next day or two and I will handle it personally. And you have a nice trip. Do you know where you'll be going?"

"No idea at all," I said. "Just someplace quiet. And peaceful."

When I signed the paper, I handed it to Lonnie. "I want you to know one thing," I said. "I am doing this because I love you. I have loved you from the moment I saw you. And I know that you may not understand it, but I am happy to give all that I have to you."

In his eyes, I could see that same look I saw the day when he was trying to figure out the numbers for the prices of gas so he could put them on the sign in front of Joe Boggs's service station. I did not give him time to speak, time to react. I reached up and put my arms around his neck and pulled him close to me. "I do this for you," I said, kissing him full on the mouth. I could feel the stubble of his beard on my face as I kissed him and he kissed me back, his lips full and firm against mine. And when I felt his hands tightening around my throat, I was not frightened at all, thrilled by the ecstasy of his kiss, telling myself only to "breathe out."

Breathe.

Out.

## LOCAL FLORIST POSSIBLE VICTIM
## OF FOUL PLAY

### Two Suspects Arrested in Connection
### with Area Deaths

Police announced yesterday afternoon the arrest of Lon ("Lonnie") Flowers and Drexel Smith, two ex-felons who moved to the area last year, in connection with the disappearance and possible murder of M.R. Vale, a local resident who operated Vale's Floral Design for twenty years and was a lifelong resident of Morris.

Police are also investigating the involvement of Flowers and Smith in the deaths of three other individuals: local businessman Roger Simmons; Sammy Hutchens, a runaway teenager from Greer, South Carolina; and Annabeth Owensby, who friends say disappeared almost three years ago.

Police traced a clue found in the Peach Bottom Motel, near Florence, to Vale's house in Morris, where they apprehended Flowers and Smith where they were in residence at the time. The body of Sammy Hutchens had been discovered on February 24 at the Peach Bottom Motel by the owner's wife, Mrs. Lucinda Galloway. The inn owner, Mr. Rex Galloway, identified a photograph of Flowers, saying he had checked into the motel on February 23 with another man.

Vale's body has not been found, but police are searching an area where Smith resided that once belonged to Ms. Owensby. Reaction to the murders among area residents has been one of shock, with townspeople describing Vale as a "quiet man who kept to himself."

Detectives have verified that Flowers and Smith

were incarcerated at the same time at Birchwood Boys Home, a facility for sexually violent youths, and again at Harnett Correctional Institution, though on unrelated crimes. Flowers served a four-year sentence at Harnett for sodomy on a minor, and Smith served two and a half years for the manufacture of methamphetamines. Both were released on parole. Flowers, who trained as a mechanic in the medium-level correction facility, worked for JB's Garage in Morris and had also been employed as a delivery man for Vale's Floral Design.

The case, which is quickly drawing national attention, is the largest murder investigation in the history of Morris, according to local authorities. Bail has not been set for either of the accused.

## . . . 7 . . .

So, now you know.

It was fairly simple, really. While Lonnie slept, I put one of my business cards into the Gideon Bible, which was in the drawer of the nightstand. Finally, a practical use for one of the damned things. I circled Psalm 94:6 in pen: "They slay the widow and the stranger, and murder the fatherless." Around the margins of the page, I had written all our names: Roger's, Annabeth's, Sammy's, mine. On the back of the card I wrote: *You will find the murderers, Lonnie Flowers and Drexel Smith, at this address.*

The media attention has been extreme as you may imagine given the nature and extent of the case. Articles entitled "Florist Killed by Flowers!" or TV segments called "A Deadly Arrangement" are not uncommon. These will undoubtedly provide many additional (and salacious) details not included here.

But as you read these articles or watch these programs and listen to the way they describe Lonnie and me, I want you to forget all the wretchedness and misery they try to inject into the story. What I hope you will remember is the softness of Lonnie's lips on mine, the sadness in his eyes, the strength of his grasp. For what I re-called in those last flashes of my life was the moment when I first saw Lonnie standing in front of the gas station, strong and simple and pure. Yes, pure. For in that moment, he held nothing for me but undiluted potential, was the unawakened dream, the eternal promise that is known simply as *before*.